The Butcher's Daughter

- A Journey Between Worlds -

A NOVEL

By

Mark M. McMillin

Hephaestus Publishing

Praise for *The Butcher's Daughter*

"... a pleasurable and action-packed read ... a delicious spin to the otherwise tired clichés of male captains ... the joy of the open seas - as well as the danger churning below - pulses throughout this rip-roaring, hearty tale of the high seas." - *Kirkus Reviews*

"... an entertaining read ... full of authentic historical events ... a defiant story, a narrative of strong will and perseverance which ultimately plummets to a tragic end." - *Readers' Favorite*

Other Works by the Author

Gather the Shadowmen (The Lords of the Ocean)
Prince of the Atlantic
Napoleon's Gold

The Butcher's Daughter
- A Journey Between Worlds -

Ode to the Queen's Privateers

Brave noble brutes, ye Trojan youthful wights,
Whose laud doth reach the center of the sun;
Your brave attempt by land, on seas your fights
Your forward hearts immortal fame hath won...

- Poet Unknown

The New World
(1535)

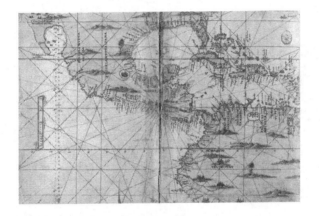

Alonso de Santa Cruz, Cartographer

Foreword

Two Graves

He who seeks revenge should dig two graves before embarking upon his journey: one for his enemy and the other for himself...

- Ancient Proverb

BOOK I

The Síol Faolcháin

Chapter One

A man - I cannot say if he was wise or not - once said to me as he gently stroked my hair, as he slowly poured honeyed words into my ear with false affection: "Hush dear child, hush. 'Tis best if you lay still. 'Tis best you accept this gift I give you now without complaint my lovely, golden dove."

I never knew this man's name. Long years have passed since I heard those vile words. They haunt me still.

Blood. I saw a lot of blood as I stepped into my father's shop.

I suppose the matter had to do with a debt unpaid, money owed to one clan or another. When I had heard the voices of

1

strange men inside our house late one night arguing with my father, I had rushed downstairs barefoot out of curiosity with a candle in my hand, dressed only in my nightgown.

And when I reached the bottom of the stairs, I saw two brutes holding my father down against his wooden cutting table while a third man, a tall, sinewy fellow standing in front of him, stabbed him over and over again in the arms, the chest and stomach with a long knife. The tall man then tossed his knife in the air with one hand and caught it by the handle with the other, as if he was performing some parlor trick, and slashed my father's throat open with one, elegant swing. Sprays of blood spurted across the room. My father's eyes fluttered for a bit before they closed on him forever.

But I am well accustomed with blood and gore. I am the butcher's daughter.

No doubt I stared at my father's three murders wide-eyed, confused, even in horror. But I did not scream. I did not cry. I did not look or call out for any help. I buried any urge to panic.

The tall, sinewy man with the knife fled when he saw me. His two companions did not. They had unfinished business. They released their grip on my father. They let his limp body slip to the floor with a dull thud and then slowly moved towards me - all smiles.

I was but twelve or so. I had never known a man before that day.

I cannot say if the man who commanded me to lie still after he forced me to the floor next to my father's torn body, the man who thought of me as his *lovely, golden dove*, was wise or not for I only knew him for the briefest of moments. You see, that man died in my arms on top of me not long after he spoke those very words to me.

My memory of that day is clouded in my mind. No, that is not quite true. I have chosen to wrap that memory in cloud. But I can, if

I wish to, remember that day - even now - with crystal clarity, in the most striking detail.

Aye, the man on top of me died in my arms when I removed his own dagger from his belt and plunged it deep into his black heart - after he had torn my nightgown open and had thrust himself inside of me. I can still hear the air escaping from his lungs. I can still smell the rot on his breath. I can still see the pupils of his eyes rolling up behind his skull as his life slipped away from him forever.

His companion had fared a little better. I stabbed him, skewered him really, through the mouth when he leaned over to pull his dying friend off of me. The blade had sliced through one cheek and pierced the other. The man screamed and fled outside, running wildly down New Market Street with the dagger still lewdly sticking out of both sides of his mouth. Not a mortal wound perhaps, but a man with scars on each cheek like that is not a hard man to find as you might imagine. Time and patience is all that is needed. A little time, a little patience, and you can easily find a man like that with matching scars at your leisure.

I can say, with absolute certainty, that this day was the last day of my childhood. But it was also the day-of-days - for this was the first day of my liberation, of my awakening, as well.

I had forewarned her gentle majesty of course. I had told her that a highborn lady, especially a queen, should not hear of such things so foul and impure.

But she ignored my warning. She leaned close to me and squeezed my hand reassuringly. "It is, dear sister," she told me flatly, "a pitiless and putrid world ruled by pitiless and putrid men, men who think of us as little more than chattel. We would know your story. From start to finish, we would know how it is you came to rule over such cruel and loathsome men in a man's cruel and loathsome world."

Yes, it is true. Sitting in a chair across from me in my drab lodgings in the Tower of London, a place of luxury compared to the dungeon I had only days before been released from, the great and mighty Queen of England addressed me, a lowly commoner and a thief, as her *sister...*

My lads forced the big man down to his knees before me. They stretched his arms out taut for me and held him firmly in place.

"Why, Captain Dowlin," I said and laughed, "you've gone and pissed yourself I see! You've gone and soiled my deck! And my crew scrubbed these planks down with holystones just this morning. They put their backs into it let me tell you. They scrubbed this deck down clean."

"Please," Dowlin pleaded, whimpering with spittle and snot running down his long beard. His eyes were nearly swollen shut from the good drubbing my men had given him. "Please, please, please..." he repeated over and over again.

"Please?" I asked. "Is that all you can say? How pathetic. I pray you can beg far better than that, especially when it is your own, pitiful life hanging in the balance. Come now, I know you can do better and I promised my lads a bit of entertainment tonight before supper."

"Please, my lady, please spare my life. For mercy's sake. I have gold. I have much gold!"

"For mercy's sake?" I asked. "No, I think not for mercy's sake. But for gold you say? Well now, you've piqued my curiosity there. And how much glittering gold is your miserable life worth to you, Dowlin?"

"Anything, name your price!"

I looked over at what was left of Dowlin's bloodied and beaten crew herded around the main mast in a tight circle. They were bound in chains, intently watching my every move, soaking in my every word. After today they would be my men.

My own lads knew the drill. They forced Dowlin down lower, exposing the back of his soft neck to me.

I stood to the side and drew my sword. "The price Dowlin - is your head!"

"Nooooooooooooo..." Dowlin screamed just before I cleaved my way through flesh and bone. With one, clean stroke, his severed head rolled grotesquely across my deck until it came to rest at the feet of his defeated crew.

And then I pointed my sword at them, the bright steel blade now dripping with Dowlin's fresh blood. "As my men will vouch," I told them, "I'm no purveyor of lies and because I do not lie I cannot say to you that killing gives me no pleasure. Your master was a wretched pig and it gave me great pleasure to kill him. Now you know why some call me *Bloody Mary*. Now you serve me and this ship - or not. You are free to choose."

The upshot of my touch of drama was grand. They all at once dropped to their knees and groveled at my feet. They all at once pledged their undying loyalty to me.

"Master Gilley!"

"Aye, Madam?"

"Introduce the new lads to our ways."

"With pleasure, Mum, with pleasure!"

Thomas Gilley was my rock. He had been with me from the beginning. For nearly two years we had crisscrossed the vast and perilous ocean together. For the past year we had sailed under Dowlin's cruel shadow.

"And our course, Mum?"

"The new lads will tell you - gladly now I should think - what our new heading is to be."

And by that of course I meant that Dowlin's men would tell us where Dowlin's gold was stashed away, or pay the awful price for their silence.

As my men went about their labors, securing the heavy guns and making repairs to shattered planks, to torn lines and sail, I went below to my great cabin, content with a good day's work. Dowlin had thoughtlessly, and without good purpose, brutalized any who had crossed his path. Men, women, children, he cared not. Yes, Dowlin was a wretched, stinking pig who often killed for sport. I had done mankind a favor by dispatching him. But in my world,

Dowlin had also been a lord and master, a prince. His death I knew could not be cheaply bought.

"An inspiring performance, Mum!" a voice called out, startling me as I stepped into my great cabin. The voice popped out from behind the door, closed it quickly and slid the bolt inside the socket.

I would not give the intruder the satisfaction of knowing that he had, for once, caught me unawares. "I'm glad you were amused," I told him flatly.

He slipped an arm around my waist and pulled me close against him. "Do you," he asked with a smile, "despise all men?"

"All but one or two," I replied and kissed him lightly on the lips. Then I reached down between his legs and grabbed him by his privates. He was already stiff and eager. I couldn't help myself and moaned with anticipation.

"Only one or two?" he inquired. "Dare I ask who?"

"Ah, you are safe for now my dearest," I answered, batting my eyes flirtatiously. "Well, at least for a night or two. You have skills, remarkable skills worth keeping."

"Aye, it was a splendid day indeed. I've always been exceptionally good at fighting, equally talented with sword, knife, or musket. I suppose one could say I was born to it."

"You are a great warrior, James Hunter," I replied honestly and squeezed him even harder. "But those are not the skills that interest me tonight. I dare say you have other skills that I've taken quite a fancy to, skills I wish to test."

"Ah, now, that is why I'm here my lady," Hunter replied and flashed his brilliant smile for me. "Not too tired from all that killing?"

"Shut up and take me you fool. Ravish me - I am hot for your wicked touch..."

Hunter obliged me gladly, with all he had to give.

I stood on the poop deck next to MacGyver, Michael MacGyver, my best man at the helm, watching the morning sun, dressed in brilliant red, rise majestically above the sea's shimmering green waters. A good, flowing wind filled our sails and the ship was cruising along nicely. We had Dowlin's magnificent ship in tow and I could hear my men with their saws and hammers working to repair her shattered rudder. It was a glorious morning. It was a *hallelujah* morning.

"Good day, Mum," Hunter said with a mischievous grin as he made his way up the companionway and handed me a mug of steaming, black coffee. "Sleep well my lady?"

"I did indeed, Master Hunter, I did indeed. And you?"

"I have no complaints. I feel most refreshed."

From the corner of my eye, I could see MacGyver crack a thin smile. A ship is a small place, too small for secrets. The whole crew knew that Hunter and I were lovers.

I savored the coffee's rich aroma for a bit before I took a sip. "What course, MacGyver? Did old Gilley even give you one before he retired to his hammock or are you sailing aimlessly about on the open sea to only God knows where?"

"We sail for the *Na Sailti*."

"Ahhh, the Saltee Islands," I said. "I thought as much."

No one had ever accused Dowlin of being clever. The Saltee Islands, lying just off Kilmore Quay between Waterford and Wexford, was an obvious choice. The islands were remote and uninhabited and not far from Dowlin's base at Youghal. Still, without a map or guide, one could roam those small islands for years and not find any buried treasure.

Hunter grabbed my mug of coffee from me and took a sip. "Dowlin's brothers," he said soberly, staring absently out at the horizon, "ghastly brutes the pair of them, will want revenge when they hear of what we've done, Mary. Righteous or not, the gods always exact a price for a killing."

Only Hunter and Gilley ever addressed me by my given name. Mary had been my mother's name. But I did not know her. She had died when I was very young. They say she had been a rare beauty. They say that before my father took her in and married her, she had been a whore.

"No doubt," I said evenly, stealing a secret moment to admire Hunter's exquisite face in the soft, morning light.

He had not yet shaved. He wore no hat and had neglected braiding his long, black hair into a queue. The breezes toyed with the loose strands, brushing them across his face. His eyes were striking blue. His chin was square and strong. I thought him the most handsome man in all of Ireland, perhaps in all of Christendom.

He used his fingers to comb the tangled mess off his forehead and then turned to face me. He gave me a puzzled look.

"Out with it, Hunter," I demanded.

"I'd rather see it comin' than get it in the back. That's all, my lady."

"I agree," MacGyver chimed in, "with Hunter."

"You agree with Hunter do you now?" I asked mockingly as I placed my hands on my hips. "As if I give a damn what you two agree on! Do I smell a mutiny brewing aboard my ship?"

Hunter and MacGyver exchanged knowing glances and chuckled. As every man in my crew knew, any one of them could speak his mind freely and without fear. Honest speech was protected by one of the Ten Rules, though precisely which one I doubt any of us knew.

Then Gilley, coming up from the main deck, stepped onto the quarter deck carrying a basket of bread from the ship's galley. The bread was freshly baked, still warm and smelled delicious.

"Mutiny is it?" Gilley asked while handing out his loaves. "Never trusted the likes of these two, Mum. Be happy to gut them both for you after they finish their breakfast. I'll hang their worthless carcasses off the main yardarm to rot. Let them serve as a warnin' to all other would be mutineers."

"Hunter," I said, "is worried about Dowlin's brothers."

"Ah, and well he should be, Mum," replied Gilley with a

serious nod. "Well he should be. Them two aren't no better than Dowlin. Worse maybe. An ill-tempered litter sprung from the angry womb of an ill-tempered bitch."

"Aye," I agreed. "So gentlemen, we must be the first to strike. And when we strike we must do so with deadly purpose..."

I stopped along the narrow path for a moment to catch my breath after the long and strenuous climb. I could see my ship peacefully riding anchor in the cove below. *Phantom* was a five hundred ton, French-built nao, ships renowned for their strength and speed. She was both square and lateen-rigged. She carried eighteen great guns cast from solid bronze - a mix of falconets and sakers mounted on rolling carriages and carronades stood neatly against her bulwarks like soldiers on parade. And fixed to iron pedestals mounted along her rails were another thirty swivels for close-quarter fighting. Sitting next to *Phantom* was Dowlin's larger ship, a fine, Dutch-built man-o-war displacing six hundred tons or better, not as swift as a nao but she was well-armed and built for rugged war. The sight of the stubby noses of her guns protruding through the open gunports - a mix of periers, sakers and falconets, twenty-four great guns in all - sent a tingle up my spine. She carried swivels as well. What a handsome sight both ships made together!

The man-o-war had been Dowlin's flagship. Now Dowlin's ship was my flag ship. Under Dowlin she had been known as *Medusa's Head.* And just to make certain that any who laid eyes on her knew exactly what ship she was, a hideous replica of the witch's head, with deadly snakes for hair and sharp fangs for teeth, adorned her high prow. No sailor roaming across the open sea could ever gaze upon that carved monstrosity without freezing in their tracks. As I resumed my climb up the cliff, I decided I would rechristen Dowlin's ship later. I would rename her *Falling Star* after the shooting star I had seen streaking outside my father's butcher's shop at the very moment my father's assailants had pried my legs apart and deflowered me. I'd pitch the witch's grotesque likeness into the sea when I had the chance.

After we reached the cliff's summit the land flattened out before us and we could see the Irish Sea in all directions for miles. Visibility was excellent. There was not a single sail in sight.

The island was little more than a desolate pile of rock and sand covered over in wild grass and patches of scrub brush. The only inhabitants we saw were small lizards scurrying about and birds, birds of many kinds and colors. Countless numbers of birds squawked and chirped at each other all across the island.

Armed with shovels and pick-axes, my new recruits led the way under a bright and sizzling sun. They were clearly fidgety and reluctant to press on, fearing I suppose that they were marching to their own graves. I gave them no reason to think otherwise. We marched in single file towards the southern tip of the island until we came upon a cluster of boulders surrounded by a thicket of thorn bushes.

"This is the place?" I asked the lead man after he stopped and surveyed the area around us. I addressed this man first because I had seen the deference the others had given him. He was also the first one to tell Gilley where we could find Dowlin's treasure.

He hesitated before answering me. I gave him a hard look and then took a moment to consider his men. "Did you, or did you not all swear your allegiance to me?"

"We did, Mum," the lead man answered.

"What is your name?" I asked him.

"Flannigan, Mum, Joseph Flannigan from Kinsale in County Cork."

"Well, Master Joseph Flannigan from Kinsale in County Cork, I did not come all this way, I did not go to all this trouble, just so I could kill you. I don't need to kill you. And besides, I don't murder unarmed men."

Flannigan lowered his head. "Beg pardon, Mum, but Dowlin was unarmed."

"Ah, a fair point you make there Master Flannigan," I said.

"*Touché*. But you are mistaken. I didn't murder Dowlin. I executed him."

I turned to address Flannigan's men. "I know Master Gilley explained things to you the other night and explained them to you clearly. Killing or harming innocent or helpless men, women or children is strictly forbidden. It is a violation of our Ten Rules. Now it is hot and this island is no paradise. Let us to business. You can help me recover Dowlin's plunder - and take your rightful share - or I can leave you all here to live on birds' eggs until some fishing trawler happens upon you. But I will not kill you."

Flannigan shook his head. "Even if what you say is true Lady Mary, we are still all dead men. Dowlin has two brothers, the Twins. They know us and they will find us and kill us all for helping you."

Hunter took a step towards Flannigan and rested his hand on Flannigan's shoulder. "Lad, you and your mates are most likely dead men already even if you don't help us. Once you reach home, Dowlin's brothers will find and kill you all just because you didn't die with Dowlin."

Flannigan's men exchanged looks all around. Heads started bobbing up and down.

Flannigan clenched his teeth, he stared at me with eyes as cold as stone. "We won't be the only game the Twins will want to feast on, Madam."

I offered Flannigan a bold and cocky smile. "Aye, the Twins, the Devil's own offspring to be sure and far more dangerous than Dowlin ever thought to be. They're more dangerous because they're smart. The Twins and Dowlin were only half-brothers I hear, same she-bitch mother but begotten from different seed."

"You know them then?" asked Flannigan.

"Not well. I saw them once tie a man down and slowly skin him alive. The poor devil's only crime was to prudently pitch some Dowlin cargo overboard during a treacherous gale to save his ship and crew from foundering."

Flannigan nodded. "Aye, I've seen some of their grizzly work up close." Then he baited me. "One brother is a big, ugly bastard,

11

strong as an ox. The other is a bit prettier, but just as big and no less strong."

"Ah, Master Flannigan, you wish to test me? I respect that. No, the Twins are nearly exact copies of each other. One is challenged to tell them apart even close-up. They're both huge, a head taller than any man I've ever laid eyes on. But one brother is a half hand taller than the other and as for appearances, well, not my taste, but they are hardly ugly."

"Apologies, Mum. Right you are. I fear your man Hunter here is right too. The Twins will come looking for us even if we refuse to help you. What then?"

"You let me worry about that. First things first. Now, shall we dig?"

Flannigan pointed to a pitted, reddish brown rock in the middle of patch of wild flowers that seemed somehow out of place. The rock, I soon realized, was not indigenous to the island. I grabbed a shovel from Flannigan's hand and started scooping out the first shovelfuls of dirt and sand myself.

Chapter Two

The queen, showing no favor or disfavor towards me, not even an inkling, narrowed her eyes slightly as she considered what I had said thus far while I paused to take a sip of water. "So are we," she asked me, "to understand that when you first decided to try your luck at smuggling, you began your venture in league with Dowlin?"

"Yes and no your Majesty," I replied. "I never actually sailed with Dowlin. Even now such a notion is abhorrent to me. My men and I sailed for ourselves, but we had to pay Dowlin a percentage of our profits, a tax or royalty I suppose one might say, for the privilege of crossing the Irish Sea."

The queen nodded. "Dowlin, by other names, was well-known to us as an outlaw and a villain. How is it you intercepted and took his ship when no one in the whole of our mighty navy could do so?"

"I intend to come to that matter your Majesty in good time."

The queen smiled sweetly at me. "It is your story, Lady Mary. Please, do continue as you see fit and proper."

"Gladly, your Majesty. Forgive me though, your Majesty. My men often addressed me as Lady Mary but, in truth, I hold no such lofty title. I'm no lady, here in England or back in Ireland."

"Oh? We think that within the four corners of our kingdom you are who we say you are."

The queen turned her head around to look over at a man sitting at a crude table in the corner of my cell. The gentleman was an older man with a pasty face and a long, grey goatee who liked to dress in black. "Sir William, we would have the title lady bestowed upon our most honored guest. Make it so."

I only learned sometime later that the queen's escort was a man named William Cecil, the 1st Baron Burghley. Cecil had a keen interest in strengthening the Navy Royal and always accompanied the queen during her visits with me in the Tower. On each occasion he sat at the table with a pen in hand, scratching my words onto parchment as I spoke.

Cecil nodded obediently, dipped his pen in the ink jar and scribbled something in the margins of his paper.

So now I was the Lady Mary and the queen's good sister. Even though this was no more than a pleasant fiction, I nonetheless felt flattered. I wondered quietly to myself whether the queen would allow me to keep my title after she took my head.

I had taken twenty men with me to find Dowlin's gold, ten of Dowlin's men led by Flannigan and ten of mine. It was not enough. Even Dowlin's men were startled by what we found. We lifted crate after crate out of the earth, filled with gold and silver coins, precious gems and pearls. We found sterling silver bowls, chalices and cutlery, finely crafted neck watches and even a large, jewel-encrusted crucifix of solid gold mixed in with other baubles of great value.

As we headed back to the ship, Hunter straddled up next to me carrying a small, wooden chest in his arms. "Did you know about all of this, Mary?"

"No," I replied. I took my sleeve to dab the sweat out of Hunter's eyes. "I had no clue what we would find. 'Tis a king's ransom."

"It will be dark soon. Climbing down that path along the cliff carrying all this loot will be tricky enough in daylight, Mary."

"You think it best then to wait until morning to return and fetch the rest?"

Hunter smiled at me. From the look in his eyes, I could tell he wanted to lean over and kiss me.

"No," he said. "I think you will do what you will do. I simply made an observation."

"Ah, and what is it you think I'll do?"

"'Tis a risk either way. Walking around on this rock at night with torches in hand could attract attention. But if we stay here through the night, who knows what we might find waiting for us in the morning."

"You dodged my question."

Hunter burst out laughing. "Ha! Ha! Ha! I never win this contest with you, Mary. Oh, very well, I'd wait until morning so I think you'll wait."

"But my plan requires us to move quickly," I said with a flirtatious smile.

"I've never known you to like it too quick before," Hunter replied lewdly with a wink.

"Money, filling your bellies and screwing is just about all men seem capable of thinking about."

"Ha! And women are so different? And I know that look. If we were alone on this rock right now we'd be naked, rolling around in the grass and moaning deliriously with wanton pleasure."

"I'd rather read a good book," I said sharply, trying to hide my smile.

"Suit yourself, my lady. I can always play cards with the lads tonight. There's bound to be a game of chance or two on deck with all this loot to gamble with."

"But then how will we discuss my plan?"

"Ah, aye, the plan. And the plan requires us to recover the rest of Dowlin's treasure and weigh anchor tonight?"

"Well, the plan might give you and me some time for other things. Gilley and the lads will have finished repairs to *Medusa's Head* and scrubbed her decks down clean by the time we return. He can lead the next team ashore whilst you and I retire to my cabin - to talk about my plan."

"I think we might have different plans in mind, dear lady."

"Oh, no, I don't think so..." I said and just to make certain I was understood, I unfastened the top two buttons of my blouse.

Hunter, never slow or dimwitted, smiled appreciatively at my cleavage.

I do not consider myself an extraordinary person. Men, I know, find me very desirable but that is of little import to me.

I do though have a gift, an extraordinary, wonderful gift. I first discovered this gift on the day-of-days, on the day I was transformed from a moth into butterfly, on the day the child in me died, on the day I was liberated and reborn a woman.

The gift I speak of is this: when confronted with a dilemma, a problem or a puzzle, my mind starts churning out ideas, possible solutions to the problem, at a dizzying rate of speed. Some have remarked on this gift; they have said that I am clever. And this is true. I am quite clever.

But I think the word clever is inadequate, too broad a term to describe this particular gift of mine. For many people are broadly clever. This gift is more refined, more limited in breadth. This gift makes me unusually adept at concocting plans and schemes.

And I've been doubly blessed. For this first gift goes hand-in-hand with a second, extraordinary gift God has seen fit to give me. Under times of tremendous stress, or even when danger is whirling all around me, my mind continues functioning with great clarity of thought, calmly, dispassionately, with little emotion to distract me.

These two gifts are what allowed me to coolly assess my options against my assailants on the day-of-days. Many ideas went through my head during those wretched, horrid moments, during my father's murder, throughout my own violation. And when I saw the knife tucked inside my first assailant's belt within easy reach, I knew what I had to do. A plan, a plan to live took root and inspired me into action.

And when my first plan succeeded - to my astonishment I must confess - I desperately needed a second plan. I needed a plan to escape. But at the age of only twelve or so, I was not especially conversant in the ways of the world.

I knew enough at least not to tarry in my father's house for very long with two dead men inside. And then there were two other men on the loose somewhere to consider, one in hiding, unscathed, and one running down the streets of Dublin screaming with a knife sticking through both cheeks. Whoever had ordered my father's killing would want me dead too. So I took what clothes I could carry, and what little money I could find, and headed out into Dublin's cold and dismal streets, alone.

My second plan was not of my own making. It was a gift from my father. He had told me that if trouble ever found me, and if he was not there to protect me, to find a man named Eoghan Dubhdara O'Malley who lived in Westport on Clew Bay in County Mayo. I was to travel to Westport on Ireland's west coast and give this man my name. That was all I needed to do. Find a man named O'Malley in Westport, Lord O'Malley, and give this man my name.

And after I ran away from my father's butcher's shop and found Lord O'Malley's home, a great estate, a castle really, he took me in and kept me for a time until he could arrange for me to stay with a family who lived down by the water's edge. I did not understand the source of this generosity at first. I did not understand until several years later.

My new father, my surrogate father, was a man named Dalton. He was not a particularly affectionate man, but over the next few years he treated me well-enough. Dalton was a person of modest means. He lived quietly in a small house with a sickly wife who rarely left her bed. They had no children. Dalton owned an unexceptional tavern down on the waterfront near the docks and was the proud owner of one, humble fishing trawler. I divided my time equally between helping him with the tavern and learning the mysteries of the sea sailing with the trawler. Between these two interests, my entire world was men.

Dalton's tavern was where I had first met Gilley. Gilley was a frequent patron and, for reasons I cannot explain, I had taken an instant liking to him as he had to me. He was sweet and kind to me, never vulgar, and shared the most wonderful stories of his days at sea with me. He had done good service with the English navy for many years. He was man to be respected. And I took pity on him. He was retired and had no family. Like me, he had been an orphan and he was alone. He found comfort in the bottle and was often drunk, or working at getting there. I looked after him and he looked after me.

The fishing trawler was where I met my first love - the sea. From the very start, on my first time out on the open water, I knew a sailor's life was for me. The brisk ocean breezes, the cool sea spray, the rhythmic movements of a ship under full sail dancing in-between the waves invigorated me. The serenity of being surrounded by blue water for as far as the eye could see soothed my troubled spirit. Travelling to foreign lands excited me.

During my days in Westport, I saw Lord O'Malley on only two occasions. The first was when I pounded on the front door of his castle in freezing rain at the tender age of twelve or so. I had travelled long and far. I was cold and hungry and underneath my street clothes I still wore my torn, bloodstained nightgown.

On the second occasion I was fourteen or fifteen, a full-grown woman and wise in the ways of the world. O'Malley had sent for me from his death bed.

I was directed to a small cottage overlooking the bay where I found O'Malley being attended to by several people who I did not know, including an ancient priest with a crooked spine. O'Malley dismissed them all with one sweep of his hand when he saw me, including the priest. He looked old and frail and had a nagging cough. I had to lean close to hear him speak. He told me that he had loved my mother very much, that she had been his one, true love before she married. He grabbed me by the wrist and squeezed with all the strength he had left and, after lowering his voice to a whisper, he confessed that I was his illegitimate daughter and that I had a half-sister whose name I did not hear. He then reached for a folded piece of paper on the nightstand with a trembling hand and pressed the paper into my own. The paper was a bank note for

£5,000 pounds sterling, a huge sum of money. Then he took one last gasp of air, closed his eyes, and died in front of me.

That money, that Godsend, inspired yet another plan. After I succeeded in sobering Gilley up, I purchased a small but sturdy Dutch fly boat with Gilley's expert help and without being swindled. The boat had been rigged for fishing. But I had no interest or experience in fishing. My surrogate father you see had never used his trawler for fishing. Dalton's interest in boats was for smuggling goods into Ireland from places like England, Holland and France, from lands as far away even as Spain, Morocco and Italy. I had travelled to all those places and had learned the business well...

It was well past midnight when the second landing party led by Gilley returned to the ships with the last of Dowlin's gold and buried treasure. But before I gave the order to weigh anchor, I sent Gilley and his men back to the site one last time with empty crates and instructed them to fill the crates with rocks and sand, bury them and then cover up any trace that we had ever been there. And when Gilley returned from that task, I gave the order to sail and we headed out across the vast and rolling sea, my home and refuge since the day O'Malley died. Once we were clear of any land, I called my officers together, as was my custom from time-to-time, for a council of war in my great cabin.

Hunter, as usual, was the first to arrive. "Good evening, my lady," he said and kissed me quickly on the cheek. "I see you've found time to mend the two buttons on your blouse."

I tried not to smile as Gilley walked in a few steps behind Hunter. "Master Hunter, Master Gilley. I trust all is well on deck?"

"All is well, Mary," Gilley said in his usual, fatherly tone. "It is a happy ship."

Hunter chuckled. "No doubt, no doubt she is with all that loot we have stowed on board."

"And the new men?" I asked.

"As I said," Gilley replied, "all appears well but these men did, until a few days ago, sail for Dowlin and Dowlin was - as we all know - more pirate than smuggler. Who knows what sins they've committed while sailing with Dowlin, or what sins they're capable of in the days ahead? None would be my first pick for a crew."

I turned to Hunter. "Hunter?"

"Thomas raises a fair point. It's impossible to know how much these men can be trusted so I trust not even one. We should put them ashore at the first opportunity and rid ourselves of them for good before they infect our own men like a cancer."

"Hmmm, and let them fend for themselves against the Dowlin clan?" I asked.

"You reap what you sow, Mary," Hunter replied coldly. "We owe these men nothing."

Neither Hunter nor Gilley were men who liked to take chances and I admired them both for it. They gave me balance against my own impetuous nature, against my lack of caution.

"Well," I said, "we need them in any case for the battle yet to come. And *Medusa's Head*, Tom, how goes it?"

"She's fit enough for an easy cruise into Dublin, Mary, no more. Smyth is a gifted ship's carpenter, but I wouldn't trust that jury-rigged rudder of his in heavy seas."

"Excellent. From today forward she'll be known as the *Falling Star*."

"You can," Hunter snapped, "call her anything you like, Mary. But men will still recognize her as Dowlin's pride and joy, as his man-o-war."

"I'll have," I said curtly, "that ghastly witch's bust removed and pitched into the sea."

"Even so, Mary, men will know her..."

"Good, let men know what I did," I said defiantly. "Most will thank me for it."

Hunter knew enough to stop. Then the rest of my officers started filing into my great cabin. As each man walked past me, I cheerfully handed him a glass of Madeira from Dowlin's private stores.

My officers, on their own accord, remained standing until I took my seat before they took their own. I paused for a moment, as I often liked to do, to glance around the table, to study the face of each man.

Thomas Gilley, a large and beefy man and balding, was the ship's master and my first officer. He was a fine sailor. He had spent over twenty years in the Navy Royal as a senior chief petty officer before coming home to Ireland and turning to smuggling with me - after I had saved him from the bottle. James Hunter, my lover, was the ship's first lieutenant, my second officer and third in command. He was also the commander of the ship's great guns. Gilley and I had found him floating in Wexford harbor one night with a knife sticking in his back. After we fished him out of the harbor's murky waters and nursed him back to health, he simply stayed with us like a lost puppy that had found a home. He had served with the French navy for a time, or so he said, and had been a soldier of fortune in the Americas for the Spanish for a year or two, though neither his Spanish nor his French was very good. Whatever the truth, he was indisputably an expert with anything that could cut, stab or go boom. Benjamin Green and Albertus Fox, both smart, eager young men and inseparable friends, shared the rank of midshipman. I had given each of them command of a gun battery and they answered to Hunter. Green and Fox had both spent a few years with the Navy Royal. And then there was Mustafa Agah Efendi, a short, wiry Turk from Istanbul who had washed up on shore in Ireland, the sole survivor of Turkish pirates whose ship had foundered on rocks off Louisburg. I had rescued Efendi from an angry Irish mob bent on stoning him after he had naively wandered into Westport, half frozen and starving. Efendi was our ship's chief petty officer. He had dominion over all the ratings and on more than one occasion he had proven his mettle. And finally there was Hadley Ferguson, the ship's navigator. Ferguson was my only officer with no formal military experience, but he was a gifted navigator with an uncanny sense of knowing when we were nearing unseen danger. He knew the coasts of Ireland, Scotland, Wales and England like no other. Ferguson had been the last to join my small cadre of officers and that had been over a year ago. Except for Ferguson, to whom I owed my life after a rogue wave had washed me overboard, my officers were all beholden to me for one reason or another. A special bond of trust and loyalty had formed between us all.

"I realize the hour is late," I said, rising from my chair. I lifted my glass. "I intend to be quick, but first gentlemen a toast. If we live long enough to enjoy it, we've all become modestly wealthy. Let us then toast to a long and healthy life so that we may all have time to spend our good fortune!"

My officers stood and raised their glasses too. "Here, here, to a long and healthy life!" they replied with one voice and tipped their glasses with me.

"Please gentlemen, be seated. Much has happened over the past few days. We took Dowlin's pride and joy and then killed him or, in truth, I killed him, and then we took his treasure. The Twins will declare a blood feud when they hear of it and we all know what that means."

"It will mean," Hunter interjected gravely, "we're badly outmanned, outgunned and outmatched."

"True, Master Hunter, true," I replied. "We can't hope take on the Twins with all their ships and men at once and whatever is left of Dowlin's clan. Still, we're hardly outclassed..."

"There is often a razor-thin line, Mary," Hunter warned, "between bold talk followed by prudent action and reckless talk leading to imprudent choices."

"The Americas, Mum?" Ferguson asked.

"Possibly," I answered, still unsure of whether I was annoyed with Hunter or grateful to him for his not-so-subtle admonition. From the beginning he had been uneasy about my decision to go to war with Dowlin. "That is an option, Master Ferguson, certainly. But we have unfinished business in Ireland and some of you, and most of the men, have families here. Ireland is our home. There is another way. We can't take on the Twins and all their might and hope to win. Master Hunter is right of course. So instead we cut off the monster's double head."

Gilley started chuckling. "So you have a plan in mind already, Mary. We all should've known. I'm curious though, how long have you had this plan rattling around in your brain?"

I gave Gilley a mischievous, prankster's smile. "Once blind greed and an unquenchable lust for blood consumed Dowlin, we all knew it would come to this someday. Dowlin had to go. The plan to crush the Twins only came to me as we were recovering Dowlin's gold at Saltee."

After I explained my stratagem, I asked each officer for his opinion. There was not much discussion though. Everyone understood that after dispatching Dowlin, a showdown with the Twins was inevitable. And then we took a vote. The Ten Rules required a vote. More, the Ten Rules required that any vote to put the ship and crew at great risk had to be unanimous.

There is nothing quite like the exhilaration - the sheer ecstasy - of setting a plan of your own making into motion and watching it unfold in choreographed sequences with near perfection. I must confess the thrill of it for me is an addiction.

I sent Gilley and a prize crew on to Dublin with the *Falling Star* to buy a proper rudder while I took *Phantom* on to Waterford, an easy sail away, to gather up more men. After departing Waterford, I sailed south for Kinsale, a small port not far from Youghal where the Twins kept their stronghold - which was as close to the Twins as I was willing to come.

Once we put in at Kinsale, I sent two men on to Youghal by horse to keep an eye on the Twins and waited. A day later I sent a few more men into Kinsale to sample the taverns and whorehouses there, not to drink or to satisfy their lust, but to spread the word that they had seen *Medusa's Head* tied up along the docks on the River Liffey with a crew not of Dowlin's own looking to purchase a new rudder. And then, for good measure, my willing gossipmongers were to say that they had heard talk in Dublin, ugly talk, that Dowlin might be dead.

Such rumors I knew would fly back to the Twins with the speed of Hermes carrying the commands of Zeus. And I knew the Twins well enough to know that they would set out immediately after hearing such talk. They would sail straight for Great Saltee to retrieve Dowlin's precious treasure before anyone else dared try. Their strength had made them arrogant and reckless. They would sail out, top speed, with notions of bloody revenge no doubt, but with little thought or care that they might be sailing straight into a war.

My spies soon returned from Youghal with news that the rumors had reached the Twins and, just as I had predicted, the Twins wasted no time rounding-up their men and making ready to sail. We set out for the Saltees ahead of them, setting into motion the second part of my plan.

If you watch and listen, you can learn a lot about men while working a tavern. There are men who pretend to be strong who are weak. There are men, for their own reasons, who pretend to be weak who are strong. Some men, weak or strong, are thinkers. More are not than are. Some men like to lead. Most like to follow. All men wear masks - though women are far better at it.

A good brawl always captured my attention. You can learn a lot about a man in a good fight. But only the best fighters ever caught my eye. And the best fighters were not always the strongest or the quickest I discovered. The best fighters held back, took time to take stock of their opponent, searching, probing, always looking for some weakness to exploit and rarely, if ever, did they attack their opponent head-on, attack their foe where he was strongest.

And simple plans are best I've learned. Less moving parts, less that can go wrong. But no plan is perfect and one must always be prepared to improvise.

"Where's Gilley?" Hunter gruffly asked me as we stood together on the aftercastle. We both had our hands cupped over our eyes, scanning the horizon, searching. *Falling Star* was nowhere in sight.

"I don't know," I snapped back. Hunter damn well knew I didn't know where Gilley was.

We had furled all sail and were bobbing up and down on the gentle swells, standing off the leeward side of the Saltees to the north. This was where we were supposed to rendezvous with Gilley. The Twins would soon be coming up from the south with their ships and fighting men to retrieve Dowlin's buried loot and we dared not let the Twins see us, lest they realize they were sailing into trap.

A decision had to be made: keep to the plan or abort? The Twins were only a few hours behind us and I had no idea how much muscle they would bring with them. Without Gilley and *Falling Star*, we might have no chance at all against their numbers.

Hunter took my hand and squeezed. "I'm sorry, Mary."

I kissed him lightly on the cheek to let him know that all was well. I knew he was anxious, not for himself, but for me.

"What, now, Mary? The Twins cannot be far away."

"We go."

"Go? We go ashore or sail on to Dublin to find Gilley?"

I chose to roll the dice. We had come too far. "Assemble the lads for me, James. We keep to the plan. We're going in."

Hunter shouted up to the two lookouts at the masthead, told them to look alive, to keep a wary eye out for any sail. And then he brusquely called all hands on deck.

I stood against the fore rail on the quarter deck and looked down on nearly two hundred souls gathered on the main deck. Good men, hard men, loyal men, men who had sailed with me, off and on, for several years.

"I won't mince words with you." I told them. "You know why we're here. We've all suffered under Dowlin's whip, some of you more than others, but we've all suffered. The high and mighty *Síol Faolcháin* thought no one could touch them. They were wrong. Dowlin the pig, a madman whose depravity knew no bounds, is dead. But we have unfinished business here this day. We may not get a second chance to catch Dowlin's brothers out on the open sea again where we can even-up the odds. You know the risks. Any man unwilling to see this fight through - say so now - and I'll put him ashore on Little Saltee where he can catch a fishing boat home after this day is finished. Speak up, no hard feelings towards any man who decides this fight is not his own."

But no one spoke. Not one man stirred.

I looked at Green and turned command of *Phantom* over to him, his first command, and had him ease our ship into the cove. I took Hunter with me and we went ashore with one hundred men armed with muskets, *pistoles*, swords and knives. We headed up the cliff overlooking the cove in single file and marched south after we reached the top while Green took *Phantom* back out to sea where he was to skirt around the northern tip of the island, just a little ways, and wait out of sight from any ships approaching from the south.

The light was fading fast and the air smelled of rain. My men and I were crouched low behind a depression, behind a natural trench that had been gouged out by centuries of rain. From that vantage point we could look down on the field of boulders where Dowlin had buried his treasure but still keep out of sight. I had first noticed this natural hiding place when we started digging up Dowlin's treasure. I thought it a perfect spot for an ambush.

Circling and squawking overhead were countless birds to keep us company as we waited. For entertainment we tossed them bits of bread and watched them dive on the scraps and fight each other. Behind us was the sea and we could hear the walruses playing and the roar of the surf crashing against the breakers below. We sat patiently in our trench for long hours. And then, off in the distance, just past midnight, we saw a long line of torches snaking its way towards us. The *Síol Faolcháin* was on the march.

"How many do you think, James?" I asked.

"Hard to say in this light, Mary. I count twenty-five torches. My guess is that every third or fourth man carries one. If that's true, then perhaps we're looking at seventy-five men or so. Maybe more, I doubt less."

I suddenly felt ill and had the urge to vomit. When I had revealed my plan to my officers at our council of war, both Hunter and Gilley had warned me that we needed two-to-one odds or better in our favor to win.

Still, we had the advantage of surprise and we held the high ground. Still, we did not need to do anything. We could let the *Síol Faolcháin* come and go unmolested and slip away into the dark later with the clan none the wiser that we had been there.

As the procession of torches slowly approached our position, I could make out the dark silhouettes of two hulking giants, a twisted pair of brutes, leading a long line of men. I was, I knew, staring at the face of Death. I felt a chill run down my spine.

Long minutes passed as the fire snake inexorably slithered towards us. I could feel my heartbeat quicken. I could feel the sweat trickling down my armpits. I could hear my own, heavy, labored breathing. I took deep breathes. I tightened the grip around my pistol. The smooth, polished wood felt comforting in my hand and as the enemy drew nearer I tightened my grip even more.

The air then turned misty and a fine drizzle began to fall as the Twins and their men reached the field of boulders, barely fifty yards or so away from us. Oblivious to our presence, they set their muskets aside and built themselves a large bonfire before they started digging.

I relished the moment when the Twins unearthed the first crate and pried the lid open. When the brothers saw the rocks Gilley had stacked inside that box they went berserk, kicking, cursing and screaming all manner of obscenities. I had to suppress the urge to giggle.

And that was the moment I had to decide. Attack or do nothing and slip away?

I did not hesitate. The choice for me was easy.

"*FIRE!*" I screamed.

One hundred muskets discharged all at once. Our first volley inflicted great carnage, more than I had dared hope. The Twins' men were huddled close together, still digging with their shovels and pick axes when I gave the order to fire. They made easy targets. Dozens fell to our cruel lead. The rest dropped their tools and their torches and scrambled to grab their muskets.

Half my men started reloading muskets while the rest started lighting the fuses to our *grenadoes* - or *grenades* if you prefer the French taken from the word *pomegranate* or so men say. We lit the fuses using lanterns we had buried in the ground to conceal the flames. But the drizzle had snuffed out more than one candle and we could only light a handful of our *grenadoes*. We tossed what we had at the boulders below. Small explosions started popping off everywhere seconds later. More men fell and groaned, dead or wounded. I saw one Twin grab a man trying to flee the chaos. The giant lifted the coward off his feet and snapped his neck in two.

We fired-off a second volley and then a third and then pitched the rest of our *grenadoes* down at the boulders. But the Twins and their men had snuffed out their torches, kicked dirt over their bonfire and had retreated behind the rocks off to the west for cover. It was too dark to tell what new damage we might have wrought.

"Mary," Hunter whispered. "We cannot stay here long. The rest of the Twins' little army back at the cove will have heard our musket fire. They'll leave their ships to come and help the Twins. We'll be trapped here with our backs against the sea and possibly overwhelmed."

"Green knows what to do. If Gilley doesn't show, if there are too many ships anchored in the cove to attack on his own, I told him to sail around the island to our position and send the longboats in to take us off this bloody rock."

Hunter smiled. I could see the pride in his eyes, the pride he had for me.

"Aye, I overheard you tell Green as much. Always have a back door to leave by if things turn ugly. Let's hope he doesn't forget about us. Let me take half the men and circle around to the left. You and the rest stay here and keep the Twins pinned down against the boulders whilst I come up behind them and out-flank their position. We have time yet. We'll fire off a volley and then rush them together, try to flush them out into the open so we can finish this."

"How will I know when you've made your run at them?" I asked. I didn't want to shoot my own men down in the dark.

"You'll know when you hear the crack of musket fire on your left," he replied with a wide grin.

I nodded and off my Hunter went, disappearing into the darkness with half my men following after him.

A few minutes later Hunter and his company opened fire and charged at the boulders. My men and I raced down the rise overlooking the field to join them. But we found ourselves charging across only empty ground. The Twins and the remnants of their shore party had already fled north to reach their ships.

All seemed lost. Our ambush had failed. The Twins were in retreat and slipping away. I was disgusted with myself. The men we had killed meant nothing. The Twins could easily replace their losses and hunt us all down later.

And then we heard the boom of heavy cannon in the distance, the boom of ship's guns, and we saw muzzle flashes light up the night sky above the cove to the north. Gilley...

One hundred strong, we took a moment to reload and regroup and then raced north towards the sound of manmade thunder. But nature chose to unleash her own, raw power just then. Terrifying bolts of lightning flashed across the sky above us, followed seconds later by the crack of heart-stopping thunder. And then it began to pour. Sheets of blinding rain hit us and hit us hard. We couldn't see five feet in front of us. Our spirited chase across the island slowed to a miserable crawl. The deluge soaked our powder too, rendering our muskets useless.

Even so, we pressed on. We had no choice.

And when we reached the cliff overlooking the cove, Hunter whistled. "By God's good grace..." he said and grinned.

The heavy rains had tapered off and in the cove below we saw six small boats sitting at anchor, ablaze and sinking. And out away, beyond the cove and breakers, in the dim light of a new day, we saw my two ships, the *Falling Star* and *Phantom*, bobbing up and down on choppy swells with sails half furled. They appeared no worse for wear. And then we saw a longboat in the water heading towards the beach, one of ours, and we hurried down the cliff to meet it.

"Bugger me, Gilley, you son of a three-legged alley dog!" Hunter shouted as the boat's crew raised their oars and let their boat glide up onto the sand. When Gilley jumped into the knee-high surf, Hunter rushed into the water to embrace him.

"Master Gilley," I called out. "You're a tad late."

Gilley, beaming proudly, doffed his hat and bowed. "No, Mum. From where I stand I would say I'm right on time..."

"Are those six boats burning on the water," Hunter asked as he and Gilley waded through the surf together locked arm-in-arm, "everything the Twins brought with them?"

"No, I fear not, James." Gilley answered. "A large war carrack got away from us in the storm. We could barely see her in the downpour. We did not know your predicament Mary so I decided it best not to give chase. I decided it best to fetch you and the lads straight away."

"Did you see the Twins?" I asked anxiously.

"Nay, Mary. We did not."

"Any prisoners?"

"None that I know of. But at first light we can scour the island and have a look around."

Hunter took in the six burning hulks and nodded. "Fine work

there, Gilley. And here I thought all your foolish stories about your time in the navy were rubbish, just braggart's gibberish."

"Well, I won't be bragging about this battle. Those wrecks you see on the water were flimsy, poorly-armed coasters. 'Twas hardly a fair match, more of a slaughter really. That carrack looked like trouble though. She looked formidable to me."

"So," I said. "The Twins brought men and ships enough to move the treasure, but didn't expect a fight. What are your losses, Tom?"

"Why none, Mary. But *Phantom* was the closest to the carrack and traded several broadsides with her. She took several direct hits as the carrack passed her by. Green is staying outside the cove to watch our flank. You?"

"Three wounded," replied Hunter.

"We've been most fortunate," I said, relieved. "There may be wounded among the Twins' men on the south side of the island."

Gilley nodded. "I'll send a company of our lads out to look for them and for any stragglers too who might be in hiding."

"Especially the Twins, Tom," I said. "Maybe they're out there lying dead or wounded somewhere, but I don't think so. The master of that carrack would never have left without them."

"I fear, sadly, you are right, Mary," Gilley agreed.

"We thought," Hunter interjected, "you were going to miss the party, Gilley."

"Aye, some fool of a ship's master rammed his ship into ours just as we were leaving Dublin Bay, fouling both bowsprits. It took some time to untangle the sorry, bloody mess."

"Intentional you think?" I asked.

Gilley scratched his chin as if it might somehow help him think. "Doubt it, but I suppose it's possible. What witless idiot would ram Dowlin's ship on purpose though? Who could be that stupid?"

Hunter cleared his throat. "Ahem, well..." he said, turning to look at me with one of his boyish grins.

Chapter Three

A dept at hiding her thoughts and emotions, I did not yet know how to read the queen. I marveled at her inscrutable manner. Her expression, like a sheet of blank parchment, revealed nothing. Even so, her eyes betrayed a kind and gentle nature as she scrutinized me dispassionately.

"Tell us now, Mary," the queen commanded. "And no false modesty either. You've skipped over a part of the story, an essential part we think. How is it you took Dowlin's ship, *Medusa's Head*, a ship larger and stronger than your own? Of even greater interest to us, tell us what drove you to loathe Dowlin so? What deep-rooted hatred spurred you on to risk everything to undo this man and his brothers? You had paid Dowlin off for nearly a year we heard you say for the privilege of crisscrossing the Irish Sea. And still you made a goodly profit. Still you enjoyed a living any prince might envy. What changed? What provoked all-out war between you and all the Youghal chieftains?"

Gretchen. Gretchen had been her name I told her majesty. I found it difficult to talk about her. I stumbled with the words.

She had been about my age when I had fled my father's house in blood, when I had found her living on the streets in filth and alone, an orphan. I brought her aboard my ship. I fed her, washed her, clothed her, doted on her and she willingly sailed with us and became a member of my crew. She was a bright and happy child. She took to the sea like a fish to water and flourished. My men adored her. Not an easy thing for a young girl to win over a ship packed tight with rough and bawdy men. I especially grew very fond of her.

One day Dowlin decided to seize one of my boats for, he claimed, unpaid tribute. That was a lie. He took one of my boats because he was jealous of my burgeoning success and this was his way of taking me down a peg or two.

As I have said, I was little more than a child when I bought my first ship with the money Lord O'Malley had given me while he lay dying in his bed. I made myself the ship's purser and hired Gilley on as the ship's master. The Dutch fly boat we acquired was a small but sturdy vessel. She was a good sailor. She was flat-bottomed which gave us the freedom to cut through shallow waters and sail up remote estuaries along the coast where we could pick up or land our contraband without drawing attention to ourselves, without any irksome interruptions. Using my surrogate father's connections in France and England, Gilley and I, and not long thereafter Hunter too, started building up a fine, little business for ourselves.

While cruising along Ireland's west coast on the Atlantic, we sailed under the protection of the O'Malley clan. But, as our business grew, we bought more ships and hired more men and expanded our operations into the Irish Sea, smuggling goods up and down Ireland's east coast. Large swathes of those waters were controlled by Dowlin and the *Síol Faolcháin* and we had to pay Dowlin tribute for the privilege of sailing through his territory.

Fool that I am, when Dowlin seized one of my boats unfairly, claiming unpaid tribute, I, in a rash and thoughtless act of defiance, rebuked and insulted him publicly. Like many in our trade, I had grown weary of Dowlin's greed. I had grown weary of his unrelenting arrogance, of his cruelty towards any who crossed or displeased him. With just one flick of his hand, whole families had disappeared in the night.

When word of my public insult reached Dowlin, he let it be known that I would be sharply punished for my transgressions. I paid his threat little heed, thought it no more than idle bluster from a buffoon. He did not own me.

And then one day *Phantom* needed her bottom graved, along with some routine repairs, and so we put in at Wexford harbor. I gave the crew their liberty and I sent Gretchen into town to buy new clothing and a few amenities for just the two of us. That was the day she disappeared. That was the day I lost my poor, beautiful Gretchen forever.

My men and I scoured the town looking for her of course after she failed to return to the ship. I thought at first she had fallen ill or that perhaps she had taken on a lover and simply run off for a few days. But there was no sign she was lying ill somewhere, no indication any harm had befallen her or that she had run off to satisfy some guilty pleasure. Before leaving Wexford, I left a letter for Gretchen with some money and instructions on how to find me with an innkeeper whom I trusted at a tavern favored by my crew.

And then, just as we were preparing to cast off our cables and drop our sails, a number of loud and vulgar men - Dowlin henchmen - appeared on the dock. They called up to me, told me that they had come to deliver a message. Dowlin had taken Gretchen they said, had snatched her off the streets and carried her down to Youghal. But she had disappointed him in bed and so he had decided to release her. They told me I could have her back if I so desired, that I could find her broken, disfigured body at the bottom of Youghal Bay.

"Hate?" I asked the queen. No, not hate I told her majesty. What consumed me, what fed my loathing and drove me on was something far worse than hate. "I know hate," I said. "I was beyond hate, your Majesty. Never before had such blind and raging fury seized me. Never before had such a mad craving to kill a man and more - to obliterate everything in this world that was ever dear to him - obsessed me..."

Loss and pain and I are old and familiar companions. But

Gretchen's death, I must confess, hit me hard and laid me low, beyond anything I had ever known before. My mind could not fathom such ungodly barbarism. Gretchen was a beautiful, innocent child. For long weeks I did not leave my great cabin. I could not eat. I could not sleep. I could not focus my thoughts on much of anything at all. Not even my love and my rock, Hunter and Gilley, could console me. But they did what needed to be done to keep our operations humming while I wallowed in my misery. I was grateful for that at least. And when I finally did emerge from my cabin, when I finally was able to rise above my great grief, I had but one thought in mind: kill Dowlin and take away his most precious possession - take away his gold.

But Dowlin would not be an easy kill. He surrounded himself with lowly sorts of all kinds, with murderers, rapists and thieves. He surrounded himself with thugs with twisted hearts who took pleasure in their grisly work. And Dowlin was the master of a magnificent, powerful warship. Smugglers mostly sail small, swift vessels with little or no armament. A few ships carry cannon, but not many and even these ships carry only small cannon. Dowlin had a powerful man-of-war. Dowlin had a ship any captain of any navy would want to command, that any pirate would envy. *Medusa's Head* was a machine of war built to intimidate and kill.

My *Phantom* was the queen of the Irish Sea. She was swift and sturdy and she too was a powerful warhorse. But she was no match for *Medusa's Head* one-on-one.

I needed some advantage. I needed some trick or ploy. I needed a plan. But for weeks none came to me. And then one evening Hunter, a virtuoso with anything that could cut, stab or go boom, gave me an idea, a stimulating, tantalizing idea...

My crew was with me. To the last man, they wanted to avenge Gretchen's death; they want to avenge the evil done. This rivalry between clans had turned into a blood vendetta. No, that is not quite true. I was the mistress of the *Phantom* and owned a small squadron of modest coasters. But I was no clan chieftain. I was a petty thief and smuggler. My men and I did not have the muscle to take on any of the clans. In truth, this blood vendetta was between me and Dowlin. This feud was personal and could only end with the death of one of us.

I sent a letter to Dowlin in Youghal, asking him to meet me face-to-face at sea, asking him for a parley. At sea because there was no place on land either of us would ever agree to meet and because at sea Dowlin would believe he was secure. I wrote that I wanted to make amends for my unfortunate outburst, for my lack of good judgment, and pay fair tribute to one of the mighty lords of the Irish Sea. I wrote that I held no grudge over Gretchen's death, but thought her end an unfortunate waste because she could have served his men as she had served my own.

All foul, filthy lies of course. Gilley had to pen the letter for me. I could not bring myself to do it.

The offer was too good for Dowlin to reject. He agreed to meet me off the tip of a spit of land called Old Head, just a few leagues south of Kinsale. But he insisted we meet aboard his grand warship - as I knew he would - and I accepted.

The night was clear and warm. The sea was in a tranquil, quiet mood.

Hunter took my hands in his and looked me in the eye. "Are you ready for this, Mary?"

"Are you ready?" I replied, trying to reassure him with a forced smile.

"As ready as I'll ever be, Mary."

"As are," interjected Gilley, "the lads and the boats, Mary. Except for Dowlin's ship, there's not another sail in sight."

"Excellent," I said. I turned to look over at *Medusa's Head*, that magnificent man-o-war, sitting only two hundred yards off our stern with all her lanterns lit. Even the witch's figurehead mounted to her prow was bathed in ghoulish lantern light. "Dowlin will only allow ten men to accompany me over."

"Ten it is, Mary," Hunter offered solemnly. "Our very best."

"If it all goes wrong, Tom, you know what to do," I said and squeezed his arm.

"Aye, protect the ship and bolt to Clew Bay."

"Good - and fifty pounds to the widow or orphan of any man who falls," I added.

Gilley nodded.

"If I fall, Mary," Hunter asked me with a grin, "would my fifty pounds revert back to you as you and Tom are my only family? If so, I think perhaps I'm being swindled."

I leaned over and kissed him on the cheek. "Don't then be a fool and get yourself killed is my advice to you."

My ten men and I piled into a longboat, set the oars and rowed across sea's still waters with a second boat in tow, with a boat loaded down with crates and barrels of different shapes and sizes. I began to fret as my men pulled at their oars towards Dowlin's ship. We were taking on an awful risk. So many things could go wrong. I tried to put my mind at ease. I tried to extinguish any doubt as I focused my attention on the soothing, pleasant sounds of water coursing over the blades of the oars. But those pleasant sounds were spoiled by another sound, by the annoying sound of a single, squeaky lantern swaying lazily back and forth from an iron staff attached to the stern of the second boat we had in tow and I began to second guess myself again.

We reached *Medusa's Head* just as the sun began melting into sacred Ireland's soft, green hills, just as a blanket of cool air settled on the water. The chill, or perhaps it was a twinge of dread, gave me goose bumps.

I willed my legs up the rungs of a rope ladder hanging off *Medusa's* side. I was the first to step aboard. I clenched my teeth and slowed my breathing down. I summoned up my courage. A crowd of men, unwholesome and unclean with smiles all around, quickly surrounded me. And there, standing at the fore rail of his grand aftercastle and looking down on me like some lord or demi-god, I saw Dowlin grinning from ear to ear.

"Welcome to *Medusa!*" Dowlin bellowed in a deep voice after the last of my men had climbed aboard. He kept his gaze fixed on me while stroking his long, black beard. "Search 'em boys. Search 'em all and be sure to liberate any weapons. Then bring the good Lady Mary up to me."

We knew better than to bring any weapons with us. Two sailors escorted me up to the aftercastle while my men, including Hunter and Efendi, were forced to remain behind, huddled together on the main deck, surrounded by Dowlin's crew. But there weren't many of Dowlin's men on deck I noted and I thought that odd. And then I understood. Dowlin had brought only a meager company with him to our little parley, not a full crew. Luck was with us so far.

Dowlin crudely looked me up and down as I stood before him and curtseyed. I could feel his eyes undressing me.

He extended his arms out with a grin. "What, no warm embrace, Mary? No tender kiss between old friends?"

"I didn't know you fancied me," I replied to put him off. But he took a step towards me and embraced me just the same. I forced myself to kiss him on the cheek. I felt woozy when my lips brushed against his skin. I would have leaned over the rail and heaved had I had anything in my stomach.

"Ah, that's better, much better," Dowlin said loudly for all to hear. "Come, Mary, let us retire to my great cabin before our supper turns cold. But first, my men seem rather lax today, or perhaps they're just shy. It's your stunning beauty Mary that has put them off and made them bashful I suspect, that has turned them into pudding. I noticed they didn't search you very well. I'll need to find my lash and reprimand the careless bastards later."

He put his hands on my shoulders. He moved them down over my sleeves, over my hips and then slowly caressed my breasts while all his men stood gawking. "Good, good. No weapons here, no weapons there. Can never be too careful, eh? Now you'll kindly lift your skirt for me so I can take a peek."

I always wear men's coarse clothing at sea. But that night I had chosen to wear a fine woolen skirt, blood red in color, embroidered with ribbons of scarlet silk. My leather bodice fit snug against my waist and I wore an open white blouse to good advantage, to accentuate my bosom. The skirt was the only one I owned and I was prepared for Dowlin's crudeness. In fact, I was counting on it. I lifted my skirt high above my waist and spun around in a circle for him several times. Dowlin's jaw went slack. I didn't have a stitch of clothing on underneath my skirt. I wore no undergarments of any kind. I could see his men down on the main deck gasp at my nakedness and ogle me with lust.

"You see, my dear Captain Dowlin," I said demurely as Dowlin tried to regain his composure. "I can't hide a thing from you."

"Mary, Mary, Mary, unlike your poor, sweet Gretchen, I'll wager you know how to please a man in bed! And then again, I've heard some say you prefer the soft curves of a woman to the hard edges of a man. What a pity if true."

"Some rumors are true and some are not," I offered teasingly. "And I'll wager you know how to make a girl coo. Look there, you've gone and made me blush. Let us to business then, shall we?"

Dowlin invited two of his officers to dine with us and allowed Hunter to accompany me. It was difficult to suppress my absolute repulsion for the man throughout the whole, nauseating ordeal. I barely ate a morsel of food or touched a drop of wine.

"Well, now, Mary," Dowlin said as pushed his plate away, finished with his meal. "Your letter intrigued me. Indeed it did. You asked for this parley. You promised to make amends. And you rowed over to my ship with a second boat in tow I saw. What does that second boat carry I wonder? What's inside all those pretty crates and barrels you hauled across the water?"

His lips curled into a crooked smile. He studied me carefully, wishing no doubt to savor my wretched humiliation.

"I brought gifts with me to heal the wounds between us, to

redress old wrongs," I answered as sincerely as I could. "And I pray in earnest that you find my gifts to your liking. But first, one gift deserves another. There should be a *quid pro quo* between friends. Gifts are best when exchanged, is that not our custom?"

Dowlin opened his mouth and burped. "I'm not particularly fond of customs. But, by all means, speak your mind."

"In exchange for my gifts, I want to reach an accord with you, with the *Síol Faolcháin*."

"Oh, and what accord might that be?"

I bowed my head in supplication. "I'm here to ask for your pardon for my careless remarks. You are a lord of the sea. You have the right to fair tribute and I must yield to your authority. I was wrong to question this. But I've never cheated you. Your men seized one of my ships, claimed I was light on payment and this is untrue - this is what roused my feminine ire."

"Even the best of friends sometimes disagree and quibble, Mary," Dowlin replied and grunted. Then he looked over at one of his officers. "Thompson, the Lady Mary claims a mistake has been made, that her account with us is balanced. She says we seized one of her ships unjustly. What say you?"

"She lies, Capt'n," the man named Thompson scoffed. He quickly craned his head around to give me an evil look.

"My lady," Hunter said indignantly, jumping to his feet, "never lies!" But Hunter's bluster, like my own lack of undergarments, was nothing more than an act, a distraction.

"Easy there, young pup." Dowlin said and placed his hand on the hilt of his sword. "Or I'll split you open between your legs and return you back to your ship missing a pair of balls. Now, Mary, Thompson here is a good man but mistakes, shall we say misunderstandings, can and do happen from time-to-time. Thompson, might there be a mistake or misunderstanding afoot here?"

Thompson sheepishly looked down at his plate. He knew his place and nodded to his master. "If you say so, Capt'n."

"Well now, there you have it! Let's put an end to this sordid business. Tell me Mary, what is this accord you wish to reach with me?"

"My lord," I said, trying to sound contrite and bowing my head again. "Keep the vessel you seized from me and accept the gifts I bring you this day but, in return, I want to sail the Irish Sea with all my ships free of any taxes for one, full year."

Dowlin erupted in a fit of laughter and slapped the table with his hand. He laughed so hard his belly shook. "Pay no taxes - for one, full year! Bless me, Mary you're a hard one! But you do have a sense of humor I must say, an exquisite sense of humor to match your exquisite beauty!"

I looked up at Dowlin sweetly, batting my eyes for him. "My lord, I'm quite serious. But you need not answer me here and now, not until after you have seen my gifts, not until after you are satisfied that you are getting the better part of the bargain by far. I want no more trouble with the *Síol Faolcháin*."

Dowlin lewdly licked his lips. "I saw some of your gifts earlier up on the quarter deck this evening. I should like to sample more."

"Oh my. You are such an incorrigible flirt, my dear Captain."

"And you, my lady, are a wicked tease."

"Well, let us see how it goes," I said and offered my hand across the table. "The hour is late and I must return to my ship for now for I have an unruly crew to contend with. But if you summon me to Youghal - in friendship - I will come and we can get to know one another better. Do we have an agreement?"

Dowlin took my hand in his and used his thumb to caress my skin. "Perhaps," he said with a slight smile. "All things are possible between friends. I will send you my answer after I see my gifts."

A sharp pain shot through my heart. I understood Dowlin's meaning. He would send me the body of someone I cared for if he was at all displeased.

He could see in my eyes that I understood. His hint of a smile blossomed into a wide grin.

It took all the strength I had to return Dowlin's soft caresses with my own, to look into his eyes with lust. "Very well. I pray you send me your answer quickly," I said and licked my lips for him. "You'll find I am not all that hard. There are parts of me that are soft and supple."

With a peck on the cheek, I said my farewells to Dowlin, collected my men and we hurried down the rope ladder to our longboat. We pushed off quickly, dipped our oars in the water and pulled with slow but even strokes. We left the second boat with all our gifts behind.

The sea was black and flat. The air was still. The great hunter Orion, with his bow in hand, hovered directly over us. I welcomed the bowman. I took his appearance as a good sign.

And then we heard the faintest splash of water, an almost imperceptible sound, near the second boat. But we thought nothing of it and continued rowing slowly - until a head popped above the surface next to me. My men grabbed MacGyver by the arms and quickly hauled him out of the water.

"Are we good, Michael?" Hunter asked in a low voice.

"We're good." MacGyver answered. His teeth clattered from the water's chill.

"Pick up the stroke, lads," I whispered, "row hard!" I turned around to look at Dowlin's ship. I could see three of Dowlin's men dangling on the rope ladder, struggling to pull our gifts in. But MacGyver had chained the second boat to *Medusa's* rudder while Dowlin and I ate our dinner and the boat wouldn't budge.

"How long, James?" I asked.

"A few minutes, more or less."

Before setting out, we had stuffed the barrels and crates on the second boat at the top of the pile with things of value, with things that would have interested Dowlin had he troubled himself to inspect our gifts after our arrival. But the bottom barrels - Hunter had packed those with gunpowder. We had left MacGyver behind on the second boat hidden underneath a tarp. After pushing-off in our longboat, MacGyver had used the squeaky lantern, the one hanging from the staff, to light the powder fuse. Once MacGyver was satisfied the fuse was burning straight and true, he quietly slipped over the side and swam to us.

"Are we far enough away?" I asked.

"Don't know, Mary," Hunter said, anxiously looking behind us. "Playing with explosives is always a tricky business. The powder can have a mind of its own. If the fuse didn't burn out the blast shouldn't be too - ."

But before Hunter could finish his thought, an earsplitting BOOM startled us. The blast's shock wave blew me off my thwart as if someone had punched me in the stomach. My heart bounced up in my throat. As I struggled to sit up, a wall of heat smacked me in the face and when I turned to look back at Dowlin's ship, I saw a great ball of fire rising into the night.

"Row! Row lads, row!" I cried out. We had to reach the *Phantom* quickly.

Smoke engulfed *Medusa's* stern. Debris went flying everywhere. *Medusa's* men scrambled in all directions, grabbing water buckets and axes and frantically tried putting out the small fires burning all around *Medusa's* aftercastle. Fire started licking its way up her Bonaventure mast and I wondered whether the whole ship might go up in flames. I frowned. I wanted Dowlin's ship intact; I wanted Dowlin and his men alive.

"Did we do it Hunter?" I asked anxiously.

Hunter kept his gaze fixed on the smoke and fire ravaging *Medusa's* stern and didn't answer for a bit. And then he cracked a thin smile. "Aye! Her rudder's been blown clean off, Mary! *Medusa's* crippled, dead in the water!"

We did not have long to gloat. A moment later we saw tongues of flame reach out across the still water for us, followed a split second later by the report of *Medusa's* heavy guns.

BOOM! BA-BA-BOOM!

Deadly iron flew over our heads. Each ball made an unsettling noise, a bloodcurdling, whistling sound like *zoozoozoozoozoo* as it whizzed past us. Even my steadfast Hunter cringed.

"Thank God," Hunter said, "they didn't load their barrels with grapeshot or we'd all be dead."

Phantom answered *Medusa*'s bluster in kind. Her guns erupted with smoke and fire.

BOOM! BOOM! BA-BA-BA-BOOM!

More shots flew by us. Gilley was covering our retreat.

Our small longboat was caught on the open water in-between two great warships trading deadly broadsides at close range. Not a pleasant place to be. We pulled harder on our oars.

Once we reached *Phantom*, we rowed past her bow and around to her starboard side to shield ourselves from Dowlin's rage. I quickly scrambled back on board with my small squad of saboteurs trailing behind me. Once we were all aboard, topmen dropped our sails and *Phantom* slowly began lurching forward. We abandoned our longboat to the sea.

When I saw Gilley standing on the main deck barking out orders, I raced over to him and embraced him warmly. "Thank you, Tom!"

"'Twas my pleasure, Mum," he replied. When Hunter joined us, Gilley clasped him by the shoulder and shook him. "By all the Saints you did it, James! You really did it! Bravo my good man, bravo!"

Hunter smiled sheepishly. "Aye, but we're not home-free, not yet, Tom."

"No, but we will be soon enough!" Gilley proclaimed with a cocky tone. "This'll be child's play now, Mary."

And that had been the plan. We didn't have enough gunpowder to blow *Medusa* up and even if we had, we had no way to deliver so much powder over to Dowlin's ship. But we had enough powder for one ship's rudder and without her rudder *Medusa's Head* wasn't sailing anywhere. She was a fish without a tail. We could sail circles around her for hours. We could pummel her into dust.

At first Dowlin and his crew were stubborn and refused to yield. Stupid men often seem incapable of understanding when they've been beaten and Dowlin was no exception.

We sailed past *Medusa's* scorched and battered stern and

circled around to cross her lightly defended bow, guarded only by a pair of measly three-pounders - and that ghastly witch's head. A dozen times we crossed her bow and poured a raking broadside into her on each pass. *Phantom's* guns inflicted a goodly amount of damage. I was elated when one shot split that damn witch's head in two.

We stayed clear of coming up alongside *Medusa*, denying her crew the pleasure of training their big guns on us. We suffered only a few random hits from her three-pounders and *Phantom* shook those light blows off with ease. But tip-toeing around *Medusa* had cost us precious time.

Pig-headed to the end, Dowlin would not surrender. He hoped he could wait us out. He hoped the daylight might yet save him. So we went in close for one final pass and swept his decks with grapeshot. A great number of his men fell dead. And then we threw out grappling hooks, snagged *Medusa* at the bow and reeled her in.

I drew my sword and led the first wave of men over the rails myself. We took the forecastle first and then charged across the main deck, slick with blood and gore, and made our way towards the stern where we encountered a handful of Dowlin's crew struggling to lower a boat in the water amidships. They tried raising the boat over the rails until they got themselves entangled in the rigging. The sight was rather entertaining and I couldn't help but laugh. They abandoned their foolishness quick enough when we closed in around them and then they fled like dogs back to the quarter deck where the rest of their mates were huddled.

We tore after them. We chased them up the aftercastle's twin ladders and across the quarter deck - and then I saw him. Dowlin was still alive. He was standing next to *Medusa's* burned-out helm along with the remnants of his defeated crew.

With his face begrimed in sweat and soot, with his clothes in blackened tatters, Dowlin looked far less menacing, far less lordly now. And just as the stars began to fade, and as the sun began to rise, my men and I closed ranks for one last charge across *Medusa's* deck to slaughter the last of our hated foe. But Dowlin knew the fight was over. He knew there was no escape. He glared at me with a mix of arrogance, loathing and disgust. He tossed his sword at my feet, surrendering his grand ship to me while plotting, no doubt, how he would kill me later.

My plan, beyond my imagining, had worked. *Medusa's Head* was mine. Dowlin's head was next...

Chapter Four

ost in thought, her majesty stood and began pacing around my cell. It was best during these moments of reflection to keep silent I had learned. I waited patiently until her highness was ready to hear more of my wretched story.

"Good, good," the queen mumbled to herself after a time. "We now have a more perfect understanding of things that had perplexed us before."

I bowed my head. "I am glad if I've been of service in some small way, your Highness."

"Let us see. You were the victim of a great, unspeakable evil at the tender age of twelve or so. After Lord O'Malley took you in, you spent your days working a tavern and learning about ships that sail the wild sea. Later, from his deathbed, Lord O'Malley whispered into your ear that you were his illegitimate daughter and he left you an inheritance, an impressive sum of money. You used this Godsend to purchase your own ship and crew and you tried your hand at smuggling. During the next few years you did well, adding more ships and men to your expanding enterprise until one day Dowlin, a jealous man, provoked you when he seized one of your vessels to take you down a peg or two. You openly challenged this clan chieftain, insulted him in public and he answered you by snatching a young girl away from you, a girl who was very dear to you. Gretchen was her name. Dowlin brutally murdered this poor child and you avenged her death by beheading Dowlin and by taking his ship and gold. Ah, but then you had the Twins to contend with. You set a trap for them at Great Saltee - but this dangerous pair of brutes survived your clever ambush, leaving you in a fine pickle."

The queen stopped her pacing in front of me, looked down and smiled. "Certainly not the happiest of stories we've ever heard, Mary. Still, by any measure, it is a most beguiling tale."

"You have summed-up the gest of things quite well, your Majesty."

"Just so, Mary. My Lord Cecil, do you have all that?"

"Indeed I do my Queen."

"Good. Let us know if your fingers begin to cramp. Now Mary, you must again summon up your courage. Please continue with your story. We would have you tell us more about your exploits. We would have you tell us more about the Twins."

We lost five good men that night we fought the Twins and all their men at Saltee. I did not know them well. One man died from his wounds from the ambush. The others were killed at sea by one, well-placed shot during the brief skirmish between the *Phantom* and the Twins' war-carrack. *Phantom* herself suffered only minor damage. We buried our fallen comrades next to nearly seventy of the Twins' own. We had thirty prisoners too, mostly wounded, who we patched up and later set free, including Flannigan and his men. Some weeks later we learned that the Twins were still very much alive, though one had lost an eye from shrapnel we heard. The Twins had fled back to Youghal, their stronghold, a place I dared not go.

Saltee might seem like a great victory, a slaughter. But no. I knew, we all knew, that we had only managed to wound the hideous beast. We had only insulted the twin-headed monster and made it angry.

In truth my plan had failed. The Twins were alive and more dangerous than before for now they knew the face of their enemy. There would be a price on my head for all the rest of my days. And the reach of the Twins was long - I reconciled myself to an early, grisly death.

Blessed with calm seas and fair winds, my tiny fleet of two made an uneventful journey back to Westport, back to our safe haven on the west coast of Ireland though I did not know if we would be welcome there. The O'Malleys had no cause to risk war with the Twins by giving sanctuary to us. Or so I had imagined.

To my surprise, our little adventure in the Irish Sea had caused barely a ripple in Westport. Our hosts were most gracious, even sympathetic to our plight, especially after I shared a portion of the spoils - half of Dowlin's treasure - with them. A heavy price to pay to be sure, but I knew the Twins would learn of it. Then it would seem as if the raid against Dowlin had been sanctioned by the O'Malleys and that suited me just fine.

The O'Malley clan, a tribe of stout warriors with a rich history in seafaring, had many ships and men-at-arms and castles in the west. They had formed powerful alliances with other clans too and were hardly friends of any of the clans who ruled the east. Even the English army gave the O'Malleys their due respect and kept its distance.

Even so, I knew we could not tarry long in Westport. Ireland has never been a peaceful, tranquil land and now the country was in the midst of great upheaval. The old Gaelic order was under siege and dying.

For generations - beyond the memory of time - the clans had been fighting between themselves for power. But in more recent times, our island has been particularly beset by change and turmoil brought from across the sea. After her majesty's father, King Henry VIII, claimed the crown of Ireland for himself in the 1540's, he quietly went about converting Irish lords into English lords, lords loyal to his royal person. And then under Mary Tudor's policy of expansion, given the quaint name of Plantation, a policy her majesty is well familiar with, English settlors started arriving on the shores of Ireland in droves. They call themselves the New English and they are given land confiscated from the Irish. These New English bring their English customs and English laws with them. They bring the Protestant Reformation. Their intolerance for all that is Catholic is strong. Their aversion to anything Irish is plain.

Oh, what a toxic brew to choke on. The Irish are a proud and independent people. They did what they always do when their independence is threatened: they took up the sword, the bow and the musket and rebelled of course.

My men and I spent the harshest days of winter at Westport hiding away under shelter. The winter gales whipping down from the Arctic were particularly fierce that year and I was grateful we could afford to remain warm and dry in port. We used our time to overhaul *Phantom* and *Falling Star* and we frequented our favorite taverns, listening to talk of war with the English and debating what to do once Eternal Spring returned to bless the land.

I lost two small vessels that winter in the Irish Sea. The ships, both galleys, were returning to Ireland from Spain and heading for a small town north of Dublin named Rush. Dowlin henchmen intercepted and seized my ships and cargo. But, by the grace of God, the Dowlin clan spared my men and set them free - unaware they sailed for me.

A young tavern wench, a demure, pretty little trinket, brought more ale and removed our plates. Between the heavy fare, the strong ale and liquor, and the inn's roaring fire, we had all fallen into a pleasant, after-supper stupor.

Hunter was the first to break the long silence. "Where away next, Mar-Mary?" he asked, slurring his words while keeping his bloodshot eyes focused on his tankard of ale. "I, I much prefers being po-poor and sailing across the briny sea than reasch, rea, rea, rich and fuckin' bored witless on land."

All my officers suddenly perked up and looked at me, waiting for my answer. But I would not decide alone.

"We all know the choices," I said. "We are living in a golden age, an age of opportunity. North, South, East or West, they all sound enticing to me - what's your pleasure, lads?"

"A decision, I hasten to point out," offered Gilley, the only one among us who was still sober, "we must not make lightly."

"Just so," I replied.

"How far Norrrth or Sou, Sou, South or East or West are you thinkin' of, Mary?" Hunter asked.

"Far enough away to lose the Twins, but not so far away we lose a chance at reaping handsome profits."

"There be the rub, Mary," Gilley said, sympathetically nodding in agreement.

Green, Fox, Efendi and Ferguson all nodded along with Gilley. But not Hunter. He smiled and winked at me instead.

"A man or a woman," he said, intentionally pushing his tankard of ale off the table, "can sail too far and fall off, fall off, off, the edge of the world Mary and disappear."

"I thought," Green asked, alarmed, "Fernão de Magalhães proved the earth was round not so long ago, that it had no edge, no great precipice? He didn't circumnavigate the globe? The earth is flat like a pancake?"

We all burst out laughing at poor Green's expense.

"Pay them blockheads no mind, Ben," I said, trying to suppress both the giggles and the hiccups as I caressed his flushed cheek with the back of my hand. "I doubt any of those ignorant baboons even knows who Magalhães was and at the very least you do. So, gentlemen, we lost two good ships last month. Trading with Spain and other kingdoms was good business for us in the past. But the Dowlin clan has cost us a pretty penny and the *Síol Faolcháin* can cause us even more woe if we stay and flaunt our disdain for their authority and power. The risks for us will only grow."

Gilley rested a hand on Efendi's shoulder. "Tell us again Mustafa about all that fabulous wealth in Persia."

"More wealth than any one man could count in a lifetime," Efendi answered in his broken English. "But why do you think

Turkish pirates sail all this way to Ireland to raid Irish ships and towns? The Ottoman Sultan, Suleiman the Magnificent, is an unbelievably rich and powerful prince and he is very jealous of his possessions. He'll not part with them easily. Not even one, meager coin. And the Mediterranean, well, its waters are fouled with desperate cutthroats and bloodthirsty marauders of every sort, especially along the coast of North Africa. No, no, my friends. We should leave the East alone."

"Well," Gilley replied, "there's nothing to the South but open water, Africa and the slave trade. Not much to the North. The Swedes have a settlement in Ingermanland at the mouth of the Neva River if you have a taste for Russian goods. But God, I hear it's cold. Hunter, you speak very little about your travels to the West, to the New World. Tell us what you've seen and done there."

Hunter took a deep breath and looked past us, staring out one of the tavern's windows as if he had found something of interest far off in the distance. "If," he finally said, "you have a taste for silver, gold, pearls, tobacco, spices, sugar or the like, the Caribbean is an interesting place. But no one can match a Spaniard in cruelty."

I squeezed Hunter's forearm reassuringly. I knew I had to tread carefully. Hunter never spoke much about his travels to the New World and when he did, he chose his words carefully, sparingly and with little joy.

"So the Caribbean, James, this is where you sailed with the Spanish?" I asked.

"Aye, mostly."

"Did you see the Silver Train?" Gilley asked excitedly. ""Is it true what they say?"

"The Silver Train is more than just legend, Tom."

Gilley looked at Hunter wide-eyed. "You've actually seen it?"

"I've more than seen it. I've traveled with it."

"Oh? Do tell."

"Aye. I was with the train in *Nueva España* - New Spain. The jour, journ, journey began at *Minas de los Zacatecas*, a city in the central part of the country, and ended in Veracruz on the coast where silversmiths melt down the silver ore from the mines into coins and bullion. I saw, I exaggerate not, mountains of silver ore, Tom. And in the south, long caravans of mules and men moved stag, staggering amounts of gold and silver up from Cartagena to a place called *Nombre de Diós* - the Name of God - a small town on the Isthmus of Panama. From those two ports the Spanish load their wealth onto the great galleons and carracks of the *flota* once a year to ship it all back to Seville."

"Mountains of silver and gold you say?" Green asked.

"I tell you Ben, you cannot imagine it. You must see what I saw to comprehend it all. The Spanish call Zacatecas the *Ciudad de Nuestra Señora de los Zacatecas*, though I would call it hell. Zacatecas is where the Spanish force the Indian peoples, men, women - even young children - below ground to work the mines. The Indians, poor wretches, make terrible slaves and die quickly in those dirty holes. The savagery is beyond imagining. Hell is a real place my friends. I have seen it."

"Did you sail with the Spanish fleet?" I asked gently, trying to nudge Hunter away from his darker memories.

"Aye, aye I did."

"What," Gilley asked, "in God's holy name did the Spanish want with an Englishman?"

Hunter cracked a smile. "I passed myself off as an Irishman as the Spanish aren't overly fond of the English. I have skills at navigation, on land and at sea, and I have a talent for mapmaking. The Spanish hired me to help them explore new territories deeper into New Spain. I traveled west with a company of *conqui*, *conquistadors* until we reached Acapulco, a port on the Pacific coast. And then we traveled north for many weeks into *Los Californias*, taking horses and pack mules with us, looking for only God knows what. Some legendary lost kingdom in the wilderness once ruled by a race of Amazon warriors is what I heard some Spaniards claim. We never found it. The expedition proved a sorry waste of time."

"You mean *El Dordo?*" I asked. We had all heard the stories of *El Dorado*.

Hunter shook his head. "No, not *El Dorado*. Myths and legends abound in the New World. *El Dorado* I suspect is one of the myths. The success or failure of our expedition north of Acapulco hardly mattered to me though. The Spanish paid me well. But, in truth, I was working for the French."

"The French?" asked Gilley. "How so?"

"The French paid me to spy on the Spanish."

"You were a spy for the French?" I asked, stunned. "Good Lord!"

"Quite so, Mary. Why so surprised? The Spanish rob the Indians of their gold and silver and the French rob the Spanish in turn, where and when they can. The French and Spanish are at war, or leastwise they were. The French retained my services to gather information, whatever I could learn."

"What happened to you?"

Hunter sat back in his chair and took a deep breath to try and clear his head. "Ah, well now, there's a story there. The *Flota de Indias*, a grand fleet of nearly sixty ships with galleons, freighters and transports, weighed anchor in early March one year and set out before the season of the *huracán*. I was with it. But storms were not our only worry. The French had more than just spies in the New World. French buccaneers infest the sea lanes between Veracruz and Seville. I sailed with the *Inca*, a slow, leaky merchantman, a caravel. In Havana, a port on the windward side of the large island of Cuba, we rendezvoused with the *plate flota* sailing up from Peru before we began our trip back to the Old World. Two weeks out from Havana, we were and blown off course somewhere north of the Lesser Antilles when our ship fell behind the main convoy, struggling against heavy seas and bucking against strong headwinds. A French twenty gunner happened upon us and ran us down. The French seized our ship and set the crew and me adrift in the boats. We rowed for weeks in those tiny boats out on the open water. The *Inca's* master was a gifted seaman though and kept us all alive. Except to take on food and water, we avoided the nearest islands because of hostile Indians. We sailed for Trinidad, but our boats gave out before we could reach that safe haven and we found ourselves marooned on - ."

Hunter abruptly stopped in mid-sentence when armed men burst into the tavern, coming in through the tavern's back door. Trouble had found us.

"There's the bitch, kill her!" an angry voice cried out.

"Assassins!" Gilley shouted and jumped to his feet.

I spun around in my chair to find a dozen men with their muskets already cocked and leveled at us. We had no chance to draw our own weapons. The intruders took a step forward with grins all around.

We all would have died that day but for the tavern's quick-witted proprietor, a man named Shaw. Shaw saved us. He was one of mine. I paid him and paid him well to watch our backs whenever we were in port.

"Another step and you're all dead men," Shaw said calmly as he came up behind the rascals with his two sons standing at his side. Shaw and his boys each held a pair of pistols, cocked and at the ready.

The twelve men spun around to face Shaw and his boys. And in that brief moment, when these brigands hesitated for just an instant to consider this new threat behind them, my men and I drew our swords and pistols. Now we had our assailants surrounded, though they held the upper-hand in numbers.

I recognized one of the men. I'd seen his face once somewhere before though I couldn't remember where. He had a distinctive red birthmark splattered across his chin and left cheek.

"I know you!" I blurted out in an angry tone, pointing my sword at him, wanting to draw attention away from Shaw and his boys.

The man spun around to face me and raised his musket at my chest. The fool killed himself.

Nearly quicker than the eye can see, Efendi reached into his sleeve, whipped out a throwing knife and sent it flying across the room. The blade buried itself in the man's windpipe, just below his

Adam's apple. He dropped his musket and crumpled to the ground wide-eyed, clutching at his throat. Shaw and his boys discharged their pistols, six shots in all, instantly filling the room with gun smoke. Hunter seized the moment. He took advantage of the confusion and leapt into the midst of the hoodlums with a sword in one hand and a dagger in the other, pouncing with the ferocity of a lion hungry for the kill. In a whirl of motion he cut one, two and then a third man down. Gilley shot a fourth man dead. Green, Fox, and Ferguson all fired their pistols too.

In less than a dozen heartbeats eleven men lay dead or dying on the tavern's cold, dirt floor. Not the noblest of places to lose one's life. The lone survivor dropped his musket and fell to his knees. He raised his hands above his head.

Hunter grabbed the man by his collar. "Who sent you?"

"Avé María, grátia pléna, avé María, grátia pléna, avé María, grátia pléna," the man repeated over and over again.

Hunter put the edge of his sword against the man's throat and nicked him. "You can deliver your prayers in person once you're dead. Now tell me who sent you or I swear by Christ I'll pluck out both your eyes. And then, if you still have a mind to be stubborn, I'll slice off your privates and feed them to the dogs. After that, if you still have nothing to say to me, I'll cut out your worthless tongue - the Spanish taught me how to make a man squeal - they taught me well my friend. Your death will not be quick or easy..."

I stared at Hunter in disbelief, unsure of whether he was bluffing or serious about his barbarous threats. But then I saw the cruelty in his eyes. I had never seen this dark side of him before. This was something new and unsettling for me. He was back somewhere in the New World again.

"Capt'n Mary," Shaw called out.

I turned and found Shaw kneeling over the man with the red birthmark on his face, the man with Efendi's knife still sticking in his throat. Shaw held a piece of paper up to show me.

"What is it, John?"

"Best have a look at this," Shaw replied.

"My God," I blurted out as I read the document.

"What is it, Mary?" Gilley asked.

"This cannot be!" Gilley exclaimed after he perused the document too. He looked at me, confused. "This is a writ signed by the High Sheriff of Dublin commanding these men to take you into custody. But these men were here to kill you, not arrest you."

"Writ, what are you talking about?" Hunter asked crossly.

"That man with the birthmark," I said and pointed, "was sent by the High Sheriff of Dublin. These are the queen's men!"

"Impossible!" Hunter declared.

Gilley handed the writ over to Hunter.

"I don't understand," Hunter said as he read the writ. He let the document fall to the floor and turned towards our prisoner. "I'm done playing with you. Speak or I'll gouge out an eye. You can pick which one. Gilley, Efendi, hold this bastard down."

"Alright, alright," the man mumbled.

"What did you say?" Hunter asked.

"Bugger me, alright!"

"Louder you scum, sucking dog!"

"Alright! Alright! On your word, before God, you'll not harm me if I talk - swear it."

"On my word," Hunter replied coldly, "before God, I'll harm you most cruelly if you don't talk - I swear it."

Hunter rested his sword on the man's shoulder while Gilley and Efendi lifted him to his feet and held him firmly. The man broke down in tears. He started sobbing like a child.

Hunter patted the man's pockets down and found a purse full of coin, too much coin for a common laborer. "You don't look like one of the sheriff's men to me. And you didn't come to arrest anyone. You came here bent on murder. So tell me, who are you?"

"My name is Joseph Gwinn."

"Who employed you?"

"I work for no one. I'm a simple farmer."

Without warning, Hunter smashed his fist into the man's nose. I heard the snap of bone.

"Ugh! What did you do that for? You broke my fuckin' nose!"

"For lying," Hunter replied evenly and tossed the man's purse in his face. The coins spilled out across the floor. "Your nose is but the first of many bones I'm going to break. I don't know any farmers with this much coin. And, if indeed you are a farmer, I'll wager your farm is not far from Youghal."

When Gwinn said nothing, Hunter moved his sword from Gwinn's shoulder up to his left ear. He slowly started slicing. Blood trickled down Gwinn's neck.

Gwinn winced and stared at Hunter horrified. "Alright! Alright! Stop, stop! I beg you. Aye, near Youghal. I have a small farm near Youghal. We're all from Youghal except for Flint. The Dowlin clan hired us. We was told to find Capt'n Mary and bring her back to Youghal. The devil take me if what I say an't so."

"Who told you?"

Gwinn looked down at the man with the birthmark. "Flint, the High Sheriff's man, the man lying over there who carried the writ, he was here to arrest the woman and bring her back to Dublin. But our orders were different. We was told to bring her back to Youghal."

"Whose orders?"

"Two brothers. They call themselves the Twins."

"And what was Flint arresting Mary for, on what charges?"

"Piracy."

"Piracy?"

"Piracy, that's all I know. That's what we was told."

"And what do you suppose the Twins wanted with Capt'n Mary?"

"They didn't say, leastwise not to me."

Hunter backhanded the man hard across the face.

"Fuck! What was that for?" Gwinn asked.

"For being stupid."

Each of the men who attacked us carried purses fat with coin. None of us could tell for certain who had given the order to kill us. We did not know if Gwinn and his mates from Youghal had been duped by the High Sheriff's man into killing us or the other way around. Against his will of course, we put Gwinn on one of O'Malley's ships bound for Italy. Uncertain of whether he had come to Westport to arrest me or to murder me, I could not kill him. By the time he reached the shores of Youghal again, if he ever did, we would be far away. As for the dead, we took their bodies out to the bay, weighted them down with stones and dumped them without prayers, without the proper burial rites due the dead. Their souls could burn in hell for all eternity for all I cared.

None of us were so naïve to think that this would end the matter. I had no means to fix the writ and it would not be long before the High Sheriff of Dublin realized he was missing one lieutenant and eleven deputies from Youghal. And once he learned that his man had disappeared in County Mayo, the High Sheriff would send more men to Westport to investigate matters further and search for Flint. After we disposed of the bodies, I summoned my officers to my great cabin for a council of war, for war was surely what we were now fighting.

Gilley was the first to voice his thoughts. "This complicates matters greatly. Piracy? For killing off a rival and seizing his ship before he did the same to us? How absurd. 'Tis a gross injustice, an affront to the laws of God and nature. And no doubt his high and mighty lordship in Dublin will add murder, even high treason against the Crown, for our supposed perfidies now. Sweet Jesus, how did it come to this?"

"The Twins," Hunter offered softly. "They pay well to have friends in lofty places. Mary, I suspect you'll not want to hear what I have to say. But it must be said. I'm sorry, Mary. The Twins have won. Not even Westport can keep us safe. Europe, the East, is closed to us and there is nothing North or South. With both the Twins and the English as enemies, we'll only lose more ships and men if we stay and fight. In the jungles of the New World there is a snake the Spanish call the *cascabela muta*, the silent rattle snake. Its venom is deadly. This particular serpent strikes quietly, without warning, and slithers off into the jungle unseen. Its victims never see it coming. Its victims never see where it goes. We must be like the *cascabela muta*. We must disappear and leave no trace."

"Disappear into the New World?" I asked. "And I pray you will tell us what the devil we would do there?"

"Unless you fancy sailing to Japan or China, aye, the New World. King Philip has imposed stiff taxes on all trade in the Americas, as did his father before him, King Charles, to help pay for all his ships and men. Smugglers do good business the Caribbean. The island of Trinidad is a particular favorite safe haven for smugglers and pirates alike. Smugglers bring manufactured goods in from Europe for Spanish and Portuguese settlors, folks who don't care to pay the king's high taxes, and then turn about and sail back to Europe with cargo holds stuffed full with tobacco, spices, sugar, wood, chocolate and the like. We could do the same."

"But you have just now warned us of the dangers of continuing our trade in Europe," Green said.

"We'll need," I said, answering for Hunter, "to approach the O'Malley clan. We'll need them as a silent partner. If we decide, one and all, to sail for the New World, we'll need to find ourselves a base somewhere in the Caribbean. Perhaps we can use Clew Island as our port-of-call here in the Old World. We ship raw goods from the New World to sell to the O'Malleys and then sail back to the Americas with whatever manufactured goods the O'Malleys will sell to us. Profits will be smaller. The hazards will be greater. Our voyages across the vast and grim Atlantic will be long and perilous. It would seem our days of ease and plenty have ended my brothers. And James, I will admit you are right. For now the Twins have won. But this great matter between us is hardly settled."

I took a moment to search the face of each man. And then, in accordance with our Ten Rules, I put the matter to a vote.

"What say the rest of you?"

All but one of my officers voted to make the Caribbean our

new home.

"Spit it out, Tom," I commanded. "What vexes you? Why do you withhold your vote?"

"I'll vote and I'll vote in favor of the Caribbean on one condition, well, perhaps on two conditions."

"Oh?" I asked, confused.

"There is," Fox quickly interjected, "nothing in any of the Rules of Ten that allows such nonsense."

"I challenge anyone to show me," Gilley quipped, "where the Rules forbid a vote with conditions attached!"

"It an't legal!" Fox protested loudly in jest - or maybe not. "There's a parliamentary decorum we must all observe. The vote is *aye* or it is *nay*. It is not *aye only if you make me the bloody king of England!*"

"Parliamentary decorum, is that Greek or Chinese?" Gilley asked.

"It means..."

"Auck, never you mind what it means, Alby," Gilley said and laughed, clearly quite pleased with himself. "You're just jealous 'cause you didn't think to do it first."

I shook my head. "Oh bloody hell Tom, very well. This argument is making my head spin. Name your price and the rest of us will vote whether to accept your terms or not. And if we don't, be forewarned: we'll toss you and your conditions over the side! If I'm to hang for piracy then, by God, I should have some fun and play the pirate before the queen's men slip the noose around my neck!"

The mood was light and all around the table my officers, even Fox, chuckled.

"Thank'ee kindly, Mum. Well now, let me see. My first condition is this: as God is my witness, and as each of you can attest truly, I've abstained from all strong drink for these past few years thanks to Mary. And I'm a better man for it. I'll not deny it. Even so, I want to taste this sweet wine I hear folk talk about made in the West Indies from exotic fruits once we reach the islands."

Hunter howled and slapped the table with his hand. "Gilley,

you old fool. You can get West Indies wine at half the taverns here in Westport! Most likely there's a bottle or two stashed away somewhere onboard the ship!"

"Stale or watered down, maybe. No, no. I want a bottle from one of those islands where folks make it fresh. I want to sit underneath one of those coconut trees in my bare feet and sip it slow. Just a bottle or two. After that I'll swear off all strong spirits again. Now and then a man's got to live tall!"

"My God," said Hunter. "This old fool is serious. And what is this second condition of yours, Tom?"

"Ah, now how appropriate you be the one to ask me, my good Capt'n of the Guns. My second condition is this: before we sail, I want to hear the rest of your story, all of it."

"An excellent choice in terms, Tom," I said. "James?"

"Oh, very well," Hunter replied with a sigh. "Let me see. Aye. The crew of the *Inca* and me were marooned on some small island north of Trinidad after our boats gave out and we were lucky for it because the French aren't shy about cutting-up Spaniards. We had no Caribbean wine as I recall Master Gilley, but we did not lack for food or water and we bided our time until a Spanish freighter bound for Seville happened by and rescued us. I fell gravely ill on that cruise, beset by tremors and fever. Sewn inside my jacket was a French letter of safe conduct, a letter I carried with me just in case I fell into the hands of the French while pretending to be in the service of the Spanish. A sailor searched my clothes looking for anything of value while I was laid low with fever. He found the letter when I was helpless. The fool couldn't read so he took the letter to the ship's master. Bad luck for me. After the master read the letter he clapped me in irons and promised to turn me over to the tender mercies of those demonic priests of the Inquisition once we reached Spain. I knew my life was forfeit. But good fortune had not deserted me altogether. A storm, a horrific storm of brutal strength, the likes of which I had never seen before and pray to never to see again, overtook us, tossed our ship savagely about for days. Matters took a desperate turn. The master ordered every hand on deck, including me, to work the sails and rigging. I must confess the Spaniard knew his tradecraft. By some miracle the ship weathered the deadly storm. Most of the crew survived. But the storm had carried us far north, had carried us up to the east coast of Ireland. The master decided to put in at the nearest port to make repairs and to rest his weary crew. The nearest port was Wexford. Good luck for me. That was when I decided it best if the Spanish and I part ways. I waited for nightfall, slipped over the side and swam for shore. I caught a knife in the back for my trouble. You all know my story from there..."

"I understand your arrangement with the French well enough, James," I said. "But I am a bit hazy on what you were looking for in the jungles of New Spain?" Hunter, I knew, was not a man who would set off into the wilderness of a strange and hostile land on a whim or without good purpose.

"My lady, I've satisfied most of old Tom's condition and the hour is late," he replied in a tantalizing tone.

"Come now, Hunter," said Gilley. "Not even whiff of a hint?"

"Whatever the Spanish were searching for they did not find it," Hunter answered with a sly smile.

I returned Hunter's smile with one of my own. "The Spanish did not find it? Ah, huh. I believe you there. But then again, you aren't Spanish..."

"How true, how true," Hunter said as he reached down and pulled off one of his boots.

We watched in fascination as Hunter took a knife, pried a seam along the top edge of his boot open and removed a long, oilskin pouch. He opened the pouch and let a thin metal cylinder encased in block of wax slip into his palm. Then he snapped the wax and cylinder in two and removed a piece of linen. He gingerly unrolled the linen across the table for everyone to see.

"A map?" I asked.

"Aye, a map," Hunter answered. "A treasure map. I never expected to return to the New World and this ragged piece of cloth is probably worthless. Perhaps it is a hoax."

"How did you come by this?" I asked.

"The story, as it was told to me, goes like so: A small unit of Spanish infantry, deserters most probably, supposedly happened upon a stash of Aztec gold somewhere in the jungles of New Spain and decided to keep it for themselves. But none of them knew how to move their wealth out of the country without being discovered. There was the problem of transportation. There are no roads in the jungles. Using wagons and mules to transport their treasure out would not be easy. So they decided to leave their find buried, undisturbed, until they could solve these problems later. A wayward priest traveling with the soldiers agreed to throw his lot in with them. The priest is the one who made this crude map. But, as you can see, it is a very poor map. Or so I thought at first. In fact the priest was quite a clever fellow. The map appears inaccurate and incomplete. It depicts certain landmarks, but none are in their proper, geographical location. The priest inked in the landmarks at random without proper relation to North, South, East or West. The *conquistadors* I served hoped that I might be able to make some sense out matters, or at least narrow down the size of the area we needed to search. We never found any hidden treasure."

"What happened to the priest and soldiers?" Gilley asked.

"An Indian raiding party caught the unlucky bastards in the open and slaughtered them all. The priest survived his wounds for a day or two and talked, or confessed his sins. The map somehow fell into the hands of a merchant. I suspect after stripping the dead the Indians sold the uniforms and gear to the merchant. The merchant found the map and thinking it worthless, he later sold it to some Spanish officer as a novelty."

"But why have you held on to this map for so long if you believe it is worthless?" I asked.

"I did not say the map was worthless, Mary. I said we found no treasure. But, while the *conquistadors* and I searched the jungles, I might, possibly, have stumbled upon the general location of where the treasure might be. I of course neglected to inform my Spanish *amigos* of this. Still, the map is flawed or it is in code and the priest and the soldiers who found the treasure are long dead. We could search those jungles for ages and find nothing."

"Why did the Spanish allow you to keep the map?" Green asked.

"They didn't," Hunter replied with another smile. "I made a copy."

Efendi startled me when he bolted upright in his chair. I thought he had been napping while Hunter told his story.

"Is this map of yours," he asked, "the copy or the original, James?"

"I kept the original for myself, of course. I left the Spanish with the copy."

"May I?"

"By all means."

Efendi carefully picked the map up and inspected the linen against the candlelight. "The oil skin and wax has served you well. The cloth does not appear to have been exposed to water."

"Why does that matter, Mustafa?" I asked, unclear of Efendi's meaning.

Efendi smiled. "Some ink can be invisible to the eye, my lady. The writing can be hidden until agitated by a chemical or heat, or even by something as simple as vinegar or saltwater. The priest may have used invisible ink to make this map. Such techniques have been used for centuries to send messages back and forth in secret."

Hunter leaned across the table and slapped Efendi on the back. "An interesting notion, Mustafa. How can we know one way or the other?"

"I have some knowledge of the art. But there are different inks made with different ingredients and the trick is to know which ink the writer used so one may determine what concoction is needed to render the ink visible. Because the errors on this map are obvious, I suspect the priest used invisible ink to hide a code needed to decipher the random symbols. Because a Roman Catholic priest prepared this map, I have some clue what kind of ink he might have used to draw this map. Of course, I may be wrong. Perhaps this map is nothing more than a joke as James has said. And this map is old, how many years James?"

"Six or seven years at least I suppose," Hunter replied. "Perhaps more."

Efendi shook his head in doubt.

"Well, we should give it a try and see," I said.

"We'll only get one chance, Lady Mary. If I apply the wrong emulsion this map will be lost forever. Even if I choose correctly, the document will most likely destroy itself within minutes. So, first we must make a perfect copy. Whatever hidden message or symbols are revealed on the original will need to be quickly transcribed over to the copy. We will need to work very fast. I will need vinegar, lemons, distilled water, charcoal and red cabbages to start with."

It was a peaceful, quiet morning. The morning watch was beginning to stumble up on deck to relieve the night watch as I leisurely strolled up and down the length of the ship to stretch my legs. A thick mist had settled over the harbor and I could barely see the other ships around us. There was a chill in the air too, a hint of fall, and I wrapped my shawl tightly around my shoulders.

Like Christopher Columbus, I had decided to take three ships with me to sail into the vast unknown to look for new trade routes, though not for the King of Spain. I had the *Phantom* and the *Falling Star* of course and I had found and purchased a large two hundred and fifty ton merchantman, the *Godsend*, in Westport. I had another dozen smaller ships sailing to different destinations between the east coast of Ireland and France and Spain. But these were mostly galleys and coasters, too fragile for the wild Atlantic and crewed by men who would want no part of the New World. So I released them all from any further obligation to me and sold the ships. I settled all my accounts to fund our new beginning.

"Mornin', Mary," Gilley said, walking up behind me.

"And a good morning to you, Tom."

"Bit nippy out."

"Aye, how goes it?"

"We're nearly ready. Three ships, three hundred men give or take, fifty-two great guns, including the merchantman's eight falconets, and eighty swivels along with enough swords, muskets, pistols, ball and powder to equip a small army. And here are the inventory lists for ammunition, gunpowder, flour, beans, rice, coffee, tea, water, lard, salted fish, beef, pork, etcetera, etcetera, and the bills of lading for the livestock and perishables yet to be brought onboard, not to mention all the tools, spare parts and our cargo of manufactured goods. 'Tis rather an impressive enterprise you've put together, Mary, especially without investors. Do you even have any money left, or are you broke?"

"The sum of all our wealth is on these three ships, Tom."

We both looked up when we heard Hunter climbing down the main mast ratlines.

"Watcha you doin' up there, James?" Gilley asked.

"Checking all the iron fittings one last time before we sail," Hunter replied as he jumped down from the rail and landed on the deck.

"Ha! Ha! You don't trust anyone do you, James?" Gilley asked.

"I trust some and some I don't. Shame on us Tom if we lose a spar or a sail to some seaman's laxness."

"And how are we today, James?" I asked.

"Fit as a fiddle, thank you kindly. And you?"

"Well enough. Tom says our preparations are nearly complete."

"I agree with Tom. The ships are sound and well-stocked. The men are ready. We can sail at your pleasure, Mary."

"That is well. I must confess though, I am savoring this glorious, cool morning. I shall miss them. I dread the oppressive heat."

"The New World can be terribly hot to be sure. But then there are the striking sunrises and magnificent sunsets, the likes of which you've never seen. Clear, emerald green waters splash up against islands lush with beautiful exotic plants and swaying palm trees lined along beaches of pure, white sand. You will see startling beauty, unsurpassed splendor, to take your breath away."

"And giant insects that bite and sting too I've heard!" Gilley scoffed.

Hunter nodded in agreement. "We aren't sailing to paradise, but neither is it hell. Europeans by the tens of thousands are flocking to the New World, giving up everything in the Old World to do so. That should tell you something."

And then we heard Efendi calling down to me from the quarter deck. The mist had thickened and I could barely see him. "Capt'n," he cried out, leaning over the rail, "all is ready."

Gilley, Hunter and I hurried back to my great cabin where we found Efendi standing at the table already waiting for us. He had set out candles, ink and pen, three large bowls of colored liquid and one iron pot filled with red hot embers.

"This is the original map," Efendi said, holding up the frayed piece of cloth Hunter had carried around with him for years. "And this other map on the table is an exact duplicate of the original that James, Tom and I drew last night with meticulous care. All is ready."

I glanced at both maps and nodded. I could barely tell them apart. "Excellent."

"Lady Mary, I cannot promise a good result. Perhaps we should wait? Perhaps we should find a priest or monk more knowledgeable in the art than me? Otherwise, I beg you for your pardon if I destroy this map for want of better skills."

I gave Efendi a reassuring pat on the shoulder. "No matter the result, you will not need my pardon, Mustafa. James, it is your map. I leave it to you to decide."

Hunter took the original from Efendi and considered the curious map for a moment. "I'm weary of carrying this ragged cloth around with me," he said and handed the map back to Efendi. "I say we try."

"Mustafa," I said, "work your magic if you can."

"Very well, my lady. James, Tom, you must be quick with your pens and transfer everything revealed on the original over to the copy with great care. You must be precise. We will only have a minute or two. Ready?"

"Ready."

Efendi took a deep breath and carefully placed the original linen in a bowl filled with yellow liquid. Next he counted to ten in Turkish, set the map on the table and pressed a dry cloth against the material to soak up the excess liquid. Then he counted again. He repeated this process with the second bowl filled with red liquid and then again with the third bowl filled with clear liquid.

"James, Tom, prepare yourselves," Efendi said nervously. "Pens in hand, *lütfen*, please, please, be ready." Then he took the map and held it over the pot of burning embers and once again he counted.

I watched over his shoulder in fascination as white lines and numbers magically appeared on the linen.

"Quickly, my friends, quickly!" he shouted excitedly. "Write! Write!"

Now it was Hunter and Gilley's turn. They studied the original for a moment or two and then started scribbling lines and numbers on the copy as fast as their hands and fingers would let them, Hunter focusing his attention on the left half of the map and Gilley on the right side.

Five minutes later, just as Efendi had predicted, the invisible ink began fading. The black ink bled into the cloth, ruining the original map forever. Hunter and Gilley set their pens aside, leaned over the copy and quietly examined their handiwork.

"Well?" I finally asked, annoyed that I even had to ask.

Both men looked up and smiled at me.

"Well," Hunter said, "Mustafa is a genius. We have ourselves a map, a good map. See here, Mary. The priest used the invisible ink to cross out certain land references. They must be meaningless. And then these numbers next to the rest are degrees, the degrees of a circle or the points on a compass. So this river or stream has been crossed out - it is a decoy meant to confuse. This lake and this small pyramid over here have not been crossed out so they must have value and the priest wrote numbers next to them. Below the pyramid is the number ninety, which I suspect is a reference to ninety degrees. These other numbers along the lines must be miles. So we will draw another map and put the landmarks in their proper order and where the lines intersect, *voilà*, that will be the place we seek. Simple, but effective."

"And does the map provide any clue of what we are looking for?" I asked.

"No, not one clue. The map is merely a guide, a guide to bring one to a certain place, a place somewhere in the wilderness. What is at this place, well, who can say? Nonetheless, the priest went to a great deal of trouble making this map. Whatever is there, if it is still there, the priest at least thought it had great value."

I embraced Efendi. "Well done, Mustafa, well done!"

"*Tesekkür ederim*," Efendi replied and bowed his head.

"I'm goin' to knock that Turk shit out of you yet, Mustafa," Gilley scolded. "You're an Irishman now lad, through and through."

Clearly quite pleased with himself, and unfazed by Gilley's playful chiding, Efendi shrugged his shoulders indifferently. As he considered his fine handiwork, his eyes sparkled, his lips curled into a wide grin...

Chapter Five

Easing his way down from the mizzen mast, Hunter casually strolled over to my side. We stood silently together on the quarter deck taking in the beehive of activity going on all around us in preparation to sail. Men were moving barrels and crates of perishables and the livestock, chickens, goats, rabbits and small pigs, up from the wharf onto the *Star* using pallets, nets and hoists. It was a new day full of promise. Then a scrawny young lad of eleven or twelve started hobbling up the gangplank with the help of a crutch propped underneath his arm.

Hunter leaned close to my ear. "Who's the boy?"

"Why that is Master William Ferrell of course," I offered evasively.

"Ah, of course it is. Master William Ferrell. How silly of me. Master William Ferrell from?"

"From Castlebar, from a farm that overlooks the old cairn to be more precise."

"You don't say! Master William Ferrell from Castlebar, from a farm that overlooks the old cairn."

"Quite so."

"You hired him?"

"Aye, I did."

"And what, if I may ask, might Master William Ferrell's skills be?"

"He can read. He can write. And he can sing and play the mandolin."

"Nooo! Truly? Most impressive! The boy can read and he can write and Master Ferrell from Castlebar can even sing and play the mandolin! How extraordinary. Fine skills to be sure, Mary. A century ago a young lad like that with his talents would have made Leonardo da Vinci proud. But I take it then he has no shipboard skills to speak of?"

"None that I know of."

"Mary! I suppose the fact that he's a cripple hasn't escaped your notice?"

"He is not a cripple, James. He has a broken leg. It will mend."

"And you took pity on him?"

"His father was killed not long ago in a hunting accident. The boy has no family. He will pull his weight in time, you'll see."

Hunter nodded and smiled. "You're going soft on me, Mary. Not good for a pirate."

"You best not go soft on me, James."

"Hmmm, what did Dowlin call you that night at supper? Ah, yes, a "wicked tease" is what I heard him say."

"Poor, old Dowlin. If memory serves, he didn't last very long after that thoughtless remark. But perhaps we can discuss this matter with more passion later, after supper?"

Hunter doffed his hat and bowed, as if I were some highborn lady. "I am at your service," he said, with no lack of chivalry in his tone. Then he took my hand and kissed it. "I am your most obedient and humble servant, *Madame*."

"Well my prince," I replied in a low and sultry voice and raised an eyebrow for him. "I can assure you that tonight you'll find me far, far more than just a wicked tease. Should you find your way into my bed, it will be my pleasure to serve you in whatever way you might desire..."

Hunter looked at me, speechless. I took pleasure in watching my rugged man blush.

I watched as broad streaks of different hues of pink and torques lit up the morning sky while my crews moved out smartly, casting off lines and dropping sail to catch the outgoing tide. It was a glorious morning. We eased our ships out into Clew Bay accompanied by flocks of squawking seagulls. Topmen eagerly went aloft and unfurled the larger square sails to give our ships greater purchase against the wind. By noon we were well into the rough and tumbly sea with rugged Ireland slowly sinking into the horizon behind us. I was not yet twenty years of age as we set out for the New World with a flotilla under my command.

Gilley had command of *Falling Star*, my flag ship, and I promoted Green to captain of the *Phantom*. The honor should have gone to Hunter but, selfishly, I wanted Hunter at my side onboard the *Falling Star*. I gave Fox command of our new freighter, the *Godsend*.

Weeks of easy sailing passed and the crew settled into a dull, but not unpleasant, routine. A sailor always gives thanks to the god or gods he prays to when his days at sea are filled with boredom. We gracefully plowed the ocean's gentle swells in close formation. The broad Atlantic had been a most hospitable hostess so far.

"Mustafa," I called out as I stepped on deck and saw Efendi at the tiller. "What are you doing there? Where's the helmsman?"

Efendi, sporting a new mustache now, flashed a broad smile at me. "He's at the privy head. It has been too long since I have held the tiller in my hands, my lady. Allah be praised, life is good."

"Allah be praised indeed my fine Turk. But do you know how to sail?"

"What's this?" Gilley interrupted as he climbed the ladder up from the main deck to the quarter deck. "An officer at the helm? 'Tis plain to see all good order and discipline has been lost aboard this ship."

Before Efendi could answer Gilley the lookout, perched high up in the main topcastle, or what some like to call the crow's nest, cried out his warning: "Sail ho!" he shouted down to us in a shrill voice.

"Where away, Master Rodingham?" Gilley called up to the man.

"Fine on our port bow, south, heading due east."

Gilley and I squinted against the sun's glare reflecting off the water, scanning the near horizon. I saw only whitecaps.

"There, Mary!" Gilley said and pointed.

"Ah, I see them now, Tom. Is there more than one ship?"

"Aye."

"It is," Hunter said as he bolted up the ladder from the main deck to join Gilley and me, "a fleet of Spanish ships."

"The *flota*?" I asked.

"The *Flota de Indias*? No. The Spanish treasure fleet is far grander and would have sailed months ago in any case. This is nothing more than a small cluster of merchant vessels. Can't tell if there is a galleon among them running escort, but I'm certain there must be one nearby. The Spanish will not trouble us and we shouldn't trouble them."

Then Hunter and Gilley both fell silent, as if they were contemplating something amiss about the ship or the crew. Whatever they were thinking, they were taking their time and seemed to be of a like mind.

"Is there some problem you gentlemen wish to share with me?" I finally asked.

"Do you see what I see, James?" Gilley asked, ignoring me.

"I believe I do Captain Gilley, I believe I do," Hunter replied, ignoring me as well and then started rocking back and forth on his heels as if was weighing some grave matter.

Gilley let out a long sigh. "I blame myself."

Hunter shook his head. "No. Nonsense, Tom. The blame is not yours or mine to bear. I blame the feisty owner of this vessel for this sorry state we're in."

"She is young and lacks experience."

"You rascals have had your fun," I said, a tad bit annoyed. "What blame would you pin on me now?"

Hunter and Gilley exchanged playful smiles, then turned in unison to face me.

"We are, Mary..." Gilley began to say and looked over at

Hunter.

"A warship," Hunter said, finishing Gilley's thought. "We must drill the crew, hone their skills at artillery. God forbid we get ourselves into a scrap and aren't ready. There's no law out here. And the *Star* is both a blessing and a curse."

"How so?" I asked.

"The *Star* will be one of the more powerful ships in the Caribbean. That's the blessing. But like a beautiful woman, men will notice her. Many will covet her for themselves and they will kill to have her. That's the curse."

"We are well-armed and our men are seasoned fighters."

"Aye, Mary," Gilley said. "They all know how to fight, but many don't have any experience in battle. We must train our lads to fight like soldiers, with one mind, as a single, cohesive unit. We must train them hard until they are prepared to face any determined enemy. Fighting like a gang of back alley brawlers will only get us all killed."

"Plainly, I've not yet grasped how dangerous this New World is that we sail to now. I am grateful to have you both. Do then what must be done."

"And where will you be, Mary?" Hunter asked.

"I shall stay here and watch. Or I can retire to my cabin if you think me in the way."

"Beg pardon, Mum, but nay," Gilley said.

I looked at Gilley, confused. "Nay? Nay, what?"

"No," Hunter said. "No you won't stay and watch. You'll report to the gun deck below with the others to begin your training without delay. Remember the first rule of command, Mary."

"Aye," I replied sheepishly. "An officer must never ask a man to do what he is not prepared to do himself."

"Good, very good. You have promise, sailor - shake a leg *Madame* before I put your name on the Capt'n's report for insubordination. Now move your lovely, little arse..."

Standing in the middle of the main deck in the midst of a crowd of men, Hunter took a deep breath and studied the faces surrounding him - and then paused to look at me. There was no smile.

He used his fingers to comb an unruly lock of hair off his forehead before he spoke. "Lads and lady, your carefree days of leisure aboard the *Star* are over. When you signed with this ship, the ship's officers spoke frankly about where this ship would sail and of our intentions. The Caribbean lures men in with her seductive charms, but her waters can be deadly. How many of you have any experience with field artillery, with cannon? Let me see your hands. Captain Gilley, looks to be about half I'd say?"

"Aye, just about half, Master Hunter."

"Very well. How many of you men have served time as gunners in the navy, any navy?"

"I count," said Gilley, "six souls in all, Master Hunter."

"Only six? Well, we shall see. We'll need gun captains. If any of you can impress me with your skills at gunnery, I'll promote you. Now all of you listen carefully. Pirates and privateers - there's not much difference between the two - led by talented captains infest the Caribbean. These men are well-armed and ruthless. They'll want what is yours and they'll have no qualms about snatching your lives away to take whatever they want. We must be ready to fight and beat all challengers. We'll train and train and train again until you drop. And then we'll train some more. Now you see our good Lady Mary in our midst. She will be working side-by-side with us and whilst on this gun deck, she is simply Mary, a common sailor and you shall treat her so. She leaves her privileges of rank up on the quarter deck. Captain Gilley, Master Efendi, gentlemen, if you please, break the men down into teams, four men to each gun - and let the games begin."

I have never been shy about getting my hands dirty as any man who has sailed with me well knows. And I have been in hand-to-hand combat and held my own. But the great guns, I must confess, terrified me and I doubt whatever look I gave Hunter that day was a pretty one.

For the first few days our drills would have been comical but for all the cuts, the bruises and damaged egos suffered. We fumbled about opening gunports, loading guns and pulling on the side tackles to ease the noses of those heavy brutes around and out over the water. No one worked together. Toes were pinched, fingers got scraped and more than one knee or elbow was cut or battered black and blue. Men cursed and fumed. Hunter seemed to be enjoying himself, especially when watching me and my own buffoonery. I was more than a tad annoyed at him in the beginning, but I held my tongue.

We practiced for hours, for days and weeks. We practiced in our sleep. We learned how to use a flexible rammer to ram a charge home and then how to ram the ball down snuggly against the charge. We learned how to prime the breech and run out the guns using the training tackle. We learned how to efficiently ease the gun around with an iron handspike to point the beast in the correct direction. We learned about windage and elevation and how to keep our linstocks always burning, even in the rain. We learned how to move in the dark and, should any man fall in battle, we learned how to keep working the guns - no matter what - as tacklemen, handspikemen, shellmen and as gun captains. The guns, Hunter repeated over and over and over again, the guns were all that mattered in a fight. We committed all the commands from *sponge your guns*, to *fire on the swell*, to *as your guns bear*, to memory. We learned how to fight on instinct, by rote, without wasting precious time on thinking. We learned how to fight as one.

And then the day finally came when Hunter, with a wide grin, gathered us all around and pronounced us ready. He opened up the ship's magazine to us and we gunners practiced the art of gunnery under his watchful eye using real ball and powder. For several hours we practiced blasting away at a small, makeshift raft *Phantom* had in tow. The raft I must admit survived our drills. No matter, the exhilaration that filled me that day, a feeling not unlike the ecstasy of new-found love, even now makes me smile.

"Are you still raw about it my darling, gunner's mate?" Hunter asked me as we laid side-by-side in my bed.

"No," I answered, savoring love's afterglow. I nestled my head against Hunter's bare chest while he gently stroked my hair.

"I'm proud of you, Mary. You handled yourself well and the lads will respect you even more for it."

"I'm proud of myself. Hmmm. How did you become so wise?"

"Wise? Ha! Not me. Wisdom belongs to priests and poets. But soldiering? Ah, well now, that comes easy to me."

"It would seem that lust, raw and uninhibited, comes easy to you as well."

Hunter laughed and ran his fingers down my arms and legs, caressing my skin as we snuggled closer. "I rather like these new, taut muscles of yours. They're erotic."

I could feel him becoming aroused again. I softly cooed. My body ached for more. "A second helping? My, my, Hunter, you have missed me. Mmm, what's this now? Oh my, I think someone's gun is already primed and loaded."

Hunter rolled on top of me. He eased himself inside me and timed his rhythmic movements, his exquisite thrusting, to the movements of the ship rocking back and forth over the ocean's gentle swells. It did not take long until he had me. It did not take long until I was moaning with wave after wave of delirious, sensual pleasure.

Bucking against the prevailing Westerlies, we made slow but steady progress. With each passing day the sun felt a little warmer against the skin.

I lost Hunter to the *Phantom* and then over to the *Godsend* as he repeated his grueling gunnery drills using up fresh victims. More *grist for the mill* he liked to say. I missed him. I missed his smile, his touch. I missed his soft caresses. I admonished myself for my pathetic weakness. A silly school girl has better sense. But the heart will do what the heart will do.

Out of the corner of my eye, I caught young Billy hobbling along the gun deck without his crutch. "Good morrow, Master Ferrell. How does your leg mend?"

The boy doffed his hat and nodded. "It mends well, my ladyship. The ship's surgeon is pleased. He has encouraged me to walk on it to rebuild my strength."

"And well you should, Billy Farrell. We must find you a suitable position on this ship so that you may earn your keep then. Report to Captain Gilley later."

"Aye, Mum."

And then, without warning - *BOOM!*

I froze for an instant, as did we all, and then I saw a puff of white smoke rising off a single gun mounted atop *Godsend's* forecastle. I could see Hunter waving at us and pointing to the sky. No, not the sky. He was pointing to a pair of wings fluttering overhead. *Land.*

"What is it, Mary?" Gilley asked as he tried to catch his breath after bolting up the companionway to come stand with me.

"'Tis a salute from our astute Master Hunter. He spied a bird flying close by. Land cannot be far off."

"Praise the Almighty!" Gilley said and crossed himself. "I feared someone had blown himself up. Well now, we've come these many leagues across the great ocean with no storms of any mention and not one soul lost. 'Tis a good omen, Mary."

I nodded in agreement. We had been most fortunate.

"Shall we signal Fox and Green to shorten sail and heave to, Tom? The skies are clear and the water is calm enough to launch a longboat. I think it best to assemble all the officers together and weigh things out."

"All the officers, Mary or just our own?"

With three ships and three crews, we had to hire more officers in Westport to sail with us, men with unproven loyalties. Gilley, Hunter, Green, Fox, Efendi and Ferguson - all tried and true - were mine.

"Right you are, Tom. Just our own."

After a hearty meal of pottage and slices of fresh pork with mellow wine - I allowed one pig on each ship to be slaughtered to celebrate the day - young Master Ferrell moved around the cabin to clear the table. Gilley had assigned the boy the menial task of ship's boy and my personal attendant, leastwise until his leg was fully healed.

I glanced around the table. Except from afar, I hadn't seen Fox or Green for nearly two months. They were both tan and lean and had grown full beards to mask their boyish faces. They looked like seasoned ship's officers now. And so they were.

Hunter unrolled a chart of the Caribbean across the table. "I suspect we're about here, a bit north of Barbuda," he said, pointing to an island in the middle of the chart. "If we continue sailing due west along this line, we'll approach these larger islands known as the Greater Antilles. Cuba, San Juan Bautista - or what traders are calling Puerto Rico now - Hispaniola, Jamaica, and the Cayman Islands are all occupied by the Spanish with large towns sprouting up everywhere. I've been to Havana in Cuba and to San Juan on the island of Puerto Rico. This string of smaller islands spread out to the east and south is known as the Lesser Antilles, or the Caribbees. I've set foot on Dominica, Guadeloupe and Trinidad but, as you can see, there are many more islands in this archipelago."

"And what of the Indians?" I asked.

"The Greater Antilles are inhabited by the Taíno, or the Borinquen in Spanish. Most are dead now, killed in war or by diseases the Spanish brought over with them from our world like smallpox. And the Taíno have not fared well in slavery. That is why the Spanish are importing Africans by the thousands to work the land. The Caribbees are ruled by a different people, the Caribs. Think of the ancient Viking raiders and you'll have some notion of who the Caribs are. They were slaughtering the Taíno and seizing Taíno land long before Columbus."

"And the Spanish haven't tried to conquer them?" I asked.

"Not with any heart. The Caribs are a proud people. They are fearsome warriors and capable mariners on the open sea. The Spanish have avoided them. Fortune has had a hand in protecting the Caribs too. Their islands have no gold or silver deposits to speak of."

"I take it we'd be too conspicuous in New Spain or Florida or somewhere along the coast of the Spanish Main?" Gilley asked.

Hunter smiled. "I doubt the New World has yet suffered many Irishmen, let alone a feisty Irish lass."

"The Spanish don't occupy these smaller islands?" Efendi asked, tracing his finger along the Caribbees on the map.

"No, not in force anyway."

"And there are good anchorages and fresh water on some of these islands?"

"Mustafa, I think we are of like mind."

"And what would that be, gentlemen?" I asked.

"If we want to be inconspicuous, Mary," Hunter offered, "we should stay clear of the big islands. The same is true of Florida, New Spain and the Spanish Main. One of these small islands in the Caribbees should do us nicely."

"And what of these hostile Indians you have spoken of?" I asked.

"We make a treaty with them. We pay them tribute for their friendship. I made certain before we sailed that we had men onboard fluent in Spanish, French, Portuguese and Italian. We'll be able to speak to the Caribs in one of those languages."

I had my doubts about the wisdom of Hunter's plan and suddenly was having second thoughts about the whole enterprise. I had not sailed all the way to the New World to kill any Indians or to lose any men in a war we had no part in. And paying tribute did not sit well with me either. Tribute is what chased us out of Ireland.

Hunter sensed my indecision. "Mary, there are risks no matter what we do, no matter what you decide. Why not explore a few of these smaller islands? I see no harm in that at least. We can sell what we brought with us and always return to Ireland if you like."

All eyes were fixed on me as I took a moment to think matters through. Hunter's quiet confidence stirred my blood just as much as his handsome, rugged face and his fine physique. I had always drawn strength from his confidence, especially from his confidence in me.

"The Caribs have no love for the Spanish I take it?" I asked.

"None."

"Let us explore a few of these islands then. We'll let the Caribs know that we mean them no harm, that we are no friends of the Spanish. Perhaps we can do some business with them once they understand we don't want slaves or land."

"Pick one, Mary," Gilley said, chuckling.

I pointed to the Lesser Antilles on the map. "Tell us what you know about these islands in the Caribbees, James."

"Not too much, I fear. Columbus explored some of them. Antigua has a fine harbor I've heard, but Columbus couldn't pacify the Caribs there and left. Columbus named this island *Doménica*, the Italian word for Sunday because he discovered the island on a Sunday. The Caribs call it *Waitikubuli* which means, or so I was told, *tall is her body*. *Doménica* is a rugged, mountainous island of great beauty. High in the mountains there is a spectacular waterfall with a deep pool of sweet, cool water flowing out from caves which is most refreshing to bathe in. Guadeloupe, or *Karukera*, which means something like *island with beautiful waters*, is where Columbus discovered the *piña de Indias* or the "pine of the Indians" or what we English call a pineapple. It is a most extraordinary and delicious fruit. Columbus named the island *Santa María de Guadalupe de Extremadura* after the image of the Virgin Mary venerated at the Spanish monastery of Villuercas in Guadalupe, Extremadura."

"And what of this island near the mainland to the south called Trinidad?" I asked.

"Ah, Trinidad is a very fine island, but the Spanish occupy the place. Worse, the pirate clans rule it. Contraband is often moved in and out of the *Puerto de España*. The Port of Spain is well-known for its bazaars and many slave markets. This is where the Spanish like to gather to buy and sell their Negroes brought over like oxen to the New World from West Africa. Some are sent to the pearl fisheries on nearby *Isla Margarita*. The rest are taken to other islands by their new masters. Trinidad is a pit of lechery, treachery and villainy. We should avoid Trinidad or, at the very least, not tarry there for very long."

I put my finger on the Port of Spain. "But this is where we can sell our cargo?" I asked.

"Aye," Hunter replied with a sigh as he thought he knew my thoughts. "That is true."

"Very well, Guadeloupe first," I said on nothing more than a whim.

We sailed due south, tacking lazily back and forth for three more days in light winds. On the evening of the third day we dropped anchor in a small bay off a small island formed by two mountains joined together by a narrow strip of land running north and south between them. The island bore the likeness of a butterfly on the chart. I gathered all my officers for supper to consider a new plan.

"Gentlemen, this is as much your plan as it is mine. Like you, I am against making any kind of permanent settlement in these islands. I confess this was not my intention when we left Ireland. But I see now that we are surrounded by many potential enemies on all sides including Spaniards and Portuguese, Caribs, the French, privateers and pirates. None of them will want us here and no wooden fort will stop any determined foe."

"Remember," Hunter interrupted, "the story of the lost fort Columbus built from the timbers of the *Santa Maria* after she ran aground on the Island of *Hispaniola*? When Columbus returned the following year, he found only ashes and none of his men. We should build no *Villa de la Navidads* in the New World."

"Quite so, James," I said. "So, like nomads in the desert, we will keep moving. We'll hop from one island to the next before we offend any host. We'll sell our Old World cargo and use the proceeds to buy a runner or two, load them up with New World materials and goods and send them back to Ireland with *Phantom* as escort. While *Phantom* and the freighters sail back to Ireland, we'll keep *Godsend* and *Star* here in the Caribbean to find and purchase more cargo for the next voyage. God only knows if we can turn a profit this way."

Gilley was the first to endorse the proposal. "I'm heartened by this bold plan Mary and I vote aye without conditions. And, I must say, if we rotate the men so they may see their home and families, it will do much to keep spirits high."

Hunter stood and nodded. "An excellent suggestion, Tom. We all know of the grim pestilence ravaging Europe like the plague. Men being men will want to fornicate with the women here, Indians, Africans or Europeans, it won't matter to any man whose blood is hot for the fairer sex. But we best remind the lads of the great pox, syphilis. We cursed the Indians with smallpox and they returned the favor with the great pox. A moment's pleasure is hardly worth a slow and hideous death. And God help the man who has carnal knowledge with a Carib woman. That man will disappear during the night until we find his body parts scattered all about the jungle in the morning. And any peace we make with these people will suffer for it. If the men know they'll be returning home every few months or so it should dampen their desires. If not, well, they best learn how to fuck a tree or I will surely fuck them for putting all our lives in jeopardy. I swear it."

And not one of us doubted Hunter's resolve, no one doubted Hunter would make good on his promised threat. Hunter never squandered time or effort on fools.

It was on the dazzling white sands of Guadeloupe where I first set foot in the New World. The early morning sky was a spectacular fusion of bold reds, yellows and purples splashed across a canvas of soft, translucent aquamarine. A crown of golden light rose above the water and I marveled at beauty surrounding us. Hunter had not exaggerated the Caribbean's seductive charms. It was, I thought, a tantalizing beginning to a promising new day.

I left my three ships anchored in the harbor's placid waters and brought sixty armed men with me in three longboats, twenty men from each ship. After we stepped into the surf, after we dragged our boats up on the sand, we fanned out along the beach under a dozen white pennants flapping in the breeze. We brought three trunks filled with gifts along and I had my men open them and set them out in front of us. Not far off to the west, nestled against the bay, we could see the huts of a Carib village with thin columns of smoke rising in the air from cooking fires. But we saw no Indians. The village appeared deserted. We stood in the sand and waited.

"What do you think, James?" I asked after some time had passed.

Hunter shrugged his shoulders nonchalantly. "We continue to show patience. They're out there, watching. They'll approach us when they're good and ready, or they'll swoop down on us with hundreds of warriors and, with our backs against the sea, well, we'll all be slaughtered in minutes."

"Not a charming thought..."

Hunter grinned. "Not to worry, Mary. They'll spare you, I have no doubt. They'll keep you alive and show you off as a war trophy."

"You are full of good cheer today."

More time passed and still we waited. As the sun began rising over the mountaintops to the east the temperature rose with it. The morning quickly went from warm to hot to uncomfortably hot and then by late morning the day turned exceedingly unpleasant and sticky. We finally sat ourselves down in the sand to rest ourselves and waited some more and then at noon, just before we all roasted, we noticed movement in the jungle in front of us - and I saw my first Indian.

Three Carib warriors, brandishing long spears, bows and

arrows, slowly emerged from the thick foliage and approached us cautiously. We stood but did not draw our weapons. Except for the chains of gold around their necks and the silver bracelets adorning their arms and ankles, the Indians were stark naked. Their ears and lips were pierced with fish bones. They had painted their skin in bright blues, greens and reds. The eldest of the three warriors stopped in front of me. His hair was more grey than black. His face was deeply wrinkled. He wore a stunning headdress made from colorful feathers, parrot feathers I think, adorned with seashells and strings of pearls. Plainly he was the man in charge. He looked me up and down, stone-faced.

Hunter tried speaking with the Carib in Spanish first and the older man with the headdress answered him in Spanish. After a brief exchange, Hunter turned to me and pointed to him.

"Mary, this is Chief Paka Wokili. His name means, I think, something like *bull* or *horns of the bull* in his language."

Hunter looked back at the Carib chieftain and introduced me. The chief acknowledged me with a nod and seemed unfazed by the prospect of dealing with woman who held rank and position. I was encouraged.

"We now have," Hunter said to me, keeping a steady smile for the chief as he spoke, "an audience with his august majesty, the King of Guadeloupe. The stage is yours, Mary."

I took a step forward and bowed my head. "Chief Paka Wokili, I am most pleased and honored to meet you. We are not Spanish. We are not Portuguese. We are Irish and we come from an island, not unlike yours, far to the east across the great ocean. We do not want your lands, we do not want your gold or your silver. We do not want slaves. We do not want to teach you about our God. God did not send us. We come in peace. We offer you our friendship."

The chief listened thoughtfully as Hunter translated my words. But when the chief offered no reply, there was a long and awkward silence between us.

"Hunter," I finally said with a smile. "Let's show the Chief his gifts."

Paka Wokili seemed disinterested in the trunks at first as Hunter tried handing the Indians different samples of the presents we had brought with us. Something then caught the chief's attention. He bent down and started rummaging through one of the trunks himself. His eyes lit up when he spotted a hand axe with a razor-sharp edge. He grabbed the axe and smiled broadly while inspecting the weapon's quality. Then he stood and pointed the axe at me and something he said made his two captains laugh. I quickly offered up a silent prayer, praying the chief had found no reason to dip the axe's blade in my blood on my first day in the New World.

"The chief," Hunter said as Paka Wokili grinned at me, "does not trust Europeans no matter what tribe they're from. He also says that no man would follow a woman as chief, as weak as women are, and that must be why your men all wear trousers, to hide our shame because we have no cocks."

I looked hard into the chief's eyes. I held his gaze and returned his smug smile with one of my own. I decided it best to show the chief, without offending him, that he wasn't dealing with weaklings.

"Tom, give me your axe."

The chief watched me with curiosity as Gilley handed me the axe tucked inside his belt. I planted my feet firmly in the sand and picked out a target. I picked out a palm tree a fair distance off and, after taking careful aim, I launched the weapon with all my might. The haughty smiles of the chief and his two captains vanished when the axe buried itself in the tree dead-on.

"The chief," said Hunter, "in a more humble tone I might add, says that everyone wants something. He says that you have only told him what you don't want. He says you haven't told him what it is you do want Mary. He demands to know our purpose here on his island."

"Tell him, James, we only wish to trade with him and with his people. Chief Paka Wokili, we wish to stay on your island, as your guest from time-to-time, for short periods to rest and to take on fresh supplies of food and water for which we will gladly pay you. We'll not build homes or forts. We'll not harm you or your people.

We'll tarry on your island in peace and leave at any time you ask us to. I swear it. We wish to buy and sell goods to the Spanish and to the Portuguese and we will pay you tribute for the privilege."

The chief reflected on my words quietly for a time. As I waited for his answer, I listened to the chirping of the unfamiliar birds hiding in the jungle, to the surf spilling across the sand, and to our pennants flapping in the breeze. Amid armed warriors from two camps, I found tranquility in the moment.

"Our good chief still has questions, Mary," Hunter said after the chief resumed our conversation. "The Spanish and the Portuguese are his enemies he says. He wants to know why he should help you trade with his enemies."

"Because," I answered quickly without much thought to show my sincerity, "many others are already trading with the Europeans settling in these lands. His Highness certainly knows this to be true because he has seen or heard of the growing cities on the big islands. The Europeans are here to stay. He can do no more to stop the European invasion of the islands than he can stop the rains from falling. But in league with us, he can at least profit from it and make his people stronger."

With a king's royal nod, we pitched our tents along the shore that very afternoon and setup camp. Later in the evening the Caribs left their village to join us for a *friendship feast* where I had my first taste of pineapple. The Caribs were a proud and handsome people I thought and proved to be gracious hosts. I enjoyed their songs and dance. I admired their innocence. Most of the women wore little more than modest cotton shorts about the size of a loincloth and saw no reason to hide their breasts. Only a few wore smocks to cover themselves. And when the women stepped into the surf to cool themselves, they stripped off all their clothing first and thought nothing of it. I worried about the resolve of my men who had gone without the tender affections of a woman for long months. I passed the word around again: we could not afford to offend or insult the Caribs in any way.

We stayed in Guadeloupe for several lazy days and nights. I

spent the time pleasurably with Hunter exploring the island's interior. On our last day in Guadeloupe, we found a pool of cool water in a clearing, a lovely spot, where we bathed and shamelessly flirted with each other until I let Hunter have his way with me - and then I had my way with him. After we returned to the Carib village, I had my men break camp and took my tiny fleet of three on to Dominica next. Chief Paka Wokili had sent a herald off in one of his great war canoes a day earlier to announce our arrival. He also insisted we take one of his nephews along with us to oversee and verify his share of any profits. I agreed to the chief's condition though I doubted his nephew would succeed in his task inasmuch as the poor fellow didn't seem to know how to count or write.

In Dominica, and then in Antigua, we repeated what we had done in Guadeloupe with nearly the same results. We now had good relations, friendship treaties, with the warlike Caribs on three islands.

With our new alliances in place, with our ships resupplied with fresh victuals and water, and with our men revitalized after a few lazy days on land, it was time to return to work, it was time to increase our wealth. We needed customers for our Old World goods and we needed suppliers for the New World goods we had yet to purchase, using whatever profits we made from the cargo we carried. I decided to try our luck in Trinidad and Tobago first.

The farther south we sailed the more ships we saw plying the Caribbean's green waters. Every vessel we passed was a freighter of one sort or another. Every vessel we encountered carried some amount of cannon. We ignored them and they ignored us. We saw no warships of any kind.

We sailed around the north-west tip of Trinidad, hugging the shoreline, until we reached the *Puerto de España* where, beyond the tidal mudflats and mangroves, we saw mud-plastered *ajoupas* sprinkled in-between large, silk cotton trees standing along the town's dirt roads. From a distance the Port of Spain had a certain charm about it. We slipped into a bay crowded with many ships and boats riding anchor and sailed past a shack with a single, naked flagpole protected by three field cannon and a low, earthen parapet. The harbor fort was the sorriest I had ever seen. A company of Carib warriors armed with sticks and stones could have overwhelmed the spot in broad daylight with ease.

We dropped anchor near the fort and I took all my officers ashore with me. The waterfront reeked, as all ports do, of blood, sweat, urine and excrement and the pungent smell of rotting fish hung heavy in the air. The thick humidity of the Caribbean and the port's narrow alleyways, devoid of any breeze, made the stench doubly potent and I suffered for it. At the center of the town we came to a marketplace filled with colorful tents and makeshift tables where merchants were peddling their wares and services of every sort and kind to prosperous men and women from around the Caribbean. And wherever the prosperous gather others, less savory sorts, are never far behind to lap up any scraps. The marketplace was packed with ruffians and I saw potential danger all around us.

I have seen Moors before in my travels to Spain. But before Trinidad, I had never seen an African in chains. I saw them in the *Puerto de España* by the hundreds, many were standing naked on the auction blocks for display. Men and women. It was plain to see some had suffered beatings. Most looked ill-kept and underfed. A few looked emaciated. I felt nauseous and ashamed. The utter despair I saw in those black faces haunts me even now.

We pushed our way through the throngs of people until we found a suitable tavern and lodge close by to refresh and rest ourselves. It looked like a place where we could make new friends. The building, four stories high, was easily the grandest one in sight, certainly bigger and better constructed than the sad, little church standing next to it. Inside, the tavern had all the essentials too: liquor, tables, games and women who looked like they knew how to please a man. I kept Hunter, Gilley and Efendi close with me and sent Green, Fox and Ferguson off to explore the four corners of the port.

"Gentlemen," I said and raised my tankard of ale. "This impoverished, little stink-hole is not quite what I expected. No matter, we shall make the best of it. A toast: to the New World, to new beginnings, to new prospects."

"To the New World, to new beginnings, to new prospects," Gilley, Hunter and Efendi all repeated in unison. We bumped our tankards together and savored our first drink in the New World.

"Don't be deceived by what you see here," Hunter said. "All around us there is great wealth. In Havana and Veracruz you will see the makings of real cities. Remember, Columbus only discovered this world less than one hundred years ago."

"*Por favor, mi amigos*," a stranger said as he stopped at our table. "*¿Estás Inglés?*"

I looked up to find a fit and handsome man wearing a fine quality, but not outlandishly expensive suit addressing us. His hat, jacket and trousers all matched. This man, I thought, wanted people to know that he had money and that he was careful with it. I pegged him for a banker.

"*Si*," Hunter answered.

"*¡Ah, muy bien! ¿Como estas?*"

"*¿Muy bien y tú?*"

"I am most well, thank you. May I sit? I would like to introduce myself."

I nodded my consent. "Of course, *Señor*. Your English is quite good."

"*Mucho gracias*," the Spaniard replied, staring at me appreciatively. "I have spent some brief time in London, mostly at the royal court to discuss matters of general commerce with the queen's good ministers."

After he took a seat he gently took my hand and kissed me on the knuckles. The man was suave, a charmer. Spanish men always are. I took no offense.

"*Señora*, I am delighted to make your acquaintance. The Americas have so few truly beautiful women to boast of. You grace

91

Trinidad simply by your presence."

"*Señor* embellishes," I protested shyly. "You are much too kind. Nonetheless, I thank you for the compliment."

"I have, I assure you, my lady, never been accused of being too kind before. Please forgive me. Permit me to properly introduce myself. I am Rodriguez Miguel de Cortés y Ovando, no relation to the great Spanish crusader, Hernán Cortés de Monroy y Pizarro, God rest his soul. I am here in Trinidad on business. My home in the Old World is in Barcelona but here, in the West Indies, I have property in both Santo Domingo and Havana."

"We are honored to know you. I am Mary. And this is Master Thomas Gilley, Master James Hunter and Master Mustafa Efendi."

"Mary?"

"Aye, just Mary."

"Just Mary? How unusual. You have no family name?"

"Alas, no, I am an orphan."

"How," Gilley interrupted and with an edge in his tone, "may we be of service, *Señor* Cortés?"

"Ah, yes, of course. I am very pleased to meet each of you. I did not mean to eavesdrop on your conversation. Three ships, ships no one recalls seeing before in these waters, and bristling with heavy cannon, arrived in port this morning. These ships are the talk of the town. I take it you good folks sailed with these ships?"

"Word travels fast in this part of the world," I said.

"*Puerto de España* is a small town."

"One of those ships is ours, yes," I offered evasively.

"Two of the vessels are warships, rather impressive warships. English navy?"

"No," Hunter replied. "Not English navy."

"You are private citizens, then?"

"Aye, private citizens we are."

"You bring a lot of firepower with you for private citizens."

Hunter shrugged his shoulders.

"You are new to the Caribbean, yes?"

"Some of us are and some of us are not," Hunter said simply.

The Spaniard shrugged his shoulders in return and removed his hat. "Ah, I see you are cautious people. And that is wise. But I mean you no harm. I feel compelled to warn you though: there are many in this part of the world who will mean you harm, no matter what master you serve. And you'll find precious little law here to protect you."

"For any who would be so foolish to try," I said boldly and narrowed my eyes, "they'll be sorry for it."

"And I can believe that my dear lady," Cortés answered, then turned to look at Hunter. "I presume you are the ship's captain?"

"I would be the ship's *master*," Gilley interrupted. "Captains command warships, not freighters."

"Ah," the Spaniard said as if surprised. "My apologies."

"You said you are here on business?" Hunter asked. "Pray tell, what business might that be?"

"His Most Catholic Majesty, King Phillip II of Spain, granted a sizable tract of land in Cuba to me. I came here to Trinidad to purchase more labor to work my *ingenios*, my mills."

"Mills, what kind of mills?" Gilley asked.

"I use the mills to process sugarcane though, ahem, that endeavor has so far not been as profitable as I would like. I do much better with tobacco. There is money in cattle too. We slaughter the herd around August each year and sell the meat to the Spanish treasure fleet before the fleet sets out for Spain. The navy pays very well for beef."

"Ah, so you are a butcher then?" I asked intrigued. "I know something about the trade."

Cortés smiled and seemed unruffled by my coarse description of his stature. "I cannot imagine you anywhere near a slaughterhouse my dear lady."

"Blood has never made me squeamish, *Señor* Cortés. Have you any knowledge or experiences with imports or exports?"

"As it so happens, I do. I do indeed. As you can imagine, vast amounts of goods and materials are exchanged between New Spain and various kingdoms in Europe. Might I know where you are from and what your business is here in Trinidad?"

"Of course," I replied. "We have just arrived in Trinidad from Ireland. And as it happens, we carry assorted manufactured goods, mostly from France and England."

"Ah *muy bien*, how interesting," Cortés said and gestured for us to lean closer. "You wish to sell these things?"

"Quite so."

"How fortuitous we meet," he continued in a whisper. "The governor of Cuba is a dear friend of mine. Well, the governor of Cuba is actually the Governor-Captain General of Santo Domingo, a man named Gregorio González de Cuenca. He is also *el Presidente* of the *Audiencia*. Perhaps I could make introductions?"

"And why would we want to meet the governor of Cuba?" Hunter asked.

The Spaniard stared at Hunter, perplexed. "*¿Que?* Why would you not? The governor is a very good man to know, my friends, a very good man to know indeed. People pay favors, handsome favors, to have an audience with his Excellency."

"And what favor do you ask from us in return?" Hunter asked.

"Why, none. You misunderstand. It is good business, *Señor* Hunter, or a chance to make good business between us. It is not every day three ships like yours, three very fine ships, sail into Trinidad. You are looking for a port of entry, no? The *quinto*, the taxes, levied by the *Casa de Contratación* of Seville on cargo being brought into the New World can be very steep these days. Spain is always in need of more revenue to pay off her debts." Cortés paused and vigorously shook his head to show his disapproval. "She is a glutton, Spain. Even the endless flow of pearls, gold and silver into the royal coffers is not enough. Her appetite to spend and spend is ravenous, is never sated."

"And the governor," I asked, "may be helpful to us in this matter?"

Cortés smiled and rested his hand over mine. "My lady is most perceptive."

"How fortuitous we have met indeed then."

"Perhaps. You do not know me. I do not know you. Even with friends and allies the New World is a treacherous place. Trust is a currency worth far more than gold here. I am not necessarily an honest man. But I am a gentleman of excellent reputation with a keen knowledge of business as my friends in Cuba and Santo Domingo can attest. I take care of my associates in business and they take care of me."

"I think I catch your meaning, *Señor* Cortés," I said. "When will you conclude your affairs here?"

"I shall return to Cuba on the sloop *Aruba* today, tomorrow, soon. I hope, if you have cause to visit Cuba, you will come to my modest *hacienda* near Havana. I am not difficult to find. Please enjoy your drinks and food. They are my gift of welcome."

"You are most gracious," I said. "Perhaps you could excuse my officers and me for a moment?"

Cortés was clearly puzzled by my words at first. And then he smiled broadly and clapped his hands. "My lady! How extraordinary! Your officers indeed! I shall wait for you outside, *mi Capitana*."

"Watcha thinkin', Mary," Gilley asked after Cortés excused himself.

I leaned over and kissed Gilley on the cheek. "Thank you, Tom."

"What the devil for?"

"For always trying to protect me. Well gentlemen, we came to Trinidad to try and make acquaintances. Brash or not, I like the Spaniard. Perhaps we should offer to return him to Havana as our guest, become better acquainted?"

"That one," Hunter said, "is lady's man."

"And you aren't, James Hunter? Oh dear, do I sense a bit of jealousy?"

"Jealousy? Ha! No Englishman with any pride could ever be

jealous of a Spaniard!"

"So you have no objection?"

"None," Hunter answered gruffly, then leaned back in his chair and folded his arms defiantly. "None at all."

"Tom, Mustafa?"

"As you say, Lady Mary," Mustafa replied, "we need to make new friends."

Gilley nodded. "Havana, Havana is where I shall have my bottle of sweet wine..."

And so we were all agreed. Cortés eagerly accepted our invitation for a free passage home and two days later we prepared our ships to sail. But I was unprepared for what happened next. Cortés pulled up alongside the *Star* in a launch packed full with twenty newly purchased black slaves shackled in leg irons, all males.

"I know that look, Mary," Hunter said as we stood together against the rail looking down at the water. "Something is gnawing at you."

"I didn't expect Cortés to bring his slaves with him. We aren't a slaver and we shall never be a slaver."

"No, we aren't a slaver, Mary. But Negro slaves are an accepted way of life here. From what little we know of Cortés, I would urge caution. I would not offend him. He could prove useful to us."

"I wasn't planning on beheading him just yet if that's your worry, James."

"I'm sorry, Mary. Are you cross with me?"

"I suppose I am annoyed, but not with you. Forgive me, James. I had no right to use such a harsh tone with you."

"Zeus's balls!" Gilley cried out loudly as he walked up behind us. "Stop this inane prattling. I tolerate a fair amount of twaddle aboard this ship. But I draw the line at having to listen to a lovers' quarrel!"

The weather turned foul only a day out from *Puerto de España*. I didn't mind. A modest storm sweeping down on us from the north-west brought sporadic downpours and a trough of cooler air. The rain and chill reminded me of Ireland and for me it was a pleasant respite from the tropical heat and humidity of the West Indies. I found the change refreshing.

We made slow progress against the contrary winds and currents though. Luckily, our guest proved to be a most engaging and interesting fellow. Each evening Cortés joined my officers and me for supper, for good conversation and a game or two of cards. We enjoyed Cortés's company immensely. But there were undercurrents too. Cortés, we all realized, was no one's fool and might prove a dangerous opponent if crossed or slighted in some way.

On the last day of our voyage the rains abated, though the sky remained overcast with thick, grey clouds and the air still held its chill. Cortés and I shared breakfast together up on the quarter deck. We enjoyed a simple meal of pineapple, bananas, fresh bread and strong coffee while standing together at the ship's bittacle. Not far off I could see Havana with many ships at anchor in her harbor and many others under sail coming in or out of port. Havana was a far busier anchorage than the Port of Spain.

"I've very much enjoyed our time together, Mary. I'm most grateful to you for your kindness and hospitality."

"It has been our sincere pleasure. We've enjoyed your gracious company. Do you, Rodriguez, know what day it is?"

"I must confess, I do not. Saturday, perhaps?"

"Why *Señor* Rodriguez Miguel de Cortés y Ovando, I'm certain you must be a good and faithful Catholic. This day is holy. Today we celebrated the birth of our or Lord and Savior Jesus Christ. It is Christmas Day. Happy Christmas, Rodriguez."

"Ah! One loses track of time out here in the West Indies. I will be severely reprimanded by my priest for failing to attend midnight mass. I will fall to my knees and beg *la Santísima Virgen Maria* for forgiveness at my next confession and all will be well. Our Blessed Mother is most understanding about such things! Happy Christmas to you, Mary."

I smiled sweetly at Cortés and handed him a leather purse. "Thank you, Rodriguez."

"What is this?"

"It is a gift, a gift from me to you, to celebrate Christmas Day."

"A gift? ¡Muchas gracias mi bonita amiga!"

"Please, have a look. I picked them up in Trinidad and I think the quality is good. But I have one favor to ask of you if you accept my gift."

Cortés peeked inside the purse and looked up at me wide-eyed. "I do not understand, Mary. I promised to introduce you to my friends, some of whom may be useful to you in business, others who have influence. I require no gratuity, no favor, for myself."

"Rodriguez, the value of the pearls you hold in your hand is thrice the amount at least of the pesos you paid in Trinidad for your twenty slaves."

Cortés raised an eyebrow. "I don't understand."

"I'm purchasing your slaves."

"My slaves? But why? If you needed slaves why did you not purchase them in Trinidad? I would gladly have assisted you, shown you how to look for quality and buy whatever you found pleasing at fair price."

"Women are curious creatures. We can be confounding and often don't understand ourselves. Will you humor me and accept my gift?"

"This is most confusing. And I must tell you, you are paying too much for my Negroes."

"I am touched by your honesty, but I also wish to compensate you for your troubles."

Cortés grinned. He held me by the shoulders and kissed me on the cheek. "How can I possibly say no, or resist your charms dear lady! Happy Christmas indeed, Mary. Will you use the Negroes on your slave galleys?"

"No. Not in the Caribbean leastwise. But rest assured I shall find a good use for them."

"You will not be disappointed. I buy the very best. These Negros are healthy and will work hard for you with little complaint."

"I doubt you not, Rodriguez."

Gilley and Hunter then joined Cortés and me on the quarter deck as the ship drew nearer to the outer bay, to the *Bahia de la Habana.* Cortés passed the time treating us to a brief history of the island.

"Havana over the years," he explained, "has become an important *villa* and port in the New World. Much of the New World's commerce flows in and out of Havana. This is where the treasure fleet assembles once a year in August or September to take on supplies before returning to Seville. Around 1560 or '61, King Phillip decreed all fleets returning to Spain must stop in Havana first. Most of Cuba's industry supports the fleet. As we draw closer, you will see three forts. *San Salvador de la Punta* protects the west entrance of the bay. The *Castillo de los Tres Reyes Magos del Morro,* named after the three great magi who followed the star to Bethlehem to honor our Lord, protects the east entrance of the bay and *Castillo de la Real Fuerza* guards the center of Havana. *Real Fuerza* is where the *Capitán General* resides when he visits. The forts are nothing more than earthworks and timber but, as you will see, *Castillo de la Real Fuerza* is being rebuilt with ironwork, stone and mortar. The castle will be a formidable fortification once reconstruction is completed. The king they say will eventually rebuild *la Punta* and *del Morro* too. Havana has attracted many a pirate over the years. It was not that long ago, in 1555 to be precise, when Jacques de Sores, a notorious French pirate, sailed into Havana and burned the town to the ground. Havana can now protect herself."

Cortés paused to wink at me. "And, of course, we have much *contrabando* trade in the West Indies, illegal trade that our good and pious king would like to put an end to. Havana is a busy port, however, and not even the king's men are privy to every ship that comes and goes. It is also true that there are many in the Americas who do not share King Phillip's fondness for taxes."

"I have," I offered with a smile, "no earthly idea what you are referring to, *Señor*."

Cortés laughed and bowed his head. "My lady, of course you do not. Such sordid matters are not fit for the delicate ears of such a beguiling and refined creature as yourself."

"How onerous," Hunter asked, "are these taxes?"

"*El Casa de Contratación* controls all trade in the New World and is responsible for collecting the taxes. The Crown assesses a twenty percent tax against all goods entering Spain from the West Indies - forty percent if the Royal Navy provides armed escort - and collects similar taxes on all imports into the Old World. These costs can make it most challenging for an honest man to turn even a modest profit."

I slipped my arm inside Cortés's arm. "Did I not hear you say when we first met, Rodriguez, that you are not an honest man?"

The Spaniard chuckled. "Bless me. Did I, did I indeed? Well..."

"Is it wise," Gilley asked, "for us to put in at Havana? We are not Spanish and we have no intention of paying any bloody, Spanish taxes."

"Quite so, Master Gilley," Cortés replied. "That is why we must introduce you to his Excellency the *Capitán General*. I would suggest you leave your merchantman and your other warship outside the bay for now."

"How long," Hunter asked, "have you had your plantation, your *hacienda*, in Havana?"

"Nearly ten years. In addition to breeding and raising cattle, we produce honey, wax, tobacco and sugar. Selling beef to the Royal Navy is a lucrative business as I have said. But I believe in tobacco and sugar. We harvest the tobacco leaves and hang them inside storage houses for curing. The process is not complicated. Demand for *cigarros* grows more and more each day. Making sugar requires additional effort but it is also profitable. We crush the cane with rollers powered by cattle or by using running water at the *ingenios*, the mills. Then we take the crushed cane and boil it down in steps using smaller kettles at greater heat each time until you are left with a thick cane juice we call molasses. Molasses is a dark, sticky mixture and as it cools sugar crystals form around the edges. I've experimented with fermenting the molasses, but the product is not very satisfactory."

"There are many *ingenios?*"

"There are three large *ingenios* in Cuba, James, and many smaller ones. The larger *ingenios* need one hundred Negro slaves or more to operate them. My *ingenio* is just outside of Havana to the south-west. I would take you there, but there is not much to see. It is a hot and dirty place with few amenities. Havana, as you shall soon discover, is still a crude *villa* though this is rapidly changing. We now have buildings with tiled roofs, churches made of stone and we are replacing our dirt roads with cobblestone streets."

"So the Negroes you purchased in Trinidad will work at you mill?" Hunter asked.

"Why no, James. Our good *Capitána* Mary owns them now."

Hunter turned to look at me. "Pardon?"

I shamelessly batted my eyes at Hunter and smiled sweetly for him. "Happy, happy Christmas, James…"

Chapter Six

n Cortés's sound advice, we left the *Phantom* and the *Godsend* outside in the bay to sail around in circles. MacGyver deftly eased the *Falling Star* in-between a maze of ships sitting in Havana's fine harbor and we let go our anchor in a quiet spot of water not too far off from shore. But I soon regretted not leaving the *Star* outside the bay. There were other warships in the harbor, not many, but impressive galleons nonetheless flying the royal colors of the Spanish king, flying the Cross of Burgundy, the *Cruz de Borgoña*, the cross they say Saint Andrew was crucified on. The navy's ensign, a simple jagged-edged cross of red set diagonally over a field of white, is oddly plain for royalty. The *Star* flew no flag, was not Spanish-built and caught the eye of many. Inconspicuous we were not. But then I reproved myself. There was no hiding the *Star*. I was right to sail her boldly into the harbor. A certain measure of cockiness was needed I reasoned if we were to survive and prosper in the New World.

As was my custom, I took Gilley and Hunter ashore with me, along with young Billy too after he begged me to let him come with us. We paid the harbormaster at the dock for the privilege of using the king's anchorage and then made our way into Havana on foot with Cortés in the lead. Billy's leg was all healed now but whoever had set the bone had done a poor job of it and he walked along with a permanent, pronounced limp.

I've heard an outrageous tale or two about cities in the New World being built with gold. Havana wasn't one of them. The town was mostly *ajoupas* huts, like the kind we saw in the *Puerto de España*, and cheaply made plaster buildings slapped together along dirt roads.

But there was evidence of change as Cortés had boasted. Money and people seemed to be pouring into the port. Havana was a vibrant, prosperous town with new construction. Buildings designed by talented architects and built to last by skilled craftsmen were popping up everywhere. We saw well-groomed gentlemen sitting next to their elegantly dressed ladies being whisked about town in fine carriages. And, unlike the squalor we had witnessed in Trinidad, the citizens of Havana made a strong effort at cleanliness. The *Cubanos* impressed me as a proud and determined people, proud of their new heritage and determined to transform their frontier *villa* into a civilized, modern city.

Cortés led us to the *Castillo de la Real Fuerza* in the heart of Havana where the *Capitán General* of Santo Domingo kept his residence when visiting Cuba. The air was filled with dust and the sounds men hard at work with heavy tools. A *conquistador* in gleaming armor, the captain of the guard, recognized Cortés and snapped to attention as we approached the fort's main gate. After the two men exchanged pleasantries the captain allowed us to pass through two massive double doors made from unhewn logs standing fifteen feet high or better. A pair of large, bronze shields inscribed with the king's coat-of-arms, one blazon for each of his four kingdoms: Castile, León, Aragon and Navarre, hung from the center of each door.

The castle appeared to be about half-built. Its walls were encased in scaffolding and we saw an army of Negro and Indian slaves, along with many prisoners, mostly French, moving huge limestone blocks into place or applying mortar to unfinished walls. Another one hundred men or more were digging a moat around the fortress's parameter with pickaxes and shovels. In the center of the castle was a courtyard with six modest but quaint wood-framed houses enclosed by a redbrick wall. The courtyard, with pretty gardens and stone walkways lined with shade trees, stood like an oasis in stark contrast to the grim, grey walls of the fortress surrounding it. Cortés led us into the courtyard and had us sit on a stone bench underneath a palm tree while he slipped inside the largest building. We waited in the shade watching the construction all around us until he popped his head out a few minutes later and beckoned us to come in.

We followed Cortés into a small parlor where a man, sitting behind an ornate desk, rose to greet us. He was a pale, reed of fellow, all bones. One good gust of wind I figured would have been enough to carry him away.

"Don Miguel de Villanueva, may I present to you *Capitána* Mary of the *Falling Star* and her two officers, *Señors* Thomas Gilley, the ship's first officer, and James Hunter, the ship's second officer. The young man waiting outside is the ship's boy."

Villanueva offered me a friendly smile. He leaned over to kiss my hand. "I am delighted to make your acquaintances. Dear lady, gentlemen, welcome, welcome to Cuba!"

"Mary, his Excellency is not here at present," Cortés explained. "But no matter, meeting his Excellency is simply a formality and he would have directed us to meet with Don Villanueva in any case."

I had to look up at Villanueva to nod my appreciation. He was exceedingly tall for a Spaniard. His face was unremarkable, except for a red goatee with a shock of grey running down the middle. He reeked of tobacco and his teeth were badly stained.

"You were most fortunate," Villanueva said as he smoothed down the red whiskers on his chin, "to have met *Señor* Cortés in Trinidad. He is held in high esteem by many in Havana, including his Excellency. Too many in the West Indies, I am sorry to say, do not share Cortés's respect for integrity in business. I would be honored if you would permit me to be your host this evening for supper but, regrettably, urgent business requires my prompt attention in Santo Domingo. A ship is waiting for me down by the pier and I must depart with haste. You are, I assure you, in good hands with *Señor* Cortés."

Villanueva turned to Cortés and clasped his shoulders. "Rodriguez, my friend, it is always good to see you. Perhaps we can all meet again in Santo Domingo soon? It is not often we have guests from Ireland in the West Indies. The people of Ireland and Spain have much in common. We share an abiding love for the Holy Church and we both despise English tyranny. *Buenas tardes.*"

"At your convenience, as always," Cortés replied and bowed.

As Villanueva left the building and stepped into a waiting carriage, Cortés led us on foot to a nearby inn to enjoy a noon-day meal. The establishment was well-furnished, clean and catered to men of substance.

"So my friends," Cortés started to say as the innkeeper brought us a basket of bread with platters of assorted cheeses. "The ports at Havana, Santo Domingo and the Port of Spain are now open to you. Provided you pay a modest gratuity, your ships fall under the protection of the *Capitán General*. I would, of course, be pleased to act as your agent."

"And why," I asked, "do we need the *Capitán General?*"

"It works like so, Mary. You and I will agree to a price, a fair price, for your cargo. You will take your ships to a certain wharf used by the navy. From there, the cargo will be off-loaded, inspected by my people and transported inland by mules and wagons. No agent from the *Casa de Contratación* will be present to interfere with our business. No official inventory will be taken. No taxes will be assessed and none will be collected. I will take care of the costs of administration, transportation and distribution. For this, for this preferential status, you will pay me twenty *pesos*, or in *thales* if you prefer, for every ton your ship weighs regardless of the value of your cargo. The *Godsend* is two hundred and fifty tons I believe you said, so the cost to you would be five thousand *pesos*. Now let us suppose the cargo has a value of one hundred thousand *pesos*. If you brought your goods in through the king's custom's house the *quinto*, the tax, would be at least twenty thousand *pesos*, perhaps as much as thirty thousand *pesos* depending on the kind of cargo you wished to import. This private arrangement I am suggesting, I must tell you, is more generous than what Villanueva customarily agrees to. He is offering this discount because you are bringing so much cargo in at once."

"An attractive offer to be sure, Rodriguez," I said with a touch of diplomacy. "But why shouldn't we simply smuggle in our goods into the islands without Villanueva and pay no fees at all?"

"You can. Some do. You, of course, would then be sailing without the *Capitán General's* blessing, without his protection, and fair game for the Royal Navy, the *Casa de Contratación* and for any cutthroat pirates. The other problem you have is this: you sail with large ships carrying substantial cargoes. Smugglers throughout the Caribbean use small coasters carrying small cargoes, cargoes that can be quickly and efficiently brought on shore and hauled-off with only a few resources in men and pack animals. Once inland, the caravans must travel across narrow, often difficult footpaths through the jungles as we have few roads in the West Indies."

"I see. And what arrangement did you make with Villanueva for exporting goods out of the Caribbean?"

Cortés smiled. "Why none. That is not his concern. That is our business. Unless you wish the protection of the king's war galleons while crossing the Atlantic, or you intend to sell your cargo in Spain or Portugal, we do not require the *Capitán General's* blessing for our exports."

"Master Gilley here," I said, "has had a yearning to wet his whistle with Caribbean sweet wine since we left Ireland. Shall we seal our pact with a drink?"

"*Sí, sí*, but of course! I prefer Spanish and Italian wines, but let me introduce you to some of the New World's best. Among the sweet wines, *Guancapo* is the most popular. It is made from different fermented fruits such as pineapples, bananas and plums. The Caribs also make a wonderful drink they call *mobbie* from fermented potatoes or sometimes with cassava, which we call *perino* or *ouicou*. *Mobbie*, I must warn you, is a potent brew."

"What's your pleasure, Master Gilley?" I asked with a playful smile.

"What do you intend to do with twenty slaves, Mary?" Hunter asked as we pulled leisurely at the longboat's oars on our way back to the *Star*.

"I don't have the faintest notion. You and Tom can sort it out. Let them know they are free, certainly. Perhaps some will wish to try their luck with us and learn about the sea. There are worse ways to make a penny. You must explain to them that we have no means of returning them back to Africa if that is their desire."

"You paid the Spaniard good money for these men and now you want to set them free?" Hunter asked.

"No, I paid Cortés in pearls."

"Ah, well that explains things proper. Pearls. Do you mean to purchase all the slaves in the West Indies and set them free, Mary?"

"Ahem, not sure," Gilley interrupted, "how the lads will take working alongside a Moor."

"Look around us, gentlemen," I replied. "We are in the New World, a world of many peoples. I'm certain I even saw a Chinaman earlier this morning walking down the streets of Havana. If we are here for any time, we are bound to have some Negroes and Indians and God only knows who else sailing with us. If they are good sailors, if they can learn and honor the Ten Rules, I welcome any who wish to join us."

"Very well," Hunter said. "I'll see to it. We already have one Indian onboard and the man insists on pulling his own weight! The lads say he is clever. They say he has taken to his new duties without complaint, eagerly in fact, and his English is improving quickly. They've taken a liking to the fellow. They've named him Henry after, I think, the dead Tudor king."

"Why King Henry?" I asked.

"Not sure. I suppose our lads assume he'll be the King of Guadeloupe someday as Paka Wokili, his uncle, has no sons. And what about Cortés?"

"Yes, indeed, what about Cortés? My own sense of it is that we may not do much better than Cortés and I think it wise for us to employ an agent. We need someone who knows these waters and understands the politics here. So far Cortés has proven himself to be who he claims to be. He seems astute. I invite any contrary thoughts on the matter though, gentlemen."

"Perhaps we should hedge our bet a little," Gilley offered. "We give Cortés cargo from one or two ships and see what we can do without him or his Excellency, the Governor-Captain General, with the rest. But Cortés did make a fair point about the risks if we try working around the Spanish."

Hunter nodded. "I think that is a sound suggestion, Tom. Send *Godsend* into port Mary and then *Phantom* next if all goes well with *Godsend*. *Star* is carrying the least tonnage for sale. Perhaps we should visit our friends in Guadeloupe. Perhaps they can help us sell off *Star's* cargo on other islands, or we can try our luck in Trinidad again."

"Gentlemen, I think we have ourselves a plan," I said. "What say you Master Billy, our ship's boy *par excellence?*"

The boy of quiet temperament for once let down his guard. He giggled.

Then Hunter turned green, leaned over the side and retched.

Gilley chuckled at Hunter's expense. "I've never known an Englishman who could hold his liquor. I tried warning him about *mobbie*. Tasted like turpentine to me. Nothin' ever good comes from making liquor out of potatoes."

Hunter put his head between his legs with a groan and ignored us. We let him wallow in his misery.

On the first day of the New Year, on the *Feast of the Circumcision of our Lord*, we offloaded *Godsend's* cargo in Havana at the wharf used by the Spanish navy. Cortés's men accepted all of it without exception and hauled the goods off in wagons and on mules. His foreman paid Green the agreed price on the spot in chests of silver and gold bullion. A few days later we sent *Phantom* in with the same result.

With Cortés's help, I took our profits and purchased two fine brigantines, displacing one hundred and fifty tons apiece. I named one ship *Westport* and gave Green command and named the other *Fair Irish Maiden* and handed her over to Fox. After taking measurements and calculating the capacity of both ships, Cortés went out and brokered deals on our behalf for lumber, silk, tea, coffee, cocoa, tobacco, sugar and spices like pepper, vanilla and cinnamon. Within a month my men were cramming New World goods into both ships until their cargo holds were stuffed full.

The success of our first voyage into the New World had so far exceeded all my expectations. I was amazed by our good fortune. But as any sailor knows - especially if his roots are Irish - a man's good luck will carry him only so far before the bitch deserts him.

Gilley set his cards down and shook his head crossly at me as we sat around the table in my great cabin. Except for Hunter and me, the others had all retired for the evening.

"God's wounds, Mary, no!" Gilley said sternly. "Hunter or I should lead the ships back to Ireland. Green and Fox are good lads, but they're young and lack experience."

"They seem capable enough to me," I shot back in a haughty tone, more annoyed with myself than Gilley because I knew he was right. But I was in a feisty mood. "Let Ben and Alby do it."

"Mary, please, Thomas is right," Hunter offered softly. "Tom or I should go with the lads. Tom is the better sailor but I am good enough, good enough leastwise to cross the Atlantic and find Ireland. And I'm the better soldier. No offense, Tom. I should be the one in command should trouble find the lads. Four or five weeks over to Ireland, a week or two to sell our New World cargo, another few weeks to purchase finished goods and then an eight, perhaps a nine week voyage back to the West Indies, God willing."

Gilley roared with laughter. "Aye, plainly I am the better sailor, James! Four weeks over, nine weeks back you say? Ha! Columbus had better times with slower vessels! I'll wager all I have the Trojans fleeing burning Ilium, Priam's pride and joy, could've rowed faster in their high-beaked biremes than you can sail!"

"You've got nothing left to wager with old man," Hunter said while pointing to Gilley's pitiful pile of coins.

Gilley considered his meager holdings and sighed.

"Very well, it is settled then," I said. "But take Mustafa with you, James."

Hunter didn't argue. Efendi was like having a guardian angel at your side.

In the morning Gilley and I stood at the ship's aft rail locked arm-in-arm, quietly watching our small flotilla set off under a dark and threatening sky. *Phantom* took the lead, struggling to make headway against the punishing waves. *Westport* followed close behind her with *Fair Irish Maiden* chasing after both of them. Sea foam exploded up and over the ships as they plowed through the relentless rollers.

I missed Hunter already. I quickly brushed away a tear before Gilley could see it. My tiny ships looked so vulnerable out on the vast and hostile sea. Then it began to pour. Sheets of pelting rain swept over us and my three ships disappeared in the mist. The darkness swallowed them whole.

"No worries, Mary," Gilley said, sensing my heartache. "Your precious Hunter will return to you within three months or less."

"I pray they all make it safely back."

Gilley gave me a reassuring hug and kissed me on the forehead. "With God's good blessing, child. With God's good blessing."

Cortés's African slaves, all twenty souls, chose to stay with me, agreed to learn how to work the ships that sail the briny sea. They seemed eager and I was glad to have my new apprentices. Billy, a curious but difficult young man, insisted on returning to Ireland with the flotilla for no particular reason I could discern. I gladly gave the lad my consent and didn't expect to ever see the moody boy again. Henry, our Carib envoy turned sailor, and turning more Irish each day, convinced Gilley and I to avoid involving his kinsmen on Guadeloupe in our business and urged us to return to the Port of Spain instead where, he promised, he could introduce us to buyers for the rest of our contraband cargo. I agreed.

And so we pointed *Star's* nose south towards Trinidad, with *Godsend* following in our wake, and fought through heavy seas at a slow but steady pace. I had given Ferguson command of *Godsend* and promoted a feisty Scotsman who called himself Jacob Atwood, a tall and handsome fellow with a wild mane of red hair, as my second officer to replace Ferguson. Atwood had signed with me back in Westport and though I had never sailed with him before, he showed great promise.

Once we reached the Port of Spain the skies began to clear and the days turned hot and humid. I paid the men their wages and Gilley gave them their liberty to go ashore.

The port was just as putrid as we had left it. Gilley and I were nearly overcome by the nauseating stench that poisoned the air all around us as we walked down the port's narrow streets and alleys. We passed luckless beggars and desperate tricksters; we passed by sick and dying men. One wretched soul who approached me for alms was covered from head to toe in open sores oozing puss. Chunks of flesh hung off his face like wax dripping down a candle. I shuddered as we walked by. He was, no doubt, a victim of the great pox, or perhaps he was a leper. Many would claim he was a living testament of God's wrath over man's promiscuity on earth, though I think it more likely the poor fellow's luck had simply ran out. Hunter had been right. The New World was no paradise and kind to precious few.

We easily found the town's square and found the tavern where we had left it, the tavern where we had first met Cortés. I declared this to be our safe haven, our rallying point if trouble found us, and passed the word along to the men. Gilley and I took a small table in a dark corner where the air was slightly cooler. We sat and had a drink or two to whittle away the hours.

And that became our routine over the next few days. We spent a miserable week in sweltering heat in the Port of Spain. Our Carib Indian, Henry, proved most resourceful though. Thanks to Henry, we sold off the rest of our Old World cargo to various merchants and smugglers around the island for very good prices. The king's good agent responsible for accessing and collecting import taxes, the *quinto*, had no objections to our business after I paid the man a gratuity - a fortune to him but a trifling sum to me - to look the other way.

And then a yearning seized me, a desire to put to sea and explore filled my soul. I did not care about the cost. I gathered all my men and like Christopher Columbus and his expedition some eighty years before, we set our sails and headed west, pushing deeper into the vast unknown. I was curious about the Spanish Main.

Sailing in ballast, we reached the island of Margarita first where they say pearls wash up on the beaches like seashells. I wanted to put in at the port of *La Asunción*, but we saw two Spanish war galleons and six armed merchantmen, naos, caravels and one sloop, anchored in her harbor. Along the docks we saw companies of men-at-arms overseeing platoons of Negro slaves neatly stacking small crates on a wooden jetty. No doubt the crates were filled with pearls destined for old Spain. Pearls, Cortés had told us, were as important to the Spanish treasury as gold or silver.

With *La Asunción* closed to us, we sailed north around the island. Three times we put in at some deserted cove and went ashore, but we found no pearls or pearl oysters or pearl beds or anything else of interest. Before sailing away from Margarita, we put in at *La Villa del Norte*, a small village of huts and one flimsy fort made of earth and wood on the coast, where we purchased supplies from Spanish locals and then departed quickly.

We headed due south next until we reached *Cumaná*, a small village on the Spanish Main nestled in-between soft rolling hills of great beauty at the mouth of the Manzanares River. The houses they say, built over the water on stilts with interconnecting boardwalks called *palafitos*, reminded Amerigo Vespucci of the City of Venice, or *Venezia* in the Italian tongue, and so Vespucci named the region Venezuela, or *Little Venice* in the Spanish.

In *Cumaná*, first settled by Franciscan friars only a few years after Columbus's voyages and recently rebuilt in 1569 by the famous pirate hunter Diego Hernández de Serpa, we were able to do some trading with the local Indians. They are one of the Carib tribes and call themselves Cumanagotos. We traded for gold, silver, pearls and for jewelry and works of art of exceptional quality and distinctive beauty. Henry once again proved himself of great value as a translator and in helping us understand the customs and culture of the Carib peoples who dwell along the Spanish Main.

We rested in *Cumaná* for several days and were enjoying a trough of cooler air when fever struck my crew and struck them hard. I was the last one to succumb to the mysterious affliction. Delirious and bathed in sweat, so cold at times I prayed for death to take me, the illness laid me low for days. At the worst of it, Gilley found a Dominican priest to administer the last rites to me, the *Extreme Unction*, when he thought it was my end. Miraculously I survived the fever. For weeks later I was nothing but skin and bones and I was grateful Hunter was not there to see me.

We lost twelve good men to the savage illness. We buried our fallen with the help of our Dominican priest and then we washed our clothes and scrubbed our ships down clean with strong soap before setting out again. I always carried ample quantities of soap aboard my ships, soap imported from Marseilles when I could get it as the French make the very best. My men tolerated this flaw in me, this desire for cleanliness. Soap, I am certain, has curative powers though none of my men believed me and scoffed. Even so, they humored me and washed with few complaints.

With clean ships and healthy crews, we weighed anchor, unfurled sail and left the death of *Cumaná* behind us. We continued our trek west, hugging the coast off the Spanish Main until we reached Maracaibo on Lake Maracaibo. The name Maracaibo, Henry told us, comes from the Carib word *Maara-iwo*, meaning *the place where serpents abound*. After we dropped anchor and went ashore we found, to our surprise, many German settlors. King Phillip's father, King Charles I of Spain, apparently had owed some German bankers money and the bankers had agreed to take colonial rights in Venezuela as payment of the debt. The bankers had heard the stories of *El Dorado*, the legendary lost city of gold, and had hopes of finding it in Venezuela. A German explorer named Ambrosius Ehinger had settled the village back in 1529, but the Spanish, being Spanish, double-crossed the Germans later and took all of Venezuela back for themselves.

We did not tarry long in Maracaibo. The senior ranking *conquistador*, a Spaniard named Pedro Maldonado, gave us a cool reception. A small fleet of English or French pirates, Maldonado wasn't certain which, had only a few weeks earlier tried to raid Maracaibo. But Maldonado and his men had been ready for them. They ambushed the pirates on the beach and forced them back to their ships with heavy losses. The sight of my ships a few weeks later, armed with heavy cannon, gave Maldonado no joy. He gave us until the next outgoing tide to resupply our ships and demanded that we leave. I could hardly blame him.

My plan, if one could call it that, other than to fend off boredom and escape the heat, was to sail around the whole of the Caribbean. The excitement of exploring new lands had seized my imagination back in the Port of Spain and neither our misfortune in *Cumaná*, nor the hostility of the Spanish at Maracaibo, did anything to discourage me. We sailed on.

Next on my chart was *Cartagena de Indias*, a town in territory of Columbia. Cartagena was founded in 1533 by a Spaniard named Pedro de Heredia. Heredia had named the port town after his hometown of Cartagena, Spain, a city founded by the ancient Phoenicians well before the birth of our Lord Jesus Christ. Cartagena was far more impressive than *Cumaná* or Maracaibo with their crude *palafitos*. After a great fire destroyed the town in 1552, the Spanish rebuilt Cartagena in stone and brick, including an impressive new building called the Palace of the Town where the governor kept his offices. The governor's power must have exceeded the Pope's own for the church standing next to his palace was little more than mud walls, reeds and straw.

The village was clean, well-laid out and boasted a fine harbor. But, like the other ports we had visited, the town's defenses were slim. Only a flimsy wooden wall reinforced with earthen ramparts and a few small cannon stood between the town and any enemy coming from the sea.

The governor of the region was a congenial man of rotund proportions named Pedro Fernández de Busto. Busto gave us a grand tour of his town once he was satisfied that we were there only to buy supplies and do some honest trading. He told us that his predecessor, Martin de las Alas, had nearly been tricked a few years back in 1568 by an Englishman named John Hawkins. Hawkins, Busto explained, had asked Alas to allow his men entry into the town so that they could sell their foreign goods in the open street bazaars. But Alas, no fool, saw through the rouse. He could see that Hawkins was no merchant and closed Cartagena's gates to the English. Hawkins retaliated by laying siege to the town but, when he couldn't humble Spanish pride after a fortnight of trying, he sailed off to look for easier pickings.

Colombia is a land rich in gold and this made Cartagena a favorite target for many a pirate over the years. But not all of Cartagena's gold came from the goldmines we learned. The Spanish had found vast quantities of the precious metal buried deep inside the tombs of dead Sinú all around Cartagena and had no qualms about robbing the dead Indians of their worldly wealth.

We spent several easy days in Cartagena introducing ourselves to potential trading partners. After we met anyone worth meeting, we returned to our sturdy ships, set our sails and headed west once more. I had a mind to visit Panama next.

"Mary. Mary... Mary, wake thyself up, Mary!"

I struggled to open my eyes and found Gilley standing over me, shaking me roughly by the shoulder. I had retired to my bed for a quick mid-afternoon nap. I rubbed the sleep out of my eyes and tried to focus.

"What? What is it, Tom?"

"Three ships have been shadowing us for some time. Now it would seem they want to close with us."

"We can't outrun them?"

"*Star* is sailing well enough. She may not have *Phantom's* speed, but she can hold her own. *Godsend* though is a different matter. With empty cargo holds she's high in the water and bouncing all around in these choppy seas. She's falling behind. Ferguson is coaxing the most out of her, but it is not enough."

"Pirates you think, Tom?"

"I know not Mary, but in these waters..."

"Right you are my good mariner! Well, we'll not give up the *Godsend*."

"No, certainly not Mary, but you best come up on deck now. Matters might turn ugly soon."

I quickly dressed and hurried up to the poop deck and over to the aft rail to look out over our stern. *Godsend* was five hundred yards or so behind the *Star* and sailing poorly. Less than a half a league behind the *Godsend*, I saw three ships with dark sails sailing abreast and tearing after us. They flew no flags or pennants of any kind. Mercifully, none of the ships were galleons.

"How far are we from the nearest land, Tom?" I asked.

"Fifty leagues or so to the south, my lady, but the winds and currents won't favor us if we port our helm and head back towards Venezuela or Columbia."

Then Atwood scrambled across the main deck and raced up the aftercastle's ladder to join Gilley and me at the helm. In Hunter's absence he was the Captain of the Guns now.

"Madam, the ship's been cleared for action," he offered in a calm and confident tone. "The guns are primed and loaded."

"Very well, Master Atwood. I see you've mounted the swivels too."

"Aye, as have the lads on *Godsend*. Prudence dictates no less."

"Master Hunter spoke well of your talents Master Atwood before he left our company. You may need to prove yourself very soon. Those three ships trying to run us down, what say you?"

Atwood glanced over the aft rail, took a moment to consider our pursuers and grunted. "Anything can happen in battle. It's the big dog that wins the fight more often than not. But a shattered mast or disabled rudder from one, lucky ball will cook our goose for certain. They're still too far off to know how many guns they carry or how many men they are. But the *Star* is as fine a ship as I've sailed on and you've got a disciplined, seasoned crew. I'd say the odds favor us if the men on those ships mean to do us harm."

Gilley nodded in agreement. "If those sons of bitches knew *Star's* strength they'd be less hasty in their approach. They must be after *Godsend*, even though she plainly sails in ballast."

"If we must fight," I said, glancing up at the sky, "the winds and currents will favor us if we come about and go straight at them."

"Just so, Mary!" Gilley said with a twinkle in his eye, looking at me with pride.

I glanced up at *Star's* white sails, trimmed well and billowing full, and again considered the wind and currents. I took in the sea around us. I took in the small, puffy clouds racing across the horizon like so many ships racing across the waves. It was a pretty afternoon. It was a good day to live I thought. It was, perhaps, as good a day to die. None of us can know our fate.

"Tom, how much time before their guns are in range?"

"Hard to tell, Mary. Most ships we've seen in the Caribbees so far, except for the galleons, carry small falconets and the like. At their present course and speed, um, I'd say an hour before they can use their bow chasers against us, if they even have bow chasers. If they don't have guns positioned forward then it will take them longer, two hours or better, before they can come up alongside us, before they can bring all their guns to bear."

I had every confidence in Gilley, and in Atwood too, but I found myself wishing Hunter was with me now. His poise and self-assurance - his confidence never wavering - was like being wrapped inside a warm and cozy blanket.

We saw a puff of smoke, a tongue of flame, before we heard the report of the first cannon. Gunners working a bow chaser on the lead vessel fired off a warning shot. The ball splashed harmlessly into the sea one hundred yards or so behind us, leaving behind a geyser of white water. Gilley had guessed well. Nearly an hour had passed before our mysterious foe could fire off a round with any hope of hitting anything.

Godsend and *Star* were sailing side-by-side now with less than fifty yards of water between us. Gilley and I had slowed the *Star* down, allowing *Godsend* to catch up. I waved at Ferguson to get his attention and pointed west. He understood my gesture and nodded. I decided to keep to our present course and ignore our pursuers for a bit.

The three caravels chasing after us were no more than one hundred and fifty tons apiece. That meant smaller crews and smaller guns, a piece of good luck for us.

"Those brazen rascals are fools," Atwood offered calmly. "They plainly have no clue of our muscle."

"Greed, Master Atwood, greed." Gilley said. "Blind greed will often undo even an otherwise clever man."

"Or just plain stupidity, Captain Gilley," Atwood replied with a wry smile. "If those louts continue pressing forward to test us, they'll rue the day they left their mother's womb once they feel our sting."

"Bold talk from a Scot!" Gilley roared and slapped Atwood on the shoulder.

The crew on the lead ship fired off a second round with no better result than the first. The shot plunged harmlessly into empty sea with barely a splash. And then the gunners from the two flanking caravels fired off their forward guns in rapid succession.

BOOM! BOOM! BOOM! BOOM!

All four shots struck empty water. Another volley soon followed and then another. With each new volley, plumes of water crept closer and closer towards us. Our enemy plainly was finished with polite persuasion. They were determined to stop us even if it meant blood.

"More proof of stupid," Atwood said and shook his head. "A waste of precious shot and powder."

"P'haps not stupid," Gilley offered warily. "I think they mean to intimidate us with their bluster. They hope we'll piss our trousers, unnerved by this rolling barrage of theirs. They hope we'll shorten sail and yield. They still don't know our strength. They still don't know what men and arms we carry."

"Nor," I added, "do they yet know the mettle of our men or of our resolve."

Another thirty minutes passed before our enemy - still sailing abreast in tight formation - was able to bring his bow chasers in range. Shots began falling all around us. Some balls flew wide to starboard. Others went wide to port. Shots fell short and shots flew overhead. A few shots fell in-between our ships. The aim of the enemy's gunners was atrocious. But with their guns now in range anything was possible.

With my blessing, Atwood had the men roll a pair of heavy guns from the gun deck back to the stern and into my great cabin. The gunners quickly removed my cabin's panels and windows and started blasting away. They quickly proved themselves the better marksmen. Our first salvos went wide and far or short and long but my gunners soon settled down and started hitting wood, though we inflicted no real damage.

And then next to me, CRACK! I shuddered. I thought I had been hit.

"God's blood!" Gilley cried out, snapping his head around. He reached down to pick up a rock the size of my hand resting at my feet. "Look'ee here, they're hurtling stones at us, Mary. It an't even round. That's why they can't hit anything. An inch more to the right though, Mary..."

I took the rock from Gilley and stared at the ugly thing that had nearly killed me. Before landing at my feet the rock had shattered the aft rail, ricocheted past my head - only by a whisker - and then smacked the base of the mizzen mast before bouncing back at me.

No, not by a whisker. Gilley took his scarf and dabbed the blood off a scratch along my cheek and crossed himself. I swallowed hard and tossed the evil rock over the side. Then I looked for Atwood.

"Jacob," I called out when I spotted him down on the main deck, whipping the men up for battle with a rousing speech. He seemed to be enjoying the moment. He reminded me of Hunter. He turned my way to look up at me. "So now we know we're in for a fight. We can't outrun these bastards. Can you tell how many guns the caravels carry?"

"Aye, Madam," he answered and rushed back to the quarter deck to stand with Gilley and me. "I sent Wilson to the main topgallant mast for a better view. The lead ship carries ten guns on her main deck with a pair of small bow chasers. She carries a pair of small stern chasers too. The ships on either side of her carry only eight guns apiece and both have bow chasers, but neither carries guns at the stern. These pirates have nothing bigger than small falconets."

"Twenty-six falconets against *Star's* twenty-four larger periers, sakers and long-barreled falconets," I said softly. "Plus we have *Godsend's* eight falconets and we have solid iron shot to work with."

Atwood grinned. "Aye, Madam. That's the gest of things. We're facing three light cruisers, not battlewagons, and I'll wager all I have we've got the better gunners. I do indeed like our chances!"

"Tom, you still fancy that notion you had earlier of coming about?"

"We can't make land Mary and there's plenty of daylight left. Your gunners at the stern though Jacob, beg pardon, haven't hit shit. If the sea was any smaller I fear your gunners would miss it too. Winds and currents would give us an edge Mary - briefly mind you - if we came about. I doubt our friends across the water would expect it."

"The gods," Atwood offered with a wry smile, "favor the bold."

I nodded. "Do they now? Well, if I remember my gunnery lessons: at one thousand yards we'll start hitting things, at five hundred yards we'll start to cause some damage and at two hundred and fifty yards we can employ the swivels, load the guns with chain and grapeshot and inflict some truly brutal damage against flesh and wood."

"Right you are, Lady Mary," Atwood said and then, with a touch of theater, he bowed to me most grandly. "And as you say, with good iron shot to work with our lads should be a bit more accurate than our foe, leastwise at long range."

More rocks rained down all around us. One shot ricocheted off our hull. Another struck the forecastle and sent splinters flying through the air.

I placed my hands on my hips. I cleared my head of any doubt. I had decided on a plan.

"You boys ready for a brawl?"

Gilley and Atwood exchanged glances, looked at me and grinned. After I told them my plan they both nodded their approval. And then I looked over at Ferguson, saw him standing at *Godsend's* helm, and I shouted my plan across the waves to him. He acknowledged me with less enthusiasm than Gilley or Atwood. He acknowledged me with a tentative nod and swallowed. But he was young. He quickly barked out orders to his crew and men scrambled up into the rigging.

I gave no rousing speech to my crew. My men knew the cut and thrust of battle, the bloody grind of war. Most had served by my side for years and needed no words of encouragement or prodding from me.

Another fifteen minutes passed before we made our move.

"About a thousand yards it is, Mary," Gilley said casually as we stood side-by-side at the helm.

Atwood nodded. He left Gilley and me on the poop deck and disappeared below to move the stern guns back to the main deck and to prepare his gunners for the turn.

More shots struck our ships. One near miss from a large projectile drenched me with a column of sticky water, soaked me through and through. Another shot struck the *Godsend* amidships and I heard a man cry out in agony.

A young Italian named Caputo had *Star's* tiller. Caputo was good but he wasn't MacGyver, who had deserted me to sail with Hunter. Gilley had to tell the Italian to steer small. Larger ships like *Star* and *Phantom* use whipstaffs below deck to turn their rudders. But MacGyver, a clever fellow who liked to tinker, had replaced the clumsy whipstaff on both the *Star* and *Phantom*, my heaviest ships, with his own mechanical contraption. His special tiller, in the shape of a wheel, allowed the helmsman to steer the ship above deck so that he could see and feel where he was going and improved the ship's handling. But MacGyver's device also required a lighter touch.

"Stand ready, Master Caputo," I said loudly. "Captain Gilley, right or left?"

"To port, Mary."

"Master Atwood!" I shouted down to the main deck. Prepare for a hard turn to port and then we shorten sail!"

"Aye, my lady!" Atwood replied excitedly.

"Master Ferguson!" I called out across the water. "Follow our lead, be ready to port your helm and shorten sail!"

"Aye, Mary! As you port your helm and shorten sail we shall do the same!"

Swarthy, bare-chested topmen spread out across the yardarms using the foot stirrups for balance in their bare feet and waited for the signal to haul in canvas while my gunners stood anxiously by their guns with burning linstocks in hand. I bit my tongue. I held my breath and waited. My duel with *Medusa* when she had been Dowlin's ship had been a simple, lopsided affair. I had won with surprise and trickery. This was my first battle with orthodox tactics. This was my first, true test.

A shot crashed into our stern. I heard glass shatter. Another ripped a hole through the mizzen sail a few feet above my head.

"Now, Tom!" I commanded.

"Prepare to port your helm Caputo, let her ease into the turn!" Gilley bellowed. He looked for Atwood next down on the main deck. "Master Atwood, we shorten sail! Caputo, bring her rudder around ninety degrees now and hold her firm once we're pointing due south."

Atwood shouted orders up to the topmen and told his gunners to stand ready as *Star* heeled sharply over. Ferguson mimicked our actions and *Godsend* turned the corner with us in nearly flawless harmony. Topmen frantically pulled the canvas in and my ships glided to a stop. Our enemy was perpendicular to us now and charging into a wall of wood, bristling with batteries of heavy cannon.

"Master Atwood!" I cried out excitedly. "Fire as you please!"

With his hands locked behind his back, coolly strutting up and down the gun deck like some lord surveying his serfs, Atwood barked out fresh orders with a voice like rolling thunder. "Take aim! Target the lead ship. Wait for the swell. Wait for it. Ready. Steady. FIRE!"

BOOM! BA-BA-BA-BA-BOOOOOOOOOM!

Ferguson gave the same order on the *Godsend*.

The deck vibrated under my feet as the guns recoiled. Clouds of smoke rose over the ship and filled my lungs with a pleasant whiff of gunpowder. A wave of elation washed over me.

Plumes of water shot up all around our enemy. Each splash marked a miss. But I saw iron shot smack wood and rip through canvas too. Like a pack of hungry wolves the enemy ships ignored these barbs. They kept charging straight at us.

"Stop your vents, swab your barrels down!" Atwood bellowed with steely-eyed determination. "Move, move, move! Jump to it! Prime and load again. Take better aim, lads. Patience. Too many wide shots last volley. Those devils coming at us want to gut you - get mean, get angry, get ugly. Give those bastards a bellyful of pain before they can do the same to you!"

Atwood's gunners answered him with hoots and hollers. They

answered him with renewed vigor. They hauled their bronze monsters in, swabbed the muzzles down to extinguish any burning residue and reloaded with alacrity and steadfast discipline. I watched the action swirling around me with satisfaction. I had a burning itch to join my men, to show off my own skills, but I was the ship's commander and my place was at the helm.

"Mary," Gilley called out, "those rascals continue sailing straight at us."

"Let them," I replied coolly and then, feeling playful, I threw down a challenge. "Atwood! Your men are sluggish today! Have they no fight left in them? Slackers all! These are not the men I trained with! Imposters, each and every one of them! Should we secure the guns and raise the white flag? Would your gunners rather I surrender this ship than fight?"

Standing in the midst of his gunners, the big Scotsman squared his shoulders back and doffed his hat towards me. He paused and gave me a puzzled look as the wind whipped through his wild, red mane. Plainly full of himself, he offered me a defiant grin.

"By your leave good lady, I'll set matters right!" he thundered, taking the bait. "You'll find no slackers, no dawdlers here today!" He roughly grabbed a handspike from the nearest gunner and used the iron rod to ease a saker around until he found an enticing target. And once he knew his aim was true, he seized a burning linstock from the gun captain. "Let me show you how it's done, lads!" he roared. He held his breath and fired.

BOOM!

Whether by luck or skill I know not, but Atwood's shot smacked the bowsprit of the lead vessel dead-on! It was a brilliant shot. The ball cracked the spar in two. The ship's jib sail went slack, floated above her port rail and started flapping in the wind like the broken wing of a bird. Men cheered.

"That's the way it's done!" Atwood boasted with adrenaline pumping hard. "No doubt every one of you can do me better! Now show me how good you are! Don't be shy! Jump to it - fire away my brave lads! Impress our good Lady Mary with your skills at gunnery!"

Gun captains leaned over their barrels and took careful aim. And when each man found his target, he brushed his linstock against his gun's touchhole. The guns belched smoke and fire and doom in unison.

BOOM-BA-BA-BA-BOOM!

The enemy's ships took a tremendous pounding. Hunter's endless hours of gunnery drills, those monotonous, exhausting exercises of his, were paying off. Still the enemy doggedly kept charging at our wooden wall. I won't deny feeling some measure of anxiety as I watched them closing with us.

Our foe did not lack courage - and he was not without a plan. At five hundred yards my opposite made his move. The lead ship, the ship in the center of the enemy formation with the broken bowsprit, continued sailing straight at us - somewhat clumsily now without her jib sail - while her two consorts peeled off. One went left and the other went right in an obvious attempt to sweep around our flank and encircle us. The enemy commander's counter-move would have been a good one had I intended to sit idly by and wait.

"Tom, Ben," I shouted after the two enemy ships coming around our flanks were well into their turns. "Unfurl all sail, get us under way!"

Topmen moved out smartly along the foot stirrups hooked to yardarms once again, oblivious to any danger. They dropped and trimmed the sails quickly. The *Star* lurched forward slowly as the canvas caught the wind. The *Godsend* did the same.

"Port your helm hard over, Master Caputo!" I ordered. Ferguson gave the same command to his helmsman and both ships made a second sharp turn, this time to the east, straight at our foe. Now we had the advantage of better winds and friendlier currents. We had seized the weather-gauge.

Atwood ordered his gunners to stuff the swivels with grapeshot and the heavy guns with chain. We pointed the noses of our ships at the lead enemy ship while a good, flowing breeze billowed out our sails. We quickly picked-up terrific speed.

"Mary," Gilley called out after finishing issuing new orders to the petty officers of each division. "You have a gift."

I felt a second wave of elation sweep over me as I nodded my thanks to Gilley. Yes, I had a gift. We were going to sail by the lead enemy ship at close range and she would be wedged in-between us, *Godsend* on her starboard and *Star* on her port, as we passed her by with all of our guns blazing. When the two captains on the flanking vessels understood my plan - and their gross mistake in tactics - they struggled to swing their ships around to come to the rescue of their brothers. But they were too far off to catch us. My timing had been exquisite.

At one hundred yards and closing fast I saw, in brilliant white, the splendid figurehead of a nude woman - or a goddess - mounted to the prow of the lead ship. The statue from head to toe was a lovely work of art.

BOOM! BOOM! BOOM! BA-BA-BA-BA-BOOOOOOOOM!

We poured iron aplenty into the lead enemy vessel as we sailed past her at close range. My gunners pulverized the enemy's hull. We fired off the swivels too and swept the enemy's decks with grapeshot, inflicting horrific carnage. I saw men fall in bloody heaps of shredded flesh. I heard the high-pitched screams and sad groans of wounded and dying men. I heard their curses too; I heard *sauve-qui-peut!* Our enemy cursed in French.

And then I saw the ship's captain standing at the helm out in the open brandishing his cutlass, indifferent to any danger, frantically directing his men in the midst of all the hot action. The man was young and handsome and I thought him very brave. When he saw me, he tipped his hat in my direction - a large, floppy thing adorned with a single, yellow plume - and bowed at the waist as our ships slipped gracefully by each other. I bit my tongue and nodded back, acknowledging my opponent's chivalry.

The ships sailed on, the enemy to the west and my own ships to the east. We parted ways and the guns abruptly fell silent. The great battle was done.

My men cheered wildly as we watched our enemy sail off to lick his wounds. "*Hoorah! Hoorah! Hoorah!*" they shouted over and over again.

I climbed down to the main deck to mingle with my crew. Elation filled my heart. I shook hands, patted backs and even exchanged a hug and a kiss or two. We did have casualties, mostly splinter wounds and lacerations though on *Godsend* one sailor suffered the worst of it when a rock bit his foot off, poor soul. Some took note of my superficial wound across the cheek and I felt embarrassed by it. The cut was nothing.

The god of war had been most kind to us that day.

I helped my men secure the guns and then had ale and spirits brought up on deck to let them celebrate. The three caravels were well over the horizon and posed no threat. And when the sun settled on the waves, we turned our ships about and resumed our voyage west.

Gilley, Atwood and Ferguson joined me in my great cabin for supper. We ignored the broken glass all around us and ate a hearty meal.

"Why so glum, Tom?" I asked halfway through our supper. Gilley had been unusually quiet, even somber.

"Not glum, Mary," he answered. "More pensive."

"Pensive is it?" Atwood asked and chucked. "Don't even know what the word means. Are you ill?"

"No, I'm not ill, Jacob. I've simply been reflecting on the day's excitement. This is a happy day I suppose, except for Schmidt who lost a foot and for those poor, wretched souls we killed and maimed. War is never pretty."

"We did not," I said defensively, "ask for trouble. Trouble found us, Tom. Trouble was forced upon us and we fought back to defend ourselves. Tell me the wrong in that."

"That is true, Mary, that is true. We didn't ask for any trouble and those scoundrels got what they deserved most assuredly. But we haven't been very good at being discreet so far since we reached the New World. Hunter was right. We're the big dog it seems and the other dogs will always want to test us, to give us a good comeuppance if they can. I worry whether we can win every battle. I wonder what will happen when we lose? Ah, but bless me, today was a good day!"

I nodded in agreement. "I am mindful of these things, Tom. Perhaps we can't win every battle. But neither can we live out our lives hiding away in some cave, cowering away in fear and scarcely living."

"How true, Mary. I have no regrets."

"I doubt those miserable fools who tested us today," Ferguson interjected, "will want to test us again tomorrow or anytime soon. I'm grateful to you Mary for your keen sense of things, for your poise in battle. You displayed wonderful seamanship and bravery and kept your wits about you under fire. Your courage inspired us all. I will never understand how it is you know these things, these things that only men should know."

"It is," Atwood chimed in and bowed his head respectfully, "a distinct honor to sail with you, my lady. You must have a drop or two of Amazon warrior blood in you."

I smiled sweetly at all three men. "You may now call me simply Mary, Jacob. You've earned the right. Aye, today was a good day. It is you three though who showed great skill and courage and inspired me and I am grateful. But we were lucky too. I know this. And no doubt there will be better and worse days ahead. I pray you will all feel as charitable towards me at the end of our cruise..."

The Province of Colón on the Isthmus of Panama was next on my list of places to see. Cortés had told us that *Nombre de Diós*, the Name of God, was one of the most important ports in the New World for this was where the fabled treasure fleet stopped to collect Spain's riches once a year. Tons of gold and silver from New Spain, Columbia and Peru, Caribbean island pearls and Venezuelan gemstones by the crate, poured into the village overland by caravan. I had an itch to see the place though I knew the great treasure fleet would still be far away assembling in Seville.

The last leg of our voyage to Panama was mercifully uneventful. We sailed into Name of God's nearly empty bay at dawn, went ashore and once again I was struck by the lack of any meaningful defenses, especially considering how much of Spain's wealth passed through this very spot. A flimsy wooden stockade sitting atop a hill overlooking the bay was the harbor's only protection. The paltry fort's garrison could barely muster a company of men and had no cannons, not one.

As we toured the town we looked high and low for God or riches but found neither one. We found oppressive humidity and heat instead, along with swarms of hungry bugs. The Spanish had built their precious town next to a swamp with a most unhealthy climate, which seemed a curious thing to do. As we strolled casually down the village's dirt roads, we passed by a many straw and mud-brick huts. The only buildings of substance we saw was one Dominican monastery, a hospital, and over a dozen large warehouses used for the treasure fleet. *Nombre de Diós* was a sleepy, dirty, place. I found the village depressing.

We learned from the locals that their sleepy, little town was not always so. When the mule trains arrived once a year to rendezvous with the treasure fleet the town sprang to life they told us. Thousands flocked to the Name of God then to ply their trades, to find work, or to revel in the great carnival, the *Feast of the Golden Bull*, where Spaniards celebrate the treasure fleet's return and Spain's preeminence among kingdoms in the world. And we heard the name of an English pirate named Captain Francis Drake. The Englishman had raided the settlement only months before, but had left empty-handed.

Finding no good reason to stay in Panama, we abruptly returned to our ships and headed for Veracruz, the treasure fleet's other favorite port of call. Fair skies and calm seas continued to bless our voyage as we sailed north and then east and then west around the Yucatán. The closer we came to Veracruz the more *tráfico* we saw cruising along the sea lanes. But we stayed clear of any traffic; we steered clear of any trouble.

We rounded the *Isla Pajaros* and dropped anchor off the island of *San Juan de Ulúa* where the *Casa de Contratación* kept a strong presence - together with the Spanish army. The Spanish had built themselves a formidable fortress of thick stone walls with massive ramparts and imposing watchtowers protected by batteries of heavy cannon on the small island of *San Juan de Ulúa*. I took Gilley, Ferguson and Atwood with me and we rowed across the bay in the longboat over to the city.

The famous Hernán Cortés had named the place Veracruz, which means *true cross*, because he and his band of *conquistadors* had landed there on a Good Friday in the year 1519. The locals though call their city the *city of tables* because when you peer down on the thatched-roof, wooden houses from the nearby heights, they resemble tables set out in neat rows and columns resembling a chequerboard. Veracruz is not like the poorly protected settlements of crude huts and dirt pathways we had seen elsewhere. Veracruz is a true city with neatly laid out homes, well-constructed buildings and wide, cobblestone streets. She surpassed all others in the New World in wealth and commerce. Wherever we turned, we saw well-to-do merchants and bustling shops. Veracruz was a place of opportunity and money, a place where we could do some business. The city intrigued me and had made, or so I hoped, our expedition around the Caribbean worthwhile.

We found a tavern favored by gentlemen of substance and mingled with the local merchants for a day or two. We introduced ourselves as honest traders looking for new markets and probed potential partners for information but, to my dismay, we soon discovered Veracruz no longer welcomed smugglers. Spain's King Phillip II and his ministers, forever craving tax revenues to pay-off Spain's many bankers, had decided to crack down on smuggling in the Americas, and on the corruption smugglers thrive on, and chose to make a royal example out of Veracruz. To enforce his will, the king had commanded his subjects to build the impressive citadel of daunting stone and heavy cannon at *San Juan de Ulúa* - as much to collect his taxes as to protect the city from marauders.

All ships entering Veracruz had to stop first at the island *of San Juan de Ulúa* to be inspected by agents of the *Casa de Contratación* who, we were informed, could not be bribed. No vessel could land goods in Veracruz or carry cargo out until the *quinto* was accessed and paid in full.

And then we heard two familiar names again. We learned that the Spanish Royal Navy had, only a few years back in 1569, trapped a small English squadron led by John Hawkins, the same Englishman who had tried to take Cartagena, along with his younger cousin Francis Drake, the same Englishman who had only a few months before visited the Name of God looking for Spanish treasure, against the walls of *San Juan de Ulúa*. Hawkins and Drake were on shore sacking Veracruz when the Spanish navy surprised their squadron anchored out in the harbor. The Spanish captured all but two ships, the *Minion* and the *Judith*, which Hawkins and Drake commandeered for their escape. Mischief seemed to follow these two troublemakers wherever they traveled. The Spanish wanted them dead.

We spent a week in Veracruz exploring, quietly learning what we could about possible opportunities and about the politics of the region. I made liberal use of Don de Villanueva's name and that of the Governor-Captain General, Gregorio González de Cuenca, even though I had never met the governor. We even entertained a number of Veracruz's more distinguished citizens aboard the *Falling Star* one evening. We treated our guests to Irish music, dance and supper. I spared no expense and entertained them lavishly. The evening was a grand success and we made a new friend or two worth having.

With our mission more or less accomplished, and restless to get underway, we purchased fresh supplies, raised anchor and pointed our ships due east, setting out for Havana some eight hundred leagues away. Havana was where I hoped to find Hunter waiting for me if God, in His mercy, saw fit to return my lover to me.

Ducking in and out of light squalls barely strong enough to be annoying, we sailed across a rough and troubled sea. I spent my evenings standing at the helm, alone, lost in thought. I had ample time to let my mind wander. Every league we sailed east brought me one league closer to Hunter. During the day I found myself anxiously pacing up and down the deck, brooding more often than not. I told myself over and over again that Hunter was just a man, a man with a pretty face and strong arms, but just a man all the same. I tried to convince myself that if he did not return to me, I could easily find another. But that, I knew, was untrue. I wanted to harden my heart. I tried and tried again but could not. And that annoyed me greatly. The little girl I had once known, the little girl who could purge any emotion at any time she wished to with little effort, was nothing more than shadow now.

Chapter Seven

ortune's fool am I. Pride. Pride walks hand-in-hand with Arrogance and Arrogance, well, she never wanders far off without her favorite handmaiden, Carelessness. Pride is a most dangerous, volatile, troublesome flaw. It is the flaw of kings and fools. Her majesty, a most attentive listener, had graciously allowed me to describe my gifts to her, of which there are but a few. But to render my story whole, I needed to confess certain imperfections in my nature as well.

I began with pride. I can no more set aside my pride than I can set aside my heart or brain. It is a part of me. There were other sins I confessed to her majesty too, including the sin of vanity, though, perhaps, this is not so great a flaw for a woman who men are easily drawn to. The queen had readily agreed.

It was pride that helped me soar. It was pride that laid me low.

I was careless in my arrogance. I failed to read the signs.

Even now I weep.

"What vexes you, Mary?" Gilley asked me as we strolled up and down the gun deck together, casually inspecting the rope and tackle securing the guns. "You've been oddly quiet these past few days."

"Why all is well, Tom, truly," I said. "I'm grateful for your concern."

"Ah, my mistake then," Gilley offered graciously, but with little sincerity in his tone.

"You look about as brown as a coconut, Tom," I said and

laughed, wanting to change the subject. "Have the tropics done the same to me?"

Gilley turned and smiled. "God forbid. No worries, Mary. You are an exquisite beauty and Hunter will think the same."

"I was not thinking of Hunter."

"My dear, my dearest Mary, lest you have forgotten: the captain of this ship, under our sacred Ten Rules, is forbidden to lie to the crew as I recall."

"Hmmm," I offered. And then Henry caught my attention. I watched him take the chip log with a length of line and walk over to the rail.

"Henry, what the devil are you doing there?" I asked him.

Henry turned to face me and broke into a wide grin.

"He knows quite well what he is doing," Atwood said as he walked towards Gilley and me to stand with us. "I taught him. Henry, be a good fellow and explain the chip wood to Lady Mary."

"Yes, yes, I use the chip log," Henry answered, speaking through his smile and using remarkably good English. He held the block of wood up to show me, tied to a reel of rope knotted at intervals of fifty feet.

"Henry has a keen passion for learning and an uncanny talent for remembering things, all manner of things," Atwood said. "Never seen anything quite like it. Henry, if you please - show our good lady."

"Step one, drop chip log in water," Henry said, still smiling. Then he stepped up on the ship's rail and tossed the wood block over the side. After jumping back down again, he reached for the sand glass sitting on top of the bittacle. "Step two, set sand glass," he said and flipped the glass over, allowing the sand to flow freely. Then, after carefully placing the glass on the rail, he watched the line play out. "Step three, count knots."

As the chip log floated away from the ship the wood block took the line with it. Henry counted the knots in the rope as they slipped through his fingers. "One, two, three, four, five, six, seven, eight. Step four, sand glass empty, Atwood, Master Atwood, sir. Henry stop counting. Eight it is. Eight knots I count."

"Very well, Master Henry, eight knots it is. How many seconds in the sand glass?"

"Thirty, Atwood, Master Atwood, thirty seconds, sir," Henry answered proudly as he began pulling the line back in.

"That is good, Master Henry. That is very good. I'll note the log book for you. One day I'll teach you how to write with pen and paper so you can make entries in the log book yourself. Off you go then. Report to Master Caputo at the tiller and see what you can learn from him. Be sure to tell Caputo I sent you."

Henry offered us another grin before he scampered off.

"Most impressive," Gilley remarked. "But do you think he knows what he is truly measuring?"

"I do indeed. I think he comprehends the concept quite well. The Carib are accomplished sailors I hear and must have some knowledge of speed and distance, however crude, to move among the islands as they do."

"And our Ethiopian friends, how do they fare?" I asked.

"More than one longs to see his family and home again," Atwood answered. "As for learning shipboard tasks and work, I've got no complaints. Every one of them has pulled his weight and I didn't see one man shrink back during the *Battle of Cartagena*. They're a tough and loyal lot."

Gilley had been the one who had insisted on giving our victory over the mystery pirate ships a proper name. We had all agreed on the *Battle of Cartagena*.

"Good," I said. "What kind of work did they do back in Africa?"

"As best I can tell," Atwood said, "two or three were warriors and hunters back home, wherever home is. The rest were farmers, craftsmen or shepherds and the like."

"Well, let's teach them how to shoot and fight. Muskets, swords, knives, cannon - all of it. Henry too."

Gilley cleared his throat. "Ahem, Mary, I'm not certain that is wise."

"Oh? And why is that not wise? Are you afraid one of them might shoot you or slit your throat one night, Tom?"

"Mary," Atwood interrupted. "The Spanish will not take kindly to seeing armed slaves."

"They are not slaves. I purchased their freedom."

"So you did, Mary, so you did," Gilley readily agreed and nodded. "But I doubt very much the Spanish will see things quite the same way."

"Gentlemen, my mind is firm on this matter. Are these twenty Ethiopians members of our crew or not?"

"Aye, Mary, but..."

"But, Tom," I said, cutting him off. "According to the Ten Rules these men must be willing to fight and die to protect this ship, to protect their mates."

"I don't think," Atwood said, "they know anything about the Ten Rules."

"Then teach each them," I replied with too much irritation in my tone.

Gilley shook his head. "Mary, please. This New World is not our world. Let's remember we are guests here. This world belongs to the Spanish and to the Portuguese. We must respect their ways. Slavery is a part of life here. If you openly flaunt your disdain for Spanish rule, well, we might need to find ourselves a new home."

"Tom, are you not the one who is fond of telling us from time to time that a man must "live tall?""

"Aye, but - ."

"But Tom Gilley, and you too Jacob Atwood, I'll not debate the matter further. We are not some toothless packet ship ferrying passengers and their trunks around. These men are soldiers and our brothers or they are not and if they are not, then we best put them ashore and be done with it..."

"*LAND!*" the lookout shouted down to us from the crow's nest and pointed to a spec of green off the starboard bow.

We had finally reached the western tip of Cuba. My heart began to flutter.

My heart sank when I did not see the *Phantom*, *Westport* or the *Fair Irish Maiden* anchored in Havana's fine harbor, known as *Puerto de Carenas*, or Careening Bay, because it is an excellent place to beach a ship at low tide to mend their bottoms. Our voyage around the Caribbean had taken ten weeks. Even if all were well, Hunter could still be weeks away. I was foolish to have had any hope of finding him or the others in Havana waiting for us.

I gave the crew their liberty and went into town to find Cortés. But Cortés was in Santo Domingo I learned and so I passed the time sampling different taverns with little to do. And then the spring rains came, monsoon-like rains. Every day it rained. Havana's streets turned into muddy streams, the town turned into a bloody quagmire. My mood turned foul. I returned to the ship and to pass the time I busied myself with menial work, with long baths in a special barrel my men had made for me, and with reading. I had copies of *The Prince* by an Italian named Niccolò Machiavelli, *Jules César* by a Frenchman named Jacques Grévin, and pamphlets about Martin Luther's work. I found them all mildly entertaining.

Midway through our third week in Havana, Cortés found me eating supper at the tavern he had first brought me to. I had Gilley, Atwood and Ferguson with me.

"Mary!" Cortés said with genuine delight. With outstretched arms he clasped my shoulders, leaned down, and kissed me on the cheek. "How lovely to see you again. And Masters Gilley, Atwood and Ferguson, welcome back to Havana. I heard you tried your luck exploring the Spanish Main?"

"Rodriguez," I said, smiling sweetly for him. "Welcome back to Havana. Sit and join us, please, and we shall tell you our story. We've missed your good company."

"*Gracias*," Cortés replied and moved a chair over to our table. "Tell me my friends, tell me about your grand adventure sailing around the Caribbean!"

We ate and drank and told Cortés our story with pleasure. We told our story the Irish way, leaving no point unsaid. Cortés was a good and thoughtful listener.

"These pirates who attacked you," Cortés said after we had finished recounting our tale, "could have been anyone. We have so many scoundrels in the West Indies. I cannot help you there. As for the fever that hit you and your men, this could have been caused by many things. Did any of the monks at *Cumaná* administer a medicine called *cinchona* to you, Mary?"

"*Cinchona?*"

"*Sí.* It is good for the malaria sickness carried by the mosquito bug. Malaria is common here. *Cinchona* is a tree found in Peru and the bark from this tree, this *fever tree* as it is known, can be ground into a fine powder and mixed with wine or water for consumption. It is a very effective remedy for malaria. I know a good apothecary in Havana and I will see that you and your men are supplied with sufficient quantities."

"We are grateful, Rodriguez. Thank you. And your voyage to Santo Domingo was fruitful?"

"Oh, yes. Routine business matters to attend to, nothing more. And I had no difficulties selling-off what you sold to me three months ago. I turned a modest profit. Your ships from Ireland have not yet returned?"

"Not yet, but soon I should think."

"I trust you will look to me as your agent, your exclusive agent, when they do, Mary."

"For only modest profits, Rodriguez? Are you sure it is worth your efforts?"

Cortés chuckled. "Well... I heard you did not do badly either. As I recall you purchased two new ships?"

"Well..."

We all laughed, raised our tankards high and tapped the pewter together with a toast to modest profits.

Cortés took a sip of ale and nodded his approval. "Ah, that is good. In a few months the treasure fleet will pass through Havana. I will sail with it. I must return to Spain. I have a wife and two young daughters with a modest estate near Barcelona to look after. If all is well at home, I hope to be back in the Caribbean before winter."

"You will bring your wife and daughters to the New World with you?" Gilley asked.

"No, no. The colonies are expanding rapidly. People are coming over to the Americas by the thousands. The king I've heard is planning to build more permanent roads, government buildings and even new and powerful fortresses, like the one you saw at *San Juan de Ulúa*, all along the Spanish Main and in the islands. The Church has already constructed a number of fine, permanent churches and has plans to build a cathedral or two in honor of our Lord and Savior. They'll be glorious structures I have no doubt. Someday we will have cities in the New World to rival any of the grandest cities of Europe. But, as you have all witnessed, life in the New World is hard and can be most cruel. My wife is a lovely woman, but she is fragile too and she would, I fear, wither and die here. A harsh land needs harsh men and women to tame it."

"What are the names of your daughters?" I asked.

Cortés's lips curled into a smile, into a father's proud smile. His eyes sparkled as he spoke about his daughters. "Ah, Isabella is my oldest and Elizabeth is my youngest. Isabella favors her mother, Marie, and she is a gentle soul. And Elizabeth, well, she favors her papa. Elizabeth reminds me of you, Mary. She will be a rare beauty someday. But she is tough and clever too. She would thrive here in the New World."

"Men," I offered, "are easily disposed to underestimate the fairer sex, the more so when they are pretty. My guess is that your wife and Isabella are stronger than you know. I will look forward to the day we meet."

"Fair enough my dear lady. I've been properly admonished. And while I stand corrected, even humbled, I know three women in Barcelona who would proudly stand with you."

A few days after our reunion with Cortés, my officers and I

were invited to dine at the *Castillo de la Real Fuerza* as Don Villanueva's guests. Villanueva was a gracious host, was thoughtful in his questions and kept the conversation light. What Villanueva knew or didn't know about the particulars of our business was not yet clear to me and I was grateful he gave me no cause to be evasive with him.

When we returned to the ships the hour was late and I was exhausted and ready for bed. I had spent the afternoon before our supper with Villanueva with Atwood on the main deck training and practicing hand-to-hand fighting with our Ethiopians in the sweltering heat. The exertion had drained me.

But when we pulled up alongside the *Star* in the longboat, a surge of energy shot through me. Standing at the rail, with a lantern in his hand I saw Hunter staring down at me with a wide grin. I bit my tongue to hide my smile. I felt my heartbeat quicken.

"Did you miss me, Mary?" Hunter called down to me unabashedly and laughed.

"You flatter yourself, Master Hunter," I said matter-of-factly. "Truth be told, we thought you dead. Atwood here would have filled your shoes nicely as Captain of the Guns. It may, however, please you to know that a day or two ago I decided to rename the *Star*. I thought we'd call her *Hunter* in memory of you."

"Ha! Ha! The good ship *Hunter*, eh? I trust you'll be denied that pleasure for a good, long while, Madam!"

As I climbed up the rope ladder and stepped up on the rail, I fought off of the urge to fall into Hunter's arms and smother him in kisses. I contented myself with an affectionate squeeze of his arm when he took me by the hand to help me down.

"Where the devil have you been, Hunter?" Gilley asked as he stepped onboard behind me. He patted Hunter warmly on the shoulder.

Atwood and Ferguson fell in behind Gilley and took turns shaking Hunter's hand. We were all relieved to see Hunter.

"We lost at least a week when *Westport* lost her rudder in heavy seas. We had to tow her into Santo Domingo to purchase a new one."

"Any complications?" I asked.

"None. The loss of *Westport's* rudder was the worst of it. Ben was crestfallen when he lost that rudder. But there was no blame to him. We've returned from Ireland loaded down to the scuppers with finished goods of high quality from many countries across Europe, even from as far away as Persia. We lost a few men to their families and had to sign on a number of new replacements. Two men died at sea, one from a bad heart I think and the other simply disappeared. And how did you scallywags and the good lady spend your time in paradise?"

"We explored," Atwood answered, "the Spanish Main much like Christopher Columbus and made a new friend or two."

"We lost twelve good men to the fever," added Gilley solemnly. "And we damn near lost Mary too."

Hunter lost his smile. He could not hide the concern in his eyes and looked at me with tenderness.

"I'm all healed," I offered nonchalantly.

Hunter nodded. "I'm glad to hear it, Mary. Well, I've returned with gifts, including some good Irish whisky. Who'll join me in a drink or two?"

"Ah, praise God, *uisce beatha*, the water of life!" Gilley exclaimed and licked his lips.

"I'm a tad woozy from a long day," I said truthfully. "Too much heat from this afternoon and too much wine at supper, but you boys go on and enjoy yourselves. No whiskey for you, Captain Gilley."

"Mary!"

"No, I've worked too long and too hard to keep you sober all these years, Tom Gilley. And that's the end of the matter. You're lucky I ignore the ale and wine. Well gentlemen, I am to bed. It's good to have you back, Master Hunter."

"I bid you a good night then, Mary," Hunter replied. "When you are better rested I can give you my full report."

The others stood by awkwardly, quietly, and made no

comment. No one offered any crass remark; none would snicker impolitely behind my back later. But they all understood Hunter's meaning.

I couldn't help myself. I tossed martial discipline over the side. I wrapped my arms around Hunter's neck and kissed him, just a peck on the check. "Good night, James and welcome back. I missed you..."

The following day I took Gilley, Hunter and Atwood with me into Havana and we found our favorite Spaniard at our favorite tavern. It was time to make arrangements for another trade. We haggled for a bit, finally agreed on a price, and ordered drinks and food all around to celebrate. Cortés wanted me to send one ship to the Port of Spain in Trinidad and another on to the port of Santo Domingo in Hispaniola to avoid so many foreign goods coming into Cuba all at once. I agreed. I wanted to try our luck in Veracruz with the third ship as I was certain our cargo would fetch the best prices there, but Cortés convinced me otherwise. Trying to smuggle contraband into New Spain through Veracruz would be too risky he said. Not even his political friends in Santo Domingo had influence over the king's stalwart minions in Veracruz. The loyalty of the *Casa de Contratación* in *Juan de Ulúa* to the king was unflinching. No *Contratación* agent there could be bribed.

Later in the evening, after we returned to the *Star*, I had Hunter all to myself. Neither of us wasted time on chit-chat.

"Do you, my lady, find my report satisfactory?" Hunter asked me with a sly grin as he rolled off me.

"Whew - most satisfactory. You haven't lost your skills in bed I see."

"You fill me with burning passion always, Mary."

"Me and half the tarts in Westport, I'll wager," I said, shamelessly baiting my lover.

"Stop, Mary. I'll not play this game with you. We pledged trust and fidelity to one another and I have honored my pledge. I've been faithful to you without exception."

I felt Hunter's sting, his rebuke. I heard the displeasure in his tone and instantly regretted my callous remark. But no woman, no matter how rich or desirable, no matter how intelligent or charming she might be, can ever feel completely secure in her position. It is a man's world after all governed by the nature and rules of men.

I took a moment to admire his lean body, his glistening flesh, in the soft light of a full moon pouring in through the great cabin's windows. I brushed an unruly lock of hair off his forehead and kissed him lightly on the cheek.

"Forgive me, James," I said in an apologetic tone. "Women can be silly creatures. We constantly crave reassurance."

"Reassurance? Reassurance of what, Mary?"

"Reassurance that we are needed, appreciated, loved," I replied.

Ahhh - there, I said it. *Love*. Neither of us had ever touched the word before.

Hunter leaned over me. "You are needed my darling Mary," he said and kissed me on the forehead.

"You are appreciated my brave and feisty captain," he said as he moved down to kiss me on the lips and then on both cheeks. He kissed my neck and worked his way down to my breasts, tenderly kissing each one. "You are, my beautiful girl," he said as he looked up into my eyes and wrapped me in his arms, "with all my heart, very much loved."

I could feel the tears pooling in my eyes. I brought his face to mine and kissed him sweetly on the lips. We lingered quietly in each other's arms. We held each other for a long while. That single moment in time was the most exquisite of my life.

Our bodies soon resumed their slow, sensual grind together. Our kisses became more passionate, nearly savage. I wrapped my legs around his hips. I squeezed him hard as his movements quickened. And when the ecstasy washed over me, from head to toe I shook, I bit down on the sheets to stifle my raucous moaning. And after Hunter had taken me again, after he had ravished me with a raw lust he had never shown before, we settled back on the pillows and held each other tightly, exhausted and content.

Hunter stroked my hair as I rested my head against his chest, listening to his heartbeat. "So," he asked me, "Atwood can fill my shoes I heard you say last evening."

"As Captain of the Guns," I replied and poked him in the ribs.

"Ah, he is a fine looking man, for a Scot, and he is strong and smart and capable."

"He is all those things. But he is not James Hunter."

"I'm sorry, Mary. Like a woman's sense of security, a man's ego can be a fragile thing."

"You need not be jealous."

"Good. I like Atwood. I like him quite well in truth and would feel some small measure of remorse if I had to dispatch him in a duel."

"Where women can be silly, men can be childish."

"How true, my lady, how true. Gilley tells me you covered yourself in glory at something called the *Battle of Cartagena*."

"I don't know about glory, James. I remember a rock grazing my cheek and landing at my feet and being drenched in seawater. Poor Schmidt suffered the worst of it when he lost his foot. But, I think, you would have approved of my actions. You might even have been proud."

"I *might even have been proud?* Mary, Mary, Mary, I'm so very proud of you already. You are an extraordinary woman..."

I had never been filled with so much joy before. I had never needed another so much. So this was love.

I was surprised to see young Billy Farrell rushing across the main deck towards me as I stood alone on the quarter deck in the early morning darkness. He was carrying a tin of hot coffee in his hands.

"Why, Master Farrell, I didn't expect to see you again. Welcome back."

"Thank you, Mum," Billy answered simply. He handed me the tin and dashed off in a hurry without another word.

"He's a quiet boy," I remarked when I heard Hunter's footsteps behind me. He wrapped his arms around my waist and started nibbling on the back of my neck while no one was watching.

"Some might say peculiar, Mary."

"He needs nurturing, that's all."

"He needs a swift kick in the arse."

Moments later, in the dim light of the new day, we saw a small boat with a single oarsman rowing towards us from shore. The boat carried three passengers, Cortés, Don Villanueva and a third man whom I did not recognize. Even from a distance I could see that the third man was dressed in ragged clothing and appeared disheveled. I could not imagine what business would bring Cortés and Don Villanueva out to my ship so early in the morning.

Hunter helped all three men onboard and tipped the oarsman. The third man's hands and feet were shackled and someone had worked him over. His face was a bloodied, bruised mess. He studied me with one eye swollen shut.

"Ah, *mucho gracias*, James," Cortés said. "Mary, please, forgive our rude intrusion."

"You are both welcome, always, aboard my ship. I assume this is not a social call. What brings you to us at this ungodly hour while the world still slumbers?"

Don Villanueva leaned down to kiss my hand. "Lady Mary, I require a very special favor."

"Oh? How so?"

"A ship, *El Camino*, came into port late last evening. I know her master. He has just returned from *Nombre de Diós* with the most distressing news. An English pirate, a pirate who is well known to us, has sacked and burned the town. Worse, he has ambushed the Silver Train!"

"Who?"

"A most despicable rascal named Drake, Francis Drake."

"I've have heard of this man. He captured the Silver Train?"

"Yes, yes. This is a catastrophe! And this particular train was very large. One hundred and ninety mules carrying thirty tons of gold and silver were taken."

"Thirty tons! Drake took it all? How?"

"Quite right, Lady Mary, he could not move thirty tons all at once. He took the gold, about thirteen hundred pounds, and buried most of the silver. The gold has a value of roughly one hundred and thirty thousand *pesos de oso.*"

"Oh my."

"Yes indeed, *oh my.* I must alert the Captain-Governor immediately. But his Excellency is in Santo Domingo."

"And you want us to sail you to Santo Domingo, but why?"

"Please, Mary," Cortés interrupted, "while we still have the tide. We could not find the master of Don Villanueva's ship. He and his crew are no doubt in town too drunk to walk or at the brothels and the master of *El Camino* refuses to sail. His ship has a cracked mast. He fears the mast will not hold in rough seas. *Phantom* is well-armed and very fast I know. Time is precious so our thoughts naturally turned to you."

"And who is this fine fellow in chains with the swollen face?" I asked Villanueva.

"He is one of Drake's men. He was left behind and is now our prisoner."

"Name's John Martin, Madam," the man said with an English accent and bowed his head to me. "I am your most humble servant. Good to be back among my own countrymen."

I ignored the Englishman and turned to Hunter. "James, can *Phantom* put to sea without delay and make Santo Domingo?"

"We aren't provisioned for a long cruise, but aye, Mary. We could be underway within the hour and make the tide."

"Good," I said and looked crossly over at Martin. "I've never been sir, nor shall I ever be, one of your countrymen."

Unperturbed, the Englishman simply looked at me with a hint of smirk on his bloodied lips, as if he knew some secret thing that I did not.

Under threatening, grey skies, *Phantom's* topmen scrambled up into the rigging and unfurled the ship's canvas. We departed Havana in haste under full sail and headed east for Santo Domingo, nearly three hundred leagues away.

Before we set out, I sent Green with the *Westport* on to the Port of Spain with one of Cortés's agents to sell our cargo there and I left Fox with the *Fair Irish Maiden* in Havana to deliver *Maiden's* cargo to Cortés's men waiting for him at the navy's wharf. The *Godsend*, *Falling Star* and Gilley were to stay put in Havana's bay. I took Hunter, Atwood and Efendi with me.

The winds were up, whipping the sea into a frothy frenzy and I had nearly forgotten how quick and nimble *Phantom* was. She plowed through the rising and falling swells with ease and we made good time. I made my Spanish guests as comfortable as possible. But *Phantom* was built for rugged war with little space for privacy or comfort and we had no fresh victuals on board to eat. Both men suffered. We tossed the English pirate in the ship's rope locker near the bow and gave him a privy bucket, a cask of water and a basket of stale bread. He suffered more.

Don Villanueva and Cortés said that the voyage between Havana and Santo Domingo typically took at least ten days. We coasted into Santo Domingo's harbor in only five.

At the mouth of the Ozama River, guarding Santo Domingo's harbor, stands *Fortaleza Ozama*. Ozama is an impressive citadel. Smaller but not unlike *San Juan de Ulúa* at Veracruz, Ozama is an imposing fort of thick stone walls, sturdy ramparts and tall watchtowers protected by batteries of heavy cannon. We parked ourselves underneath the shadow of the Ozama's big guns, as safe a place as any, and dropped anchor.

While Don Villanueva scurried off to find the Captain-Governor with his distressing news, Hunter and I followed Cortés to tour the city - and to make arrangements to sell *Phantom's* cargo of contraband. Santo Domingo was the New World's first city we learned and there, at the *Gateway to the Caribbean* as many liked to call it, I felt the raw power and majesty of Spain in the New World for the first time.

Santo Domingo is a real city, not some crude village of straw and mud huts. She is grander than even Veracruz and she is a city of many firsts. We walked along the first street built in the New World, the *Calle de Las Damas*, and saw the New World's first cathedral, the *Basilica Santa Maria la Menor*. In 1542 Pope Paul III had elevated the church to the lofty status of a cathedral where, they say, the remains of the great man himself, Christopher Columbus, lay buried. And we passed by the New World's first castle, the *Alcázar de Colón*, an impressive structure of white stone and handsome arches built in 1510 by Columbus's son, and the island's first viceroy, Diego Columbus. We spent a lazy day exploring Santo Domingo, the city of many firsts.

In the evening Cortés invited Hunter and me to his home for supper and I felt flattered by the intimate gesture. His house was spacious and well-built with stone and plaster and had a tiled roof. The house boasted luxuries like glass windows, tiled floors and a water closet imported from Córdoba. The kitchen stood apart from the main house in a separate stone building with double brick chimneys. Not far from the kitchen we saw several shacks for curing meats and tobacco as well as living quarters for Cortés's slaves.

When I complimented Cortés on his household slaves, who treated Hunter and I like royalty, who were most courteous and well-mannered to us in every way, Cortés explained that his household servants were *Negros Ladinos*, African Moors who had been born and raised in Castile surrounded by culture and etiquette - unlike the *Negros Bozales* who had been brought to the New World in chains from Africa to toil in the fields and work the mines like beasts of burden and who knew nothing about European social graces. And then there were the *Negros Criollos*, Negros born in the New World. Cortés explained that the *Criollos* were often of mixed blood, the bastard children of their Spanish masters. Some *Criollos* enjoyed the status of *Ladinos* and some did not. My thoughts turned to a young boy I had seen outside the kitchen earlier. He was a fair skinned child with dark and curly hair. I wondered about him but did not ask.

A handful of gentlemen of substance, men who weren't afraid to invest in tax-free imports, soon joined us for a delicious dinner of smoked pork, plantains, Spanish rice and *boniatos*. And for desert, I had my first taste of sweet chocolate, or *chocolātl* in the original Aztec tongue. Cortés's servants served it warm, poured over slices of banana and prickly pear and chunks of pineapple. I closed my eyes and softly moaned with guilty pleasure, savoring my first spoonful. The men all chuckled, amused by my reaction. Then we retired to an outdoor veranda where Cortés served us after-dinner cordials and handed out cigars. And when we were all feeling mellow, Cortés proceeded to auction off *Phantom's* cargo. I struck good bargains with the highest bidders.

I held the lantern for Hunter as he unbolted the lock. The stench nearly bowled me over when Hunter opened the rope locker's door. Hunter grabbed the Englishman by the collar and yanked him to his feet.

"Who are you, Master Martin?" I asked, covering my nose and mouth with a handkerchief. "I would know your story."

"Why, as you can see, Madam, I am a man in need of a fresh privy bucket," the Englishman answered cheerfully with a thin smile.

I grit my teeth, unamused. "Ordinarily, I appreciate humor in a man. It shows intelligence. But you, sir, best tip-toe lightly with me. I'm in no mood for puerile humor and we have no time for idle banter. Are you or are you not a pirate, a common criminal, as the Spanish claim?"

The Englishman shook his head. "Pirate maybe my lady though the term privateer suits me better. But common? No, never. Never in my life has anyone accused me of being common."

"You sailed with Drake?"

"Yes."

"How is it," Hunter asked, still holding the Englishman firmly by the collar, "you were separated from your crew? Privateers don't often leave their own behind."

"Hunter is it not? James Hunter?"

Hunter looked at the Englishman with surprise. "What of it? Our paths have never crossed. You don't know me."

"No, perhaps not, but I know of you. You did some interesting work for the French not too long ago in the Americas."

Hunter turned to look at me. Few men knew anything about his past.

"And you, my lady, you had some trouble in Westport awhile back, or so I've heard. It is also rumored you have O'Malley blood."

I could feel my cheeks burning. I could feel my temper rising. I'm certain my face turned bright crimson. How could a stranger know such things?

"Master Martin," I said with an edge in my tone. "Let us speak plainly. Perhaps you don't fully understand your predicament. In the morning the Spanish will come to fetch you off this ship and then you'll dangle from the end of a rope until you're dead. That is if I don't turn you over to Mustafa first. He's the fellow standing over there in the shadows. Mustafa is a Turk and what he can do with a knife will, well, I best not say lest your balls shrivel up and you foul yourself and God knows how badly you reek already."

"Well, Madam, there's no denying I'm in a fine pickle now. A Spanish noose around my neck or a Turkish blade you say? Those are my two choices?"

"I think," Hunter said impatiently, "the man wants to die, Mary."

"No, Master Hunter, I have no wish to die, certainly not today and certainly not by the hand of some stinking Spaniard."

"Tell us then," I demanded, "and be quick about it. Who are you? Deserter, spy, provocateur, saboteur, thief, murder, pirate or privateer? And, fair warning, my patience is quickly waning."

"Truth be told," the Englishman replied casually, as if he

didn't have a care in the world, "I am just clumsy. It was night when we took *Nombre de Diós*. There was fighting in the streets and in the houses when we torched the place to cover our retreat back to the ships. The winds picked-up. The flames spread faster than we had expected and I got separated from Drake and the others. There was much confusion. And then I was struck from behind in the head by something heavy and fell to my knees, unconscious. When I came to in the morning, I found myself chained to a post outside the town's fort. I was not the only prisoner. I watched the Spanish behead the others."

The Englishman leaned down to show me a nasty gash across the back of his head to help prove his story. His hair was matted down in dry blood.

"Why did the Spanish let you live?"

"I cannot say for I do not know, Madam. Certainly my appointment with my executioner will not be much delayed."

"You must have some clue why the Spanish kept you alive and brought you here to Santo Domingo. What is special about you?"

"I was the only English prisoner. The others were French or Cimarrons."

"Cimarrons?"

"Cimarrons, former Negro slaves who've escaped their masters and have signed with Drake and others to fight the Spanish."

"So?"

"So, we seized tons of gold and silver. The Spanish must believe Drake buried most of it in the jungle somewhere as it would have taken us days to transport that much weight over to the ships. That's a fair assumption. The Spanish must think I know where Drake buried it."

"And?"

"And? And I truly do not know what Drake did with all of it, Madam. Drake divided his forces. He and his crew took the loot. I went with the French and Cimarrons. Our mission was to set the town on fire as a diversion for our escape and I did not see what Drake and his men did with the treasure. No doubt they carried what they could back to the ships and buried the rest somewhere along the coast."

"You are not," Hunter said, "some lowly seaman, friend."

"No. I never claimed to be some lowly seaman. But I will not say more. Aye, you can torture me and I will talk. All men do. But I'll only spill out gibberish with my guts. Better death than to betray my allegiance."

"Allegiance to whom?" I asked.

The Englishman took a deep breath and exhaled slowly. "Lady Mary, I will tell you who I am not. I am neither a deserter nor a pirate. I am not a murder or a thief. And I am certainly not your enemy."

I looked at Hunter. "Hunter?"

It was Hunter who had persuaded me to speak to the Englishman before the Spanish came to take him.

"I find it most curious," Hunter replied, "that he hasn't begged for his life or promised us gold if we set him free. He's no pirate or brigand on the run. I don't care to see a fellow Englishman dance at the end of a Spanish rope. But, I don't know Mary."

I looked the Englishman up and down. "Mustafa, please bring me clean water, soap, some bandages and a bottle of whiskey so that I can dress the prisoner's wounds. Best bring a needle and thread too. Master Martin - if that is even your true name - what will you do if I set you free?"

The Englishman cracked another thin smile. "I'm known as a rather resourceful fellow in some circles, circles that might interest you. If you release me, I will find my way off this bloody rock and you, you my dear lady, will have a friend for life. And that Madam is no small matter..."

In the morning the officer of the watch came to my great cabin. He woke me to inform me that the rope locker was empty, that our prisoner had escaped. The Englishman had, the seaman reported, somehow found a way to remove his shackles and then used the iron to pry the hinges off the door. I immediately had my men search the ship from top to bottom, but the Englishman was long gone.

"I shouldn't worry about it, Mary," Cortés said as we sipped our morning coffee on the quarter deck together. He paused to remove a cigar from a breast pocket inside his jacket. "The Englishman could not have gone far. He has no money, no friends and no resources. He is alone."

I put my hand to my mouth to hide a grin. Martin had money, money I had given him.

Cortés mistook my gesture for unease or something else and tried to reassure me. "The garrison at Ozama will send out patrols immediately. Rest assured, they will find him."

"But Don Villanueva entrusted that rogue to my care," I offered in earnest. "I am embarrassed that I have lost his prisoner, that I have failed him. Don Villanueva will be most displeased. He will have good cause to find fault with me and I can hardly blame him."

"Nonsense, Mary! The blame is hardly yours alone to bear. The man was able to pry apart inferior Spanish iron before he forced the door to your rope locker open. In any case he was nobody, a lowly sort, and he will be caught in a day or two and swiftly hanged - or he'll die in the jungle. Either way he is dead. Please, I beg you, think no more on this."

"Thank you, Rodriguez," I said while I removed a lantern from the rail to light his cigar for him. "You are a dear friend."

And I knew, if I would have let him, Cortés would have kissed me at that very moment. But I excused myself to see to my duties as the ship's owner, or so I said.

Don Villanueva remained behind in Santo Domingo when we raised our anchor and dropped our sails. Nothing more was said about Martin. Cortés came with us. We cruised west of the city for just a little ways to a quiet, little cove to offload *Phantom's* Old World cargo. We moved the goods in the early evening light from ship to shore where Cortés's men, with torches in hand, were already waiting for us. After we finished transporting every crate and every barrel, the gentlemen who had purchased our goods at Cortés's auction paid us with large sea chests filled with silver *escudos*, gold doubloons and pieces of eight. We counted our treasure on blankets laid out across the sand and then sailed back to Havana in ballast with Cortés, richer than when we had left.

"A good evening to each of you," I said as I glanced around the table with all my officers present.

Falling Star, Phantom, Godsend, Westport and the *Fair Irish Maiden*, all my ships, were anchored close together in a quiet spot of water off the island of Guadeloupe. Yes, I had chosen to return to Guadeloupe after I felt too many prying eyes on us in Havana. Chief Paka Wokili had gladly accepted the gifts we brought him after his nephew Henry - now our man - vouched for their worth under the terms of our pact, under the terms of the friendship treaty between the Irish and the Carib. The chief graciously allowed us to set up camp on his island and my men, all in high spirits, happily pitched our tents along Guadeloupe's idyllic shore.

"I seek your good counsel, gentlemen. We've done exceedingly well in the New World thus far. Good Fortune has smiled broadly on us. The first order of business is to consider welcoming Masters Jacob Atwood and Michael MacGyver into the fold. Jacob, you're first. Our rules require a unanimous vote by this assemblage. Are you willing to swear an oath, a blood oath, to me and to the men around this table if they accept you as a brother?"

"Aye, I am."

"Good. And will you honor, on your life, the Ten Rules?"

"Aye, I will."

"Then stand and give us your binding oath now with God as your eternal witness."

"I swear, on my life, to faithfully honor the Ten Rules. I swear this to each of you and before Almighty God as my witness."

I had placed a dead fish in the center of the table earlier. I pulled my dagger from my boot and stabbed the fish, leaving my dagger imbedded in the table. "Excellent. Understand this Jacob Atwood: I will, by Christ, hold you to your sacred oath."

"I understand full well, Mary."

"Very good then. What say the rest of you? Are we all agreed to accept Jacob as one of us, as our true brother, or does any man here desire to express his objection?"

Gilley was the first to cast his vote. "Jacob has proven his mettle. I say aye."

"You have my blessing too, Jacob," Hunter offered next.

And one-by-one my other officers around the table followed Gilley's lead and voted to accept Atwood as one of us. I was well-pleased that my brothers thought as much of him as I did.

"Welcome to the clan, Jacob," I said.

As was our custom, Atwood knelt before me and I anointed his head with seawater - our lifeblood - and then I kissed his hair. When I stood, all stood with me. "The meaning of the skewered dead fish is plain enough and the seawater is our *aqua vitae*," I said and raised my glass of whiskey. "To life," I toasted and drained my glass. All my officers did the same.

I repeated the ceremony with MacGyver. He was a gifted mariner and tinkerer, but it was his steadfast bravery setting off the powder kegs against *Medusa's* rudder that had won him our admiration.

"Now, then, to business. As the mistress of this little enterprise of ours, I have the right to appoint command. Thomas Gilley, you are the most senior among us, the most experienced, command of *Falling Star*, our grandest ship, is yours and the gallant Michael MacGyver, the newest officer among us, shall be your first officer. Michael, watch and listen well to Tom and someday you'll have your own command, of this I have no doubt. James Hunter, you shall take command of *Phantom* and Jacob Atwood shall serve as your first officer. Hadley Ferguson shall keep command of *Godsend* and

Albertus Fox, the *Fair Irish Maiden* is yours. And Benjamin Green, command of the good ship *Westport* goes to you. You masters of the merchantmen can choose your own first officers as you see fit. And Mustafa Efendi, I have not forgotten you. You my fine, brave Turk are a far better soldier than sailor and unto you I give command over all the ratings on every ship. The men will obey your will or else."

"Mary," Hunter asked with a droll smile. "I think I understand the hierarchy of things well enough, but pray tell us what will you do?"

"Oh, I'll be here and there, watching you hooligans closely to protect my investments. Now, we'll divide any profits with one-third to me as owner and one-third to me again as investor, which I'll use to increase our wealth. The remaining one-third will be divvied up as follows: captains of the warships, Tom, James, you will each receive eight shares apiece. Masters of the merchantmen, Hadley, Albertus and Ben, you will each receive seven shares. All second officers, Michael, Jacob and Mustafa, you each will receive six and one-half shares apiece. The rest of the pie shall be divvied-up among the men, each according to his rank, as you, my officers, deem fit and proper. Does anyone disagree or wish to offer a better proposal?"

"Mary, you and I go back a ways," Gilley said. "And I've made a tidy fortune with you. Ours is a dangerous profession, but live tall I say! I think this arrangement is most reasonable and fair."

"A few more successful runs between the Old and the New World like this last one," Hunter added, "and you'll have the most loyal crews in the whole of Christendom."

"It is settled then," I said, content. "So, our good friend Rodriguez Cortés is making purchases of New World materials for us in Havana. Tom, the honor is yours to lead the merchantmen back to Ireland this time around once the ships are loaded. We'll need to rotate the crews to give each man his turn to see family and home again. Cortés said -"

I stopped in midsentence when we all heard a sneeze outside

my cabin door. Efendi jumped to his feet, opened the door and found young Billy standing at the threshold. Startled, Billy stared up at him in horror.

"Oh, sorry, Lady Mary," Billy offered sheepishly, looking down at his shoes, embarrassed. "I came to clear the table."

"Thank you, Billy, but it is late and you may turn in now," I said. "These plates and glasses can wait 'til morning."

"Very good, Mum. Thank you, Mum."

"I accept," Gilley said as Billy disappeared up the companionway while Efendi closed the door, "my charge to cross the ocean blue with our precious cargo, Mary. It'll be good to see lovely Ireland again and fill my lungs with cool, fresh air. How long does Cortés require?"

"He told me he needed two weeks or so to make all the necessary arrangements for us," I answered.

Hunter stood to stretch his muscles. "Mary, do you intend to keep *Phantom* and *Godsend* here?"

"I thought I'd keep *Phantom* in the Caribbean, aye, but send *Godsend* on with Gilley. Cortés was confident he could buy enough with the money I gave him in advance to fill all three merchantmen and maybe a little more."

Hunter yawned. "And you intend to do what in the Caribbean to pass the time? I see that restless look in your eyes, Mary. Explore the lands to the north or south or do you intend sail around the Spanish Main and continue on to China to finish Columbus's great quest?"

"Nothing so bold, James. But I suppose you're right. My eyes betray me. I do crave some adventure. Do you, my wily provocateur, still carry that map of yours around?"

Chapter Eight

eady notions of adventure filled my head in Guadeloupe. Fully rested and eager to set out again, we struck camp a week after our arrival. We set out with the tide for Trinidad in force. I had a powerful man-o-war, a large, fast nao, one caravel and two sturdy brigantines all under full sail and nearly four hundred men under arms. Even by Old World standards we made an impressive sight. We tacked against a lively south wind and contrary currents the entire voyage and made poor time. But we were in no hurry. After we sold the rest of our cargo off to one of Cortés's associates in Trinidad - for a handsome sum - we returned to Havana to find Cortés to negotiate new business.

When we reached *Puerto de Carenas*, Havana's superb bay, we saw many warships riding anchor, including several magnificent Spanish galleons. I was certain we were looking at Spain's fabled treasure fleet. We shortened sail and I took Gilley and Hunter with me in the longboat over to the *Westport*, a small ship the Spanish navy would show no interest in. We sailed *Westport* into Havana, leaving the rest of my fleet at sea.

We found Cortés at his favorite tavern eating an early supper of roasted pork and black beans and sipping Spanish wine. He greeted us warmly and after supper walked us down to the waterfront and to a small, empty storehouse where he once again delivered.

"What ships did you bring with you into the harbor, Mary?" Cortés asked as he counted out the gold and silver we brought with us. We paid our Spanish partner half up front and half on delivery as was the custom.

"Only *Westport* and her holds are empty. We sold off the rest of the cargo in Trinidad."

"Ah, *muy bueno*. The navy is inspecting all ships entering and leaving Havana."

"The harbor is crowded. Are the ships we saw in the harbor from the treasure fleet?" I asked.

"No, no. The treasure fleet is far grander! The ships you saw will support Admiral Pedro de Valdés's fleet once he arrives. I am told the king is sending Valdés here to hunt down the Englishman Drake. The Spanish Court was none too pleased with the loss of the Silver Train at *Nombre de Diós* as you might well imagine."

"Ah, I see," I said. "So once Valdés's arrives with more ships, he'll take on supplies and scour the Caribbean looking for Drake?"

"I am of course not privy to the admiral's specific instructions, but yes I should think so," Cortés answered, pausing to admire a gold doubloon in his hand. He held the coin up in his fingers against a shaft of golden sunlight pouring in through a hole in storehouse's roof directly above our heads. The large coin glittered in the light. "New World gold has a powerful allure. For years Spain and Portugal have been fighting off pirates in the New World. These rogues come from France and England mostly, but some sail from other countries too. The English pirates have become more brazen lately and there are those who suspect they operate in these waters with Queen Elizabeth's secret blessing. There is even talk of open war with England."

"That could complicate matters for us, Rodriguez."

Cortés looked at me and smiled. "Yes, and so we must use more care. That is why there is no cargo here. That is why we must sail on to Old Havana."

"Old Havana?"

"Old Havana, yes. A few years after Columbus's voyages, *Conquistador* Diego Velázquez de Cuéllar founded the town of Havana along the *Rio Mayabeque* on the south side of the island. But Old Havana is a small port and when gold was discovered in *Nueva España*, and the treasure fleets started sailing between the two worlds, the early colonists moved here to the north side of the island because of the *Puerto de Carenas.*"

"Yes, I see. Spain needed a deep water port large enough to support the treasure fleets. The fleets can assemble in Havana and take on supplies before making the long and arduous voyage home across the Atlantic. Havana is ideal."

"Precisely, Mary. Havana is ideal. Old Havana is mostly ruins now, but it is less than thirty miles away by land and the roads are good so this is where I sent our cargo bound for the Old World. There will be more cargo waiting for you at Santo Domingo."

"*Excelente, Señor* Cortés."

Just as Cortés had predicted, Spanish officials did indeed board *Westport* before we sailed. A customs agent from the *Casa de Contratación,* along with a young lieutenant of the Royal Navy, inspected *Westport* from stem to stern, saw her empty cargo holds, found nothing irregular in her registry papers, and let us go our way. After we rejoined my little fleet waiting for us outside the harbor, we sailed west and then south and then east around the windward coast of the Island of Cuba until we reached a poor, forgotten seaport of neglected buildings and ruins. We saw Cortés's men, a mix of laborers and slaves, waiting for us along the docks with wagons and mules loaded down with materials from all across the Spanish Main.

Not one to forego life's comforts, we found Cortés sitting in the shade under a white canopy near the shore at a table with platters of food and bottles of wine already set out. Behind him stood a pair of Negro slaves holding fans, moving the still air around for his comfort.

"¡*Siéntate a comer, esta muy bueno!*" he called out to me as I stepped out of the longboat. He waved me over to join him.

"This is most civilized," I said and laughed.

"We do what we can to maintain a dignified life even in this hostile country."

I plopped down in an empty chair next to Cortés and we passed the time eating and drinking and exchanging frivolous chitchat as men labored in the sweltering heat to load the ships. The meal gave me no pleasure, but I did not wish to offend my host. My men would understand. They had seen me get my hands dirty plenty. They had seen me sweat and bleed. But I wondered what Cortés's men and his slaves must have thought of us, relaxing in the shade, being pampered like Egyptian royalty as they toiled in the heat.

Once the cargo was loaded onto the ships, I paid Cortés the balance due, thanked him for his hospitality and we agreed to meet again in two or three months' time after my fleet made its way back to the New World with Old World goods to sell. Now all the risk was mine to bear.

I stood between Gilley and Hunter on the *Star* as the crew made ready to sail. I linked my arm inside Gilley's, a man who was dear to me like a father, and held him close. "According to our good *amigo* Cortés," I said, "you will meet a man named Miguel Hernandez in Santo Domingo. He will make all the arrangements for the rest of our cargo. Here is a receipt from Cortés to prove payment has been made in full. And then it is off to Ireland you go and I pray we find you well in two or three months' time. We'll all rendezvous back in Guadeloupe."

"No worries, Mary," Gilley replied and patted my arm reassuringly.

"Do you want Hunter, Atwood or Efendi to go with you?"

"Nay, Mary. MacGyver is first rate. And besides, if you plan on traipsing through the jungles of New Spain, you'll need those three ruffians with you."

"Fare thee well then, Tom. You must return to us safe and sound."

"With God's good grace I shall, Mary, with God's good grace."

"We should," interjected Hunter, "discuss that little pleasure trip of yours, Mary."

"What is there to discuss, James?" I asked in a defensive tone. I already knew what Hunter would say.

"You're a strong and a strong-willed woman, Mary, as tough as nails in body and mind and you command the respect of all the men for it. But the jungles of the Isthmus of Panama and New Spain are no place for you. The *conquistadors* are some of the hardest, toughest, bravest men I've ever marched with and many of them don't survive the jungle. The jungle is merciless. She is a killer."

Gilley nodded. "James, you've given sage advice - for all the good it will do you."

I kissed Hunter on the check. "Aye James, for all the good it will do you..."

Once Hunter and I were back on board the *Phantom*, we waved Gilley off as a lively wind pushed his tiny flotilla out to sea under fair skies. Hunter and I stood quietly at the rail together, hand-in-hand, watching our ships sail east for Santo Domingo and then on to Ireland beyond. We watched our ships until they turned into little specs, until they disappeared over the far horizon. And then I gave the order to pull our anchor in. My men turned the capstan singing a bawdy, spirited shanty. And after they lashed the anchor down to the cathead with sturdy rope and chain, they went aloft to set the sails and the ship began to stir.

I took the tiller firmly in my hands and eased the *Phantom* out into deeper water. I pointed our ship's sharp nose west towards New Spain and sailed us out to sea under a blood red sky. I sailed us into a setting sun...

Chapter Nine

nglish pirates had left very little of *Nombre de Diós* standing. Drake and his men had put the torch to the entire village just as Martin had said. Drake had ordered his men to burn everything to the ground. They had destroyed *Nombre de Diós* with purpose. I thought that curious. Drake was not content to simply steal Spanish gold and silver. He seemed to hate the Spanish too and I wondered why. We passed by charred ruins, replaced by crude, makeshift huts and tents. We passed the sorry, little fort we had seen a few months back up on a hill overlooking the bay, the fort that had no cannon. Drake had gutted the fort with fire too. Even the hospital and the Dominican monastery had not escaped his English wrath.

I led my men, one hundred strong, one hundred of my very best handpicked by Hunter, through the streets of that broken town while sad-faced villagers turned out to watch us with trepidation. I felt pity for them. There would be no treasure fleet this year, no *Feast of the Golden Bull* to celebrate Spain's preeminence among nations. There would be no money from other provinces flowing into the pockets of those who called *Nombre de Diós* home.

I left Atwood behind in command of *Phantom* with a skeleton crew. He was to return in two weeks' time to fetch us or, if we were not back by the end of three, he was to sail on to Cartagena and wait for us there. Cartagena was to be our rallying point if things went wrong for us in Panama.

The Name of God's garrison commander, a feisty, little fellow with a wild mustache, approached us in the middle of the town with a puny squad of men in tow. The captain demanded to know our purpose in Panama and refused to let us pass. I told him we were off to find the fabled city of *El Dorado* and he laughed. He laughed in my face as if I was a fool. But after we paid the villagers for our supplies and for as many good mules, donkeys and machetes as we could find - after I filled the commander's purse with silver - he grudgingly waved us through. We marched under a blazing sun in single file down a dusty, dirt road and headed for the jungle just beyond the town. When I spun around to take one last peek of the sea before we disappeared into the wild, I caught the commander standing at the edge of his village still watching us. I could see in his eyes that he had written us off as dead.

"Don't think our good captain would wager any money on our safe return, Mary," Hunter said casually as we walked side-by-side at the head of the column. "I don't think he expects to ever see us again."

I kept my eyes focused on the narrowing path ahead. On either side us was stagnant water, swampland, and thick foliage. Insects started coming at us in droves.

"Would you like to remain in town and wait for us?" I asked.

"Only if you stay behind with me and we find ourselves a sturdy bed," Hunter answered, smiling.

"You best save your strength for the task ahead, Captain James Hunter. If we're not dead in a week, or at each other's throats with knives in two, we'll see about the other..."

We marched for several days in stifling heat looking for something that might make sense out of Hunter's map. We walked in our heavy clothing drenched in sweat. We scratched our skin raw from the swarms of insects tormenting us and most of us had been hit with the runs. I would gladly have paid gold to take a cold bath in fresh, clean water. We were all miserable. On the third day I had Hunter cut my hair, down to the roots, which provided me some relief from my suffering.

We ignored these hardships and pressed on, still uncertain of what we were looking for. But then, on the fourth day out, off to the side of the path and covered over with vines and plants, a pile of white-washed rocks caught Efendi's eye. He fell out of the column, carefully brushed aside the overgrowth and smiled. Someone had purposefully set the small rocks out in the shape of a crude cross. Hunter and I and half my men had blindly stumbled past the spot.

Hunter took a knee and retrieved his map, orienting the cloth to the cross. "My God," he murmured. "I had little hope that this map was anything more than a hoax."

"What is it, James?" I asked as Efendi and I peeked over Hunter's shoulder.

"Look, Mary," Efendi said and pointed to a small cross on the map next to a trail.

"Foolish me," Hunter said as he traced an imaginary line over the map with his finger. "I thought this mark was an *x*, a symbol for what I knew not. But it must be these stones laid out along the trail. I suspect we are looking at what is meant to be a needle pointing north, not an *x* or a cross. If we cut through the jungle here, we should come to these ruins. At the ruins we turn west and follow along this river or stream depicted over here for a short way until we reach this hill. At the hill we turn south until we find this."

"What is that?" I asked.

"I know not, Mary. We can only hope we'll recognize it when we see it, if we see it at all."

"It looks like a pencil to me."

Hunter grunted. "Let's hope not."

"How far, James, do you think?" Efendi asked.

"I'm not certain, Mustafa. If the priest had any sense of scale when he drew this map, we should have a better idea once we find these ruins. But the Isthmus of Panama is a narrow strip of land so these distances cannot be very great. And then again, we may be looking for something no more real than the myth of *El Dorado*."

"Should we," I asked, "leave the mules and some of the men here?"

"It is tempting to go in with just a scouting party, but I dislike the notion of splitting up our men out here." Hunter glanced over at Efendi. "Mustafa?"

Efendi nodded in agreement and pulled his machete from his belt. "Our muskets, balls and powder are on those mules. Our rations too. We can't carry all that weight on our backs while wield these."

I looked down at the stone needle pointing north, pointing into the thick jungle beyond the trail. Our journey, I realized, had so far been easy. I hesitated. My muscles ached, my bones were weary. I had never felt so tired. I had never been so filthy.

"You still want to push forward, Mary?" Hunter asked, sensing my hesitation. "Why don't you take ten men and return to town, let Mustafa and me press on from here?"

I grit my teeth. I blotted out any thought of weakness and grabbed Efendi's machete from him. "This way you say?" I asked and pointed.

"Aye," Hunter replied with a long sigh, pulling out his own machete. He followed me into the wall of leaves and vines with our men and pack animals falling in close behind.

Hacking our way through the thick foliage was slow, tedious work. Painful blisters covered my palms and feet. All of us were caked in grime and soaked in sweat. The sound of dripping water, an incessant, most irksome noise from condensation running off the leaves surrounded us. But at least we found the heat more bearable the deeper we traveled into the jungle. The sun could not penetrate through the treetops. The bugs became less of a nuisance too. I suppose we had become too filthy to feast on. By noon on the fifth day we stumbled onto the stone ruins of a small, abandoned Indian village, or what may have been an outpost.

"This," Hunter said as he looked down at his map and held out his compass, "must be the place. I hear running water over there. That must be the stream. I am encouraged."

"Let's push on," I said in as strong a voice as I could muster, desperately trying to mask my exhaustion.

Hunter nodded. "Mary, you would make any *conquistador* proud."

I smiled. "James, whew, you need to stand downwind!"

"A bit ripe am I?" Hunter asked and chuckled. "But you, my lady, are hardly any better. Let's go and find that hill..."

Efendi, standing next to me, started chuckling too. But then, in a blur of motion, he roughly shoved me aside, whipped out his dagger and launched the sharp-edged steel past my head.

I spun around to see what had spooked Efendi and saw, only a few paces from my feet, an enormous snake with Efendi's knife sticking in its neck, pinning it to the ground. The hideous black and tan creature hissed at me as it wrapped itself in coils, struggling to set itself free.

Hunter took his machete and quickly cleaved the monster's head in two. "The Spanish call it a *terciopelo*, the Spanish word for velvet," he said gravely as he recovered Efendi's knife, wiping the blood off on his sleeve before handing it back to Efendi. "Its venom is very deadly."

I beat down the urge to vomit and quickly gathered-up my things. Hunter formed the men up and we quietly pushed on to the sound of gurgling water.

When we reached the stream the ground turned flat, was clear of any brush, and we were able to pick up our pace. We started making good time. The trees thinned out along the way and for a while we could see the sky above our heads. A light breeze caressed our skin and spirits rose as we trudged along the clearing.

We did not need to travel far. The hill, not more than twenty feet high and oblong in shape, was not hard to find. There was only one. The hill seemed oddly out of place and we supposed that men had made it. Hunter thought that perhaps the hill was an Indian burial mound.

We left the hill undisturbed and turned left, heading south back into the jungle, and our journey turned hard again, even worse than before. The farther in we walked the soggier the ground became until we found ourselves trudging across thick muck and then through knee-deep water. Every step we took soon became a battle against the mud sucking at our shoes and boots. Mules and donkeys brayed. Men grumbled. Still we pressed on.

When night closed in around us, we lit our torches, tightened our belts and continued marching forward. We had no choice. There was no dry ground to rest on. We marched through the swamp all through the night, sometimes in waist-deep water, and well into the next morning, munching on cold sea biscuits and dried, salted meat or what the Incas call Ch'arki in their Quechuan language.

"Let us hope," Efendi said, "that Tom and the lads are having a better go of things sailing across the Atlantic. I walked through the Syrian dessert once. The journey was brutal and nearly killed me. This, I think, might be worse."

I took in the dirty, exhausted faces of my men. "Captain Hunter."

"Aye, Mary."

I raised my voice so that all could hear me. "Are we lost?"

"Nay, Mary. But this marsh land is not on the map. If this land is newly flooded, even if we find the spot we are looking for, we'll never be able to dig anything up out of it."

"Which way, James?"

"Straight ahead as best I know."

"Lads," I said and pointed my machete from man to man. "I am, if you care to hear the truth, bone-weary, hungry and in a foul temper. I'm more miserable than I've ever been. I'm tempted, so very tempted, to turn around and quit. How I long to be back out on the open sea aboard our sturdy vessel with a cool, fresh sea breeze blowing in my face! I suspect all of you feel about the same. But we've come this far. We must be close. You've heard the whispers. You've heard the rumors and they are true. We're looking for buried, Aztec gold, gold stolen by Spanish deserters. We need to find dry land and then, if it is God's will, we'll find the gold. Are you with me?"

"There's no doubt we're all with you, Mary!" Hunter proclaimed loudly, waiting for no man's answer.

Hunter turned around and took up the march, plunging us deeper into the jungle. The rest of us fell in quietly behind him and we resumed our exhausting struggle against the sucking mud and thigh-deep water. More than one man cursed after he tripped over a hidden tree root or stumbled on a rock and fell headfirst into putrid water. My imagination ran wild with thoughts of water snakes.

By noon on the next day we mercifully found ourselves back on dry land. We stopped to make camp to rest and to eat a hot meal.

"Fine speech back there, Mary," Hunter said as he stretched out on the ground next to me. He laid his head on his backpack and closed his eyes. "Inspiring, really."

"I wasn't sure they'd all follow us," I replied. "I know what you will say: never give an order unless you are confident it will be obeyed. Well, no matter, I thought - ."

But I stopped my mindless prattling when I heard Hunter snoring.

I plopped myself down next to him and closed my eyes as well. But, despite my fatigue, I couldn't sleep and so I made the rounds among the men. I offered words of encouragement here and there and helped dress a wound or two. And then I walked off a ways beyond our camp to find a quiet spot where I could relieve myself in privacy. And as I squatted with my trousers down around my ankles, I saw something odd through the brush standing in-between the trees and I smiled.

"Mary, Mary," Hunter said, shaking me. "Up you go sleepy bones. We should try and cover more ground today while we still have the light to navigate by."

I rubbed the sleep out of my eyes and yawned. "What's your hurry, James?"

"Beg pardon? I'd say we're all most anxious to find whatever there is to find out here and then work our way out of this shithole."

"I had the most wonderful dream. I dreamt of chocolate."

"Mary..."

"No need to be testy, James. The object we are looking for on the map..."

"Aye? What of it?"

I gave Hunter a coy smile before answering. "I know what it is."

Hunter looked at me as if I were ill. "Oh? I pray you tell us, Mary."

"It's a small, stone obelisk."

"A small, stone obelisk? Is it now? Fascinating. And how did you come by this revelation? Was the obelisk in your dream too?"

"Don't be silly," I replied in a playful tone. I raised my arm and pointed. "I've seen the obelisk. It stands about a hundred paces or so over there..."

Hunter stared at me dumbfounded for a moment, processing what I had just said, and then turned to the men. "Quick lads, grab your shovels and your pickaxes and follow me! Snap to!"

The obelisk, the only manmade object in sight, stood about nine feet high in the middle of a small clearing, but surrounded by many trees. We could have easily missed it. The monument, or whatever it was, had been chiseled from a single block of white, polished stone. Stars and gods and strange beasts not of our world adorned the pillar's four sides. The craftsmanship was exquisite. We started digging all around the obelisk. We searched and dug for hours with nothing to show for our efforts except for empty holes.

And when the light began to fade, we put aside our tools, lit our fires and rested. I looked around the campfires and saw one hundred dispirited faces. There was no song, there was no laughter. We were all too miserable and tired.

Hunter and I sat on the ground side-by-side and shared a meal of salted beef and a little wine mixed with water.

Hunter poked me playfully in the ribs. "I truly thought you were touched in the head for a moment when I woke you earlier, Mary."

"If we did this all for naught, the men will indeed think me quite mad."

"I think the Aztecs were mad to place that ridiculous carved stone pillar out here in the middle of fuckin' nowhere," Hunter replied in a weary voice.

Efendi, having set the night watch, having made the rounds with the men, came over and sat down beside us. "The map has been true so far, Mary. Who would go to such effort only to play some silly child's prank? No, I think not. The priest who made that map was here. I feel it in my bones."

Hunter removed the map from his shirt and studied it once again. "Perhaps we are missing something. Maybe to the priest the obelisk itself was the treasure, not any gold."

Hunter handed the map over to Efendi.

"This is," Efendi said, scrutinizing the map carefully, "a faithful reproduction of the original. I am certain of it."

I sighed. "Well lads, in the morning we can dig some more and search the area for clues. I don't know what else to do."

"Huh..." Hunter uttered, absently staring at the fire. He had a puzzled look.

"What is it, James?" I asked.

"Well, what Mustafa says is true. We made a precise copy of the original."

"So?"

"But we didn't copy the inscription on the obverse side of the map."

"What?" I asked, crestfallen. "There was more? But the original is lost to us!"

"Aye, but I still remember what was written on the back of the original. I gave it no thought at the time and it probably means nothing."

"And?"

"It was the name of a person actually. The name *Luke* was scribbled across the back of the map."

"No, James," Efendi said, correcting Hunter. "The name *Luke* was written on the reverse side of the map, yes, but someone also added the number one hundred and nineteen below the name."

"*Luke* and *one hundred and nineteen?*" I asked. "How odd. What could it mean?"

"Could Luke have been the priest's name?" Efendi asked.

"I suppose his given name could have been Luke, Mustafa, but unlikely," Hunter replied. "He was a Spanish monk and probably went by Pedro, José, Miguel or something of the sort. We shall never know. Well, we best get some sleep. Tomorrow will be another long day."

In the morning the rains came, cold, biting rains out of the north swept over our camp and we were all more miserable than before. Still we dug, probing the earth, and searched. We methodically expanded our digging farther and farther away from the obelisk in concentric rings. We dug all day long and found nothing. Our holes quickly disappeared in water and mud. Spirits plummeted.

As dusk settled in around us, I gathered all of my men in a circle. "We're all feeling wretched and supplies are running low," I said, frustrated. "It is not in my nature to quit a thing once started. But, well, unless one of you bright lads has some worthy thought, I'm at a loss what else we might do. We can't dig up the whole world. Captain Hunter, let's have a look at that map of yours. Let's pass it around so that every man can take a peek. Perhaps one of you will see something that James, Efendi and I have missed."

Hunter passed his precious map around and every man took a hard look. But no one had a word to say.

"Very well," I said. "James, pass the map around again. Think lads, think. I should mention that this map is a copy of an original. Someone, probably the priest who drew the map, scribbled the name *Luke* and the number *one hundred and nineteen* across the back of the original."

I had barely finished my words when a tall, lanky seaman, a man named Pike, Henry Pike, stepped forward. He had sailed with me for years.

"*One hundred and nineteen* you say, Lady Mary?" Pike asked.

"Aye," Hunter answered for me. "What of it Pike?"

"Might you mean eleven and nine, Capt'n Hunter?"

"Eleven and nine?" Hunter asked. "I suppose, why?"

"And you say a priest made this map?"

"Aye, Henry, now you know the whole story," Hunter answered, clearly growing irritated. "I trust you are amused."

"Amused? No, sir. Why I believe the inscription is a reference to chapter eleven, verse nine from the Gospel of Saint Luke, Luke the Apostle, from the New Testament. It is a favorite of many."

It was if a bolt of lightning had struck me in the head and I at once knew that Pike had solved the last part of the riddle. "Please, tell me one of you God fearing lads brought a Bible with him?"

Pike held up his hand. "No need, Lady Mary. I know the chapter and verse by heart: *"And I say unto you, ask, and it shall be given to you; seek, and ye shall find; knock, and it shall be opened to you."* The Gospel according to Luke, chapter eleven, verse nine."

Hunter threw up his hands, disgusted. "Well, that's just jolly now, clear as pixie shit."

"Let me see that map again," I asked excitedly. "James, look, look here. Could it be that the priest drew the pillar on its side, pointing north, and not standing straight up as one would naturally assume looking at this map?"

"Knock, and it shall be opened to you," Hunter mumbled to himself. His eyes suddenly lit up. He glanced down at the map in my hand and chuckled. "Damn, my brain must be numb!" he said loudly for all to hear. He grabbed a dozen men and hurried over to the obelisk. "Push lads, not too hard, easy now. Let's test it, see if she'll tip over on this side to the south."

My men pushed. The obelisk didn't budge.

"Right. Good. Now, let's swing around to the opposite side and try again to move her, tip her over towards the north. Let's see if she'll give up her secrets this time. Gently now..."

The men pushed again. To our astonishment the obelisk creaked and groaned and started moving. The stone slowly started tipping over on its side on hinges hidden underneath its base.

And as my men lowered the obelisk on its side, ropes and pulleys running through a pair of hollow tubes set below the earth went taught and the ground, a hundred feet off - one hundred and nineteen feet to be exact - gave way. My men and I rushed over to the spot to have a peek. And there, stashed inside a crudely constructed wooden vault six feet down in ankle-deep water, we saw a dozen European-made chests. My men quickly lifted the chests out of the vault and set them on the ground side-by-side. We crowded around in a circle, mesmerized as Hunter pried the first lid open. Our jaws went slack when we saw the glittering bars of silver and gold stacked neatly inside the chest.

We paused outside of town. The prudent thing to do, I knew, was to bury our treasure somewhere outside of town and come back for it another day as Drake had done with most of the silver he had stolen from the Silver Train. But I was too worn down by fatigue to care and the Spanish garrison charged with protecting the Name of God was but a meager collection of riff-raft that couldn't stop us.

I sent a squad of men ahead, down to the beach, to make certain our *Phantom* was somewhere close-by. We were three days late but Atwood, that wonderfully stubborn Scot, had decided to linger off-shore for just a little while longer. We pulled our sacks of supplies and our chests of treasure off the mules and donkeys and emptied their contents out along the road. Then we re-stuffed the burlap sacks with our precious gold and silver bars and discarded our supplies and empty chests in the swamp.

My men and I, a filthy, sorry lot of stinking flesh with open sores and wounds, wearily trudged through town in single file in our torn and ragged clothing. We looked like a company of *desperadoes* on the run and the villagers kept their distance. We found our longboats where we had left them and after we piled our booty onboard, we piled ourselves in too and pushed-off before the captain of the garrison could come by to wish us farewell - before he could satisfy any curiosity he might have about the burlap sacks we carried bulging at the seams. We left our pack animals, our tools and the rest of our supplies behind as parting gifts.

"Good Lord!" Atwood exclaimed, looking down on us from

Phantom's rail as we pulled our longboats up alongside. When I started up the rope ladder, he laughed. "I could smell you heathens all the way from shore. What is that awful, dreadful stench? Did you fall into a shitter? And what happened to your hair, Mary? You're nearly bald!"

"We have a good story to tell, Jacob." I said brightly.

"Well, you and your lads will not step aboard this vessel before you bathe, I swear it! God only knows what vermin you carry with you. What a sad collection of misfits you be."

"We bear glad tidings, oh my Captain," I replied playfully. "You may find us more appealing, our odor more fragrant, once you see the gifts we bring."

"Indeed? A tantalizing proposition. You've piqued my curiosity. Oh very well, Madam, if you are bearing gifts and wish to share - then I say welcome aboard."

And then, on a childish whim, just as Atwood reached for my hand to help me over the rail, I leapt off the rope ladder. I plunged feet first into the water below with a great splash.

My men howled and cheered and those who could swim soon stripped off their shirts and shoes and joined me. The sea had never felt so good. For modesty's sake, I swam around the rudder, over to the ship's starboard side, so that my men could strip-off all their putrid clothing. After Hunter swore on his life that he would rescue me when I was ready, I did the same. I discarded every stitch of fabric.

Once I was back onboard the *Phantom*, after I had properly washed every inch of me with soap and dressed in fresh clothing, I went up on deck and found the whole ship's company assembled, silently staring at the dozens of burlap sacks heaped around the main mast, patiently waiting for me. The world was still and at peace. I listened to the rigging blocks clattering in the breeze, to the water slapping up against the hull. I could hear the pintles grinding in their gudgeons. I took in the faces of my men and savored the moment of our sweet triumph, a moment I knew that would be etched in my memory forever. Hunter, washed and clean-shaven, casually strolled towards me to stand by my side. I had to suppress a terrible yearning to fall into his arms and slip my tongue inside his mouth.

"Lady Mary," he said loudly for all to hear, pointing to the pile of burlap sacks. "Look, look at what you've done!"

The crew broke out into wild cheers, stamped their feet and applauded.

"I had," I said, after the men had quieted down, "a little help. We never would have found what is in those bags without the cleverness of three men. Captain Hunter, Master Efendi, and Master Pike, would you please step forward and do the honors? Show the rest of the lads what shiny things we hauled out of Panama's dismal swamps!"

The three men proudly walked to the main mast together, grabbed a sack and spilled its contents out across the deck. Those who had not yet seen our riches, those who had stayed behind with Atwood, gasped.

"As owner and investor," I said, "my share as you all well know is one-third and one-third again of all we take. But, on this occasion, I'll only take my one-third share as owner. I hereby forfeit my one-third share as investor. That amount will be divvied-up among all of you in proportion to your rank. Master Pike, without your love of the Scriptures, without your devotion to your faith, we may never have found this pretty metal. I hereby triple your share."

Phantom's crew went berserk with hoots and hollers. Men tossed their hats up in the air and cheered. It pleased me to see them happy. It pleased me to keep their loyalty.

As men dispersed to see to their duties and to store our treasure below, Atwood rattled off commands to get us underway. Topmen raced up the ratlines and soon we had a good sea breeze rounding-out our sails, stretching the ship's canvas taut. The gentle winds nudged us out into deeper water and pushed us east towards the Caribbees.

I went to the helm to stand with Hunter, Atwood and Efendi. "Is it more or less," I asked, "than what we took from old Dowlin?"

"Oh, I'd say quite a bit more," Hunter answered. "Each gold bar is worth about five hundred and fifty *pesos*, maybe more, which is equivalent to about two hundred and twenty-five English pounds I think. The silver bars are worth, give or take, thirty-five *pesos* apiece. As luck would have it though, this ship is blessed with at least two men onboard gifted in mathematics and it just so happens they are standing with us."

"Indeed, Jacob and Mustafa are good at mathematics? How fortunate. And what is their opinion?"

Hunter traded glances with Atwood and Efendi and laughed. "Well, Jacob here calculates our stash to have a total value of about fifty thousand *pesos*. Mustafa disagrees. He believes the figure is closer to only forty-eight thousand *pesos*. But, here's the rub: a Scot they say will lie to inflate his worth to trick you where a Turk will lie to hide his worth to cheat you. So my guess is the proper value lies somewhere in-between."

"And what would forty-nine thousand *pesos* be in English pounds?"

"Roughly, about twenty thousand, two hundred pounds sterling I should think, give or take. Not a bad haul considering a common seaman makes only about eight ounces of gold a year."

"Ah, so you too have skills in mathematics, James?" I asked with a smile.

Hunter winked at me. "Oh no, not me, my dear lady. I am but a simple soldier. Numbers tend to numb my brain. Over the years I've barely been able to keep track of all the ships I've sailed with and a running tally on the number of wenches I've bedded..."

On our way back to Guadeloupe, we put in at *La Asunción* on the Island of Margarita, the port that had been closed to us before. We had time to kill until Gilley returned with the fleet and I was curious to see more of this island they say is mother to countless pearls. *La Asunción* is a pretty spot, a sleepy town with white beaches surrounded by soft, rolling hills of green. But the town has very little commerce. The Spanish use the island to harvest pearls and not much else. I saw no pearls and soon grew bored. We took on fresh fruit and water and quickly weighed anchor, dropped our sails and headed on to Trinidad next, not my favorite port-of-call, but I thought it wise to try and make new friends whenever and wherever we could.

The Port of Spain was as we had left it, a horrid, filthy stink-hole. I assembled all hands on deck and reminded them about the penalty for betraying clan secrets and about the price they might pay for a single night's carnal pleasure - the great pox - and then I let them loose on the population with three days' liberty. My officers and I spent our time making acquaintances with merchants and traders in town and relaxing at our favorite tavern on the square.

And then one afternoon a man, a man familiar to me, strolled into the tavern. He strolled into the tavern with swagger wearing a fine suit, newly purchased, along with a wide brimmed hat, a distinctive floopy hat adorned with a single, yellow plume. I recognized the dapper gentleman at once. This was the pirate who had attacked my ships off the coast of Cartagena. I kept my face hidden in the shadows and considered how best to kill him.

"What is it, Mary?" Hunter asked me after returning to our table carrying two tankards of ale. "Looks like you've seen a ghost."

"No ghost, James. I see trouble standing nearby in flesh and blood. That man, the one standing at the bar wearing the expensive apparel and the large hat with the long yellow feather..."

Hunter slowly craned his neck around towards the bar. "I see him, but I know him not."

"I do. He's the pirate captain who attacked us on our way to the Name of God a few months back."

"Ah-ha. Shit. Mary, I beg you, start no mischief here. We know nothing of this man or who his friends might be."

"No worries. You are right, James. We need to study our enemy, understand his strengths and weaknesses before we strike with deadly purpose. I will have my vengeance though."

"That's my woman..."

"Am I your woman?"

"You know the answer to that question already."

"Hmmm. Perhaps, but a woman yearns to hear it."

"Perhaps if you stood before me naked, without a stitch of clothing on, I might know better how to answer you."

"Oh? Well then, leave your drink, bring your lust and follow me upstairs. I took a room for us earlier..."

After spending three days in the Port of Spain with nothing to show for our efforts, I recalled my crew and we sailed out to sea with the next tide. We headed north for Guadeloupe. Along the way we passed by a string of small islands scattered across the sea like so many gems or pearls. Many of those islands are too small for names, too small for anyone to live on. I realized I had been a fool, taken an awful risk, pulling into the Port of Spain with our special cargo still on board. So I decided to find a safe, deserted spot to bury it all until the day came to pay the men their fair shares and spend the rest.

I saw Billy busy tightening down the swivel mounts on the rails for Efendi and called out to him. "Billy, pick us out a lucky island! I intend to bury our gold and silver."

The boy eagerly dropped his tools and climbed up on the main mast shrouds. He shielded his eyes from the sun's glare with his hand and started searching for our lucky island in earnest.

I stood at the helm with the tiller in my hands. The ship was handling well and I was relishing the moment. The skies were turning overcast and it smelled of rain, but the cooler air only invigorated me. And then I saw Hunter scurrying up the fore mast and the image of his naked body, his fine physique, pressed against my own flooded all my thoughts. I could feel my cheeks turn flush.

My moment's secret pleasure was interrupted when Atwood straddled up next to me. "Should I ready the longboats, Mary?"

"Aye, and bring our loot up on deck too. All of it."

"Straight away, Mary. Should I have one of the lads relieve you at the helm? Will you be goin' ashore?"

"I think not. You and Hunter see to things. I'm quite content to stay with the ship and rest my weary bones a bit."

"There, Mum!" Billy called out and pointed excitedly.

The island Billy found for us, a spec of dirt, couldn't have been much more than one hundred acres across and I wasn't certain whether it was even on the map. There were a score of small islands all around us, but it was easy to see why Billy had chosen this particular rock. In the center of the island stood a cluster of four palm trees, curving around each other in a most distinctive way as if they were dancing in a circle and embracing. They formed a natural marker.

"Well done, Master Ferrell," I said. "Jacob, if you and James are of a like mind, that we can find this place again without much effort, then you have my blessing to lower the boats away and you know what to do."

"With pleasure, Mary."

I put a man in the chains with a lead line to call out the water's depth and eased *Phantom* in as close to land as I dared. At fifty yards or so off shore I gave the order to let go the anchor and the ship came to a graceful stop. The water was clear enough to see the bottom. Schools of colorful fish circled around our anchor.

Hunter and Atwood took two longboats and a small launch, men, shovels and our loot, now packed inside sturdy chests of oak reinforced with iron fittings, and rowed across the gentle surf over to the beach. Atwood returned an hour later with all the men and the two longboats, leaving Hunter behind with the launch to finish drawing a map of the island. After Hunter returned we resumed our voyage north.

The next morning our days of easy sailing abruptly ended. The winds suddenly shifted, from west to east to east to west and the swells began rising and falling with mounting power. I took in the sky and did not like what I saw. The clouds were hanging low and moving fast and started swirling around in a most peculiar way. The color of the sky turned from gray to a dull, sickly yellow. And then it started to drizzle with chunks of intermittent hail.

"Mary!" Hunter cried out, racing towards me from the main deck as I worked the tiller.

"What is it, James?"

"Nothing good comes out of the east," he said. "We must prepare ourselves."

I scanned the horizon in all directions. "You think what blows our way is more than a summer storm?"

Atwood and Efendi, having seen Hunter's haste to reach me, soon joined us at the helm.

"What is it, Mary?" Atwood asked.

"I know not. Ask Hunter."

Hunter had is eyes fixed on the heavens.

Atwood moved next to him and did he same. "James?"

"I pray I am wrong. But this yellow sky, the clouds moving counterclockwise and the hail - I've seen this peculiar phenomenon before"

"And?" I asked.

"The last time I saw a sky like this a *huracán* soon followed."

"A *huracán*?" I asked, alarmed.

"Aye, Mary."

"What do we do? Come about and make for the Port of Spain? It's not far off, no more than one hundred leagues away I'm certain."

"No. If what blows our way is a *huracán*, we'll never make it to Trinidad. We must stay well clear of any land and head for open water. We take our chances out at sea in deep water or we risk running aground and foundering on one of these islands."

Out of nowhere a terrific bolt of lightning split the sky open directly above our heads followed instantly by a horrific clap of thunder. We all froze. The ungodly din raised the hair on the back of my neck and sent a shiver down my spine. The winds picked-up full of rage, whipping the sea into an angry, frothy beast. Our ship pitched and rolled with mounting violence. The light drizzle gave way to showers and the showers gave way to sheets of blinding, stinging rain. We braced ourselves for the worst.

"Jacob, Mustafa, rouse the men, all hands on deck!" I said, nearly screaming to be heard over the wind's shrill whistle. The noise was most unsettling. "We set the storm sails, double lash the heavy guns, secure all the hatches and tie anything down that can shift or move."

"We move out smartly lads," Hunter added, "and do what Mary says quickly. Then you best remember how to pray to whatever god or gods you favor."

After Atwood and Efendi spun around and hurried off below to fetch the men, Hunter pulled me into him, held me tightly and kissed me hard. "With everything I have, my whole heart, truly I love you, Mary," he said as if he were saying goodbye, as if this was the end. Then he raced after the others before I could say a word, not even taking a moment to let me kiss him in return. I'd never seen fear in Hunter's eyes before. I'd never heard him say farewell.

When Atwood returned he took the tiller from me. The brawny Scot was the strongest man among us by far. We pointed our ship's nose into the wind and tried sailing farther out to sea. And when darkness closed in all around us, when the winds howled so fiercely it hurt our ears, when the ship's planks and timbers groaned so badly we thought she was breaking-up, we offered up our prayers and braced ourselves for death.

After cresting each massive roller, *Phantom* plunged deep into the bottom of every trough. As her nose disappeared beneath the waves each time, I took a deep breath and prepared myself for a cold and unhappy end. But then, when her bow reemerged to scale the next new roller, I found my courage again. It was a wet and wild ride.

When Hunter returned to the quarter deck, he held me firmly around the waist with one arm and kept his balance with the other wrapped securely around rail. I knew he wanted me to go below. But I would have none of it. I had not forged my reputation of steel in a world of iron men by cowering out of sight from danger.

Our nao smashed her way through the heaving seas. She

fought tenaciously for her crew and my hopes began to rise as the hours past. But when night fell the sea had more to show us. Towering waves, twenty footers or better, assaulted us on our starboard flank. Walls of water came crashing down over the rails, ruthlessly knocking our poor ship to and fro. Men lost their balance and went flying. Many suffered cuts and bruises and there was a broken bone or two. More than one sailor went down with the *mal de mer* and spilled his guts. No one slept. I must confess, never have I been more terrified than during those harrowing hours I lived through the raw, awesome fury of the *huracán*.

When morning finally broke, when the sun peeked through the clouds with shafts of golden light, the winds subsided and the sea again turned calm. I was stunned we had survived. We could see the huge and terrifying storm behind us moving off to the north-west, hurrying on in the direction of Hispaniola and I thought of our Spanish friends.

Phantom, bruised and battered maybe but seaworthy still the same, had held herself together. She had brought her crew safely through - a testament to the remarkable skills of her gifted, French craftsmen. After making some quick repairs, my weary men and I eased our disheveled ship into Guadeloupe's small harbor a few days later. Mercifully, the storm had spared the island. Once we landed on the beach, men fell to their knees and kissed the ground. I saw a few men weep.

And when Chief Paka Wokili came out to greet us, I paid him his fair tribute - a fortune to him, a trifling sum to me - and he rewarded me with a grand smile. I had a hard time explaining to the chief though that Henry was not dead, that he had gone off with the fleet to see our fair island across the ocean. We raised our tents along the shore and spent our days in Guadeloupe waiting anxiously for Gilley. For all we knew the *huracán* had devoured Gilley and all my ships and men.

Two weeks after our arrival though, as I took my morning stroll along the beach, four familiar, handsome vessels suddenly appeared through the early morning mist. The ships glided across the silvery waters of the bay and dropped anchor next to *Phantom*. And then I saw, standing tall on *Star's* grand forecastle, my greathearted Gilley, a man who was dear to me like a father, waving and smiling at me.

I hurried back to our camp to start breakfast. I gathered all my officers around the fire as the longboats floated in. And as was my custom when we were all reunited, I cooked and served each man as they traded their stories in turn, each tale growing bolder than the one before it. Billy sat on a tree stump near us, took out his mandolin and began playing old, Irish folk tunes. He chose haunting melodies set to sad and wistful lyrics that tell the story of our people. He had a soft touch and a strong voice and I saw more than one tear-stained cheek around our campfire.

Gilley slapped his knee after Hunter and Efendi finished recounting our adventures in the jungles of New Spain. "Whoa, Aztec gold! You actually found it with that wretched, old map of yours, eh James? I was wondering what happened to your hair, Mary! Did we take as much loot as we took from Dowlin?"

"More," Hunter replied. "How is it you escaped the *huracán*, Tom?"

"*Huracán?* We sailed through no *huracán*. We saw a massive beast a fair distance off to the south. Even so, I'm not too proud to say we swung our ships to the north and ran. Praise God we did. One of the storm's tentacles caught us a few hours later. We sailed through heavy seas and waterfalls of rain for one day and a night. You weathered the storm safely on the island I take it?"

"Ha!" Hunter scoffed. "What fun would that be? Mary sailed us straight through the monster's heart and laughed as waves as big as mountains crashed down all around us! We sailed through no mere storm - we sailed through the *huracán*..."

Gilley looked at me in disbelief. "Good God!"

"You can't believe everything a sailor says," I said nonchalantly while moving around the fire to pour more coffee. "What news in Ireland?"

"The same, more or less," Gilley answered with a weary sigh. "The English continue settling Ireland like the Spanish are settling the New World - displacing the natives as they do so. And like the Spanish, they are moving in none too gently. There is a lot of bloody fighting, mostly in the south. The Irish lords are slowly, methodically, being crushed by the iron fist of that English usurper sitting on the thrown in London. Then there is the Reformation. The Protestants grow stronger and bolder by the day. The land we saw was not the Ireland I once knew. Ah, but as for business, we were most successful. All four ships are burdened down with Old World finished goods, which should fetch us a pretty penny."

"You hauled finished goods half way around the world to fetch us a pretty penny you say, old man?" Hunter asked playfully. "That's your boast? Why we purchased our gold, gold enough to buy a kingdom, at the meager cost of a few mosquito bites and Mary's shorn hair! Now that's how one turns a handsome profit I'd say my good man!"

Gilley yawned. "I've suffered enough of this English braggart. I've heard a lot of bold talk about this Aztec gold and silver but have yet to see one coin or a single bar."

"I'd worry far more," I said sweetly and leaned down to kiss Gilley on his bald head, "if James tries to convince you that we pitched our treasure over the side to appease a cruel god's temper."

"I only needed," Hunter interjected, "to sacrifice Gilley's share to the blue-maned king of the sea. Gilley may be poor, but the rest of us will make out quite nicely, Mary."

We spent the next few days cleaning and repairing our ships and then we set out for Santo Domingo on the Island of Hispaniola. We all agreed it best to keep the fleet together. We sailed out in force.

Once we neared Santo Domingo though I took only the *Phantom* inside the port so as not to make the Spanish nervous. I knew the treasure fleet had to be somewhere nearby in the Caribbean and the Spanish I assumed would be on high alert. We moored our ship underneath the watchful eyes of the Spanish garrison and their batteries of heavy cannon at Ozama and after a customs agent from the *Casa de Contratación* came aboard to inspect our empty holds, I took Gilley, Hunter, Atwood and Efendi with me into town to find Cortés.

Santo Domingo was not as we had left it. The town had been ravaged savagely by the *huracán*. I was saddened to see houses flattened by the wind. We saw many others with walls still standing but no roofs. Ferocious winds had ripped away the straw and tile. Some homes had simply vanished without a trace. Everywhere we walked we saw debris littering the roads. We passed by broken chairs and tables, pottery and clothes and countless branches, leaves and fronds. On the edge of town some frightful force had mowed down a swath of trees deep into the jungle. How anyone could survive such devastation seemed a miracle to me.

As luck would have it, we found our friend Cortés at his home on the edge of town. Except for a few minor scratches across his face he seemed uninjured. His house appeared undamaged.

"Mary!" Cortés exclaimed as he met us at the door. He smiled and waved us inside with genuine enthusiasm. We embraced and exchanged kisses on the cheeks. "Praise be God, you are alive and well!"

"We are all well. And you?"

"Good, good. I am fine and as you can see my house was spared. I have a few broken windows in the kitchen from a fallen tree but, all-in-all, I was most fortunate. Come in, come in my friends. This is my second *huracán*. I pray I never see another. You know the word *huracán* has no Latin root? We Spanish took the word *huracán* from the Taíno word *huracan*, which means storm, and made it our own. Not the only thing we've taken from these poor natives is it?"

"And what," I asked, "took down all the trees on the west side of town?"

"Ah, a *tronada* or what I've heard English sailors call a *ternado*, a funnel cloud of intense power spawned by the *huracán* touched down. This *Devil's Breath*, as we call it, ripped through the town killing many good people, destroying homes and shops and then cut a path through the countryside. The *tronada* did more damage than the *huracán*."

"This New World is a cruel and hostile world," I offered softly.

Cortés led us to his parlor and poured each of us a glass of wine. "No more so than the Old World I think, Mary. Death stalks each of us and has no prejudices. The dark lord of the underworld is never far away. But let us abandon such morbid thoughts! You had a successful voyage I trust, Captain Gilley?"

"We did, we did indeed," Gilley answered. "We returned with superior quality goods that I'm confident will be of interest to you, goods that will fetch you excellent prices. We even brought back crates of Spanish wine to sell, my friend."

Cortés nodded his approval. He insisted we stay for supper and his household staff, his *Negros Ladinos*, once again treated us like royalty. After supper we retired to Cortés's veranda where Gilley provided bills of lading for everything we had and, after a bit of friendly haggling, Cortés and I reached a fair bargain for it all. I agreed to make one delivery down the coast, a few miles away from Santo Domingo as we had done before, one in Old Havana and another in the Port of Spain. Even with Cortés's cut, and the money needed for labor and bribes, our profits were extraordinary. I did not, of course, tell Cortés that. He was making plenty.

With our business concluded, I said goodnight and returned to the ship with Efendi. Gilley, Hunter and Atwood remained behind with Cortés to enjoy more drinks and cigars, the stink of which I found nauseating although, I must admit, I tried a pipe once and thought the experience pleasurable.

In the morning my three warriors stumbled back to the ship locked arm-in-arm, more sloshed than I had ever seen them. I had to suppress a smile. I loved Gilley and Hunter and we were all growing fond of Atwood. I was glad to see the bonds of friendship strengthening between them.

"You're late!" I called down to them from the rail in mock anger.

The three men clumsily navigated across a short plank stretching from the dock to the ship until Gilley fell to one knee and retched.

"*Christ* what a mess!" I chided him.

"For pity's sake, Mum!" Gilley pleaded, struggling to stand with the help of his two accomplices.

"Shhh, I implore you, Mary," Hunter said and put a finger to his lips. "Not so loud."

I ignored his pathetic plea and continued to have my fun. "Shhh? Is that what I just now heard you tell the mistress of this ship? Shhh? Good God, if I had any sense I would have all three of you tied to the main mast and flogged for your unpardonable insolence, as punishment for your deplorable behavior! Get our good Captain Gilley below to the surgeon and you two, Captain Hunter and Master Atwood, report to me at once in my cabin! And for honor's sake I hope you didn't let the Spaniard best you!"

Hunter suddenly turned green, leaned over the plank and emptied his stomach too. Atwood appeared nearly as unsteady.

"Christ Almighty!" I cried out, more worried than mad and rushed down to the plank to tend to my wounded. I helped them below to their hammocks and let them sleep off their misery. And as my wounded rested, I gave the order to cast off lines and we eased the *Phantom* out into the harbor where we set our sails to rendezvous with the fleet standing off in the distance a league or two away.

"Mary!" Ferguson called out to me as we approached the *Godsend*. "Two merchantmen sailed by not but an hour ago. Both masters said the same thing: the treasure fleet is on the move, sailing east for Seville along the north coast of Hispaniola. The merchantmen accompanied the fleet a-ways and then peeled-off for Santo Domingo. We have time to sail around the leeward side of the island to catch a glimpse if you are so inclined."

"The fleet is this far south?" I asked, confused. We had always heard from Cortés and others that the treasure fleet, after leaving Havana, always sailed north, hugging the east coast of Florida to catch the favorable winds and currents there before turning east for Spain.

"Storms blew the fleet south."

"Well, let us have a look then!"

And that is what we did. The distance wasn't far.

After rounding Punta Cana on the eastern tip of Hispaniola, the power and grandeur of Spain suddenly appeared before us. The treasure fleet was moving under full sail in a line that stretched across the water for several miles. We counted sixty good-sized merchantmen of different types in all, along with a number of smaller transports carrying passengers and their baggage. And we saw at least six galleons running escort too, magnificent galleons, each one a four-masted, triple-decker. The sheer majesty of the spectacle took my breath away.

After Spain's prestige and glory turned north-east and sailed off into the horizon, we came about and returned to the waters of Santo Domingo where we found Cortés's men waiting for us on the shore in a small inlet to the west of the city, the one we had used before, and delivered *Westport's* cargo. And then we set out for Old Havana where we offloaded *Fair Irish Maiden's* cargo first and then *Star's* cargo, again into the hands of Cortés's agents, to men we didn't know. We finished our journey in the Port of Spain where we met more of Cortés's men and offload *Godsend's* goods on a desolate stretch of beach to the leeward side of the island.

Each transaction went smoothly. Our methods had become routine.

We kept in communication with our Spanish partner through letters and I advised Cortés of our success. I always sent two letters in duplicate to Cortés, one to his *hacienda* in Havana and the other to his home in Santo Domingo because we never knew which of the two places he might be. The Spanish run a reliable system of small packet vessels in the Caribbean, sailing from port to port with passengers and bags of letters and small parcels without interference from pirates. Even pirates have a need for mail I've heard. Post riders pick the letters and parcels up at the docks and then ride inland to deliver the mail to the proper recipients.

We passed the time in the Port of Spain overhauling our ships in thick humidity and punishing heat while we waited for word from Cortés. We needed payment for the Old World goods we had just delivered and instructions on where to pick up our New World cargo for the return voyage back to Ireland. Once the work on the ships was completed, we passed the time relaxing at our favorite tavern on the square.

And then - to my surprise - Cortés walked into the tavern one day. He pulled up a chair and sat down at the table with Gilley, Hunter and me.

Chapter Ten

ppearing both agitated and distracted, Cortés seemed peculiarly different. He was not his usual cheerful, chatty self. But then again, neither was I.

Earlier that morning I had walked down to the water alone to refresh myself in the cool surf. I had stripped off all my clothing and waded out a ways into neck-deep water. The world was quiet and at peace. The sunrise was a masterpiece of bold reds, purples and splashes of soft blues. I thanked God for my Good Fortune. I relished my quiet moment. And then, no warning, I was attacked. I was attacked most viciously. Something stabbed me over and over again with searing, awful pain. It happened so fast I barely caught a glimpse of the animal's purple tentacles as it swam away from me. And then I saw another. A pair of Portuguese man 'o wars, or maybe it was a cluster of three, had stung me on my legs, on my thighs and across my back and stomach. Worse, I failed to read the signs...

"Are you ill, Mary?" Cortés asked me as he took a laced handkerchief from his pocket and dabbed the beads of sweat off his brow. The air, even inside the tavern, was stifling. "You look pale and, forgive me, I don't mean to be indelicate, but you keep rubbing your legs and stomach."

"No, I am not ill. I offended a fish. At least one Portuguese man 'o war attacked me this morning while I was relaxing in the surf."

Cortés grimaced. "Ewww, I've heard the wounds are very painful. The skin will swell and bubble and then itch. You will be miserable for many days. But the man 'o war's venom is rarely fatal."

"Lucky me," I said and took a sip of ale.

Hunter and Gilley both looked at me with worry. I dismissed their concerns with a flick of my hand.

Cortés explained that he had come to Trinidad to see an old friend who had fallen gravely ill. He was clearly in a hurry and so we did not press him for more.

"Well, I do not have much time," he said coldly. "Other matters require my immediate attention back in Santo Domingo. I must depart with haste after I pay my respects to my dear friend. To business then?"

"Of course," I replied.

"All the arrangements have been made. The money and the cargo for your ships will be ready for you in Old Havana in two weeks' time. You should sail without delay."

"You will have all of it in Old Havana?" Hunter asked, surprised.

"Sí. Is this a problem?"

"No," I answered weakly. I had trouble focusing. My skin felt like it was on fire and I was beginning to feel nauseous.

"Good, I am sorry for the change to our usual arrangements," Cortés said gruffly. "But this could not be helped for reasons we can discuss at a better time. It is possible that I shall see you all in Old Havana in two weeks, but I would not count on it." And with that, Cortés abruptly excused himself and left.

We wished the Spaniard a safe journey and after we finished our drinks, I had traded-in my ale for some awful concoction the barkeep had given me to settle my stomach, we too left the tavern. We spent the rest of the day combing the streets of the port to gather all our men.

"I hope," Gilley said, standing at the rail with Hunter and me as we watched the crew move the last of the fresh provisions onboard the *Star*, "*Señor* Cortés knows what he's doing. It seems queer he won't be in Old Havana with us to oversee matters, to insure the trade goes smoothly, especially with so much at stake."

Hunter nodded. "Aye. This is a lot of material to assemble in one place. I'm surprised he could hire that many wagons and men."

"No matter," I said. "It makes things easier for us."

"Do you still intend to lead the fleet back to Ireland yourself, Mary?" Hunter asked.

"Aye, why not?" I replied a bit too sharply. I was feeling poorly, worse than at the tavern. I blamed the heat of the noonday sun. "It will be autumn soon. I long to breathe in Ireland's cool, crisp air, to watch the leaves change color. I trust you boys can manage things here for a spell just fine while I'm away."

"Ha!" scoffed Gilley, "You can have cold, dreary Ireland. I rather prefer palm trees now and the warm, Caribbean sun."

"Well," I began to say, struggling to answer Gilley with something clever. But then my world started spinning around me and I collapsed.

I remember very little after that. But I do recall the black pit. I recall the pit most vividly. Black men, not Negroes, but men dressed in black robes with ravens' heads - black eyes, black beaks and feathers - grabbed me with their black claws and beat me mercilessly for hours. Then they bound my hands and feet and gagged me using live, black snakes for rope and tossed me into a deep pit, into a tar pit as black as night. Bloody and bruised, they left me there to die. I laid in this pit covered in sticky tar in agony for more days than I could count. All seemed lost until the snakes took pity on me and released me. They slithered underneath my body, lifted me up on their backs and carried me to the top of the pit where I was able to crawl back into the light. And then I heard a voice, a familiar, comforting voice calling out my name.

"Mary, Mary," I heard this voice say over and over again. I felt something cool being pressed against my forehead. When I opened my eyes I saw my shining, beautiful Hunter leaning over me with a candle in his hand. He smiled.

"What happened?" I asked as I lifted my head up off a pillow to look around. I was on the ship, lying in my bed.

Hunter softly stroked my hair. "You've been unconscious for some time."

"Unconscious? Was I injured? I'm I dying?"

Hunter, my hardnosed man of rippling brawn, took his finger and brushed away a tear running down his cheek. "No, I think not. I think the fever has at last broken. You'll live, praise God, you'll live."

I could feel the ship rolling on the swells. "How long have I been out?"

"You've been unconscious for four days and then some."

"What?"

"Aye, four days, Mary. The ship's surgeon thinks the poison from Portuguese man 'o war is causing your affliction. Your body is covered in welts and blisters where the tentacles stung your skin. It's as if someone had taken a lash and savagely whipped you raw all over. The surgeon has no medicine for this. But Henry said there is a Carib woman in Guadeloupe who can help. We're sailing for Guadeloupe now under full sail."

"Oh, aye, the man 'o war. Where's the fleet?"

"Gilley is sailing for Old Havana with *Phantom* and the rest of our ships to meet Cortés's men. He'll pick up our money and cargo and then it's off to mother Ireland for Gilley and the lads. You can do the honors, lead the fleet, next time around after you've recovered."

"Oh," is all I could manage to say. I didn't have the strength to say more and settled back down on my pillow.

Hunter took my hand and offered a loving smile. "Gilley and I almost came to blows over who would stay with you and who would lead the ships back to Ireland. I won. Rest now..."

I did as Hunter asked. I closed my eyes and drifted off in sleep.

When I awoke again I found myself inside a tent, one of ours, set-up along the shore with an old Carib woman sitting by my side. The old woman offered me a toothless grin. It was night and there were many lanterns and candles set out all around me. The air was thick with smoke and pungent incense.

"Who are you?" I asked. But the old woman wouldn't speak.

Hunter pulled the tent's flap back when he heard my voice and stepped inside. "Mary!"

"James, where are we?"

"We're in Guadeloupe."

"And who is this woman?"

"You don't remember?"

"No. Remember what?"

"We thought we lost you."

"Oh? Why?"

"Port of Spain, the Portuguese man 'o war?"

"Oh," I said, struggling to remember. "We were on the ship?"

"Aye, but the fever came back. This woman saved your life. She is a healer. It was Henry's idea to bring you here to her. Nothing the ship's surgeon tried helped you. He gave you what little Paracleus's laudanum we had onboard, but the medicine only made you retch. Nothing we did eased your fever for very long. The skin all over your body turned black and blue and blistered. I began to fear you had the Plague."

"We were with Cortés in Trinidad..."

"Aye, that's right. He left for Santo Domingo and Gilley left for Old Havana."

"And then I fell into a pit."

"A pit? What pit?"

"Oh, never mind. We're in Old Havana?"

"No my darling girl, we're in Guadeloupe."

"Oh, aye, aye, so you said. And the others?"

"Gilley should be well on his way to Ireland by now with our ships loaded down with New World goods."

"And *Star* is anchored in the bay?"

"Aye, indeed she is. Now let's try to get some broth in you. You haven't eaten in over a week."

Even the simplest tasks exhausted me at first. I was weak and thin. My trousers wouldn't stay on my hips. Each day Hunter made me walk and swim. Each day we went a little longer and a little farther around the island and slowly my health and strength returned.

Of my closest officers, only Hunter was with me and we had less than one hundred men. The rest had sailed with Gilley.

I sat on a blanket in the sand next to Hunter near the campfire as we shared a meal of roasted pig and corn and boiled squash. I even felt well enough to have a thimble full or two of mellow wine. Our men were doing the same around their campfires stretched out along the shore. A fair number of Carib men, women and children turned out to join us in our modest feast. The camp settled into a merry mood with soft music, dancing and laughter.

A gentle breeze with a hint, a tease, of autumn blew off the water from the north. The stars were bright and clear. The evening was delightful.

Hunter refilled my mug. "You are looking much better, Mary."

"I feel much better."

"Are you up for a new adventure?"

"Certainly. You have some thoughts?"

"I do indeed. When you are fit and able I will share an idea or two that might amuse you."

I leaned close to his ear. "Well," I whispered, "I should rest then. But first, perhaps you could row me over to the ship? I think I might be well enough for one small adventure in my bed..."

BA-BA-BA-BA-BOOM! BOOM! BOOM! BOOM!

At first I thought I must be hallucinating from a relapse of the fever. I bolted upright in my bed when I heard the boom of heavy cannon all around us. Hunter did the same. It was still dark outside. We threw on clothes, grabbed our weapons and rushed up to the main deck.

Ugly, wretched war had found us. War had caught us napping.

I froze in horror when I saw the dark silhouettes of three ships sitting in the bay blasting away at our camp with their great guns. Our flimsy tents along the shore were exploding in balls of flame, one after the other. I could hear the screams of wounded and dying men, my men. And then I saw a fourth ship, a large carrack, emerge out of the darkness. She was sailing towards us with angry men lined-up along her rails; she looked nearly as formidable as the *Star*. What few men I had onboard the *Star* with me, less than twenty souls in all, scrambled up on deck with swords and muskets in hand. But we had no chance against the numbers lumbering towards us.

"Mary," Hunter said. "Quick now, slip over the side and swim to shore. Run into the jungle and hide. We'll hold them off as long as we can. Go now!"

"No! I'll not slink away in the night like some craven coward."

"Mary!"

And then I saw the face of my enemy and at once I understood. Two hulking brutes, two giants, stood on the quarter deck of the war carrack sailing towards us, goading their men on. The shorter brother wore an eye-patch. The *Síol Faolcháin* had crossed the Atlantic to find and butcher us!

"Look, James!" I said and pointed my sword at the giants.

"*Jesus!* The Twins! But how?"

Then Billy stumbled on deck, dragging his gimpy leg. He carried no weapons and seemed in a hurry to reach the rail.

Hunter raised his pistol at him. "Billy! Stop!"

Billy spun around to look at me. His eyes were filled with terror. His cheeks were stained with tears.

"I'm sorry, Lady Mary. I'm sorry, so terrible sorry for what I done!"

His body started shaking. He broke down and sobbed. Ignoring Hunter, he turned away to climb up on the rail.

"Billy!" Hunter shouted and cocked the hammer on his pistol back.

But I placed my hand over Hunter's wrist and pulled the barrel down. "No, James. He's only a boy."

"He's a fucking traitor! He's old enough to die!"

"You can't be certain of that. What does it matter now? We'll both be dead soon enough. I pray there is a life after this one, a life we can share together. I love you, James Hunter. With all my heart and soul I love you."

We heard a splash of water after Billy jumped.

Hunter seized me in his arms. "And I love you, Mary. Survive this night, I beg you. Whatever you must do to keep your life - swear to me you will!"

After I reassured him with an empty nod, he kissed me hard and released me. He turned his attention to the Twins. Their carrack was less than fifty yards away and gliding slowly towards us. Hunter raised his pistol and shot into the crowd of men. A sailor at the bow with a grappling hook in hand groaned and tumbled into the black water.

We had no time to ready the great guns. We had no time to raise the anchor or to set our sails. Hunter quickly formed the men up in a skirmish line behind the bulwarks and we fired off several volleys through the gunports before the Twins' ship coasted up alongside us. Our situation was hopeless.

The ships struck hard. I lost my footing and fell against the skylight, hitting the back of my head. I could feel warm blood trickling down my neck from a gash across my skull. I tried to stand but felt woozy. And then a wave of men yelling curses poured over our rails and pushed my own men back. My crew fought bravely, desperately, but were easily overwhelmed and surrounded. When I finally managed to stand, I ordered my men to lower their weapons. The Twins wanted me, not them, and I hoped I might somehow purchase their lives by surrendering my own. My men obeyed. The Twins' men moved about disarming us.

Then the Twins leapt over the rail together. I looked for Hunter but didn't see him. When the Twins saw me, they smiled.

Then Hunter emerged from the shadows near the forecastle with his sword raised above his head and charged at the taller Twin. The giant, holding a sword in each hand, towered over Hunter and grinned. I wanted to fall to my knees and cry. Hunter had chosen to die hoping, I suppose, that his death might satisfy the Twins' thirst for blood and save me. His attack was suicide.

The two men squared-off and started trading light blows, testing one another. A stillness settled over the deck as all eyes turned to watch Hunter and the Twin go at it.

The fighting pair warily circled around each other for a bit. And then both men viciously jabbed and lunged at one another. Steel struck steel. The giant had the strength and girth of a bull and quickly took control. He attacked with unrelenting rage. Hunter, quick and strong, parried every thrust, blunted every blow, but still the brute kept advancing, forcing Hunter back.

And then the Twin landed a savage blow with a hard kick into Hunter's chest. Hunter stumbled backwards until his back slammed against the main mast. The giant moved in for the kill. I put my hand to my mouth and gasped.

But before the Twin could reach Hunter, Hunter, in a burst of speed and energy, pushed himself off the mast, launched himself into a summersault and barely missed slicing the brute's head off. The Twin somehow blocked the mortal blow at the last second. Even so, a trickle of blood ran down the monster's cheek from a cut across his brow. Hunter's blade had nicked him.

Hunter savagely pressed home his attack with raw power, slashed away with blinding fury, forcing the Twin back on his heels. The giant's grin vanished when he couldn't regain his balance. He suddenly knew he was fighting for his life. He glanced over at his brother, looking dazed and confused.

Then Hunter made an awkward turn. At first I thought he had twisted his ankle or slipped and had lost his balance. Worse, he had let his guard down. The giant saw his chance and with all his ungodly strength he thrust his sword at Hunter's heart. But the big man's blade found only empty air to stab at when Hunter deftly stepped aside. Hunter's timing had been flawless. Before the giant could recover from his error, Hunter whipped his sword around and plunged his steel deep into the giant's massive chest. The blade ripped through lung and pierced the monster's back. The Twin dropped his swords and sank to one knee.

Then the one-eyed Twin stepped forward. He pulled his pistol from his belt and without a word shot my Hunter dead. I watched in horror as Hunter fell. The Twin had his men pick my poor Hunter up and pitched his body over the rail like garbage. I did my best - for Hunter - not to falter. I hid my tears. I tried to be strong. I prepared myself for death.

Our captors bound our hands. They took my men below but kept me on deck and tied me to the main mast. They left me there alone. I watched a dozen boats with teams of men move towards the shore. And after the Twins secured the beach, two louts came for me. They tossed me in a boat and rowed me to the island. I couldn't tell in the dark how many of my men had been killed as we stepped onto the beach. Some I reasoned must have survived the barrage and fled into the jungle. The few bodies I did see, as my captors hustled me towards the only tent still standing, had been carved-up by grapeshot. It was a quick, if gruesome death. It was a better death I knew than what was waiting for me inside that tent. My two escorts, one on each side of me, dragged me by my arms inside where the one-eyed Twin was waiting.

"Ah, Mary, Mary, Mary," he said with a crooked smile. "How happy I am you're alive. How I've longed to see you, to touch you, to feel your soft skin against mine."

I looked at him defiantly in the eye as his two lackeys held me firm. My thoughts turned back to the day of days and I smiled. This animal could hurt me. He could make me scream and beg and he could kill me. But he could never truly break me. He could never make me yield. Never. And if there was the slightest opportunity to kill him, even wound him, I would.

He circled around me like a predator about to devour its prey. "You won't be smiling long, my love. I am, you know, a cultured man. I am fluent in Italian, French and Spanish and I speak tolerable Latin and Greek. I appreciate fine art and music. I appreciate beauty in all its forms. You are an exquisite beauty. What a sinful waste it would be if I were to exact my revenge on thee here and now. But then again, my, my, my, well I know what a deadly, poisonous bitch you are."

He stopped in front of me, ripped my blouse open and laughed. "Ahhh, I knew it! Your breasts are perfect, like two beautifully shaped melons. Your nipples are not too big and not too small. Everything about you Mary is nearly flawless. I even like this short hair of yours. It is most becoming."

Then he took a dagger from his belt and placed it against my cheek. He ran the tip of the blade playfully across my lips, down my chin, down my neck and around my nipples. I closed my eyes. I clenched my teeth. My muscles tensed as I braced myself for pain. But I refused to beg. I tried to hide my fear. I bit my lip to keep it from quivering. I had the urge to pee and squeezed my legs together.

"Well my dearest Mary, did you know there is a bounty on your head?" he asked and wagged a finger in my face. "Tsk, tsk. You've been a naughty, naughty girl. You've committed piracy on the high seas back in Ireland. You've killed the queen's good men. How can I carve you up on this fucking island and still collect the bounty? Your flesh will putrefy before I can get your body back to England. No, no, I will not kill you. Not here. Your life has more value to me than your death - for now. I'll let the English kill you and they will pay me for the pleasure. You'll be drawn and quartered at Smithfield. Your body parts will be dragged across the four corners of England. They'll stick that lovely head of yours on a pike outside the Tower. I doubt any man will want you then. Oh Mary, my deadly, little viper, what a painful, grisly death you face, eh?"

I opened my eyes and looked down at the one-eyed monster's brother sitting in the sand in the corner of the tent. His shirt was soaked in blood and he was whizzing his breath away. He would not last through the night. This was Hunter's parting gift to me. Again I smiled.

The one-eyed Twin turned to look over at his wounded brother. He understood my thoughts.

"You needn't concern yourself with him. He'll live or die. What of it? Let's concern ourselves with you. You've lost everything, Mary. Your ships, your gold, your men, your precious lover Hunter too, all lost. Ah yes, the gold - Billy told us where to find it, where you buried it. Very soon it will all be mine."

I ignored the pig and glanced over at Billy. He was standing in the corner opposite from the wounded Twin, still dressed in his wet clothes and shaking. I finally broke my silence.

"Why Billy, why? What insult did I ever give you or your family?"

Billy looked away, ashamed, and did not answer me.

"Oh, Mary let him be," the one-eyed Twin said softly. "The poor lad is embarrassed as you can plainly see. Where's your heart, your kindness? Have you none at all? Billy was working for me from the very start. I killed his father and held his sister ransom. Then I broke his leg, just to get your sympathy, to inspire you to hire him aboard your ship. Well, in truth it is my dead brother's ship is it not? Breaking the boy's leg was a nice touch don't you think? It was my idea to use him as my mole. And when you sent him back to Ireland, he came running back to me. He told me everything to save his sister. Come over here, Billy. That's a good lad. No reason to be shy around our sweet and gentle Lady Mary."

I could see the tears pooling in Billy's eyes as he slowly shuffled towards me. I was glad Hunter had not killed him. He was just a boy, a poor, abused boy trying to protect his sister.

"You've done well, Billy," the one-eyed Twin said as he wrapped one arm around Billy's shoulder and hugged him close. "I'm proud of you, my good lad. Have you ever seen breasts like these? No? Cat got your tongue, boy? No matter. I forget how young you are. Well here we are Billy. You've done everything I've asked of you and as your reward you are free to join your sister. Off you go."

A spray of blood splattered across my face and breasts as the wretched pig sliced the boy's throat open with his dagger. Billy stared at me in shock, crumpled to the ground and died.

"Ahhh, he was just a boy!" I blurted out and started crying.

The one-eyed bastard drove his fist into my stomach without warning. I doubled over in pain and couldn't breathe.

"Do not question me, I did the boy a favor!" he screamed. As I struggled to catch my breath, he wiped his dagger across my skin. He smeared Billy's blood over my breasts and hands. He roared with laughter as he looked me up and down. "There now, look at this! Ha! Ha! Ha! How fitting, Mary! Billy's blood is on your hands!"

I bared my teeth and lunged at him, hoping to rip out his throat. But his men held me fast. The Twin backhanded me so hard across the face I nearly fainted.

"Still yourself, Mary! Restrain your temper, bitch! Don't you see? Poor Billy would've been tormented all the rest of his days had I not shown him my mercy. We put dogs down, put them out of their misery, for less. Well, I'm not quite certain you heard me before, listen carefully now Mary: I... have... taken... all... your... ships..."

"You lie!" I said, spitting the blood pooling in mouth out on the sand. The one-eyed Twin's savage blow had split my lower lip. "My men are on their way to Ireland."

"No, no, Mary. We are friends. I would never lie to you. It's all true. And I want you to suffer knowing how colossal are your blunders before I hand you over to those putrid English shits. Old Havana? Isn't that where you sent your precious fleet? Aye, Old Havana it was and that is where we surprised your men as your ships sat defenseless riding anchor in the bay. My ships flew the King of Spain's royal colors, the *Cruz de Borgoña*, and I had this wonderful Spaniard with me too, a knowledgeable pilot who showed me the way. Poor, stupid Gilley, he hesitated when we pulled into the bay. He wasn't sure what to do. He let us come in close. The fool never even ran out his guns. After we took your ships, with hardly a shot fired mind you, I had Gilley bound to the main mast and, aye, you know what happened next. I took my time killing him. I used this very blade to filet him. Good God could that old sot squeal. I can still hear his pathetic cries for mercy ringing in my ears. Oh yes, that old drunk was not too proud to beg."

I lowered my head. I could feel all my strength draining from my limbs. All was lost. My poor, dear Gilley, dead. Hunter and Gilley, dead. All my men, dead. My body began trembling. Tears streamed down my cheeks.

The one-eyed Twin looked over at one of his men. "Bring the Spaniard to me!"

"Ohhh..." I offered meekly moments later when two thugs dragged Cortés inside the tent. The one-eyed Twin was right. My blundering had indeed been colossal. For the first time in my life, I knew the utter shame of absolute defeat, of total humiliation. The feeling was supremely wretched, ugly and unnatural. For the first time in my life, I wanted to fall down and die - not to escape to Heaven - I yearned to be no more. I yearned to cease to exist.

"Mary," Cortés called out to me, dropping to his knees and sobbing. He clasped his hands together as if he were in prayer. "They took my wife, my daughters. I had no choice. I did, I did not know it would come to this. I swear."

He saw Billy's dead body sprawled across a patch of blood-drenched sand and swallowed hard. "The boy, Mary, the boy is the one who betrayed you Mary, not me, never me. I am sorry, so very sorry."

"It's alright, Rodriguez," I said and tried offering him a reassuring smile. "You were right to protect your wife and daughters."

"Spaniard," the one-eyed Twin barked. "You and your arrangements with the Captain-General might be useful to me in the future. Spain and England I think will be at war before too long and God how I hate the fucking English. That makes us allies and nearly friends. You are free to go your way."

"And my family?"

"Your family? Why I'm no barbarian, sir. I never laid a hand on them. But I have men in Barcelona who will look in on them from time to time. If you ever cross me, well..."

"And Mary?"

"She's hardly any concern of yours. Now leave us. I suspect you're too squeamish for what will happen next."

After he made the sign of the cross, Cortés quickly crawled backwards until he was outside the tent. I wasn't certain whether to pity him or curse him as I watched him leave.

A man then popped his head inside the tent and told the one-eyed Twin that Carib warriors were massing in the jungle not far off. The giant nodded and turned to me again.

"Well, damn. It seems that we must cut our pleasant reunion short. So now you know most everything, Mary. Did you really think you could kill my brother, take his ship, steal our wealth and we'd let you sail away scot-free? Does your arrogance know no bounds? I've stripped you naked. I've taken everything from you. *Everything* I tell you. And Mary, I want the world to know..."

"Kill me you pig and be done with it," I offered defiantly, mumbling the words through my swollen, lower lip.

He laughed. "No, no, no. Kill you? No, I will not kill you. I know you are not afraid to die. Perhaps you even welcome death, eh?"

The rumbling sounds of a Carib war chant filled the tent. The Carib were not far away.

The Twin looked at one of his men holding me and jerked his head around. "Have the men ready the boats and then bring it to me."

The man snickered at me as he disappeared outside. I understood the man's glee when he returned a moment later with red-hot poker in his hand.

The one-eyed Twin took his dagger and cut through my trousers and undergarments. He ripped off all my clothes until I stood before him naked. He grabbed the poker and brought it close to my belly, close enough so I could feel the heat, then slowly moved the poker up along my torso until he reached my face, all the while grinning.

"Now Mary, truly you do stand before me naked. Your body is

exquisite. Your beauty is like none other. I dare say Venus would be envious. I should pass you around to my men but, being the diseased, rancid trollop you are, I fear you'll infect them all with the great pox, or something worse. I wanted to spend more time with you, show you what I can do with a razor, but I'm in a bit of a hurry so this will have to do. This is the mark of the sea serpent. It is my mark, Mary."

I turned my head away and closed my eyes.

But he grabbed me by my chin and yanked my head around. "Look at it damn your soul or I'll burn out both your eyes! That's it, that's my pretty. Look at it. This serpent is the symbol emblazoned on my banner and I expect you to bear it proudly for me until the end of your miserable days. This, you filthy bitch, is for our brother..."

And when the beast pressed the searing, hot metal against my skin, when he pressed the branding iron over my left breast, next to my heart and held it there, my flesh began to smoke and sizzle. I heard myself scream, and then I fainted.

When I came to, I found myself on a strange ship under sail, imprisoned inside a rope locker. The space was cramped, dark, hot and stuffy and when I tried to move my arms a terrible, shooting pain passed through my chest. And then I remembered the red-hot poker with the sea serpent brand. I pulled my blouse back and saw a bloody, round wound over my left breast, next to my heart. The wound looked infected. I couldn't help myself. I broke down and wept. Why had the pig just not killed me? Of course I knew the reason why. He wanted me to suffer pain worse than death. In this the one-eyed Twin was most successful.

I took in my new surroundings and tried to find something I could use as a weapon, not for my jailors, but for myself. With every breath I took death, my own death, ruled my every thought.

Time passed by slowly, painfully, in that rope locker as the ship plowed through the rolling sea. After my jailors had shut me in that locker they never let me out, not once, not until we reached Waterford one month later. And even then I was only outside long enough to be transferred, bound in chains and shackles, over to another, smaller vessel. All my hard muscles had vanished. My body was frail and stiff. I struggled with even walking.

But once this second ship put to sea, my circumstances improved dramatically. The ship's master was appalled at my condition and he had a kind heart. I was thin and pale and dirty. The iron shackles had rubbed the skin around my wrists and ankles raw. My clothes were filthy and in tatters. He took pity on me, unshackled me and even had his men make a simple tub for me to bathe in. He gave me fresh clothing to wear and an ointment for my wounds. I ate what the crew ate and I was permitted to roam freely about the deck. My health greatly improved over the next two weeks.

"You are," the ship's master asked me as we stood together at the rail midway through our journey, "Bloody Mary, Lady Mary from Westport, are you not?"

"Some call me by those names, aye."

"Ah."

"If you know who I am, why have you treated me with such kindness? Many think me wicked."

"I had a younger half-brother once, a fine, fine young man. He sailed on one of your ships a few years back."

"Oh?"

"Poor lad was lost at sea."

"I'm sorry to hear of it. What was his name?"

"Benjamin Jones."

"Benjamin Jones. His name sounds familiar, but I knew him not. If you wish to do me harm, if you wish to exact your revenge on me now, you go about it in a most peculiar way, sir."

"No. I hold no grudge against you, Madam. The sea takes who she will take. You paid a sizable stipend to his widow and to his two young daughters, my nieces, after he died. That money was a tremendous Godsend to his family."

"I am glad to hear of it. May I know your name?"

"The name is Crook, Madam. Charles Crook."

A warm and wonderful peace suddenly, inexplicably, embraced me as I knew, at that very moment, that what I was about to tell the ship's good master would absolutely come to pass. I blurted out the oddest thing.

"Well Master Charles Crook, when I am free, after I rally all my ships and men, I shall remember your kindness. I shall show you and your men my gracious mercy should our paths cross again. Your masters though are doomed."

Crook stared at me dumbfounded. He offered no reply.

A few days later Crook turned his ship into the Thames and we sailed up river until we reached the docks in London proper where English soldiers armed with long halberds and dressed all in black, mandilions, doublets, leather jerkins, paneled trunk hoses, nether stockings and feathered hats, all black, were waiting for me on the wharf. They led me away on foot in chains and tossed me into a dark and most depressing dungeon.

And yet, as I took in my grim surroundings, against all reason, I refused to accept that my life was forfeit. I refused to accept that death swinging from an English gallows - or worse - would be my sad and unfortunate end. I was born for more.

BOOK II

El Grande y Felicisima Armada

Chapter Eleven

eading books had become tiresome. I rose from my chair next to the window and moved over to the small table in the corner of my cell where I resumed my work sketching things, things that I had seen in the New World. I wasn't a particularly good artist with a stylus or with colored chalks, but I found drawing a pleasant distraction to while away the hours. My notebook was nearly full with fair renderings of ships and castles and lush Caribbean islands, with Spanish *conquistadors*, noble Africans and fearsome Indians covered gloriously from head to toe in war paint.

It had been some weeks since her gracious majesty's last visit. Nonetheless, I was certain the queen would come to see me at least one more time, to discuss, if nothing else, the whereabouts of whatever might be left of Dowlin's treasure or of buried, Aztec gold.

And after another month of idle waiting the day finally came. The jailor unlocked the door to my cell and commanded me to rise. But I was wrong about my visitor.

A man wearing a dark blue cloak with a hood he used to conceal his face slipped into my cell. I noted the sword and scabbard strapped to his side and the dagger tucked inside his boot. The jailor locked the door behind him and I prepared myself for the worst. Even little princes can disappear forever in the Tower without a trace they say. And then the man pulled his hood back to reveal his face and I gasped. I felt woozy and nearly fainted. I stared hard into his eyes too stunned to speak. My body began to tremble.

"Mary..."

"My God, my God, how, how?" I asked and started sobbing.

He caught me as I fell into his arms. We embraced and traded fast and furious kisses until I buried my face in his chest, crying uncontrollably. For long, dark months, heartache, shame and guilt had consumed me, had worn me down until I felt nothing. I had become little more than an empty shell struggling to get through each day. Now a flood of emotions overwhelmed me, nearly knocking me off my feet.

Hunter held me close and gently stroked my hair. He let me weep. After I calmed down he kissed my forehead, raised my chin to look at me and smiled. I could see the warmth, the reassurance and compassion in his eyes. I could feel his love envelope me. He kissed my cheeks. He used his thumbs to brush away my tears.

"Mary, Mary..." he said tenderly.

I stared at him, still uncertain. For a fleeting moment I wondered if might be going mad.

"How, James?" I asked again, struggling to understand. "I saw you die!"

Hunter laughed. "Did you now? Did you indeed? Odd, I don't feel dead. It was not my time. I have too much living yet to do! Mary, Mary, Mary, I will die an old man in my own bed with you, I pray, lying at my side."

"But, I saw the one-eyed Twin shoot you down. I saw his men toss your body into the sea!"

"The Cyclops shot me true enough after I ran his brother through and his men did indeed toss me overboard, thinking that I was dead." Hunter paused to unbutton his shirt and showed me a round scar. "I'm no ghost, Mary. The fool should've put a lead ball between my eyes, just to make certain I would never breathe again."

"My God, you were only wounded."

"Aye, the ball struck a rib and broke it. Hurt like hell, but the wound was hardly mortal. After they tossed me overboard I held my breath for as long as I could and played dead. And then it was an easy swim in the dark to shore. I ran past the camp and quietly slipped into the jungle."

"Did any of the lads make it?"

"More than I dared hoped at first."

"How did you make your way back to England?"

"Ah, our good man Henry helped us out there. The attack infuriated Chief Paka Wokili. A handful of his people were killed I'm sorry to say. The Twins knew better than to linger on his beach for very long and left Guadeloupe without searching the jungle for the rest of us. After my wound healed, the old chief agreed to lend me a pair of war canoes. I took as many men as I could with me, about twenty in all, and left the rest behind under MacGyver's charge. We rowed for the Port of Spain and there we parted ways. Some of the lads stayed in Trinidad. Some signed on with ships sailing for Europe as I did."

"How amazing. I'm sorry, I'm so terribly sorry for what I've done, James. How, how will you, how can you ever forgive me?"

"Forgive you? For what you've done? Oh no, no, no, Mary. You did no wrong. This wrong was done to you. It was done to all of us. And that twin-headed monster shall pay dearly with their miserable lives for it - I swear it."

"I was arrogant and careless. I was a fool."

"No, Mary. You were bold and fearless. And you were betrayed."

211

"I let them shoot you down."

"No, no. Not so my darling girl. Stop this now. You are punishing yourself unfairly. There was nothing you could have done for me or me for you. I saw the men holding you down on the *Star* as the taller brother and I dueled. The Twins concocted a nearly flawless plan. And yet here we are. We live and we are reunited. God favors you, Mary."

"I don't think God favors any of us, James. But tell me now, and be quick about it too before the jailor returns to take you away from me. What are you doing here? Have they arrested you? On what charge?"

Hunter chuckled. "No arrest, no charges that I know of. The High Sheriff of Dublin and his men found me wandering about Waterford asking questions about you. I knew you were alive. Carib warriors saw the Twins bring you ashore, take you inside a tent for a time and then row you back out to one of Twins' ships. Waterford is where I learned the Twins had served you up to the English. The queen's men insisted I accompany them to London. But they informed me of no charges. They placed no irons on me and as you can see, I have my sword and daggers and carry two pistols stashed against the small of my back. In truth, these men treated me with great deference. They were most cordial."

"What then?"

"I know not. What I do know is that the Constable of the Tower promised me no one would disturb us until the morning."

"The queen's work," I said.

"You've acquired some interesting new friends, Mary."

"Friends? No, James. Though the queen has treated me most kindly, she will turn me over to her royal prosecutor after I no longer amuse her. And once her prosecutor is finished with me at trial, he'll introduce me to the queen's royal executioner."

"Let's not worry about such matters now. I'm hardly privy to the queen's thoughts or designs. But I doubt your purpose here is to amuse her. They say she is most wise. They say she is quite clever. Hmmm, I wonder?"

"Wonder? Wonder about what, James?"

Hunter grabbed me by the arms and smiled. "'Tis a mystery to me, my dearest Mary. But be of good cheer - the queen would hardly show this much interest in you today only to hand you over to her headsman tomorrow."

Hunter then started unbuttoning my blouse.

I placed my hands over his to stop him. "No, James."

"Hush now, I know what he did," Hunter said softly and gently brushed my hands aside. He opened my blouse and glanced down at my breast. "Ah, well now, we've both been scarred. This is a mark you should take pride in."

"What?" I asked dumbfounded. "I shall carve this hideous scar, this abomination, out of my flesh if I happen upon a knife or piece of broken glass."

"You see a scar? No, Mary, no. You are wrong, so very wrong. I see a badge of great courage. You should embrace this mark and be proud."

"Courage?" I asked, confused. I broke down and started sobbing all over again. "The one-eyed pi... pi... pig killed Gil... Gilley and all the others. He took, took, everything from me and then, then, he dis... disfigured me with his... his mark to... to... to complete my, my humiliation. This scar is meant to... to... remind me, to, to show all others that I'm, I'm, his property."

"Aye, Tom, Ben, Alby, Hadley and many good lads are dead and our ships and wealth were taken. We grieve for the loss of our fallen brothers. But here I stand and you have men who will rally to your side and fight for you! Aye, the one-eyed pig left his mark on you - so take it for your own, raise it on your banner when you shout your battle cry! Where's the mighty lioness who led us from the Old World into the New, who bested pirates and took us through swamps and jungle, never wavering, not once, to find lost, Aztec gold? Where's the lioness who stole my heart and fused it with her own?"

His eyes turned misty. He seized me in his arms with mad passion and kissed me hard. I yielded to his lust. I surrendered to my own burning desires. We furiously stripped off our clothes and tumbled into my bed. We shamelessly made love ruckus and sweet, again and again. We giggled like adolescents discovering love for the first time. When our ardor became too loud the jailer rapped on the door to ask us if all was well and we laughed. But once we had satisfied our cravings of the flesh, after our bodies were spent and could do no more, we held each other quietly, silently, for a long while, savoring our exquisite moment together in love's afterglow. And then we talked. We talked all through the night - a night I feared might be our last together.

In the morning, as shafts of golden light poured in through my cell's small window and settled on my pillow, the jailer came as promised to take Hunter away from me. I marshaled every ounce of strength I had as Hunter kissed me farewell. I watched in silence as he walked off. I refused to shed even a single tear. When the jailer closed and bolted the door to shut me in, I was again alone.

The days passed into weeks and I grew more despondent, worse than before. Hunter had given me hope and hope is a dangerous thing in a place like the Tower, especially when both mind and heart are fragile. One day a voice in my head said to me: *Mary, to win everything, you must lose everything first.* This voice repeated these same words to me over and over again. I could not shake them. At times I wondered if I was perhaps again delusional with the fever, or going mad.

And then the day arrived when her august majesty, the Queen of England, returned to the Tower to visit me. I stood and curtsied with sincere respect. She took a seat across from me as she always did and Wexford, her faithful consort, took his place at the small desk in the corner of my cell to record my words with pen and paper. She looked at me dispassionately and began our conversation by asking me to clarify certain portions of my story here and there. I obliged her gladly. But after I had finished answering all her questions, a great silence fell between us. The queen seemed distracted by other, weightier matters. Or perhaps she was considering all that I had said and was having doubts about my story. There was no sweetness in her manner. I began to fret.

"What," the queen finally asked me, "are we to do with you, Mary?"

"Your Majesty?"

"What shall be your fate, girl?"

"I know not, your Majesty. I suppose a trial, a verdict of guilty certainly and then I'll be hanged or beheaded for my crimes."

"And does this prospect trouble you?"

"Not greatly, no. I have seen the face of death before. I should have been its victim long ago. I should have died that day I witnessed my father being murdered in his shop. I should have died at sea a dozen times or more. And I should have died on the beach at Guadeloupe that night the Twins attacked my camp and took me. Every day has been a gift, a blessing. Perhaps your Majesty might indulge me, might consider one small favor though?"

The queen arched an eyebrow. "Oh, a favor you say? A royal favor? And what favor might that be?"

"I would not care to have my body left on display for all the world to see rotting away in a cage at Wapping for many months. Perhaps your Majesty could find it in her noble heart to show me some pity, allow my body to be buried at sea?"

"Pity, pity for you, dear sister?" the queen scoffed. "Ha! We think not! Your time here in the Tower has muddled your senses. Why would a beautiful woman with title and possessions, a woman with wits and cunning in abundance, need any pity from us? We pity those poor wretches who have crossed you, whose bones lay scattered across the ocean deep."

I was taken aback by the queen's words. I did not know what to say and so I said nothing.

"You seem oddly willing to embrace death quick enough, Lady Mary. Or perhaps I should address you as Captain Mary? How can this be so when you now know your Hunter is alive and well, a man we've heard you say on more than one occasion that you are very fond of?"

"Knowing he is alive and well but out of reach has eased my pain but a little."

"Ah, we supposed as much. Now, tell us, you spoke of crimes. Let us have frank and honest speech between us. What crimes should you be tried for precisely? What high crimes have you committed to warrant a hanging at Execution Dock or a beheading at the Tower?"

"Beg pardon? Your Majesty has heard my story."

"Indeed we have. You have told us tales of murder, treason, kidnapping, rape, theft and pillaging. Which one of these heinous crimes are you guilty of?"

"I've killed, your Majesty. I have killed many men."

"Ah, yes. So you have told us - in striking detail. But the law is often very tolerant about killing. Isn't that so my right and trusty Lord Wexford?"

Wexford laid his pen down on the desk and cocked his head to one side before he looked over at me. "Quite so my Queen, quite so. Why, a kingdom may go to war and solders must kill. That is no crime, your Majesty. A man may rightly kill to defend himself, his family, his hearth, his home and certainly these matters are not crimes. A king or queen may execute subjects for treason to protect the realm. Neither is this a crime under our laws. A person may - ."

Wexford stopped in midsentence when the queen raised her hand to cut him off. "Thank you, my Lord Wexford. We understand your point quite clearly. Yes Lady Mary, we have heard your story and we have been a most attentive listener. Some months ago we charged our High Lord Marshal with the task of examining your story too and he could find no flaw in it. You have been remarkably candid and honest with us - more than many, even amongst some at court in whom we place great trust. Indeed high crimes have been committed, but not by you."

"I don't understand, your Majesty."

"Oh come girl. A clever woman can always recognize another

clever woman. Do you think us daft?"

"Certainly not, your Majesty."

"Good. Then give us a little credit, Mary. You've committed no crime against this kingdom, well, none leastwise that would warrant a hanging. Your dabbling in smuggling is of no interest to us. You've lived and survived most of your years in another world, in a dark and dangerous world where people live and die by dark and dangerous rules. You've killed men, true, men who deserved killing for their wickedness and perfidies we think. As we see things, you've done our realm a good service. It is you, my dear, who has been the victim of murder, rape, kidnapping and violence."

I must have looked at the queen in shock. "So what is to be done with me?"

"We would see the mark," the queen commanded.

I hesitated for a moment. But when the queen frowned at me with displeasure, I stood and undid the lace to my blouse and reluctantly exposed my breast for her.

The queen stood and pulled my blouse back off my shoulders. She considered both my breasts and then focused her attention on my scar without emotion.

"This Twin was right in this at least, you are an exquisite creature, now what to do with you indeed?" she said and began relacing my blouse for me. "Your Master Hunter is right my dear. You must take pride in this mark. You must take this mark for your own. As for what is to be done with you, well, you are to be released on the morrow and we shall issue you a royal pardon for any past transgressions. We have one condition, however. We must have your word that you will never take up arms against us."

A sudden flood of emotions overwhelmed me. I fell to my knees before the queen, bowed my head and wept.

The queen leaned over and kissed me on the head. "Do you love this Hunter of yours?"

I wiped the tears from my eyes before looking up at the queen. "With all my heart I do your Majesty."

"And we are assured he is worthy of your love. Go to him. Find a quiet place to live. Raise a family. Do this with our blessing. But if you return to the sea you love Mary, you tempt fate and we fear for your wellbeing. It would distress us greatly if any harm befell you as we have become very fond of you."

"Is it your command then, your Majesty, I not return to sea?"

The queen smiled. She held my chin in her hand. "No, it is our wish, nothing more. You have O'Malley blood. We know you are a free spirit with a fiery heart. We know you have debts to settle too. A man shall visit you tomorrow. If you choose to return to life at sea Mary, you must do so on his terms. Our interests must not be in opposition."

"Your Majesty is most gracious."

"Did you know you have a half-sister named Grace O'Malley, or *Gráinne Ní Mháille* in the old Gaelic? She is causing us some mischief in the Irish Sea of late."

"I know her not, your Majesty."

"No matter. Do we have your word that you shall never take up arms against us?"

"You do, your Majesty," I said and kissed her hand.

"And if you again have warships and men-at-arms at your beck and call, do we have your word that you will defend your Queen should evil from across the seas threaten our royal person?"

"I swear it."

"Good. If you will give us your binding oath on these matters later with the customary formalities, then all can be forgiven my good, my most precious sister. We shall miss you, Mary..."

Just as the Sovereign Queen of England, France and Ireland and the *Fidei Defensor* had promised, a man came to visit me the next day, a man with the harsh countenance of a strict schoolmaster, a man with a familiar face. I struggled to understand.

"Madam," the Englishman said as he removed his fine hat and bowed before me most elegantly.

"You!"

"I go by many names but *you* is hardly one of them," he replied with no humor in his tone. "One of my names is John Martin as you may recall. In Santo Domingo you showed me kindness, my lady. You spared my life and put money in my pocket. You gave me a sporting chance. Even though you asked for nothing in return from me in Santo Domingo, I am here to repay my debt."

"I would be most indebted to you, sir, if only you were able to show me your kindness. I take it by your fine apparel, by your cockiness and by the fact that you have privileges inside the Tower, that you are a gentleman of substance and influence. But you should know sir that I have the queen's attention and she may yet be fond of my neck."

"Ah Madam, you have wits to match your charm and beauty. You do not trust me and it is well that this is so for I am not a man to be trusted. But you underestimate your friends. And I assure you, I am indeed your friend. That much you can trust. I was the one who first whispered your story, what I knew of it at least, into the queen's ear and I am here now as the queen's good servant."

"I see," I said. "And how, may I ask, do you serve the queen cooped-up in the Tower with me on this fine day?"

"Did the queen not say to expect me?"

"Her majesty told me a man would come to visit me though she did not say his name. On this, however, she was most clear: her majesty intends to release me, to grant me a royal pardon. But if I choose to return to sea again, I must do so on the terms this man gives me."

Martin removed a rolled parchment from his coat and undid a red ribbon, letting the parchment unravel. "Quite so, my lady. I am the man the queen spoke of and I have in my hand a *Letter of Marque and Reprisal* signed and sealed by Her Royal Majesty on this very day. There is an undeclared war being waged between England, France and Spain, in part over the New World, a world you have become well-acquainted with. If you accept this commission, you are pledging your allegiance to the Queen of England, France and

Ireland. You sail the seas and oceans as an English privateer."

"A privateer?"

"Yes. It is a most dangerous and short-lived business for amateurs and fools. But for those who can sail and fight, for those who are clever and can keep their wits about them during moments of great peril, the work can be most lucrative."

"I can sail and I can fight."

"Yes, I know. Your skills at sea have not gone unnoticed."

"I can willingly pledge my allegiance to England too and unlike some at court I suspect, my pledge will have value. But many of my men will not give the same pledge if it means fighting against their Irish kin."

"Yes, I anticipated this conundrum as did the queen. Her majesty is interested in humbling Spanish arrogance and checking French interests in the New World which grow stronger by the day. The New World brings new world politics, Mary. You and your men will not be required to fight against your own countrymen. But neither, my lady, can you fight with them if their fight is against the queen."

"I see. Pray tell me sir, who are you exactly?"

"Exactly? Exactly I am a man of many faces, many names and with many assorted talents. When first we met I was a man in need of a fresh privy bucket as you might recall. But let me answer you more plainly in this way if it will help you any: I count among my friends Francis Walsingham and I am to the queen, professionally, what your Hunter is to you."

I knew the name Walsingham. He was rumored to be the queen's spymaster. "Hmmm... How very interesting. Will your travels take you back to the New World then?"

"I should think so, yes."

"Well, I can sail and I can fight as I say. There are even some who think me clever. But I have no ships and without ships I'd make a poor privateer."

"Ah, allow me to remedy this unfortunate circumstance, at least in part. There is a respectable sloop moored down by the docks at Gravesend. She is old and a bit clumsy, but she is seaworthy. It is a start. I inspected her myself some days ago. She is, with the queen's blessing, yours."

"How will I find this sloop?"

"Oh, I suspect you'll have no difficulty there. I can't resist giving you a hint though: look for a yellow-gold ensign flying off her bowsprit staff."

"I'll need men to sail her."

"I shouldn't worry about that."

"Is she armed?"

"Alas, no. But you are a resourceful woman. Ah, that reminds me. I have a second gift for you, Lady Mary. I have it on good authority that there is this very fine nao, French-built, being repaired and reconditioned at Waterford after suffering some minor damage recently when she ran aground. She bears a striking resemblance to a ship once known as the *Phantom*, or so men say."

"Indeed? Do you know the brothers who call themselves the Twins?"

"I know of them."

"Are they in the queen's good graces?"

"Certainly not."

"The *Phantom*, laid-up in Waterford you say?"

"So I said."

I took the *Letter of Marque and Reprisal* from Martin's hands and countersigned the document on the corner table using the very pen Lord Wexford used to transcribe my story for the queen.

"What happens if the Spanish capture my men or me as we raid the Spanish Main?"

Martin took the original commission back and handed me a copy. He took my hand and kissed it. "The Queen will deny the authenticity of the document you hold in your hands of course, claim this copy was forged."

"Ah, of course. The Spanish hang pirates."

Martin finally cracked a smile. "Indeed they do, Madam. Our adventures into the New World are not for the faint hearted. I must take my leave of you now Lady Mary and you must make ready to depart these dreary quarters and regain your freedom. Your past sins have now been forgiven. You are reborn. Have a care with your new life dear lady. I pray we meet again, as friends and allies always. I wish you Godspeed in your new journey..."

As the outer doors of the Tower closed behind me, I stepped out into a fine and pleasant snowfall. The entire city was blanketed in unspoiled, white powder. The lamplighters had already made their rounds. It was dark and London's streets were deserted. I stood outside the Tower and filled my lungs with clean, fresh air. I took a moment to relish the glorious taste of freedom.

I had no plan except to find a certain sloop flying a yellow-gold ensign. I had no money for a carriage or for a ferry boat and so I started walking. I buttoned up my coat against the evening's chill and hid my dagger, both coat and dagger were parting gifts to me from the Constable of the Tower, and then I crossed the river and headed east for Gravesend. The walk though was more than I had bargained for. By the time I finally reached my destination my legs were wobbly and the souls of my feet were burning.

My mind continued churning out ideas at a furious pace as I walked up and down the docks at Gravesend, searching for a sloop flying a yellow-gold ensign. I needed men. I needed money. And I would need a plan to exact my revenge. Yes, revenge - bloody and swift - ruled my thoughts. Jesus preached forgiveness and love they say. He gave the Old World the New Testament. But I would return to the New World with a sword in one hand and the Old Testament in the other and God could sort out the right or wrong of it on judgment day. *Lex talionis*, the law of revenge, a fashionable new expression in London, is what I had in mind.

Martin was right. The sloop was not hard to find, though I had passed her by three times. The yellow-gold ensign Martin had spoken of hung limp against the staff, caked in ice and snow, and I had missed it.

When I stepped onboard the sloop, three men startled me as they stepped out of the shadows. I planted my feet firmly and swiftly drew my dagger, unafraid. If this was the queen's plan to quietly see me disappear, so be it. But I would not go easily, not without a fight.

"Easy there, woman!" Hunter bellowed and laughed. Atwood and Efendi rushed to my side to embrace me. My heart soared. Delirious with joy I kissed and hugged them both. And then, to my annoyance, I broke down again, weeping like some silly girl.

"We have a hot meal and warm clothing waiting for you below, Mary," Hunter offered cheerfully and took my hand.

"Oh, I am indeed chilled to the bone and famished too!" I replied. "English weather does not suit me and the walk was long. Your gifts are most welcome!"

Hunter laughed. "You walked? I would have thought your high and mighty friend would have brought you to us in her royal barge."

"She gave me freedom. I am content."

We went below to the ship's galley to share a meal and to tell our stories in turn. Hunter had even thought to bring wine and plenty of it.

Atwood and Efendi had been on shore with most of the men in Old Havana they told me, helping load the cargo onto the barges, when ships flying Spanish colors entered the bay. The Twins - who my men at first thought were the Spanish coming to intercept a few smugglers - struck fast and hard with hardly a shot fired, easily overwhelming Gilley and the rest of our men onboard the ships. Atwood and Efendi, powerless to help Gilley, could only watch from shore as the Twins seized our ships and executed all my officers. Gilley, Green, Fox and Ferguson, all very dear to me, were butchered. When the Twins launched boats carrying platoons of men to storm the beach and seize our cargo, Atwood and Efendi gathered the remnants of our men and scattered on foot north towards Havana where they later found a sturdy ship to steal for the long and perilous voyage back home to Ireland.

"How many men can we muster?" I asked.

"Two hundred, perhaps a little more, Mary," Atwood said. "But we'll need a larger boat than this old tub and we'll need money for provisions and heavy guns. Do you have anything left, Mary?"

"No. My only treasure in all the world is you three men unless, of course, any of you wish to pursue better prospects. I'll hold no grudge."

Atwood grunted. "Did the English torture you in the Tower?"

"No. Why do you ask, Jacob?"

"Something has addled your brains. Better prospects indeed! We are bound by the Ten Rules or have you forgotten?"

"No, I haven't forgotten," I said and reached across the table to squeeze Atwood's hand. "Thank you, Jacob."

"Good, we're with you whatever your plan might be Mary. But I pray it includes running down those dogs who call themselves the Twins and snuffing out their lives."

"One Twin may be dead already," I offered. "Hunter ran him through the chest and when last I saw him he was nearly dead. But aye, the Twins are prominent in my thoughts. There will be a reckoning, I swear it."

Efendi whipped out his knife and let it fly across the table, hitting the cabin door dead-center. "I am with you always, Mary. Allah rewards those who forgive. But the *Quran* also teaches that the recompense for an evil is an evil like thereof. We owe the Twins a pain or two and I will hone my skills for the day we catch them crawling out from whatever filthy lair they hide in."

Hunter reached under his chair and produced a swatch of yellow-gold cloth folded neatly into a triangle. "If you accept this gift, my lady," he said, while spreading the material out across the table. "Then I too am yours to command."

I stared at Hunter's gift with mixed feelings of joy and sadness. His gift was an ensign of yellow-gold with a red sea serpent emblazoned in the center, the same serpent the one-eyed Twin had burned deep into my flesh, a sea serpent poised to strike.

I nodded. "Aye, your terms are satisfactory. I embrace this

mark as my own, as my coat-of-arms. This flag shall be our victory banner."

"Excellent!" Hunter said with a grand smile. "Have you a plan, Mary?"

"We gather as many of our men as we can and then we sail on to Waterford."

Hunter's smile instantly vanished. "Mary, please. You aren't thinking of attacking the Twins in their own stronghold?"

"Hunter, have you lost your senses?" I asked teasingly. "Attack the Twins where they are strongest? God forbid! But there is something that belongs to me in Waterford and I shall have it back."

"Why not ignore whatever has caught your fancy in Ireland?" Atwood asked softly. "If the English catch you again they'll hang you or lop off your head for certain. Perhaps it is best if we simply leave the Old World behind us - quietly - without risking any more trouble?"

"What we do in Waterford, gentlemen, we do with the queen's good blessing," I replied. I removed the letter of marque from my coat pocket and unrolled the parchment over Hunter's yellow-gold ensign.

"English privateers, eh?" Atwood asked, absently scratching the stubble on his chin as he perused the commission.

"Aye," I replied. "There's a storm coming to the New World, a great and terrible storm of guns and soldiers. We saw this storm brewing when we smuggled goods in and out of the Caribbean. The French, the Dutch and the English, are all envious of Spanish wealth and power. Even the Germans and one or more of the Italian kingdoms have made claims in the New World. Only God knows who will prevail in the end. But fate has chosen the side I fight for now. The queen granted me a royal pardon on the condition I never take up arms against her or oppose her interests. I agreed to her majesty's terms. I gave her my solemn pledge and I will honor that pledge and so my allegiance must be with the English. But you gentlemen are free to choose as you like, to go your own way. The Ten Rules do not address this extraordinary circumstance and hence none of you are bound by them here. I release you from your oath."

"As I said, we are with you, Mary," Atwood repeated. "We are with you, staunchly so. But I don't know how the lads will take to sailing for the English as privateers."

Hunter grunted and rolled his eyes.

"Whatever flag flies off our mizzen gaff," I said, "is of little consequence. We sail for ourselves. The queen assured me that we would never be required to fight against our own. Her majesty's natural enemies are Spain, Portugal and France."

Hunter picked up the letter of marque and chuckled. "Stealing from the Spanish or the French I doubt will offend any of our men."

Chapter Twelve

ime to go I told myself and took a deep breath. I had over one hundred and fifty men-at-arms with me, men we had rounded up mostly from County Mayo after sailing from England to Westport. Most were tough and seasoned sailors, battle-harden veterans, men who had sailed with me in the New World or back in the old days when we were free spirits, crisscrossing the Irish Sea with impunity.

Phantom, renamed *Mary's Folly* some had heard, had been removed from a floating dry dock earlier in the day and was sitting peacefully at anchor out in the middle of Waterford's bay. The streets of the city were quiet. The sky was clear and studded with all the brilliant stars in heaven. Not the best of nights for lurking about on the water, but not the worst of nights either. I could see my breath in the crisp, cold air as I gently worked the longboat's tiller. My men rowed quietly, pulling at their muffled oars with even, measured strokes towards our target. We moved across the bay likes swans gracefully moving across a still pond with barely ripple made. We saw no sign of *Medusa's Head* and I was grateful because we could never hope to take that ghastly brute on without a lot more men.

I had twenty lads with me in one boat and Hunter had another twenty more with him in the other. Atwood stayed behind with the sloop and our reinforcements.

We raised our oars and silently glided up alongside the *Phantom* in the dark unnoticed. Efendi was the first to spring into action. He shimmied up the anchor cable and carefully eased himself over the rail. A moment later we heard a soft groan and then a dull thump, followed by another and then another and we knew Efendi's sharp knives had done their deadly work. It is well for men to fear the night. With the ship's night watch of three down, Efendi dropped a half dozen lines over the side and waved us up.

I kept ten men with me on deck while Hunter took the rest and went below to round up any stragglers. My squad moved with purpose, raising spars and unfurling sail and then to save time we cut the anchor cable. I grimaced at losing that anchor. A new one would cost me a pretty penny later. It is odd the things we think about sometimes.

After I gave the signal, Atwood eased the sloop in close, just in case my plan went awry and we needed extra muscle - or if everything went truly wrong and we needed to escape. But our first venture into lawful piracy and murder was rolling along smoothly. We quickly had *Phantom* secured and underway.

I took the tiller in my hands and pointed the ship's nose east, towards the open sea. Nothing, or so I told myself, could stop us now.

Hunter bolted up the companionway wearing a victory smile. "Found twenty souls below Mary, all sleeping soundly in their hammocks. We bound and gagged each one without too much fuss."

I nodded and let out a sigh of relief. We truly were going to make it.

"Any provisions onboard, James?"

"Not enough to get us to the West Indies."

"Well then, we have some hunting to do - Master Hunter."

Hunter laughed and went aloft, climbing all the way to the crow's nest to have a look around. When he reached the top, I watched him attach an ensign, my battle flag, to the masthead. The yellow-gold banner, with a red sea serpent poised to strike emblazoned in the center, unwrapped itself and fluttered freely in the light breeze. I must confess I felt a twinge of pride. I slipped my hand inside my blouse and touched the hideous scar over my left breast. My thoughts turned to that awful day an ocean away and to those I'd lost. I could feel the tears pooling around my eyes. But the sorrow didn't last. Neither did the pride. I needed to focus on the task at hand dispassionately, unburdened by any emotion. Yes, the sea serpent was now mine and I had retaken *Phantom* - but I would not be content until I had taken much, much more.

And then - no warning - there was a terrific BOOM off our starboard bow, followed seconds later by a number of smaller explosions and popping sounds. I flinched. We all flinched. My first thought was that somehow all was lost. I snapped my head around just in time to see a small storehouse on the docks vanish in a ball of smoke and flame. Debris went flying everywhere. Bits and pieces of wood, metal, glass and stone peppered the water all around us.

I looked up at the masthead and caught Hunter grinning down at me like some puerile, schoolboy prankster. Before we had launched our assault on *Phantom*, Hunter had disappeared for a time with the longboat and ten men, rowing for the docks. For what purpose he had refused to tell me.

"Good God, Hunter what have you done?"

He cupped his hands around his mouth. "Why nothing, Mary," he shouted down to me. "Some fool must have been careless in storing his gunpowder in that shack. I love a good explosion - don't you? Look, look Mary! Rockets are shooting off! How splendid! Waterford is sending us off with fireworks, she sending us off in style. What a grand victory celebration this is, all in your honor!"

As I watched the red and white rockets lighting-up the night sky all around us, I was stricken with the giggles. The send-off was indeed grand. It felt good to laugh again.

Once we reached the sea, we shortened sail and Atwood transferred most of his crew over to me using the longboats we had in tow. *Phantom* would need men to work her great guns for what I had in mind next. Then we headed north to prowl the Irish Sea, to look for ships belonging to the Twins.

Phantom was mine again. But now we needed money to provision her. With a single shot across the bow, we snagged five meager vessels in rapid succession and one real beauty, a three hundred ton caravel with graceful lines. One ship was English and we let her go. Another vessel was hauling legal cargo out of Dublin and we let her go. The other four, including the caravel, belonged to the Twins or to rival clans and were loaded down with smuggled goods. We kept this plunder for ourselves. Our prisoners talked freely and we learned that the taller Twin, the one Hunter had run through the chest in Guadeloupe, had recovered from his wounds and was still very much alive. I was almost glad to hear it. I wanted the pleasure of finishing him off for myself.

The Twins would discover that they were missing several ships soon enough, including the powerful *Phantom*, and we dared not linger in hostile waters for very long. We had to work fast. So we laid on the canvas and took our prizes, top speed, on to Liverpool in the midst of a driving snowstorm. We pushed the vessels hard. After we reached Liverpool, I kept the handsome caravel for myself but sold the other ships and their cargoes off cheaply. We used the proceeds to buy provisions for our long voyage back across the barren sea, for our expedition back to the New World.

But before we set our sails to leave England behind us, I gathered our prisoners on the wharf with snow flurries whipping all around us. I scrutinized the face of each man, looking for anyone from that night of bloody slaughter in Guadeloupe. I saw no one familiar.

"You may all live or you may all die together this day," I told them as I shivered against the cold. Not even my heavy coat and scarf could keep me warm. "I wish to know if any of you were with the Twins in the New World."

No one uttered a sound.

"Very well, I'll have the swivels loaded with grapeshot and I'll splatter your guts all across this wharf. Grapeshot is an ugly way to die."

"We're merchant sailors, not soldiers," a faceless voice cried out.

"None of us have been to the New World," another man

added.

"No? Tell me this at least: how many ships did the Twins take with them to the New World?"

"Four, they took four ships," a third man offered. And then a fourth man readily agreed and soon there were a number of heads bobbing up and down, nodding in agreement.

I decided these men had no reason to lie about how many ships the Twins had taken with them to the New World. "You tell those two pillicocks when you see them next," I said, placing my hands on my hips, "those twin pigs you call your masters, tell them Bloody Mary has risen from the dead."

I leaned close to Atwood's ear. "Jacob, the Twins did indeed have four ships when they attacked us in Guadeloupe. How many ships attacked you in Old Havana?"

"Seven, Mary. So the Twins must have had help from our Spanish friends. But we paid the Spanish plenty. Why, I wonder?"

"I wonder why myself."

"Do you recognize any of these men?"

"No, Mary."

The snow changed to sleet, into a thick, heavy slush, as my men and I boarded our ships. The gooey mixture started clinging to the rails, to the masts and rigging. Ships across the harbor were transformed into delicate crystal, into lovely ornaments floating on the water. No one would be following us in such weather. We left our bewildered prisoners behind on the wharf stranded along England's cold and dreary shores. They looked like icicles. But just before my men cast off the mooring lines, I went to the aftercastle where there was a wooden placard nailed into a beam just below the fore rail. Chiseled across the placard in counter-relief in gold lettering was the inscription: *Mary's Folly*.

I took my knife and pried the placard off. I went to the rail and tossed the wood over to the crowd of men huddled on the wharf. "A parting gift," I told them. "Something to remember me by. And I shall well remember you. I've seen your faces. I've marked each of you well. You can all keep your lives today but, if I catch you with the Twins tomorrow, well, I wouldn't count on God for any mercy..."

Our journey across the broad Atlantic was quick and uneventful. After we reached Guadeloupe, we glided into her quiet bay and dropped anchor near the shore. We saw a crowd of several hundred men, women and children assemble along the beach, curious to see who we were. Most were Carib, but we also saw a number of Irishmen and Moors mixed in.

I sat at the bow of the lead boat as my men dipped their oars in the water. I recognized MacGyver first, waving wildly at me. And standing next to MacGyver I saw Henry beating his bare chest - newly tattooed with a sword crossed over a battle axe - and yelling up at the sky, beside himself with joy. I was thrilled to see them both.

MacGyver rushed out into the surf to help me step off the longboat. "Mary! My God, I can't believe my eyes! You're alive! You're alive! And you've come back!"

"Michael, it warms my heart to see you well," I said as we waded through the knee-high surf together locked arm-in-arm.

Then Henry rushed over and surprised me when he wrapped his arms around me and embraced me warmly. He knelt before me, took my hands and kissed them both.

"My goodness, Henry! 'Tis good to see you too!"

"Lady Mary, Lady, Mary, welcome home!" he said. And when he stood he broke into a huge smile, flaunting his new teeth for me. He had filed his front teeth down into sharp points and I wondered if the rumors about the Carib were true. Some say they are cannibals. No matter. Yes, I thought, I am home.

"It is good to be back, Henry. Why the tattoos?"

"Paka Wokili has no sons. I will be chief after he returns to the sky. He has said. His word is law."

"Oh? Congratulations my liege. You are now Prince Henry!

Chief Paka Wokili, will he agree to see me?"

"Oh, yes, yes, Mum. I am sure, I am sure."

"Good. I must try to make amends with our great friend and host."

"What is amends?"

"Peace."

And then the rest of my men, marooned on Guadeloupe for long months, surrounded me. They took turns shaking my hand or embracing me and more than one tough-nosed mariner broke down and wept.

"How many are we?" I finally asked the crowd.

"We are forty-two strong, Mary," MacGyver answered. "We buried thirty-one of ours and eleven Carib after the ambush. The rest of our lads set out on the ocean in war canoes after James left. We haven't seen any of them since."

"Let's hope," Hunter said as he and his crew dragged their longboat up on the beach, "they were as lucky as me finding a way home."

And then Chief Paka Wokili, wearing his magnificent headdress but not a stich of clothing more, emerged from the jungle with his royal retinue in tow wielding his long spear. I raced over to him, fell to my knees and wept before him.

"Please, Henry," I said. "Tell the chief I beg his forgiveness for bringing death and violence to his island."

After Henry finished translating my words, the chief gently laid his hand upon my head and spoke to me in a soft and soothing voice. "Lady Mary," Henry said. "Chief Paka Wokili says take strength from your anger. Then you must sit on your enemy, um, no, no, you must step, aye, you must step on your enemy. You must step on his throat and pull out his heart."

I looked up at Chief Paka Wokili and narrowed my eyes. "The day will come," I promised, "when I will cut off his pig head. I swear it."

The chief nodded in satisfaction. He whispered something in Henry's ear, lifted me to my feet and embraced me.

"Lady Mary, Chief Paka Wokili makes honor. You today and forever his daughter."

Now I was the daughter of a king and the sister of a queen. I took the chief's hands and kissed them.

We pitched our tents along the narrow shore and set up camp among the swaying palms. I wasn't concerned about the Twins, not yet. Even if they had a mind to follow us, which I doubted they would do with any haste as they knew I would be waiting, we had a two or three week head-start on them at least. We prepared a magnificent feast on the beach. We built large bonfires and slaughtered pigs and sheep. We ate and drank to excess and exchanged our stories in turn with care. We offered-up our prayers to our fallen comrades too and wept until we could weep no more. And after we had had our fill of good food and mellow wine, after we had let our grief run dry, I gathered my officers around me. Hunter, Atwood, Efendi and MacGyver all plopped themselves down next to me and we held a council of war. We needed a plan.

I rolled a chart of the Caribbean out across the sand and searched the faces of my brothers. "Well?" I asked.

"We should sail here first," Hunter said, tapping a string of islands to the south with his finger, islands lying between Concepcion and Madinina, the place where we had buried our Aztec gold.

I gave him a puzzled look. "Why, James? There's nothing there."

Hunter smiled. "Are you certain?"

"I watched the one-eyed Twin slit poor Billy's throat after Billy told him where to find the gold. The Twins would never have left the New World without it."

"The Twins," Hunter said, "should have slit the boy's throat after they retrieved the gold, not before. Maybe they found that rock in the middle of the ocean, maybe not. But I didn't bury the gold all in one place."

We all stared at Hunter, dumbfounded.

In the morning we broke camp and returned to our ships with

haste. I handed Hunter command of the *Phantom*. The Twins had lavished money on reconditioning her. Waterford's gifted shipwrights had re-rigged her masts and spars to carry more canvas and she was even swifter than before. The caravel, which I decided to name the *Carib*, had proven herself a good sailor. She was rugged and well-built, but she had no heavy guns and she wasn't the fastest ship. The sloop, the queen's gift to me, was fast and agile, but she was too small and old for my purposes and carried no cannon. The men dubbed her the *Abuelita*, the *Old Lady*, and that was fine with me. I had nearly two hundred fighting Irishmen to crew my three ships plus another nineteen fierce Carib warriors newly recruited by Henry. And I had my twenty steadfast Moors. All my Africans had survived the ambush and chose to stay with me. As for heavy arms, we had eighteen great guns, a mix of falconets and sakers, and another thirty swivels we kept stored below.

Under clear skies, with a brisk wind coming down from the north, my tiny fleet of three weighed anchor and we headed south. Hunter and I had the *Phantom*, Atwood and Efendi took the *Carib* and I gave command of *Abuelita* to MacGyver. It was an easy sail, though it took some effort to find our island. Two of the four crossed palm trees were missing, swept away by some storm we supposed, perhaps even by the very same *huracán* we had barely survived after our first visit. We had to sail around in circles for hours before we found our precious island.

We lowered a boat in the water and rowed ashore with no other sails in sight. Hunter and Atwood started digging underneath the two twisted palms in the middle of the island while the rest of us looked on.

"Are you certain this is the spot?" I asked after they had dug out a pit down to the waist.

"Aye, Mary," Hunter said frustrated, breathing heavily. He took his sleeve to wipe the sweat off his brow. "Are you certain this is the right island?"

"As certain, no more and no less, as you, James Hunter."

"Ah, *touché*, you make a fair point there my lady. Well, we're not finished yet. Let's take a look around. Spread out and look for a green rock, a smooth, round rock that looks a bit like a turtle's shell."

We all joined Hunter in his search for his unusual rock. After an hour of staring at grass and sand and common rocks, I thought Henry was going to explode into a thousand pieces when he found a smooth, green rock shaped like a turtle's shell. He went berserk, jumping up and down, hooting and flapping his arms like a bird. He had found the rock buried underneath a foot of sand.

After inspecting Henry's find Hunter broke into a wide grin. "That's the one, Henry! Good man, well done!"

Hunter and Atwood grabbed their shovels and started digging anew. Before noon we were lifting wooden chests out of the earth, four in all, each one filled to brim with Aztec gold.

"The fuckin' Twins have taken the rest," Hunter said. "I'm mystified how those double half-wits found this place with two of the twisted palm trees missing. They must have searched and dug up every one of these little shit islands for days. Well Mary, the Twins may have taken the lion's share, but this isn't a bad haul, eh?"

"Ah, I think the phrase "lion's share" is meant to mean all of something, not a portion," I said teasingly.

"Beg pardon?"

"In Aesop's story the lion claimed the whole kill for itself as I recall, not a portion..."

"Who's Aesop?" Hunter asked with a bewildered look. "And what lion?"

"Never you mind, James Hunter," I said and kissed him lightly on the cheek. "This is quite a find, my compliments to your cunning, sir - well done!"

"This is," Atwood said, reaching down to run his fingers over the bars of gold, "indeed a king's ransom. I remember now you stayed behind on this spec of sand after you sent the rest of us back. I supposed you had taken a nap after you drew your map. What possessed you James to bury these four chests apart from all the others?"

"A nap? Come now, Jacob, you can speak plainly we are now kin after all..."

"Ahem, well, truth be told James - only for a fleeting moment mind you - the thought of some skullduggery crossed my mind. But you returned to the ship empty-handed. I took the liberty of searching your boat."

"Ha! Ha! Excellent! I respect you for doing so! Damned if I know why I buried this stash away from the rest, Jacob. I did it on a whim. I suppose the thought of being double-crossed crossed my mind. Not all our men are loyal."

The big Scotsman laughed and turned to look at me. "Well damned lucky for us you did! I don't think Hunter would trust his own mum, Mary - if in fact he ever had a mum. Not this man of countless secrets."

"Atwood," Hunter replied evenly, "you betray your own envy. I hear you Scots prefer the tender affections of sheep over those of a woman. Tell us now: what sheep gave birth to you?"

"Such outrageous slander!" Atwood exclaimed with false indignation. "As I point of honor I should dispatch you in a duel here and now. This shovel would do the trick. I did not know my father but, as you can plainly see from my strength and beauty, he must have been a god, leastwise a demi-god."

"What say you, Mustafa?" I asked when I saw him crack one of his rare smiles.

He cocked his head to one side. "I've always thought you island folk a strange and hostile people!"

"I must agree with you, Mustafa," I said and laughed. "Well then, we have unfinished business to attend to. Shall we, gentlemen?"

We had gotten no further in our plan while sitting around the campfires in Guadeloupe than planning to find our treasure. But I swore to my benefactor, the Queen of England, I would cause her enemies some woe if I chose to roam across the great oceans again. I knew where I had to start and gave the order to set a course for Old Havana on the island of Cuba. But before we left our treasure island behind, I had the men pull the ships in close and tie them off together, *Abuelita* to *Phantom's* starboard and *Carib* to her port, and I called all hands on deck.

Under a sky of royal blue, with our three ships rocking lazily back and forth over soft ripples of shimmering green, I leaned over the quarter deck's fore rail and peered down on all my men. I cleared my throat and smiled. "Lads, as you know, after the Twins served me up to the English, her Majesty the Queen took pity on me. She granted me a royal pardon for my past transgressions and then she released me on this sole condition: if I chose to return to my life at sea again, I had to swear my allegiance to her. I had to promise to never take up arms against England while she reigns. You now have that same choice to make. A royal pardon for your loyalty and you can continue sailing with me, or we can part ways here and now. The queen has given me a commission, a letter of marque, to engage and destroy her enemies. We have her leave to raid the Spanish Main. Our smuggling days, for now at least, are over. But for those who wish to join me, our days of privateering have just begun. For any who wish to pursue other interests, I'll give you the sloop to do with her as you wish. No hard feelings if that is your choice. You are all free men."

I glanced over at Hunter and nodded. "Captain Hunter, you are my senior officer now. You are the first in line. I will begin with you. Will you swear your allegiance to the Queen of England and turn privateer with me? If not, I shall pay you your fair share of the gold and do the same for any man here who wishes to join you."

"Join you as a privateer you say, Madam?" Hunter asked.

"Aye."

"Well now, there's hardly a choice to be made there. But I know not this Queen of England you speak of. She never once showed me any favor or offered me a kind word. She never put a coin in my pocket or any food on my table. I'll swear my allegiance gladly, but my allegiance, always, is to you, Lady Mary."

I am certain I gave Hunter a most disapproving look. Those were not the words I wished to hear. And well he knew it as I could plainly see when he defiantly folded his arms and offered me an impish smile.

"If we prey on Spanish ships in these waters, our allegiance must be to the queen," I replied sharply.

But Hunter insisted on being difficult. "Again my allegiance is to you, my lady. If your allegiance is to the Queen of England, so be it. In the end is not my unwavering pledge of loyalty to you the same as your pledge of allegiance to the queen?"

Exasperated, I bit my tongue and nodded. "Oh very well *Master* Hunter, I'm honored you will join me. Captain Atwood, you are next in the chain of command. What say you?"

"You have my allegiance already, Lady Mary. I am bound to you by the Ten Rules, as are we all. But I will gladly swear my allegiance to you again before all these fine witnesses on this glorious day if it would please you for me to do so."

Now I had two troublemakers on my hands toying with me for all my men to see. And so it went down the line. All the rest followed Hunter's cue and swore their allegiance to me. Not one man, not one, had any desire to part ways with me. Of course I was grateful; of course I felt proud.

"What was that about today?" I asked Hunter later after he snuck inside my great cabin.

"Mary, the men believe in you. They are loyal to you, not to some pampered, English princess a world away. It is folly to ask a man to swear an oath to some cause he has no stake in or to a person he does not know. So long as we plunder Spanish ships and wealth, and give the queen her rightful share, I rather doubt her majesty will have any qualms about why or how we do it. I pray you are not too cross with me."

He slipped an arm around my waist, drew me closer to him and started kissing me on the neck. I should have shown him my displeasure and thrown him out the door. But I was hardly immune from his beguiling ways, his animal lust. I desired his touch too much.

"I should," I said, "not encourage future impertinence by

rewarding you."

He began undoing the buttons on my blouse. "I dare say you will not regret encouraging me. Allow me, my lady, to show you the full, *hard measure* of my, ahem, *impertinence*."

I surrendered to his naughtiness. I surrendered to my own yearnings, burning hot and fast. I moaned when his tongue found mine. I cooed softly as he slowly slipped a hand inside my trousers, opening me, tenderly caressing me with his fingers. With unselfish patience, my lover set his mind to indulging my every need, indulging my every sensual pleasure.

We made an easy sail across the green Caribbean to Cuba. By mutual agreement of all my officers, we hauled down our yellow-gold banner - with its distinctive red sea serpent emblazoned in the center - and sailed without flags or banners or pennants of any kind. We had no wish for fame. We had no desire for recognition. My past arrogance had cost us dearly and so now we slithered across the poisoned sea like shadows on the water. Anonymity was our friend, stealth our stock-in-trade.

We found a deserted cove along Cuba's southern coast and dropped anchor before sailing on into sleepy, Old Havana. There was no reason not to sail directly into Old Havana except for my need for a little more time. Old Havana was where Gilley, Green, Fox and Ferguson had all died. Gilley had perhaps been near his natural end, but the others had been in their prime. My heart ached for all of them. I assembled my officers in my great cabin. I did not know what to do about Cortés. But Cortés was the sole reason why I was returning to Cuba.

"Thoughts, gentlemen?" I asked. "You all know why we've returned to Cuba."

Atwood was the first to speak. "He betrayed us, Mary. What is there to discuss?"

"He claimed he was coerced," I answered flatly. "He was

desperately trying to protect his family. Perhaps the Twins even tortured him to bend him to their will."

"Rubbish," Atwood replied, unmoved. "Did you see any wounds on him when you saw him in the tent?"

"No."

"And even if what Cortés told you was true, in whole or in part, why did the Captain-General of Santo Domingo send three armed ships to Old Havana with the Twins?"

"We were," Efendi offered, "double-crossed for the gold."

"Cortés," MacGyver interjected, "didn't know about the gold, Mustafa."

"No," said Hunter. "Not at first perhaps. But Billy did."

I went around the table and refilled each man's glass with wine. "But I am," I said in a weary voice, "unclear how Billy got word of the gold to Cortés?"

Hunter shook his head, uncertain. "I'm not sure, Mary. Perhaps Billy told Cortés about the gold when Cortés met us in Trinidad and perhaps Cortés passed that tidbit of information on to the Twins after he returned to Santo Domingo. It is possible the Twins didn't even know about the gold at first but thought they needed more muscle, more ships, to take us on and cut a deal with the Captain-General for a share of any spoils. Or perhaps they cut their deal with Villeneuve. Who can say? We only know for certain that the Twins sailed into Old Havana with the help of the Spanish to seize our ships, to destroy our operations in the Americas."

"Why?" Efendi asked. "We paid the Spanish well. Why would the Spanish favor the Twins over us unless the Twins seduced the Spanish with promises of treasure?"

Hunter nodded in agreement. "That is the golden question."

I sighed. "Gentlemen, I still have doubts about the depth of Cortés's complicity."

Atwood persisted in his condemnation of Cortés. "Mary, Cortés is dirty. No question about it in my mind. He could have said less to the Twins. He could have done more to protect you without endangering his family."

I stood and rested my hand on Hunter's shoulder. "Bring the Spaniard to me - alive," I commanded in a testy tone and abruptly adjourned our meeting. I could not think of Cortés without thinking of his daughters too.

Three days later I walked into a small, abandoned building next to a wharf along the water, into a building that had once been used as a warehouse for the ships that frequented Old Havana long ago. The air inside stunk of rotting wood and putrid water. A good portion of the building's roof had caved in. I saw Cortés sitting in a chair in the middle of the building. He was naked and blindfolded. His hands were tied behind his back. Those had been my instructions.

Following our council or war, Hunter, Atwood and Efendi had purchased horses and ridden on to Cortés's *hacienda* in Havana. If Cortés wasn't there, he would be in Santo Domingo or in the Port of Spain. We would find him. But finding Cortés proved easy. My men found Cortés at his *hacienda* sleeping soundly in his bed. They subdued the Spaniard without a fuss, unawares, and returned him to me alive and unharmed.

Cortés did not know who his abductors were. He looked up when he heard my footsteps. Hunter, Atwood and Efendi followed me inside.

"*¿Quién está ahí?* Please, who is there?"

"Ah, the little worm can speak," Atwood said in a muffled voice.

"English? *Por favor, Señor*, please, please who are you? There is some mistake!"

"The better question," Hunter asked, disguising his accent, "is who are you?"

"*¿Que?*"

"Who are you?" Hunter repeated.

"I am Rodriguez Miguel de Cortés y Ovando. I am a respectable citizen, sir. My business is in farming and ranching, in imports and exports."

"No," Hunter said. "No, you are not Rodriguez Miguel de

Cortés y Ovando. You are a filthy, foul, disgusting little shit, a *mierda*. You are nothing but a whore who sells himself to the highest bidder."

"*¿Que?*"

"Tell us," Atwood demanded. "Tell us about the Twins."

"What?"

Atwood leaned in close, coming nose-to-nose with Cortés. "You play games with me friend and I'll cut you slow. You'll curse your mother for ever bringing you into this world."

"I don't know. I don't know. What is the Twins?"

"Not what," Atwood corrected, "who, who are the Twins?"

"I swear, I do not know."

"Two huge Irishmen, nearly identical brothers," Hunter interjected. "One wears a patch over his eye."

"Ah, yes, yes - you must mean Romulus and Remus! Yes?"

"Good God!" Atwood roared and laughed. "You're joking? Truly, they call themselves Romulus and Remus, after the Roman twins suckled by a she-wolf?"

"*¡Sí!*" Cortés replied and pissed himself. "Romulus and Remus, the Irish giants."

"You've met them?" Atwood asked.

"*¡Sí!*"

"Which one is Romulus?"

"The brother who wears the eye patch is Romulus."

Romulus and Remus. I had always only known them as the Twins. I looked down at the pathetic man in front of me sitting in a puddle of his own urine. I felt no pity. I nodded to Hunter to continue.

"And who," Hunter asked, "is the woman who calls herself Lady Mary?"

"She is dead I think now. She was from Ireland."

"You did business with her?" Atwood asked.

"*Sí*, a little."

"What business?"

"She, she had ships. She brought goods from Europe to the

Americas."

"You mean she was a smuggler."

"I, I don't know. Maybe."

"Maybe? Huh... And why do you think she is dead?"

"The Irish brothers, they took her. I heard they took her back to Ireland."

"Why?"

Cortés started squirming in his chair. "They did not say."

"They had ships and guns?"

"Yes."

"How do you know they took her? How did they find her?"

"I, I, I only know what I have heard people say."

"I warned you friend about games," Atwood said in an ugly tone, then back-handed Cortés across the face.

Cortés winced.

"You're lying."

"Please, please... There is some mistake I tell you!"

"We know you met the Twins in Santo Domingo. They asked you questions about Mary and you gave them answers. Yes? Do not lie..."

"Yes, yes, they threatened to kill my wife and daughters in Barcelona if I did not cooperate with them. I did not answer their questions freely."

"Cooperate you say?" Hunter asked. "Did you sail with the Twins to Old Havana?"

"No."

"No? To Guadeloupe then to find Mary?"

"No, no, no."

"No? So how do you know Mary is dead?"

"I, I, just assume she is dead. I haven't seen her or any of her men for many months."

"What do you know about Spanish ships attacking Mary's ships in Old Havana?"

"Why, nothing, Señor."

"Nothing?"

Cortés tested the ropes that bound him. He was sweating profusely from every pore. "I, I, I know nothing about these things."

"Are you certain?"

"Please, who are you?"

"We're asking the questions," Hunter said, followed by a fist into Cortés's stomach.

"Ugh! *Señors, por favor*, why, why do you do this? What harm have I done to you? Please..."

When Hunter raised his fist again to strike Cortés, I grabbed his forearm. I knelt down next to Cortés. I cupped his balls in my hand and then I began to squeeze.

"*Ahhh*, no, no, please, please..." Cortés pleaded.

I squeezed harder. I squeezed until he arched his back in agony, straining against his ropes. "How good it is to see you again, Rodriguez," I whispered into his ear and removed his blindfold.

He snapped his head around and looked at me in terror. His eyes were bulging from their sockets. "Mary!"

I released my grip around his testicles and stood. "Aye, Rodriguez. I'm alive and well. Mustafa, your knife, please."

After Efendi handed me his knife, I took the blade and wedged the edge against Cortés's privates. "A man is not a man without his cock and balls. Are you a man Rodriguez?"

Cortés started sobbing. "Please, Mary, please."

"Please, what? Are you begging me to stop or is there something you wish to tell me? Because if you are begging me to stop I care not and I will leave you here with my companions to do with you as they like. They don't seem very fond of you. On the other hand, if you wish to talk to me, then talk and I will stay and listen."

"Please, please do not hurt me. I will tell you anything you wish to know, Mary, anything."

"Then be a man," I said as I ran the cold, steel blade across his scrotum. "No more lies, Rodriguez."

"Yes, yes, no more lies."

"Swear it."

"I swear to God, no more lies."

"Good. You just might survive this day with your cock and balls attached. But I give you fair warning Rodriguez: I haven't quite decided what to do with you just yet. James, Jacob and Mustafa here I do believe want to carve you up and feed you to the fishes."

Cortés looked at each of us in turn. He was panting so hard I feared his heart might burst before he could tell us his story.

"Let us begin anew," I said softly. "Calm yourself, Rodriquez. You sailed with the Twins, with Romulus and Remus, to Old Havana. You were with the Twins when they attacked my ships after my men went ashore to pick up our cargo, true?"

"Yes, but I was a prisoner."

"A prisoner?"

"Yes."

"How so?"

"Mary, the Irish brothers had men in Barcelona watching my family."

"Ah, so you said. But you haven't answered my question."

Cortés broke down again. His shoulders shook, his chest heaved up and down as the tears began to flow. "They broke into my home. They force, forced me to go with them."

"Oh, they forced you?"

"Yes, I swear it."

"Very well. Let's see how this plays out. And the Twins had four ships?"

"Yes."

"And there were three Spanish ships in the harbor too?"

When Cortés hesitated I slammed Efendi's knife into the chair, barely missing Cortés's balls. I left the knife imbedded in the wood, quivering.

"YESSS!" he screamed.

"How did the Twins come by three Spanish ships?"

"I do not know. But Villeneuve, Villeneuve was somehow involved."

"And after the slaughter in Old Havana, you were with the

Twins in Guadeloupe when they ambushed me? Come now, don't be coy. After all, I saw you in the tent that night."

"Yes, yes, but I did not know the Irish brothers would harm you."

"Hmmm... You blamed the boy Billy that night for talking, for betraying me?"

"Yes."

"How did you learn about the gold?"

"I, I..."

"No more lies, Rodriguez. I grow weary of our game."

"Billy, Billy told me about the gold when we last met in Trinidad. I sought him out. I told him the Irish brothers had sent me and that is when he told me about the gold. He believed the gold would save his sister."

"I see. And the Twins had you lure us to Old Havana where they would be waiting?"

"Yes."

"And when the Twins did not find me or the *Star* in Old Havana, they sailed to Guadeloupe to find me."

"Yes. After, after, they took your ships they, they tortured Gilley and then the others. Your men were very brave. Gilley would not tell them where to find you, neither would the others. But the brothers knew to look for you in Guadeloupe anyway. They tortured your men for pleasure."

When I heard Gilley's name, I had to pause for a moment. I felt my lower lip start to quiver. I felt the mist rolling across my eyes. I bit my lip and turned my back on Cortés. I would not let him see me cry.

"There had to be another who betrayed me besides Billy," I said matter-of-factly after I had composed myself.

"I, I don't think Billy meant you harm, Mary. But there is more to the story than just the gold, yes? These men despise you, Mary. The Twins said you killed their brother and stole his fortune back in Ireland."

Cortés's words cut me to the quick. I took a moment to weigh things out. There was truth in what he said. Perhaps Cortés and Billy were no more than victims. But then again, no. I spun around and railed on him. "Damn your eyes Rodriguez! You don't have the right to ask me questions! Now, there was another, yes?"

"Yes."

"Who? Who else led the Twins to you and then helped them find me? Who else betrayed me?"

"I do not know his name."

"One of my men?"

"Yes."

"What did he do?"

"In Trinidad he sought me out and handed me a letter to deliver to the Irish brothers."

"What did the letter say?"

"I do not know, Mary. The letter was sealed. I swear it."

"Describe him."

"He was a short man with a beard. He had long, black hair and a flat nose. A small piece of his ear, his left ear I think, had been nicked in a fight, or in an accident."

"Dundee!" exclaimed Hunter. "How did you know, Mary?"

"I didn't know until now. Billy only returned to Ireland once with you and the fleet. I wondered if perhaps another betrayed us too, somehow fed the Twins information. Go now and fetch our good Master Dundee for me."

Dundee had been one of the newer men we had recruited before sailing for the New World. I knew him only as an able sailmaker.

Hunter and Atwood soon returned dragging Dundee in-between them. They muscled Dundee over to me and held him fast.

"Is this the man, Rodriguez?" I asked.

"Yes."

I turned to Dundee. "Why?"

Dundee didn't answer. He didn't protest or deny a thing. He looked down at Cortés, saw the knife sticking in the chair against Cortés's testicles and looked away. He found comfort in staring at his shoes.

After we returned Dundee to the ship and tossed him in a cargo hold, we went back to the warehouse to finish our chat with Cortés. When he looked at me I could see that something inside him had broken. He spilled his guts; he started blabbering like a child and told us everything. I believed his story about his family, about needing to protect them. I could have forgiven Cortés for that. Cortés told the Twins what he knew about my enterprise in the New World to save his wife and daughters. But the Twins had also seduced him with Aztec gold. Cortés had cut a deal with Villeneuve to lend the Twins ships and men to trick my men in Old Havana in exchange for a share in the gold. This was an unpardonable sin, a sin I could not forgive. Cortés understood. He started whimpering again.

Still, I did not kill him. I took his little finger instead. I held his finger firmly while Efendi sliced it off.

"There, there now," I said as Cortés screamed and sobbed hysterically. I moved around behind the chair and began massaging his bare shoulders. "Hush, now my dear, hush," I whispered into his ear. "Shhh, shhh, shhh... The worst is over, Rodriguez. I will let you live. Your finger though is mine. Your loyalty is to me now. From this day on, until the day you die, you will do what I say when I say and you will do whatever I say without question or compromise. For if you fail me, I'll come for you and I will find you and I'll let Efendi here finish what he has started. He'll cut you up in little pieces, starting with, well, you know. Do you understand me?"

"My fam, fam, family?"

"Your family never offended me," I said as I undid his bindings. "And as anyone who knows me will attest: I do not harm or threaten women or children, not ever. The Twins though are far less squeamish about who they threaten, maim and kill. Alas, it is clear you do not truly know me for if you did you never would have betrayed me - certainly not for the devil's own offspring or for a few pieces of fucking gold."

Freed from his bonds, Cortés pressed his bleeding hand against his chest to numb the pain, to staunch the flow of blood. "I, I understand."

I walked around the chair and undid my blouse in front of him. "Good, Rodriguez. Look at me. If it gives you any comfort, I've been maimed too. The one-eyed Twin, Romulus, gave this beauty mark to me after you left the tent that night in Guadeloupe. No doubt you heard me scream when he seared my flesh with a hot iron. No matter where you go, I can always find one handsome Spaniard missing a little finger on his left hand. Should I take your other little finger from your right hand too, just to be certain you understand me?"

Cortés glanced at my breast and quickly looked away. "No, no, no... Please, Mary."

"Very well then. I will let you keep your life in exchange for your loyalty, for your undivided loyalty to me. Do we have an understanding?"

"Yes."

"Swear it before whatever god you pray to."

"Before God, I swear it, Mary. You have my loyalty."

"We shall see. Do you recall our first meeting in Trinidad?"

"Yes, of course."

"As do I, Rodriguez, as do I. I remember your advice to me that day. "Trust," you said, "is a currency worth far more than gold here.""

"Mary, Mary, I, I, I..."

"Never mind. Had you heeded your own good advice we would not be here now. One last matter before I send you on your way. You owe me a substantial sum of money, money for my lost cargo, money for the ships taken from me and money to compensate the widows of my dead and then there is the interest to consider - and I want it Rodriguez. I want it all..."

The Ten Rules were quite specific. The Ten Rules required a

unanimous decision by each and every man. We tethered our three ships together in the middle of Old Havana Bay and my officers assembled all three crews on deck before breakfast. Dundee was brought up in heavy chains and I took my position on the quarter deck, standing against the fore rail.

"This man, one of our own," I said in a loud voice for all to hear, "has betrayed us. Because of this man's treachery many of our brothers are dead, our ships and treasure taken. The choice is yours to make. The Ten Rules are most clear: punishment by death at sea or the offender must be marooned on the nearest land, forever banished from our sight. This man, I cannot bring myself to even say his name, neither admits nor denies the charge against him. But the evidence of his crimes is plain and strong."

I looked down on Dundee. "Prisoner, you have the right to speak. You have the right to defend yourself. This is your trial."

Dundee shook his head and refused to say a word. He refused to even look at me.

Hunter took a step forward to stand by my side. "Those for death, say *aye*. Very well. Those in favor of leniency, say *nay*. Very well. Lady Mary, the vote is unanimous."

"Indeed I see that it is, Captain Hunter. Prisoner, the vote by one and all is death. Before I accept the sentence, one last time I ask you: do you have anything to say?"

Dundee finally looked up at me. Not defiantly or in anger or even in fear as I had expected, but with a peaceful countenance about him.

"Only this, Lady Mary: I'm sorry for what I done. I never meant you or any of my mates any harm."

"Well," I replied without emotion, "I never meant to take your life away when you signed on with me back in Westport either. But there it is."

I gave a nod and two burly men hustled Dundee to the side. They forced him to step up on the rail bound in heavy chains. He took one last look at the world around him and then, without another word, he jumped overboard on his own. With a splash of water he was gone.

I turned to look at Cortés standing against the mizzen mast only a few steps away wearing a forlorn expression on his face like that of a lost, little boy. I waved him over to me.

"Rodriguez, I would have you come and stand by me as we prepare the ships to sail. I wish to enjoy your good company again. I wish to resume our wonderful conversations about politics, history, religion and life. Tell me first my dear, how does your hand mend?"

Chapter Thirteen

efore noon we were weighing anchor and setting our sails to catch the morning tide. The currents did the brunt of the work and gently pulled us out to sea. I was standing at the bow drinking my morning coffee, stealing a moment's solitude, when I saw, on the far horizon, the sun just beginning to peek above the waves. I watched in fascination as she made her steady climb into the early morning sky betwixt two billowing thunderheads, enormous dark beasts, the largest I had ever seen. The titans - nearly identical twins - closed in on the rising sun on both sides like two huge pincers and devoured her, blotted out her glory, before she could reach the lofty heavens. A shudder ran down my spine. I wondered if the gods were sending me a new omen.

We set our course for Santo Domingo next for this was where Cortés kept his money. Santo Domingo was the place where I also hoped to find Villanueva. I had questions for him, questions that needed to be asked in person.

I sent MacGyver with the nimble *Abuelita* on ahead, followed by Atwood and the sturdy *Carib* while I fell in behind them both with the deadly *Phantom*. My thought was to offer-up the unarmed *Abuelita* and *Carib* as bait should we happen upon any Spanish ships worth plundering along the way. We made a peaceful, if slow, passage north under threatening skies in choppy seas.

I went below to the galley and returned to the poop deck with fresh coffee for Hunter. I found him at the helm quietly working the tiller. With his feet planted firmly on the rolling deck, with his gaze fixed on the far horizon, he was a match for any of the fearless knights of old, the epitome of a man who would give all he had and never yield. And as the winds whipped through his hair and spray came over the rails, showering him in seawater, I felt my knees go weak. He made a handsome sight.

Hunter took a sip of coffee and nodded his appreciation. "Weather's turning, Mary."

"Aye, doesn't look too threatening. *Huracáns* don't strike in the winter months, or so they say. Perhaps we'll be alright."

"I'll have the lads rig the ship for foul weather nonetheless."

"A prudent order, my Captain."

"So, we take Cortés to Santo Domingo, he pays us the money he owes us and he pays us damages too and then we try to snag Villanueva while we're there. And then, well, I'm a bit fuzzy on what follows next?"

I laughed. "I know not. I thought you might have some clue?"

Hunter didn't return my laugh. "Mary, we've been extraordinarily lucky so far. But we're beset by enemies on all sides. Our lives will be cut very short indeed if we meander about these waters aimlessly for too long."

It began to mist and then the drizzle came. A cold and biting rain soon replaced the drizzle. I leaned my head against Hunter's shoulder and wrapped my arm around his waist as he continued working the tiller.

"Let us suppose," I said, "we were free to go anywhere we desired. Where would we sail to my love?"

Hunter kissed my hair. "To the north, I think. Great tracks of land lie to the north of New Spain and Florida."

"And do what?"

"Build homes, plant crops, farm our own land. Establish a settlement and live in peace, far away from any kings or queens and the games they like to play."

"That is a pleasant fiction, my dearest."

Hunter sighed. "Aye, I suppose, I suppose it is."

We exchanged puzzled looks when we heard a commotion down on the main deck. I went to the fore rail to see what all the fuss was about and saw Henry with his Carib brothers, nineteen in all, dressed in rugged, European clothing.

Henry had the Caribs drawn up in two neat, parallel lines with one line facing the other. Each man held a sword in his hand. Henry was teaching them how to fight. He saw me and smiled and then resumed drilling his raw recruits. Henry was no less a warrior now than any Irishman on board. The Carib were renowned for their bravery and ferocity in battle, but my Caribs needed to master Old World ways. Henry understood. He knew that whatever plan eventually inspired me, there would be blood.

We landed at night along a secluded stretch of beach some three miles west of Santo Domingo's harbor to return Cortés to his home. I left the fleet in MacGyver's care with orders to sail on to Guadeloupe if any trouble found us. I took Hunter, Atwood and Efendi with me and we walked with Cortés straight into the jungle with torches in hand. We headed north and continued walking until we stumbled upon the path cut by the *ternado*, the *ternado* spawned from the awful *huracán* those many months ago, and then we turned east. That path, I knew, would lead us straight into the city. When we emerged from the jungle an hour later the streets of Santo Domingo were dark and deserted.

"I will take," I told Cortés as we approached his house, "only what you owe me, money for my lost cargo, money for my ships and restitution for the widows of our poor dead plus a little extra for interest because your payment to me is late. I will collect the rest - as reparations - from Romulus and Remus when next I see them. Do not try and cheat me - or I will take everything you have."

"No, no, I will not."

"Oh? And why will you not?"

"Because, Lady Mary," Cortés answered, instinctively grabbing his hand with the missing finger, "the Twins have no scruples. They are cruel. But you are clever."

"So?"

"I fear you more than the Twins."

"Why?"

"I can take my family away from Spain. We can flee and hide

from the Twins. I am confident of this. I have good contacts in many countries. But I am less confident we can hide from you, not for very long."

And I knew Cortés was telling me the truth. He understood his lesson.

Cortés gave us two chests of Spanish gold *reales* and three larger ones of silver along with a thick wad of bank notes for the rest, notes issued by his Spanish bankers. Hunter and Atwood protested loudly when they saw the notes. Neither man trusted paper. I too was unsure. But Efendi urged us to reconsider. Such negotiable paper he said, if authentic, was as good as gold or silver and paper was easier to transport, easier to hide. After inspecting the notes carefully against the candlelight, Efendi pronounced them genuine. Hunter and Atwood shook their heads in doubt.

Then Efendi surprised us all with his knowledge of banking. Two rich and powerful families, he explained, both Jewish, controlled most of the banks in Iberia. Because of the Inquisition, Jews were either converting to Christianity to save themselves from persecution, the *cristianos nuevos* as they were called, or simply fleeing Portugal and Spain altogether for more tolerant lands. The Marrano family had decided to become *cristianos nuevos*. They chose to remain in Iberia and some say they still practice their Jewish faith in secret. The Mendès family though chose to flee Iberia for Istanbul, taking their enormous wealth and banks with them. Under the protection of Sultan Suleiman the Magnificent the Mendès family was safe and prospering and the integrity of international banking had suffered only a little. The notes Cortés handed us were from the House of Mendès. Impressed by Efendi's wisdom, Hunter and Atwood gave our Turkish friend from Istanbul a hardy pat on the back and apologized for ever doubting him.

"Now, Rodriguez," I said as took his wounded hand wrapped in gauze in mine. "Let us have plain speech between us. Under any law I know of we have every right to kill you for your wickedness and treachery. I do not think you evil though and, but for the Twins, I'm certain we'd still be fast friends and good trading partners. You are free to return to the life you had before we snatched you away from your cozy bed in Havana. But remember this: in return I may, from time-to-time, call upon you for a favor or two and you will give me your unwavering loyalty when I do."

Cortés surprised me when he bent down on one knee and began sobbing. He took my hands and kissed them.

"Mary, Mary, I am so ashamed. You never did me any wrong. Yes, you have my loyalty. From my heart, I thank you. I thank you for your mercy. I shall remember what you've done for the rest of my days - I swear it!"

"Good, good, those are the words I long to hear Rodriguez and now we are friends again," I said and lifted him to his feet. "And as your friend, as your very good friend, when I find the Twins I promise you they will sorely regret the day they threatened your wife, your daughters..."

Before we departed Cortés's house, we learned from one of his slaves, a Castilian *Negro Ladino*, a handsome woman with kind eyes and fine, grey hair, that we had just missed Villanueva. I had secretly slipped her money during my last visit to Santo Domingo and now, unbeknownst by Cortés, she worked for me. Villanueva had left the West Indies for Spain only a few days earlier the woman told me. So I borrowed six brawny field hands from Cortés and two mules to help us carry our heavy chests and before the break of dawn we retraced our steps through the jungle and back to our ships. After stowing our gold and silver away, along with our paper notes, we weighed anchor and set off at first light. I left the mules behind but took Cortés's six Negro slaves for myself of course.

For no particular reason I knew of, I decided to return to Guadeloupe. In Guadeloupe at least we had friends who would help us with fresh provisions. To my dismay, I still had no plan. A day or two sitting on the beach underneath the swaying palms I thought might help inspire me.

"Lady Mary, Lady Mary!" I heard a voice call out excitedly as I slept. And then the voice rudely began shaking my shoulder, forcing me to prop myself up on an elbow and pop one eye open.

"Henry?"

"Captain Hunter sends me. To hell you must go!"

"Excuse me? To hell I must go you say?"

"Mmm, no, no, no. To helm, to helm you must go my Lady Mary."

"'Tis the middle of the night, Henry. Oh, for the love of Christ, very well. Go and tell your captain that I am on my way."

"Ha-ha! Yes, yes. Henry can do it! Henry can do it!"

Those were Henry's favorite words. *Henry can do it! Henry can do it!* We heard him say those words each and every day, like some daily prayer, although when he said them they sounded more like: *Enry can tu it, Enry can tu it!* I managed a smile for him and shooed him away with my hand so that I could wash my face and dress. He disappeared up the companionway in a burst of energy with the giggles.

The night sky was clear. The air was calm. The moon was a sliver shy of full.

When Hunter saw me step on deck he pointed to a silhouette dancing on the water, the silhouette of a single ship sitting in Guadeloupe's harbor with all her lanterns lit.

"Spanish?" I asked, wrinkling my nose.

"Perhaps, hard to tell even in the moonlight," Hunter replied.

"Have they run out their guns?"

"Not sure. I don't think so though, Mary. We're still a bit far off but I don't see any burning linstocks, just the lanterns. This doesn't feel like an ambush. Even so, we should be cautious."

"Indeed we should. Double the watch and wait until first light before we enter the bay?"

"Aye, wait until first light and double the watch. Clever girl."

I tried to stifle a long yawn. "I don't feel particularly clever. I'll fetch us a dram of *uisce beatha*."

"Ah, a glass or two of *aqua vitae* would do nicely, take the damp chill out of my bones. Thank you kindly, Mary."

Unable to sleep, I kept watch with Hunter through the night sipping on good Irish whiskey. At first light we found a fine brigantine of one hundred and fifty tons or more with all her sails rolled-up and secured, quietly riding anchor in the bay. She was well-armed and flying English colors.

I sent Atwood east and MacGyver west to circle around the island to look for other sails. After they returned and hoisted green pennants from the mizzen gaffs, the signal that all was clear, I eased *Phantom* into the bay under half sail with our guns primed and loaded, with my gunners standing at their stations ready to spring into action at the first hint of trouble.

"You there!" a voice cried out to us from the brigantine when we came to within fifty yards. "What ship are you?"

Hunter cupped his hands over his mouth. "The better question my good man is what ship are you?"

"We are the *Queen's Grace*."

"You're English?"

"Aye, we are English."

"State your purpose here. What are your intentions?"

"We are looking for a band of Irishmen led by a woman who calls herself Lady Mary. She is known to frequent these waters. *Quid pro quo*, stranger, who might you be?"

"I am Mary," I cried out to the shadowy figure speaking to us. "Now you have found me. Who might you be, sir?"

"Ah, Lady Mary, 'tis John Martin."

I squinted against the early morning glare for a better look. "Ah, so it is. Small world. Will you join us for breakfast, John Martin?"

"'Twould be an honor, Madam. I shall have a boat lowered away and be over directly."

As Hunter reached down over the rail and helped Martin on board, a longboat from the *Carib* pulled-up alongside us, followed a minute later by a launch from the *Abuelita*. I had invited Atwood, Efendi and MacGyver to join us.

"What brings you across the storm-tossed sea to the New World, Captain Martin?" I asked.

"Oh, I beg you, no lofty titles for me. I am simply Master Martin. But please, call me John. Her Majesty Queen Elizabeth inquires about you, Lady Mary."

"Does she now?"

"Indeed she does."

"I'm flattered. This is Captain James Hunter, whom you met once before when you were our honored guest in the ship's rope locker."

"Ah, well I remember," Martin said and warmly shook Hunter's hand. "I am honored to make your acquaintance again, and under much more agreeable circumstances, Captain Hunter."

"Likewise," Hunter replied.

And after Atwood, Efendi and MacGyver joined us on the quarter deck, after introductions and pleasantries were exchanged all around, we went below to my great cabin for a hardy meal of fresh baked bread, eggs and smoked ham while my gunners kept to their stations with their guns trained on the *Queen's Grace*. I had learned my lesson.

Martin, a short, stocky fellow with broad shoulders, a full beard and long black hair, ate enough for two. He was alert and he was shrewd during our conversations. His eyes, neither cruel nor kind, were always flittering about assessing the world around him. His temperament never strayed far from serious; his expression never varied much from austere.

"What news from England?" I asked cheerily as I went around the table pouring more coffee.

Martin nodded his thanks for the coffee before answering. "All is well in England. The realm is at peace. Trade is good. There have been no plagues or famines of late and the queen's health is excellent. Her majesty is enjoying a most glorious and prosperous reign."

"I'm glad to hear of it."

"There was talk before I sailed from London about some

skullduggery in the Irish Sea a few months back. Perhaps you've heard something about these matters?"

"No, I don't think so. What kind of talk?"

"It would seem that some new, upstart pirates are on the loose seizing unarmed merchant ships and kidnapping and terrorizing their poor, beleaguered crews, six vessels in all so far. One or two of the ships were English but the pirates set them free, giving no explanation for their benevolence. Most peculiar. And, if you can imagine such a thing, these same brazen rascals towed the rest of their plunder straight into Liverpool where the Navy Royal has ships on station!"

"Liverpool? Whatever for?"

"They kept one carrack for themselves but sold the other three, along with their illegal cargoes, off at auction to Liverpool merchants in broad daylight! A rather ugly business to be sure."

"My, my, my, I can't imagine such audacity!" I said. "Spanish rascals no doubt or perhaps even wayward Moors up from North Africa."

"No doubt one or the other," Martin agreed with a thin smile.

"I pray the Navy Royal catches these marauders with haste, that justice is swift and sure. Piracy puts us all at risk."

"Oh, I suspect these villains are long gone and out of reach, Lady Mary. Perhaps they are even here in the Caribbean now, somewhere nearby, as we sit comfortably in your cabin enjoying our leisurely breakfast! Even so, I was glad to see your gunners at their stations when I boarded! Ah, and then there was some curious doings over on the other side of the Irish Sea in Waterford at about the same time. Whether the two matters are connected or simply a fluke well, who can say?"

I did my best to look surprised. "Good gracious, there is more?"

"Quite so. A small storehouse down by the docks used to store gunpowder blew, making quite a mess, and rumor has it the Twins are missing one warship, a nao, that had, only the day before, been taken out of dry dock near that very storehouse."

"Good God! Only a fool with a death-wish would insult those two gruesome brutes."

"My thoughts exactly, Lady Mary, my thoughts exactly. This is, I must say, a very fine nao you have here. Has she been recently reconditioned too? Well, no matter. She seems well-built and carries an impressive array of heavy guns on her main deck. I can certainly attest from personal knowledge that her rope locker is most sound. Is she swift and nimble?"

"None faster, none more nimble."

"I believe you there. I'll wager in the right hands she would do good service against even a Spanish galleon. And the *Carib* and *Abuelita*, do they carry any heavy cannon?"

"Alas, no," Atwood answered. "Both vessels be good sailors, but they are only freighters. The *Carib* is rugged enough to carry guns, but the *Abuelita* is too small."

"I see. The *Carib* looks sound enough, a well-built carrack, and you should give thought to arming her. Well, with each passing day relations between the great kingdoms turn more confusing, more sour. Tensions are rising. Spain for instance has complained to her majesty, quite bitterly in fact, about the constant raids on Spanish shipping and Spanish towns in the Caribbean and the Azores. The Spanish accuse Englishmen of leading many of these attacks. Her good and pious majesty of course condemns any form of lawlessness. She especially deplores acts of piracy on the high seas and has informed the Spanish ambassador of this in no uncertain terms and on more than one occasion."

"The queen is most wise," I said and nodded. "Tell us, if you can, what brings you here to the New World, Captain Martin, I'm sorry, forgive me, John, with your own well-armed battlecruiser?"

"In her generosity her majesty allows me, from time-to-time, to slip away from Court to attend to my family's own commercial interests. I am the queen's good servant, but a man must still earn a living and put food on his table."

"Oh, and what, if I may ask, is the nature of your family's business here in the New World?"

"Why plundering Spanish ships and property of course."

"It is well," I said as I turned to consider Hunter and Atwood. Both men were standing with me on the forecastle, enjoying a round of after-supper spirits. The ship's lanterns had been lit, the night watch had been set and all was quiet onboard the *Phantom*. A full and radiant moon slipped in and out of the clouds. A pleasant breeze kept the humidity tolerable. We could see the Carib cooking fires along the shore. We could hear the strange sounds of the jungle floating across the water to us.

"What is well, Mary?" Atwood asked.

"It is well to have a plan."

"Martin," offered Hunter, "didn't leave you with much of a plan, Mary. "Go forth," he says with a grand sweep of his arm. "Humble Spanish arrogance," he says with the hint of a smile and tells us to "help yourselves to Spanish wealth." And then he sails off looking for Drake. God's blood, what foolishness is this? That's hardly a plan."

"I know that look, Jacob," I said, ignoring Hunter for the moment. "Out with it."

"Ahem. Well, Mary, I wasn't with you, James or the others of course when you went after Dowlin. But when I heard about your parley off Old Head near Kinsale and your adventure at Saltee, I thought my God, now there's a captain I could fight for! Of all things, there's a woman I could fight for! And here I be. *In for a penny in for a pound* they say. Where you go Mary, with whatever plan you devise, I will gladly follow. This is who I was meant to be."

Hunter drained his glass. "Sweet Jesus, you can lay it on thick, Jacob."

The big Scot laughed and slapped Hunter on the back. "Ha! Ha! Mary has no greater patron than you, James Hunter. We need to put food on the table just like our new friend Martin. I say: let the Spanish pay for it. Let's pick an island, any island, and play

263

pirate. These islands are ripe for the plucking."

I stepped in-between the two men. I slipped one arm around Hunter, the other around Atwood and held them close. "The Island of Margarita is not far off and *La Asunción* is a pretty spot. Gentlemen, I have a taste for something beautiful, something lustrous, elegant and girlish."

"Look up," Hunter commanded, "I give you the full moon, good lady. Is she not lustrous and elegant? Is she not beautiful and feminine?"

"A thoughtful and generous gift to be sure James. But I was thinking of something at bit more attainable, something I might wear. I was thinking pearls."

"Silly me," Hunter replied. "Very well. At first light, I'll summon Mustafa and Michael for a council of war."

I jumped when Hunter pinched my bottom. "Owie!"

"Are you all right, Mary?" Atwood asked, unaware of what Hunter had done.

"I'm fine, fine. Some horrid thing bit me."

"Not much wind tonight," Hunter said. "Those stinging gnats are out again. What do the Spanish call them?"

"*Mosquitos*, little flies," the stout Scot replied. "Well, the mornin' will come early. I best return to my ship, offer up a few prayers and catch a wink or two. I bid you both a good night."

"If I find what bit me," I said, "I'll crush the damn thing. In the morning then Jacob. Sleep well, good night."

At breakfast, with all my officers, we held a council of war and then readied our small fleet to sail. We finally had ourselves a plan, a good plan, and one and all were excited to sail across the open sea for Margarita. We set out at once.

Kinkae stood before me bare-chested on the quarter deck. His ebony skin glistened in the warmth of the sun's golden light. He had tattooed a coiled lash around his arm, a reminder of his former days in bondage. The tattoo was new. The African was as black as night and ruggedly attractive. His lean body was all hard muscle. A natural leader, he had assumed the role of petty officer over the other Africans with my blessing. Disliking the word Negro because of the taint it carried, I chose to call the Africans my Moors. These were the men I had purchased from Cortés for a bag of pearls and I was glad to have them. I caught myself staring at Kinkae's fine physique for a moment too long. I had to cover a smile with my hand and look away.

"How do things go for you Kinkae and your people?"

"Life is good, Lady Mary."

"Ah, your English is improving."

"Thank you, Lady Mary."

"You and your brothers are free men and yet you continue to serve this ship."

"Yes."

"We are about to go to war with the Spanish. There will be killing and a lot of it I think."

"Yes."

"Ah, ha. Then you and your men are with us?"

"We are all with you, Lady Mary. You are life."

"Life? No, no. I am your employer, nothing more."

Kinkae took in his surroundings. He considered the ship under full sail. He took in the crew moving about and then considered the sea around us.

"You are," he said and slapped both hands on the rail, adding power to his words, "life, Lady Mary! And this is good."

I was about to reject his overly generous remarks again. But then I saw the tears pooling in his eyes, the slight quiver in his lower lip. I placed my hand over his. "Very well, Kinkae. I accept your gracious words. Let us talk of other matters. Have you ever done any acting?"

"Acting?" he asked me with a puzzled look.

After I explained my plan, and his part in it, Kinkae offered me a broad smile. He squeezed my hand and quickly disappeared below, eager to prepare his division.

"Handsome fellow," Hunter remarked, walking up beside me.

Well I knew Hunter was baiting me. "Aye, a girl could lose

herself to those muscles."

"Should I be jealous?"

"Not at all, Captain Hunter. I've seen you naked. I've seen your muscles and no girl would ever ask you to leave her bed. You've grown a tad soft though in the middle, mister. Some honest work shoulder-to-shoulder with the lads down on the main deck for a week or so would whip you into fighting trim, would harden-up those muscles."

"Ah well now, Madam, there is hard and then there is hard again," Hunter replied with a sly smile. "It is all a matter of understanding the body's critical functions."

"You mean like the heart, the brain and the lungs?"

"A bit south of those regions."

"Good grief you are a bawdy fellow, sir!"

"Should you call for me later, Madam, I will show you bawdy. I will show you hard..."

My God, I thought silently to myself, *how much I love this man.* I wondered if other women loved as much. I wondered if men and women loved in the same way.

Sailing under fair skies, we cut smoothly through the calm waters of a grey and empty sea. My plan was simple. My plans were always simple. Complexity means clutter and my mind flinches at clutter as my body will flinch at a pot of scalding water when too close. We had transformed *Abuelita* into a slaver and MacGyver was to sail her into *La Asunción* with Kinkae and his Moors bound in chains. And as for me, well I had been demoted. I was nothing more than a lowly cook's apprentice now if any outsider inquired. A female captain, a female captain privateer, a female captain privateer parading around in the Caribbean would hardly pass for discreet. Gone were my days of vanity, of carelessly, arrogantly, flaunting my prowess.

The *Abuelita* went in first with Hunter and MacGyver, followed an hour later by the *Carib* with Atwood and Efendi. The *Abuelita* was in port to market her cargo of Negro slaves. The *Carib* was in port to take on fresh provisions. I held *Phantom* back, less than a league off the coast, where I waited for the signal.

The signal was easy to spot when it came. Hunter fired off a rocket over *La Asunción's* modest fortress. I took the tiller and guided *Phantom* into the bay with our guns run out and my gunners at the ready. *La Asunción's* small harbor was nearly deserted. Only a few fishing trawlers and an old barge or two were anchored in her waters. *Abuelita* and *Carib* were tied up against the main dock and I steered *Phantom* in behind them.

I cropped my hair up inside my hat and was, from head to toe, clothed like a common sailor. After we secured *Phantom* against the quay, I took fifty well-armed men with me and raced up a hill towards *La Asunción's* fortress where I found Hunter and Kinkae standing at the gate, smiling. The exhilaration of the moment filled me with indescribable joy.

"The fort," I asked, winded from the run up the hill and gulping down air, "is secure?"

"The fort is ours," Hunter replied proudly. "After we walked Kinkae and his Moors inside in chains and set them loose, we easily overpowered the garrison without spilling any blood. The town is ours as well. Jacob and Efendi are searching the shops and storehouses now. MacGyver is inside the fort spiking all the cannon."

"Anyone hurt?"

"So far, not one man. Not one shot fired. The Spaniards were caught unawares and accepted the change in their fortunes with aplomb."

"You've rigged the fort's powder magazines?"

Hunter laughed. "Mary! It's hardly like you to ask frivolous questions. The fort's powder stores will go *ka-boom* after we leave."

I rested a hand on Kinkae's shoulder. "Well done, Kinkae!"

He broke into a wide grin. "Thank you, Lady Mary. I like this acting."

"Excellent!" I said and laughed. "We shall need to find another role for you to play soon, something worthy of your natural talents!"

We snapped our heads around when we heard the rumblings

of a skirmish brewing down by the harbor. We heard crack of sporadic musket fire.

"You finish here, James," I said. "I'll meet you down at the docks. Whatever is left to do, you best be quick about it."

Hunter and Kinkae hurried back inside the fort while I took my men and raced down the hill where we found Spaniards, two dozen strong and dressed in full battle armor - metal helmets, gold breastplates and greaves - forming-up into a battle square next to the docks. *Conquistadors.* They seemed determined to block our way back to our ships. They made an impressive sight in their polished armor, brandishing their long pikes. Spanish bronze and spear tips glittered in the strong sunlight.

I could see Atwood and Efendi in the center of town rallying their men, one hundred souls in all. They were preparing to rush the battle square. The Spaniards would all be slaughtered.

I formed-up my own company into two lines. The front rank fell to one knee. The second rank stood behind them. We faced the Spaniards with our muskets pointed at the sky. Atwood, Efendi and their men hurried over to join us. My one hundred and fifty seasoned veterans, with muskets at the ready, stood against twenty-four *conquistadors* in gleaming armor with pikes and swords and pride.

I stepped out in front of my men. "*Rendir!*" I cried out to the Spaniards. "Yield!"

"Honor forbids it," a voice in the center of the Spanish square shouted back to me in English.

"Honor is about to rob you of your lives," I said. "No good purpose is purchased by your deaths here today."

"State your name!"

"Odd you think it fit and proper to make demands of us, from men far stronger than you. But if you must know, I'm John, the captain's steward. My captain is presently up at the fort disarming the garrison and spiking the fort's cannon. You'll find no help from that quarter if that's your plan. I expect our captain will be down directly and once he sees this sad demonstration, as honorable as it may be, he'll waste no time killing you. He'll blow you all away like dust."

"And who is your captain, boy?"

"Nobody. Nobody is his name."

The Spaniards looked uneasily at the force arrayed against them.

"And who are you?" I called out.

"I am Captain Ramirez Menendez from Cordoba," the voice replied.

"Well, Captain Menendez, take your men and fall back to the town before my captain returns. His moods are, well, unpredictable. Go now and live to fight for your king another day. This day belongs to us. Lads, make way. Let these fine, brave soldiers pass. No need for any bloodletting."

Menendez took a moment to mull things over, then gave the order for his men to shoulder their pikes and fall back into the town. We let them slip away unmolested.

Then Hunter and his men started pouring down the hill like a wild mob.

"Jacob, Mustafa, any booty?" I asked.

Efendi smiled as Atwood lifted a leather satchel off his shoulders and let me have a peek inside. I saw dozens of pearls.

"And there's more, Mary," Atwood said. "Not many, it is not a fortune, but it is enough to call today a good day."

And then BOOOOOM! Every man flinched when the fort's magazine blew. When we spun around we all saw a column of thick, black smoke mixed with cinders and ash rising above the site. And then an instant later we heard a second, softer BOOM behind us. I spun around again and saw white smoke rising from one of *Phantom's* guns with Henry standing next to it. I had left Henry behind with his Caribs to guard the ships. He was frantically waving at me.

"Quick lads!" I said. "Something's amiss. Back to the ships! Not a moment to lose, run!"

It was easy to see what had spooked Henry once I stepped back onboard. Six ships flying the royal colors of the Spanish navy were sailing out of a fog bank straight for the bay. The lead ship was a fair-sized galleon, a two-decker and well-armed with huge red crosses emblazoned on her sails. She was not the largest galleon I had ever seen nor was she the smallest. She was a handsome craft. The other ships in the convoy trailing behind the galleon, five ships in all, looked like freighters. The convoy was still a good bit off and I could not yet tell whether any of the merchant ships carried heavy guns.

Scores of Hunter's men were still running down the hill while Atwood and his men scrambled across the docks to reach the ships. Some tripped over themselves and more than one man lost his footing and stumbled or was bumped off the quay and took a tumble into the water. But for the danger we were in I would have burst out laughing at all the buffoonery unfolding around me.

I debated what to do. Wait and hold the bay until all my men were back onboard the ships, or sail out now with what I had before we were cut off from the open sea? I could return later with the *Phantom* to pick up any stragglers - had we discussed a rallying point at some village on the other side of the island. I cursed my own stupidity. I had no good plan to fetch my stranded later.

And I cursed my soft heart too. I couldn't leave Hunter behind.

"Henry!"

"Yes, Lady Mary?"

"Quickly now! Take your lads aloft and start unfurling sail! As fast as you and your men are able!"

"Henry can do it!" he said eagerly and rushed off like a madman, barking out orders in Carib as he raced past his men.

I looked at my crew spilling over the rails, trying to get back on board. "You men coming aboard - to the guns! We'll ease her out into the bay some and cover our brothers on land. We need to give the others time to reach their ships."

Once enough of my men had climbed back on board the *Phantom*, we slipped the mooring lines and pushed off. I shouted to the men stranded on the docks, told them to get themselves over to the *Carib* or *Abuelita*. I took the tiller and maneuvered *Phantom* out into the bay. Long minutes ticked by like painful hours. There was hardly any wind to fill our sails and precious little current to steer by. The bay was like a stagnant pond. *Phantom* was handling as sluggishly as I had ever seen her. I couldn't coax any speed out of her at all. I cursed my foul luck. Farther out at sea, with a good, stiff breeze to fill their sails, the Spanish convoy was moving at a fairly good clip, heading straight for us in a single line.

It was plain to see we weren't going reach deep water in time so I slowly brought our ship around to face the Spanish with our guns already primed and loaded. We had one advantage: the Spanish navy did not yet know our purpose. They did not yet know that we had come to raid *La Asunción*. I looked back at the docks and saw *Carib* and the *Abuelita* finally moving out into the water. And I saw the plume of smoke rising higher and higher above the fort. If nothing else, the Spanish would be on high alert after seeing the smoke and ready their own heavy guns for action - I prayed only the galleon had them.

I used Niccoló Taraglia's gunner's quadrant with a plumb bob to measure out the range. Hunter had purchased the newfangled device in Ireland on his last voyage and had taught me how to use it. When the galleon came to within one thousand yards or so I gave the order fire. The great guns thundered, belching smoke and flame.

BOOM! BOOM! BA-BA-BOOM! BA-BA-BA-BOOM!

I had my gunners target the lead ship, the galleon. We peppered the sea all around her with geysers of white water.

"Again!" I cried out.

My gunners worked like demons, swabbing muzzles down, reloading and taking careful aim. They moved with purpose, they moved with gusto and then patiently waited for my command.

"Hold, wait for it, steady... and... *FIRE!*"

BOOM! BOOM! BA-BA-BA-BA-BOOM!

Every shot but one splashed harmless into the sea. My men erupted in a great cheer when that single ball struck the galleon's bow!

Then the galleon made a sharp, ninety degree turn to bring her own impressive firepower to bear. Her crew ran their guns out smartly and fired off a broadside. Well over a dozen shots screamed above our heads. Several shells hit the docks behind us and a few landed in the town. Spanish aim was atrocious.

My men fired-off a third salvo and with a larger target to shoot at their marksmanship improved. Two shots struck the galleon's hull. Others punched holes in her canvas. But when I scanned the galleon for damage, I found none.

The Spanish answered us in kind. Dreading iron's deadly kiss, we cowered behind the bulwarks when we saw the tongues of flame and smoke reaching out for us. We weren't too proud. We braced ourselves for pain.

BOOM! BOOM! BA-BA-BA-BA-BOOM!

Three shots struck our hull hard. I heard one plank crack. One ball smacked the deck in front of me, ricocheted over the rail and landed in the water with a splash. Another half-dozen shots went high, whistling past our heads and ripping through our sails. The Spanish gunners had settled down. Their marksmanship was improving. We were in a fight I did not know if we could win.

But then, a moment later, while the galleon continued to hold her station, the rest of the convoy turned around and I breathed a sigh of relief. The freighters were only lightly-armed. The galleon's crew realigned their sails and her helmsman ported his helm to follow the convoy north. The galleon was only protecting her little chicks. Her captain had no appetite to engage us in slugfest. I could hardly fault him. My plan had been the same. We named this brief skirmish the first battle at *La Asunción*.

The *Carib* pulled-up alongside us as my men secured the guns. I saw Hunter standing in her main mast shrouds, every inch of him proclaiming proudly: *I am the triumphant hero.* He had earned the right. We had all earned the right to savor a moment's glory.

"Well," Hunter called down to me with a broad smile, "that was most entertaining!"

"More entertaining," I said, "than what I bargained for. I can still feel my heart lodged up in my throat."

Atwood, standing tall at *Carib's* tiller, looked my way and laughed. "Nothin' a drink or two to wash away the brine won't cure, Madam!"

The *Abuelita* then pulled-up alongside the *Carib*. MacGyver, less brash than his brothers, contented himself with a friendly wave.

"Let's muster the men on deck and take a count of heads," I told all three men. "Find Efendi, oh, there you are Mustafa. Mustafa, call the roll and make certain we haven't left any man stranded on shore. Then we'll all rendezvous back in Guadeloupe."

Once all hands were present and accounted for, we floated out into deeper water where our sails caught a good, stiff wind. We left fair *La Asunción* behind us and made an easy passage back to our favorite port-of-call. But before we went ashore, we circled around the island to look for other sails. We all knew the Twins, their black hearts craving bloody vengeance, would return someday to Guadeloupe's waters looking for us. I was hardly any different.

After I sent lookouts up into the mountains to keep a watchful eye on the sea, I paid homage to our good friend and ally Chief Paka Wokili. I walked into his village with a swagger in my step and handed him a small bag of pearls, a fortune to him, a pittance to me, and then pulled him aside to cut a deal, to make a private arrangement just between the two of us.

Later in the evening the chief held a magnificent feast for us in honor of our great victory over the Spanish at *La Asunción*. I was flattered of course, but our great victory was as insignificant to the Spanish Crown as the chief's bag of pearls was to me.

When the feast came to an end, we said our farewells and returned to our ships. We could not risk making camp in Guadeloupe again and so we sailed for an island a bit south of Dominica, to an island Henry told us was quiet, secluded and had good water. The island, when we found it, wasn't even on our charts. It had no name and so I gave it one: I named it Gilley.

With our ships anchored close by, we pitched our tents along the shore near a stream of fresh water. And then, underneath a sky of brilliant red and orange, I gathered all my officers, which included Henry and Kinkae now, around my campfire for a council of war. I passed around bottles of mellow wine, wine Atwood's men had liberated from taverns in *La Asunción* during our raid, and tossed another faggot on the flames. The wood hissed and crackled back at me.

After Henry and Kinkae gave their binding oaths of loyalty and trust, after I stabbed the dead fish to a piece of wood and anointed their scalps with seawater - our lifeblood - and kissed them on the hair, we accepted one African Moor and one New World Indian into the clan. Then it was time to reflect on our mistakes, mistakes that could have undone us all.

"Well now," I said, "our little excursion into *La Asunción* was nearly a disaster. We let the Spanish sneak up on us with no plan of escape. Had those freighters carried heavy guns, or had the galleon's captain had bigger bollocks, we might all be sitting in a Spanish jail this night, waiting for our executions in the morning. The blame is mine."

Henry looked at me. "What is bollocks?"

MacGyver howled and grabbed his privates. "Your stones, lad, your balls!"

"We're all," Atwood said softly, staring at the fire, "to blame Mary, leastwise those of us with military service. We were sloppy."

Hunter nodded in agreement. "She's a seductress, the Caribbean. She'll lull you into complacency with her beauty and kill you later in your sleep. We must resist her charms, harden our resolve if we are to survive this place."

I grabbed a bottle out of Atwood's hands and took a long swig. "Well said, my good lads. We must start thinking and acting like soldiers. We are soldiers. Indeed, we are soldiers on a military campaign."

Efendi startled us when jumped to his feet and drew his sword. "We start this very night. I'll double the watch on each ship and in the camp. Let's put out every campfire, snuff out every candle and every lantern. We must be invisible. Our enemies could be lurking anywhere."

Atwood grabbed his bottle back and sighed. "You're a cruel one, Mustafa. Ha! You Turks always are. But I can find no fault with what you say. You see to the camp, Mustafa, and I'll see to the ships. I'll return to the ships tonight with more men to stand watch - I'll take enough men to man the great guns if needs be. From this day forward, we keep half the men on the ships, just in case trouble should find us. As you say Mary, we are indeed soldiers on campaign."

I yawned. "I am proud to serve with each of you. Goodness I am tired. Tomorrow then. We rise early and break camp at first light."

"And then?" Hunter asked.

"And then we sail for fair *La Asunción*."

"*La Asunción?*" Hunter asked. "Again? What the devil for?"

"Because," I answered. "I'll wager the captain of that galleon - that brave, devilish Spaniard who had the gall to stand and fight - turned his ships around after we departed to complete his mission at *La Asunción*. The Spanish will not expect us to return so soon. I want that galleon and her guns."

When Hunter rolled his eyes at me, I blew him a naughty kiss. I turned away and went back to my tent to turn in for the night.

The sounds of a man moaning in pain awakened me in the morning. I quickly dressed and traced the sounds to a tent pitched next to the stream. Inside I found Hunter knelling next a sailor lying on his back while he applied a wet cloth to the man's brow.

"What is this?" I asked and dropped to my knees next to Hunter.

"It was Murphy's wish that only a few of us knew of his affliction. He was adamant you not know, Mary. He felt ashamed. He has the great pox. He's taken a turn for the worse. He can barely piss and when he does the pain is unbearable for him. His water recently turned black and he has a frightfully high fever."

I took the cloth from Hunter and dipped it into a basin of

cool, clean water. I tenderly dabbed the beads of sweat off Murphy's face. He was burning up. Lesions and a nasty rash covered his whole body.

Murphy looked up at me. His eyes were worn and yellow. "Good lord, are you an angel?" he asked.

I forced a smile for him. "No, my dear Pat, no. You are such a tease. It is only me, Mary."

"Ohhh, Mary. Lady Mary, they've shot me all up. I think they've shot me dead."

I looked over at Hunter. "He's been shot?"

"No," Hunter whispered in my ear. "The unlucky wight is slowly going mad."

"Is there anything we can do for him?"

"I'm afraid not, Mary. There is no medicine for this."

"No chance he might recover?"

"*Nada*, none. If the fever doesn't kill him, when his pain becomes too great, his heart will simply give out."

"How long?"

"Hours, days, weeks, there is no way of knowing. But he will suffer and suffer badly until his end."

I looked back down at Murphy. "Pat, you chose a most excellent spot to place your tent and rest. You are next to a good stream with living waters flowing out into the boundless sea. We have no medicine for your pain, but we will make you as comfortable as we can - or - we can help you sleep and end your pain. The choice is yours and yours alone to make."

Murphy grimaced and started moaning again.

"Oh merciful God, I want to sleep," he said weakly. Then he grabbed my arm and tried to lift himself. "Avenge me, Mary! Kill 'em bastards who shot me up, will you?"

"I will. We'll bury you here, next to the stream and the ocean. It is a peaceful, lovely spot. We'll name the stream Murphy's Creek. Now close your eyes and sleep my friend..."

After Murphy closed his eyes, I gave Hunter a solemn nod and Hunter gently placed his jacket over Murphy's face. He pressed one hand against Murphy's mouth and pinched Murphy's nose with the other. Murphy hardly struggled as Hunter choked the life out of him.

After we assembled all the men and buried Murphy's body, I offered only a few words. I did not know the man well, in fact none of the men knew Murphy well. I invited Pike, our man of Holy Scriptures, to offer up a proper prayer. The service was simple and to the point. Then we broke camp, returned to our ships and headed south for *La Asunción*.

When I stepped out on deck to stretch my legs, I found Hunter hunched over the chart table. He offered me the slightest of nods and I could tell that something was amiss, but I bit my tongue.

"I don't," he finally said, "want to die alone and unloved."

His words took me aback. I had never heard Hunter say such a thing before. I would never be a mother, but at that moment I felt a mother's love. Hunter's fear, his naked vulnerability, touched my very soul. I felt the urge to coddle him as if he were my child.

But with men all around us going about their work, I could only take Hunter's hand discreetly in my own and massaged his skin with my thumb. "You won't die alone or unloved my precious man, I swear it."

And then the skies turned angry, followed by cold and numbing rains. Whitecaps soon popped up all around us. Spring, eternal in her beauty, but temperamental in her ways, had finally returned after a long and peaceful slumber. From the north raucous winds whipped the sea into an evil frenzy. Our little ships struggled against the heavy seas and toiled against gusts of punishing wind. Though we had seen far worse, this gale was unrelenting and dragged on and on. We lived in wet clothing soaked in seawater. We didn't sleep or eat cooked food. We were cold and miserable for many days and nights.

After the gale had finally spent herself into oblivion, after we passed through the last of the rain and a morning mist, *La Asunción* appeared before us like some lovely, sparkling jewel set against a sky of stunning, cobalt blue. She looked no worse for wear. And in the town's small harbor we saw one familiar Spanish galleon, not the largest galleon I had ever seen nor the smallest, secured against the main dock with chain and sturdy rope. She was a handsome craft. Five familiar merchant ships sat anchored nearby in the bay. Our spirits soared.

I stripped *Carib* and *Abuelita* of most of their men and we sailed straight into the harbor with *Phantom's* guns run out, already primed and loaded. There was no need for finesse or parlor tricks. This was an attack of brute force, surprise and speed. I intended to take us in, pick the Spaniard's pocket, and sail us quickly out again.

We had already spiked the fort's cannon during our last visit to *La Asunción* and I supposed that most of the galleon's men would be in town drinking and whoring about as sailors on liberty are wont to do. And I was right. The galleon's decks were nearly deserted when we eased-up alongside her.

Hunter and his men, two hundred strong, hiding out of sight below deck, sprang into action when I gave the signal. They boarded the galleon with swords and pistols drawn. No battle cry was raised. No champion's taunt was offered. They boarded the galleon in silence. But not me. I was just the cook's lowly apprentice now. I was just a spectator and forced - by solemn promise - to remain behind on *Phantom*.

Hunter made his way up to the galleon's forecastle to direct the assault from there while his fighters poured across the galleon's decks like an irresistible, rolling wave. My heart filled with pride as I watched Hunter and my lads in action. Hunter's men overpowered and disarmed the ship's watch with ease and then went below where they found another twenty souls off-duty enjoying a hot breakfast. They hustled the bewildered Spaniards topside and forced them to join their sad-faced shipmates standing idly around the fore mast.

The galleon was ours without one shot fired, without any alarm sounded. We accomplished all of this in broad daylight in hostile waters.

After Hunter's boarding party stripped the galleon's skeleton crew of any arms, Hunter set them free. No purpose was served in kidnapping the king's good men. While the Spaniards sheepishly wandered back into town, with no urgency in their step, Hunter's men moved out smartly. They quickly slipped the galleon's mooring lines and readied her guns for action. Topmen scrambled up the shrouds like tree monkeys, nary a slouch among them, nimbly spread out across the spars using the foot stirrups for balance and went to work setting the galleon's sails.

And then Spaniards by the score, marines, sailors and *conquistadors*, an angry mob plainly bent on killing, suddenly came gushing out of the town. The mob rushed down the dock, heading for the galleon but when my lads took the swivels and fired a whiff of grapeshot above their heads, when the Spanish saw one hundred muskets lined-up along the bulwarks pointing down at them, they lost any ardor to advance. I saw the proud Captain Menendez in the crowd again, looking uncertain of what to do. I felt a twinge of pity for him. After all, he had been forced to swallow a double dose of humiliation by my hand in less than one fortnight. At least now he had a galleon's captain for company.

Hunter barked out orders calmly, inspiring all around him. His topmen let the square sails drop, sails emblazoned with the scarlet crosses of the great Iberian king, and the galleon lurched forward as her poor, deflated crew looked on from the quay, powerless to stop us.

I eased *Phantom* out into the bay, swung her nose around and headed out to sea. Hunter did the same and followed me with the galleon. And as we sailed past the five freighters anchored in the bay, my men smiled cordially and waved at the Spanish seamen standing along the rails, gawking. The freighters were tempting targets, but I had no wish to offend Good Fortune with gluttony. We left these prizes behind for another day. We had what we had come for. Our second raid of *La Asunción* had been lightening quick with no blood spilt on either side.

With no one scrambling to try and catch us, we shortened sail an hour later and my fleet of four came to rest on the open sea in a tight circle. The gale we had sailed through earlier had broken

North Wind's cold grip and the day was turning uncomfortably hot and muggy. Flushed with victory, my men were too excited to care.

"My compliments to you and your prize crew," I called over to Hunter under a scorching sun. "An extraordinary feat-of-arms!"

Hunter put his hands on his hips and began strutting about the galleon's quarter deck like some proud peacock. "Child's play, Madam!" he boasted.

Atwood, an exceptionally agile athlete despite his size, grabbed a line and swung himself out over the water from the galleon to the *Carib*. "Don't let it go to your head," he shouted over to Hunter with a stern voice, all for fun. "You had some help."

"Not from you, I didn't," Hunter replied playfully. "When last I saw you, you were headed below to change your soiled trousers. I trust by now your bowels have settled down!"

The men roared with laughter.

"Lady Mary," Atwood asked indignantly, "how long must I suffer these outrageous barbs from this English dog? From a man who, speaking of trousers, is *all mouth and no trousers!*"

"Now, now, boys," I said, beaming. I did not know how many galleons King Phillip of Spain had or even if he would notice that he was missing one. But this was a good and memorable day. "Play nice. Does this prize have a name, Captain Hunter?"

"She does, Madam, she does indeed. If her papers are authentic, she's the good ship *El Cid*."

"How does she handle? Is she a good sailor?"

"She's soundly built, Mary. But she's too high off the water and too slow and cumbersome for our purposes. Weatherly she is not."

"Anything of interest down in her holds?"

"Other than stores of rotting food and a good supply gunpowder, we haven't found a thing. We have some crates and barrels to open yet."

"What of her guns?"

"Like the ship herself, they're old and of inferior quality I'm afraid. I wouldn't trust them."

The months had slipped by since we had sailed from Ireland. I had men who wanted to be paid. I had men who wanted to see their homes and families again. And now I had a galleon I couldn't use. Still, she might be worth a pretty penny at auction. And I needed to refit the *Carib*, convert her to a warship or sell her off and buy a proper battlecruiser. I couldn't auction-off the galleon or refit *Carib* in the New World. And the *Abuelita*, well, she was too old and small to be of much more value.

"We'll put in at Guadeloupe to take on fresh provisions and then we set a course for England. After we conclude our affairs in London, we'll sail on to Ireland and visit Westport where I'll pay the men their shares and release them to tend to their homes and families."

My words were greeted with a rousing cheer...

How does one ask for an audience with the queen? Who does one even approach to ask for an appointment with royalty I wondered? I had no clue.

Our voyage east across the ocean to the Old World had been fast and pleasant with fair weather as our loyal companion. In contrast, we found London blanketed in fog and cold drizzle when we landed. The chill cut right through me and I could feel the sniffles coming on. I did not like the city. I did not like any city.

I walked through London's dreary streets sneezing my poor head off with Hunter and Atwood at my side. Along the way we stopped at a tavern or two to quench our thirst and warm ourselves and to learn the whereabouts of the Admiralty's offices. I needed to auction off my prizes and give the queen her rightful share. But I did not know what formalities were involved. We eventually learned that the Lieutenant of the Admiralty, the presiding officer of the Council of Marine, was the man to see. The Council had been King Henry VIII's creation some years back to oversee his Navy Royal.

We did not meet with the Lieutenant of the Admiralty of course. We were lowly, Irish ruffians of no importance to anyone.

We were rudely handed off to some minor clerk instead, to a baldheaded, disagreeable little runt of a man with badly stained teeth who I did not much care for. I bit my tongue and suffered through his ornery disposition and lack of prudence all the while hoping to never have dealings with him again. He kept insisting, in the most tedious fashion, for proof of legal title for the ships I wanted to auction off, for ships that we had stolen! And he had no clue what to do with the bag of fine pearls I handed him. I finally decided matters for the poor fellow. I left him with a one-third portion of the pearls to be delivered to her majesty and I was precisely clear with him, informing him that her majesty and I were well-acquainted and that he could lose his head if even one pearl went missing. The fool professed to understand. We came to the same arrangement with my three prizes. One third of the proceeds would go to the Crown, one third of the proceeds would go to our investors, which was me, and the rest would be paid to my men in shares according to each man's rank. I made no mention of the gold. That was ours by right, prior to any arrangement I had made with the queen.

We sailed away from dreary London two weeks later richer for our efforts. The galleon had sold for a small fortune, the *Carib* for a pretty penny, and the poor *Abuelita*, well, she brought in nothing more than the price of scrap, but I was glad to be rid of her just the same.

Now my fleet was down to a single ship and we were terribly over-crowed. I had to share my great cabin with all my officers who slept on the hardwood deck wrapped in blankets. Worse, I was denied the pleasure of Hunter's touch. Mercifully our cruise was short. We put in at Plymouth on the south coast of England first where we had heard there were some very fine ships for purchase if you had the coin. We found two, both caravels of two hundred and fifty tons or better. One was French-built from the shipyards at Boulogne and I was thrilled to get her because the shipwrights in Boulogne, as any savvy mariner knows, make the finest ships in the world. The other had been built in Italy and she was a rare beauty.

Neither vessel carried any cannon, but I knew where we could find some ordinance across the Irish Sea.

Once we reached Westport, I paid the men their shares and every man was thrilled. No one had expected the hefty amounts I handed out. And then I released the crew to their homes and families. I gave them thirty days, no more, to be back onboard the ships if they wanted to sail with me again. The choice between the Old World and the New World was theirs to make I told them, always, and there would be no hard feelings either way.

For the next thirty days I was miserable. The weather was cold, wet and depressing. I found myself longing for the warm breezes of the Caribbean and that surprised me. But worst of all I was alone. Hunter had abandoned me to visit an ailing sister in Dublin, his only living kin. Atwood, I learned to my surprise, had a wife and six children in Scotland and he took off for home. MacGyver had family in Waterford and Efendi, well, he simply vanished to God only knows where. That left me with my Caribs and Moors to keep me company and none of them could engage me in interesting conversation for very long or hold his liquor. So I spent my time inspecting and fixing little things on the ships - and I found my heavy guns. About the Twins on the east coast, there was precious little information.

Twenty chilly, lonely days passed before my men began trickling in. Only ten or so appeared at first and then twenty, and then thirty and so on. But by the thirtieth day we were still twenty-five men short and both Hunter and Atwood were among the missing. I delayed our voyage back to the New World for another five days. On the sixth day, Atwood finally found his way back to me looking fit and jolly and then on the seventh Hunter magically appeared with most of the stragglers drifting in behind him.

"I'm a bit surprised," Hunter told me later as we cuddled in my bed to celebrate our reunion, "that you didn't sail without me."

"I had a mind to," I replied. But we both knew I was lying.

"My sister, her name was Anne, took a turn for the worst just before I was about to leave her. A few days later it was her time. I had to stay and bury her."

I caressed his face and held him close. "Yes, I know. I received your letter. I'm so sorry, James."

"No need for sorrow. Like Murphy, she was in great pain. I pray she is in a happier place. I'm grateful I was there to comfort her at the end. She had no one else."

"I could never have sailed without you."

"You are Mary, I say it simply, a joy to my heart. I love you with my whole being, with all I have to give."

"And I love you, James Hunter, with all my heart."

"I know. I know you do and I have some poor understanding of how hard it is for you to love. I'm a very lucky man."

I rolled over and kissed him sweetly on the cheek. "It is easy with you," I told him with an honest heart. We held each other tightly until we slipped quietly into a deep and blissful sleep.

Chapter Fourteen

Rounding the dark, forbidding shores of Roonagh Point, we must have made a splendid sight to the hundreds of fishermen trolling the waters between Clare and Inisturk islands in their little herring busses, dragging their drift nets across the waves to snag themselves a livelihood. We were three powerful battlecruisers sailing in formation, moving out swiftly, skimming across the waves under full sail with colorful pennants flying from every masthead and large flags of ridiculous proportions waving off the sheets and lines. One of the flags was my battle ensign of course, the red sea serpent poised to strike on a field of yellow-gold - purchased by me in blood. The pageantry was grand. But the show was strictly for our own amusement. We'd haul down every pennant, haul down every gaudy flag and streamer too and stow them all away in the lockers before we ever flaunted them in the Caribbean again.

Before departing Westport, we removed the figureheads from all three ships. We painted the hulls and superstructures black; we painted everything above the waterline tar black, including the masts and spars. We blotted out any colorful art work and obliterated every decorative carving. We removed anything that made our ships stand out. We craved anonymity and practiced stealth as we glided across the deep and boundless sea.

Sailors are a superstitious lot by nature. Bad luck it is to step aboard a vessel that has no name. So, before setting out, we christened our new ships and on this occasion I let my men choose whatever names they took a fancy to.

Hunter and I again had the *Phantom*, now a twenty-two gunner after I added four more great guns, and she was still the queen of ships. Command of the French-built caravel, now armed with eighteen heavy guns and thirty swivels, went to Atwood. His men christened her *El Rojo Diablo* because of her dark-grey sails with streaks of subtle crimson which, in a certain light, looked like burning charcoal. MacGyver took command of the Italian-built beauty, mounting sixteen heavy guns and twenty swivels. MacGyver and his crew named her, quite fittingly I thought, *La Mia Bella Donna*, but for simplicity's sake we all called her *Bella*.

Yes, our squadron must have made a magnificent sight as we left the Old World behind us. With a lively wind to speed us along our way our three grand warships, cruising in a line with our high flying banners and sails billowing full, would have made any admiral in any navy proud.

Most of my veterans had reenlisted with me. But we had taken on new men too. We didn't know the mettle of the new men and my veterans had grown soft. My captains would not let such men - not the raw recruits or my veterans tested by rugged war - sit idly by as we lazily plied the blue waters of the Atlantic. Not when we were sailing into trouble. And so we resumed the grueling gunnery drills and combat training. We practiced for hours and days and weeks, relentlessly honing our skills with the great guns, sharpening our expertise at swordplay, with musketry and knives. We practiced until our limbs gave out. We practiced until our minds went numb. We practiced until our captains said *enough* and proclaimed us ready.

As was our custom, we put in at Guadeloupe once we reached the warm waters of the green Caribbean. We found Chief Paka Wokili waiting on the beach to greet us with his royal entourage standing close by. He embraced me warmly after I jumped off the boat and stepped on shore. We distributed many presents to the chief and his people. A good number of our gifts were quite expensive too, unlike the cheap baubles we had seen others from Europe hand out. The Carib were delighted. And as was his custom, Chief Paka Wokili called for a great feast of welcome to be held in our honor.

But after my Irishmen had had their fill of food and drink, we said our farewells and hurried back to our ships. We could no longer risk tarrying on Wokili's lovely island for very long. We had enemies all around.

We turned the capstans to raise the anchors. We dropped our canvas to catch the wind and eagerly sailed off. Not to sail to other islands to rest ourselves or to look for gold or treasure, no, not this voyage. It was if some witch had cast a spell over me. A sudden desire for hot action filled my soul and spurred me on. I wanted to meet the Spanish out on the open water. I wanted to test ourselves; I wanted to test our mettle against them. I wanted to know if we were good enough to be privateers. I had the ships. I had the guns and the men and I owed the Spanish a pain or two. But the masters of the New World were hardly slouches at cruel, hard combat and I had always avoided engaging the Spanish toe-to-toe before. I do not know what possessed me, what madness drove me on to fight the Spanish head-on.

We knew the waters off Trinidad and the Port of Spain were usually teaming with ships. This is where I decided to try our luck first and no one disagreed with me.

"Mary," Hunter asked as we walked along the main deck together, inspecting the batteries of guns. "What has come over you of late? You are like a woman obsessed."

"Am I?"

"Well..."

"Please, speak plainly."

"Aye then, you are."

"Does that trouble you?"

"No, Mary. We've crossed the vast stretches of a perilous ocean to fight and snag ourselves some prizes. All the men know this."

"And?"

Hunter shook his head in frustration. He did not know what to say.

I squeezed his arm to reassure him. "Please, James, you need not worry yourself, not on my account. Women can be fickle. We don't always understand ourselves."

"I suppose this is true, Mary. But there is something else at work here. Of late you seem different, beyond what you have just described."

"Ah, I see. Well then, there are I suppose two Marys. There is the Mary who loves her man more than her own life and then there is me again who can take a life, the Mary who cut off Dowlin's head without hesitation, without regret or sorrow. And as we sail into the vast unknown, purposefully looking for trouble, I am Mary, Bloody Mary, who stands ready to sever heads. I am Mary who yearns to kill those who mean us harm, to kill those who double-crossed us. Are you so different my brave and handsome prince?"

"No, I suppose not. We are alike in this. We share, I think, a quiet, measured ruthlessness."

"I sometimes think we are more than just lovers, James. I often think we are kindred souls, you and me. Aye, a quiet, measured ruthlessness perhaps says it best..."

We passed many sails as we drew nearer to Trinidad. We saw many freighters from different countries. We saw Dutch, Italian, Swedish and French ships along with, no doubt, a number of smugglers mixed in. But I had no wish to harm former colleagues, to injure merchants struggling to turn an honest profit. We let them all pass by unmolested. And then twenty-five leagues or so west off Trinidad, we sighted a heavily-armed Spanish nao cruising towards the Port of Spain and she was fair game.

Her master, no fool, became suspicious when he saw three ships bristling with heavy cannon bearing down on him. He had his men lay on more canvas and he did his best to scaddle into port. The nao was a clumsy brute though, built for hauling cargo, not speed, and we easily overtook her.

I gave young MacGyver first honors. *Phantom* and *Diablo* held back, standing watch, while MacGyver drove *Bella* close-in. His men shortened sail, let *Bella* gracefully coast-up alongside the nao and then snagged her with a pair of sturdy two-flue irons and pulled her in. I watched the fun from *Phantom's* helm with Hunter at my side. We stood together underneath a canopy draped over the aftercastle, fashioned by my men out of sailcloth to protect my tender skin from burning.

MacGyver led a boarding party over the rails and disappeared into the bowels of the nao for an excruciating length of time. When he finally reappeared on deck he waved at us, giving the signal that all was clear. MacGyver had his men lower away the nao's small launch and rowed out to me.

"Mary," MacGyver called up excitedly from the boat, all smiles. "She's Spanish as we thought. She's carrying livestock, pigs, chickens, even cattle, but not much else."

Hunter burst out laughing.

"What amuses you, my good Captain?" I asked.

"We've sailed an awfully long way for a stinkin' pig boat!"

"What's her condition, Michael?" I asked, unfazed by Hunter's contrarian mood.

"Wouldn't waste any time on her, Mary. She's old, she's fat and slow."

I turned to Hunter. "What say you, Captain James Hunter?"

"There's no money in leaky, old boats or in pig shit. Same for chicken and cow shit too I'll wager. I'd set her crew adrift, beach the nao and let the animals go free. Then I'd torch the fuckin' boat. Nothing here has value. Our good friend Martin ought to at least appreciate a good English bonfire using Spanish wood and sailcloth."

"James Hunter, you are much too cross on such a glorious morning. Not every ship we plunder will be loaded down with Phillip's treasure."

Hunter rolled his eyes. "I am not cross my lady, nor do I yearn for any treasure on this *glorious* morning as you call it. But neither do I fancy being one of Martin's pawns and risking our lives for this."

"No, you are right of course," I said brightly, then turned and looked down at MacGyver. "Michael, what say you then?"

"I am of a like mind with James, burn her."

"So be it then. See to it, Michael. You are in command."

After MacGyver and his men rowed back to the Spanish nao, after they hustled her crew of twenty into the nao's launch and set them adrift with only one set of oars, they beached the old freighter on a quiet spot of shore. They released the animals next, lit torches and set the nao on fire. Tendrils of thick, black smoke quickly wrapped themselves around her planks and timbers. The old wood hissed and popped and crackled at first. Then fire shot up out of the hatches and crawled up along the masts and sails. The whole ship went up in flames like kindling.

Not long after we burned the Spanish nao to her keel, and not far off, we ran down an unlucky slaver from Africa. Well, unlucky depending on one's view. I sent Hunter over next, hoping to improve his foul mood. He gave the slaver's small crew the ship's boat and set her Negro cargo free, over one hundred souls in all. We could not take them with us so Hunter gave the Africans muskets and a compass and told them to head due south for the Spanish Main where they could disappear into the jungle. I gave my own Moors the chance to join them if they wished to. But no man did. And that surprised me. My Moors were veteran sailors now and could have easily found their way back to Africa with the slaver. But no. Every man chose to stay and cast his lot with me.

We waved farewell to the world's new free and brought our own ships around. I decided to take *Phantom* into the Port of Spain to see what we might learn.

We dropped anchor in the harbor, as the docks were overcrowded with ships and boats of every kind, and rowed ourselves ashore. I took Hunter, Efendi, Henry and Kinkae with me. Or rather they took me with them. I was still just a ship's boy, a lowly cook's apprentice now. I wore men's clothes, nothing new for me, and Hunter smeared soot across my face. We paid the harbor master his due for the privilege of parking our vessel in his harbor and then Hunter and I walked to our favorite tavern on the square. The others went about the town to watch and listen. We were on reconnaissance.

After several rounds of drinks, Efendi, Henry and Kinkae walked through the tavern door and plopped themselves down next to Hunter and me. Except for turning tipsy on good German wine, Hunter and I had accomplished very little. The tavern was quiet and slow. Even the tavern's stable of pretty strumpets, with their brightly painted faces and flaunting seductive apparel that left little to the imagination, weren't winning over much action.

"How goes it lad's?" I asked.

Mustafa shook his head and helped himself to my wine. A devout Muslim, intolerant to the ways of others, he was not. He drained the cup in one gulp. "I heard no talk of any interest, Mary. What about you and James?"

Hunter grunted. "We've had no luck either. Not much happening here, though I find myself a poorer man than when I first arrived this mornin'. I'm indebted to our cook's good apprentice here for ten pieces of eight if you can imagine such a thing!"

Efendi grinned. "You are the sorriest gambler of any of us. What wager did you lose this time, James?"

"The score is two to four in my favor," I said, correcting Hunter before he could say another word. "And so you owe me twenty, not ten pieces of eight you scoundrel. Hunter bet the tavern's fine ladies would flock to him, offer him their soft caresses, their tender affections, over me, over just a stupid ship's boy."

Efendi howled with laughter. He laughed so hard tears rolled down his cheeks. Henry and Kinkae smiled, amused by Efendi's reaction though it seemed clear neither man understood our humor.

"Henry, Kinkae," I said after Efendi had regained his composure. "All is well?" Both men nodded and winked at me when Hunter and Efendi weren't looking.

With nothing to show for our efforts, I took my ships and we headed west for no good earthly reason. Sailing around Trinidad in tedious circles had sapped me of my patience. My restless soul yearned for hotter action. Neither the pig boat nor the slaver had satisfied my appetite for more.

We decided to try our luck with a visit to the Spanish Main. I chose Cartagena as our next target. Blustery winds filled our sails as we eased our ships out into deeper water. The strong gusts propelled us over rolling whitecaps at a tremendous rate of speed. Puffy, white clouds in countless numbers raced across the sky ahead of us. The air was crisp and clean and spirits soared.

Halfway to Cartagena we sighted four armed merchantmen and one four-masted galleon, a magnificent vessel, all heading south in a cluster. This was the fight I had been itching for.

Atwood brought *Diablo* in close to *Phantom's* starboard while MacGyver steered *Bella* up alongside our port. All three crews moved out smartly to ready the ships for action. The air was thick with excitement.

"A glorious day to be out on the water, lads!" I cried out to my captains. "The way I see things the wind favors us if we go at them south by south-west at an angle and get ahead of them. I'd rather go after the mother hen first in the rear of the convoy, chase her off or disable her, and then devour her little chicks in turn. But we lose speed and time if we try to come in behind the convoy. And then it is a race to the nearest port. What say you, my good captains?"

"If," Atwood replied, "we try cutting them off to the south they'll turn west I suspect, attempt to flee that way. That should suit our purposes just fine I think."

After inspecting the guns, Hunter left the main deck to stand by my side at the helm. "I like the odds, Mary, and the plan."

I turned to MacGyver. "Michael?"

"*Woo-who!* Let's get crackin'!"

I laughed. "That's the spirit boys! Jacob, Michael, if that galleon gives us any trouble, James and I will give her a taste of iron and hold her off whilst you two go after the freighters."

Hunter arched an eyebrow and smiled at me. "That galleon just might prove to be a challenge, my lady."

I had a sudden urge to kiss my man but settled instead on returning his smile with one of my own. "What's this now? The great Captain Hunter, having doubts on the eve of battle? Nonsense! I have the utmost confidence in you and in your men. Those cocky Spaniards will soil their trousers once they see you coming."

Hunter put his hands on his hips and laughed. "About the Spaniards shitting and pissing their britches, I have no doubt. But not because of me, oh no, no, no. It is when they see you at the helm my Amazon Queen, that is when they'll want to cut and run! I pray though we're all smiling at day's end. The odds may favor us, but war is a dicey business, Mary."

"So you and Jacob keep reminding me. Your wise counsel is always most welcome, sir - let us get to it then. We all know the drill. We all know what needs to be done..."

And off we went like dogs on a foxhunt. Three ships sailing abreast chasing after five sailing in a row. We set our course south by south-west and charged at the Spanish with all the sail the spars and masts could carry. Our ships had never sliced through the water faster. The winds and currents both favored us.

I went to the bow to get a better view. I could feel my body soaking up energy from the sun and the sea. I relished the sensation of the cool spray splashing against my face and the warm wind whipping through my hair as we closed the distance with our prey. When I turned around to take in my crew, I saw men bustling. Half-naked topmen, their lean bodies bronzed by the Caribbean sun, were aloft trimming sails to coax all the speed there was to coax out of *Phantom* while the gunners went racing about the deck, readying their long-barreled falconets and sakers for action. Dozens more scurried between decks bringing up ammunition and powder from the ship's magazine below along with muskets, swords and the swivels from the ship's armory. The crews on *Bella* and *Diablo* were busy doing the same.

The action swirling around the ships filled me with exhilaration. I was, God help me, born and bred for war.

Once we were within two thousand yards or so of the nearest vessel, the Spanish commander realized outrunning us to the south was hopeless. Just as Atwood had predicted, he turned his fleet ninety degrees to starboard and headed due west. The move bought the Spanish a little time, no more. We adjusted our course too and before long, with our faster ships, we were sailing in the wake of the Spanish squadron. With each grain of sand slipping through the hourglass we closed the distance with our reluctant prey.

At one thousand yards we opened fire with our bow chasers mounted on the forecastles. We started lobbing iron at the nearest ship, a two-masted merchantman. She was plump and slow, the slowest vessel in the Spanish squadron, and she had been falling farther and farther behind.

At one thousand yards we couldn't hit her. At eight hundred yards we couldn't hit her. At six hundred yards we punched a hole or two in her sails. But at five hundred yards - my gunners started smacking wood. The freighter had eight guns of modest size sitting idle on her main deck, but her crew couldn't bring their guns to bear without turning their ship to face us. The freighter had no chasers, her gunners had no answer for our salvos. At two hundred yards my gunners couldn't miss and the merchantman promptly struck her colors. My men - all three crews at once - raised a tremendous victory cheer. I signaled Atwood to follow me and ordered MacGyver to shorten sail and snag the freighter. I wanted MacGyver to put a prize crew aboard the merchantman and then follow us as best he could to help us run down more victims.

But how quickly fortunes can shift and change. In the blink of any eye the western horizon turned dark and then turned very dark and menacing. Within minutes the sky went black all around us, as black as night, and the winds began to howl. Sheets of stinging rain began pelting us on all sides. The sea churned with anger. With little forewarning, a freak storm swooped down upon us, unleashing an unholy vengeance on our heads. Even the bravest among my crew felt fear's bite. None of us had ever witnessed such a precipitous shift in the weather before.

Hunter rushed about the ship like a madman, helping men tie things down, securing whatever they could. They double-lashed the guns and went aloft in the ferocious winds to take in all our sail, saving all but one. The winds shredded the main topgallant to tatters before my men could reach it.

We had to let the Spanish merchantman go. The heavy seas made it impossible to board her. The Fates robbed me of a prize. I could see the Spanish fleet turning, resuming their former course to the south and my merchantman scurried after her sisters. The Spanish had chosen to make a desperate dash for the nearest land.

I stood at the fore rail and I caught Hunter's attention as he rushed around the main deck barking out orders. I made a circle in the air with my arm and he understood my meaning. He pointed south, the direction the Spanish were taking, and vigorously shook his head *no*. He pointed north and shook his head *no* again and did the same when he pointed to the east. Finally he pointed at the bow. Three times he pointed to the west, nodding *yes* each time. I understood his meaning and grimly nodded in return. Our only chance to save ourselves was to rush headfirst into the jaws of the vicious maelstrom, no matter how grave things seemed.

Our good ship *Phantom* was knocked violently to and fro for hours. We nearly capsized twice. We lost sight of *Diablo* and *Bella* in the dark. Not even when blood curdling shards of light split open the sky did we see our friends and brothers across the water, not even a glimpse. I feared the worst.

The storm battered us roughly about from dusk to dawn. Teams of men took turns at the chain pumps, emptying out streams of bilge water. How none of our guns broke free from their lashings, with tons of seawater cascading over our rails, I know not. Gilley had always said that Hunter was one of the finest mariners he had ever known. It was Hunter's keen skill and cool courage that night that saved us all. Of this I have no doubt.

By early morning the sea and sky, both grey and still

unfriendly, had quieted. My heart rejoiced when I saw the *Diablo* a league or two off our starboard bow limping towards us. Her rigging was a mess. But we saw no sign of *Bella* and my stomach started churning. Hot tea was my only breakfast. The crews worked feverishly repairing only what was absolutely needed and then we brought our ships around to scour the ocean to the east, to look for MacGyver and his men or whatever flotsam and bodies we could find.

But a good and gracious God favored us that day. We found the *Bella* an hour later, intact, bobbing up and down on lazy swells with all her sails furled. Even from a distance it was easy to spot the problem. *Bella's* mizzen mast had snapped in two. The great stick's top mast was floating in the water alongside *Bella*, entangled in its own rigging. Amidships we saw a gaping hole in her side. Two guns had broken free, had smashed through the bulwarks and plunged into the sea. Some of *Bella's* men were working in-between piles of debris and stacks of spare lumber patching the hole in her side while others were busy trying to improvise a temporary mast as best they could.

"Glad tidings, Michael," I shouted as *Phantom* and *Bella* drifted past each other. "It warms my heart to see you alive and well, Michael."

"Let me tell you, Mary, I thought for certain we'd all perish. What a short-lived but mean-spirited gale she was!"

"Can you manage until we find you a proper mast?"

"Aye, I think so. We'll know soon enough. We lost two men, swept overboard with the guns during the night."

"Oh, I am sorry to hear of it. Who?"

"Thompson and Sweeney. Good men."

Even from afar I could see the guilt in MacGyver's eyes. "Thompson and Sweeney. Pity. We shall honor the memory of both men in the evening after supper, give them the proper burial rites. We had better luck on *Phantom* and Atwood lost no souls. You have the smallest ship. You have by far the toughest challenge in heavy seas. You saved your ship and crew with brains and daring. Fine,

fine sailing by any measure, Michael."

"Thank you kindly, Mary. It was quite a scare. Any sign of the Spanish?"

"No, not a hint. But I can't imagine surviving those monstrous rollers coming at me dead amidships and heavy in the water with cargo."

"No, nor can I. Poor devils. 'Til supper then."

After we offered up our prayers owed the dead, we put our ships back into fighting trim and set out to the west again mid-morning on the following day. We did not sail far before we ran across another vessel. We spotted a single ship just before sundown and hurried towards her while we still had the light. She was a heavily armed caravel of good size but, like *Bella*, she had been dismasted in the storm. Her main was missing, though strangely her crew seemed in no great hurry to fix things.

But when we pulled up alongside the crippled ship, I grinned from ear-to-ear. I could hardly believe my good luck.

"Why that's the son-of-a-bitch!" I blurted out and pointed.

"What?" Hunter asked and dropped a length of rope he had been coiling around his shoulder to come and stand by my side.

"That smug fellow sitting against the stern, the one with the large, floppy hat decorated with a single, yellow plume resting in his lap and drinking a bottle of wine, that's the vermin who attacked us off *Nombre de Dios*. That's the dirty rascal I pointed out to you that day we were in the Port of Spain at the tavern on the square."

Hunter pushed his hat back off his forehead to have a better look and whistled. "Why so it is, Mary. I remember now. He's the dapper Frenchman who likes wearing outlandish hats with yellow feathers. Well, well, well now - this reunion between the two of you should be most entertaining!"

The man with the gaudy hat glanced up at me as my men tied our two ships off at the stern. I could see he recognized me. The imbecile looked at me and smiled! I could hardly believe the bastard's gall. He didn't seem at all distressed to see me. He turned his attention back to his wine as if he hadn't a care in the world and ignored me.

With their ship dead in the water, surrounded by three battlecruisers, his men made no hostile move, made no attempt to ready their heavy guns for action. My lads slid two planks over the bulwarks to make a narrow passageway.

"English?" The Frenchman asked nonchalantly as I stepped aboard his ship.

"Irish," I replied coldly.

I could feel the Frenchman's eyes on me. I'm sure I must have blushed. The Frenchman was as handsome as Hunter, or nearly so.

"Oh dear, this is most embarrassing, *Mademoiselle*," the Frenchman said as he sprang to his feet. "You have caught me at a most awkward moment."

"I should say so," I said and looked over at the stump in the middle of his ship where a main mast had once stood.

The Frenchman followed my gaze over to the stump and laughed. "Ohhh, that? No, no, no. I mean nature calls and I must take a *pissier*. If you'll excuse me, *Mademoiselle*. I'll hurry right back. I promise."

The rogue thrust his bottle into my hand and hopped up on the rail. Then he undid his trousers and started relieving himself in front of me! My jaw went slack.

"Ahhh!" he uttered and turned to smile at me. After finishing his business he buttoned up his trousers, jumped down from the rail and took his bottle back. He bent a knee and bowed. "That is so much better. French wine always goes straight through me, worse than German ale!"

"Who are you?" Hunter asked as he stepped aboard the Frenchman's ship.

"*Pardon, Monsieur?* You do not know?"

"No."

"Ah! Impossible! *Comment cela se peut-il?* How can this be? But I am famous in these waters!"

"You don't say?"

"But I do say! I am Guillaume Le Testu, the master of this ship and your humble, most obedient servant."

"Testu? Is that so? You look damn good for a dead man. It might interest you to know that the Spanish captured Testu at *Nombre de Dios* after Testu and Drake robbed the Silver Train. Drake and Testu took some thirty tons of gold and silver - or so the story goes. The Spanish didn't waste time with a trial and beheaded Testu on the spot. Your head appears to be still attached."

"*Oui, oui*. What you say is true. That Testu, poor fellow, is dead. I am the son. You must be Hunter. I've heard of you. And you, my gracious lady, are no doubt, Mary."

"Aye, I am Mary and you, sir, are a pirate and scoundrel," I replied, struggling to keep an even tone. I had to resist the urge to draw my sword and disembowel the man in front of his crew despite his charms.

"Pirate? Scoundrel? No, no, dear lady. I am no pirate - my men and I are free spirits, we are buccaneers, nothing more!"

"Buccaneers?" Hunter snapped. "How quaint. The Devil take me if there's a whit of difference between the two!"

"Well, perhaps we can discuss the matter over supper? Different words used to say the same thing can nonetheless have different connotations, don't you agree? There are nuances to consider. If nothing else the word buccaneer certainly sounds more respectable, more appealing than pirate!"

Hunter scowled at the Frenchman. "Trade wits with me here and now lad and you just might find yourself trading blows with me later at the point of a sword."

Testu clapped his hands together. "*S'il vous plaît*. Please, please my friends. You are my honored guests. *Je suis désolé*. I meant no offense."

"Guests?" I asked and scoffed. "I think you mean to say that as my prisoner you wish to beg me for my mercy, sir."

"Prisoner? No, no. And I do not beg for mercy. I beg to differ. We fight a common enemy. Why, we should sail together!"

"Sail together?" I asked sharply. "Great God, you've got spunk."

The Frenchman looked at me, genuinely puzzled. "Why, why should we not sail together?"

"Are you serious? You attacked my ships awhile back, not far from these very waters. We are enemies. Sail together indeed, ha!"

The Frenchman threw his hands up and laughed. "That was before I knew who you were. Besides, you got the best of me that day if I remember. Not many do."

"And I've got the best of you today as well."

"How true, how true. The gods are spiteful creatures and can be quite heartless in their perverse desire for amusement. I piss on them! At our prior meeting you were the mistress of a handsome galleon, yes? I thought you Spanish. Not many Irish in these waters, even fewer Irish with Spanish galleons. Alas, no harm done."

"Prior meeting? Is that what it was? My God, sir, you are loose with your choice of words. And no harm done you say? We traded broadsides. You lost men to our iron that day, on the day of our *prior meeting*. No raw feelings?"

"Why, nooo! None at all. We live and we die and how we live and die defines us. My men lived well. My men died well. *C'est la volonté de Dieu*. It is God's will. You were, I understand, only defending yourself."

I was finding it difficult to dislike the Frenchman. "Well then, let's just say that I don't like or trust the French. There's a fine, fine reason not to sail together."

"*Pardon*, my lady? Why is this so? I am like the brawny lion. You are the sleek jaguar. Our kind are always on the prowl. You and I were born to hunt! It is our nature. What a fighting pair we would make! What is not to like?"

Testu then noticed a tall, lean Blackamoor standing near the capstan. "Ah, Maurice!" he called out to the man, who was busy banging away at some metal part with a hammer. "There you are *mon ami*."

"Sir?"

"Go and find that damn cook of ours!" Testu growled, continuing to speak in tolerable English. "Tell him to sober up and light the galley fires. And then bring me more wine! We have honored guests onboard and I wish to entertain them properly with a proper meal. Make sure the old fart sobers-up first, Maurice. Only then is he allowed to light the galley fires. Better yet, you best do it for him."

The Blackamoor nodded with a smile and disappeared below.

"Maurice is a Cimarron, a former slave. He is my first officer. He is a wonderful number two, a fine, fine sailor. Our cook on the other hand is a disagreeable, little dwarf of a man, but he is a magician with cuisine. He can create the most delectable treats when he puts his mind to it. I swear that Italian sot could make boot leather taste good. At tending fires while drinking, well there Antonio's skills are somewhat lacking. He nearly set the ship ablaze a month ago. Lady Mary, Captain Hunter, you and your officers will of course join us for supper, I insist! Later you can have my head if that is still your wish."

It pained me to admit it, but the Frenchman was beginning to win me over. Even Hunter, I could tell, if grudgingly, was warming up to him.

In the morning, following an evening of excellent food and wine and pleasant conversation, we took Testu's broken ship *Aphrodite* in tow under the watchful eye of the splendid, nude likeness of the goddess mounted to her prow. I had agreed to take Testu as far as the Port of Spain, the only port where Testu could show his face, or so he said. The Spanish I knew had indeed turned a blind eye to much of the Caribbean's lawlessness in Trinidad in hopes of pacifying a handful of pirates and smugglers. Under an unspoken, sometimes uneasy truce between the two factions, Trinidad was neutral ground. Rescuing Testu was a small price to pay to buy his friendship I thought, or perhaps even a sliver of his loyalty, however fleeting either his loyalty or friendship might be.

We used our time in the Port of Spain to make general repairs to our ships. We even found a sturdy, new mizzen mast for *Bella*, though I paid too much for it. But whenever the ships needed anything, I never skimped on money.

With the work overhauling our ships nearly completed, my officers and I joined Testu at the tavern on the square for a last meal together. The tavern was far livelier than when we had left it a few weeks earlier. The place was packed with men drinking, playing cards or dice or sampling the establishment's abundant carnal pleasures. I was surprised to see several sailors of my own sex among the crowd. They were taller and stockier than me and looked capable of holding their own.

It was at the tavern that my past, again, caught up to me. Henry and Kinkae, nearly inseparable friends now, stood at the tavern's door and waved me outside.

"What was that all about, Mary?" Hunter asked me after I returned to our table and took my seat.

"Oh, not much. The lads had a question about purchasing iron mast fittings for use as spares."

Hunter furled his brow, he glanced at me askew. "A question about iron fittings? At this hour?"

"Aye, iron fittings. In the morning let's gather the men. We sail for Santo Domingo. We sail with the next tide."

"Santo Domino? But before we snagged Testu, we were sailing for the Spanish Main. Why this sudden change of heart, Mary?"

"Think little on it, James. Drink and be merry. As you've heard me say once or twice before, women can be fickle. We often don't know the *why* of it ourselves."

We left our new friend Testu in Trinidad and found Cortés where we had left him, in his home in Santo Domingo. It was well past midnight when I quietly slipped inside his bedroom. I gingerly sat on the edge of his bed with a loaded pistol in my hand. He didn't stir until I took my fingers and started gently combing the loose strands of his glossy dark hair back off his ear.

His eyes popped open at my touch. He bolted upright in his bed. He looked at me in terror.

"Mary! Sweet Jesus!" he said, putting a hand over his heart. "You startled me!"

"How is my favorite Spaniard? You are well I trust, Rodriguez?"

A glint of moonlight pouring in through the bedroom window reflected off the silver barrel of my pistol. Cortés eyed the weapon carefully.

"Ah, forgive me," I said and eased the pistol's hammer down. "This is not for you, my dearest. I find comfort in keeping it close, especially when I hear the names of the Twins floating about."

"They are not here, Mary, I swear it!"

"I do not doubt you there, my friend. I did not think to find them in your bed. Still, the dolphins whisper to me. The seagulls sing to me. They warn me. They say the Twins are near."

"Yes, yes! But I had no means of getting word to you, to warn you of their plans. I did not know where you were. I received a letter from these wretched brothers only recently. They wrote to tell me that they would depart Ireland soon. They will sail to the Caribbean with large quantities of contraband, or so they said."

"They inquired about me, yes?"

"Yes."

"And you said?"

"Nothing, Mary! I wrote no reply. I swear it!"

"Relax, Rodriguez, relax. I believe you. They sail with two ships: *Medusa's Head* and the *Pilum*, yes?"

"Yes."

"Their only interest is in smuggling goods and finding me?"

"No. They intend to put in here, at Santo Domingo, to see the captain-general. The captain-general will then accompany them to Havana."

"What intrigue is afoot there I wonder?"

"I cannot be certain. But it is no secret there are many in Scotland and Ireland who would support Catholic Spain in any war against the heretic, Tudor queen. Her Protestant faith is the devil's own work. With God's blessing, it will be her undoing. His Holiness will burn her at the stake."

"Oh? How remarkable. When did God judge Elizabeth a heretic? And pray tell me, how did you come by this divine revelation? The Almighty confides in you? I've heard of no such judgment."

"No, but - ."

"Well, never you mind, Rodriguez. I did not come here to quarrel or debate religion with you. I am indifferent on the matter. But I do smell an opportunity. Whilst the Twins are dillydallying here in the New World, I shall return to the old one. My men have families to look in on. But I will need cargo for my ships. I do not sail for charity. Same arrangement as we had before?"

"Yes, of course, of course. But everything I have is in Havana."

"Aye, everything you have is in Havana. So it is time for you to dress my good man. My ships are nearby. We sail tonight; we leave now."

"For Havana?"

I took Cortés's hand in mine, his right hand missing a small finger, and gave him a puzzled look. "But of course Havana you silly goose. Where else would we sail to in the middle of the night?"

"But, Mary, I have vouchsafed those goods already to another."

"Aye, I know. But to whom I wonder?"

"Well, I, ahem, I ..."

"'Tis alright, Rodriguez. You may say it."

"To, to, to the Twins. I could not refuse them. What, what will I tell them when they see my warehouses empty?"

"What will you tell them, indeed? Hmmm. Tell them a rival, a competitor, forced you to sell it all to them on pain of death. Or tell the Twins that agents of the *Casa de Contratación* surprised you and confiscated everything. Or tell them a *ternado* swept it all away. Tell them anything you like - except the truth. And when they do ask you about me, you will tell them that I panicked when I heard they were coming to the Caribbean. You will tell them that you have it on good authority that I fled to France in terror. Do you understand?"

Cortés nodded.

"Say it."

"Yes, yes. I understand, Mary. You fled to France in terror."

"Good, now dress," I said sternly and gave him back his hand.

And then, as if on cue, Mustafa stepped out of the shadows, holding Cortés's trousers.

After leaving Havana, with our ships loaded down to the scuppers with Cortés cargo, cargo vouchsafed to the Twins, we made good time sailing east across the poisoned sea. And as I stood on the beak-head at the prow watching the dolphins play, I knew somewhere out on the vast horizon the Twins were sailing west, sailing past us in the opposite direction. And though I could not see them, and they could not see me, I could feel our fates colliding. A chill raced down my spine. I shuddered at the premonition.

But then, as the sun melted into the sea off our stern, as bright and lovely Venus - a joy to every mariner - ascended high into the heavens, Hunter snuck up behind me and kissed me on the neck. He started nibbling on my ear and I felt my knees go weak. And when he wrapped his arms around my waist in the fading light and held me close, a wonderful, comforting warmth filled me, expunging my earlier disquiet.

"Mmm, you wish to warm my bed?" I asked as I savored our tender moment.

"Nah, I need you to step aside woman so that I can use the head."

"Oh? Well after you finish your business at the head you can go and do whatever it is lonely men do at night when they have no woman to satisfy their cravings. Your loss, sailor. The worse for you considering the desires of this woman are on fire..."

He slapped my bottom as I walked away with a smile on my lips. I went to check on the night watch and then retired to my cabin to wait for Hunter.

After a quiet supper with just the two of us, Hunter stretched out across my bed with his hands locked behind his head, staring absently up at the ceiling planks. "Do you think," he asked me, "Cortés will betray you?"

"No," I replied as I stood in front of him and began caressing his inner thigh. "Cortés has made no move against us. He has remained, so far, faithful."

"How can you be so certain, Mary?"

"A woman's intuition perhaps?"

"A woman's intuition my arse! Now that I think of it, of late you seem to be a step or two ahead of the rest of us. It is uncanny what you sometimes seem to know. I thought it was just good luck or a fluke at first. What is it you know now that the rest of us do not?"

"Now?" I asked as I undid the buttons to my shirt. "Now I know my body aches for your attention."

Hunter raised an eyebrow, but not over my obvious attempt to seduce him. "Ah-ha, why you sly, little fox!"

I let my shirt fall. I slowly undid my trousers and let them slide off my hips. I stood before my lover naked, filled with raw and eager lust.

"I've been deprived of your cock for too long," I said, yearning to feel his touch. But he seemed oblivious to my lewd advances. He seemed content to let me beg him for what I needed.

"Ah, I should've understood matters sooner," he said and slapped his forehead. "I've seen how you talk in whispers and exchange silent nods around Henry and Kinkae at times. Those two have helped you establish a web of spies throughout the Caribbean using Caribs and Moors. True? But of course it's true. And you must be using Chief Paka Wokili's war canoes to ferry messages back and forth between the islands. Ha! Our good chief is a participant in your little ring of agents!"

I licked my lips seductively and purred. I climbed into the bed and straddled him. He pretended to ignore me so I slowly began grinding my hips against him. "God, you're slow-witted tonight, James."

Still my man snubbed me. But I could feel him stir. I could feel his manhood rising. I could feel the wetness between my legs. I could feel my own ecstasy slowly building.

"Inspired, Mary. Ingenious really. Why keep this a little secret from me and the others?"

I undid his belt and pulled his trousers off. I leaned over him, slipped my tongue inside his mouth and lingered there for a moment, just long enough for the promise of something more. "Because, Henry and Kinkae both made me swear I would keep our arrangement secret."

"Suspicious buggers aren't they? What do they get out of it?"

I unbuttoned his shirt. I kissed his neck, his chest and worked my way down to his stomach. "I promised Kinkae that I'd purchase the freedom of any of his people who helped us. Esmerelda, you know the woman, the Castilian *Negro Ladino* in charge of Cortés's household, she is in our employ. She uses the money I give her to help her people. Chief Paka Wokili likes the quality gifts we give him and what we pay him in tribute. Henry asked for nothing. He seems inspired by the sheer sport of it. Now relax my love. I want to inspire you."

Hunter continued staring into space; he continued ignoring me. "Clever. How many spies do we have, Mary?"

I did not answer him. And when I took his stiff rod in my hands and began pleasuring him, he mercifully stopped asking me silly questions.

We arrived in Westport safely and sold off our cargo for a tidy sum. I had of course sworn off smuggling but did not think the queen, if she ever learned of this small infraction of her rules, of my brief fall from grace, would mind too much considering the pearls I had left behind for her in London.

I gave two months' liberty to all my men. Hunter, Atwood and Efendi went on to County Cork and Youghal to make certain the Twins had left Ireland for the New World and to learn whatever they could about our hated archenemy's plans. And I, reluctantly, agreed it was best for me to venture no farther than Westport and keep myself to the shadows.

I spent most of my days in the taverns along the waterfront where the talk was mostly of rebellion. Queen Elizabeth's father, King Henry VIII, had claimed the crown of Ireland for himself during his reign of course and the English ever since had taken a heavy, brutal hand in humbling Irish pride. But England wanted far more than just Ireland's rigid obedience. The English wanted the island for themselves and were colonizing Ireland as the Spanish were colonizing the New World - by displacing the indigenous population just as Gilley had said - under the policy of Plantation. English soldiers had begun the purge with the *cúige* of Ulster in the north and then invaded Munster to the south, deposing the Gaelic nobility and handing their lands and titles over to the new English nobility.

The English wanted more than just land and titles though. They wanted the soul of Ireland too and brought the Protestant Reformation with them. As English settlors poured into Ireland by the thousands, they purified the island with sword and fire. Christendom's two jealous gods were at war. Both gods had men under arms and were willing to shed blood to possess and pacify Ireland. I heard tales, evil tales, of whole families, men, women and children, being slaughtered.

And I heard the name Francis Drake again. He and another man named Norreys, Sir John Norreys, had landed at Rathlin Island to the north and stormed a castle there held by the rebellious MacDonnell clan. After Drake and Norreys's men cut down all the castle's defenders, taking no prisoners except for the ringleader MacDonnell, they searched the nearby caves, rounded up the women and children in hiding and forced them off the cliffs. They say hundreds of Catholic Scots perished in the massacre. The say Drake forced MacDonnell to watch the slaughter of his people.

I listened to these grisly tales of horror dispassionately for I did not see myself as Irish or Catholic. I had no stake in any of it. Jealous kingdoms had butchered their neighbors for land and wealth and power for centuries. No earthly being has the strength to stop it. Not even the gentle lamb of Bethlehem from what I've seen and heard has the clout to change things.

Still, it would be untrue to say that I was untouched by the slaughter of innocent women and children. God knows I have killed. I've killed men without a twinge of repentance, without the slightest guilt. But I shuddered at the thought of murdered children and their poor mothers. Only the stoniest heart could hear of such evil and feel nothing.

It was a cold and drizzly morning as I walked down Quay Road. I tightened my cloak around my shoulders and quickened my step.

"By the grace of God!" I heard a voice call out behind me. "Mary?"

I spun around to find a man, an elderly man short in stature and plump around the waist dressed in the plain, brown robes of a friar staring at me. We had just walked past each other. He looked at me in disbelief.

"Mary! Dear God, I thought I was mistaken, but it is you! Do you remember me, Mary? 'Tis Thomas, Mary, Friar Thomas!"

The friar took both my hands and held them affectionately for a moment as I struggled trying to remember his face. I remembered the name.

"Friar Thomas? Friar Thomas from Dublin?"

"Aye! Friar Thomas from Dublin. There's but one of me in Ireland though I be the size of two! When first I saw you across the way I thought I had seen a ghost. Then I crossed the road to have a better look. God's mercy, the resemblance is striking. Bless me, you are your mother's daughter. If she were standing with us now you'd be a matching pair."

I leaned close and kissed him sweetly on the cheek. He had been a good friend and priest to my father after my mother passed.

"Do you still have a weakness for strong ale?" I asked.

Friar Thomas rubbed his generous paunch and beamed. "Your memory is sound. I sometimes wonder in these troubling times, as I grow old and foolish, if God is truly Catholic. Perhaps He is a Lutheran or one of these new Puritans or something else altogether?

God help us if He's a Muslim or a Buddhist! But no matter what His church, surely He must enjoy good ale! Lead the way my sweetest, dearest Mary!"

"What brings you to Westport, Friar?" I asked as we walked along the road.

"I have kin here. My brother is a cooper. He and his wife have three healthy sons and two lovely daughters and I'm very fond of all of them. I come to Westport to look in on them from time to time. And you, Mary, I thought you dead or worse after they found your poor father - God rest his soul - murdered with no sign of you. What happened, dear child? Where have you been all these years?"

"Ah, I wish I could tell you that my story will require a goodly amount of ale and time but, in truth, there is not much to say. I simply ran away."

"And you live here in Westport?"

"No, no. I dabble in trade and shipping here and there, nothing very exciting I'm afraid. My life is rather boring. I'm only passing through Westport until I find new work."

"Oh? An unusual occupation for a woman, trade and shipping. You're not married?"

"Good heavens, no. I spend most of my days at sea. My shipmates are my family."

The friar grabbed my arm and we stopped walking. "Ah! I must be daft! Ships and trade - smuggling by another name - and you frequent Westport, the O'Malley stronghold. Of course, now I see things plainly. You know the truth of it then, about your father?"

"Yes."

"You know that John Kelly was not your natural father?"

"Yes."

"And after his death you made your way here to Westport. Kelly must have told you what to do, who to see, in the event he came to a bad end. You went to see Lord Eoghan Dubhdara O'Malley?"

"Aye."

O'Malley was the last of his kind, the last of the Kings of

Umaill. You are of royal blood, Mary."

"Father, listen carefully to me now. 'Tis best you never speak of these things again, not to anyone, for your sake as well as mine. I must keep to the shadows. I must walk lightly and leave no footprints behind. There are those who would see me dead. These men would have no qualms about killing a friar too if his killing led to me."

I could see in Friar Thomas's eyes that he understood. He had never been anyone's fool.

He bit his lip and nodded. "I will say only this and then no more about these matters. Your mother was very dear to me. You are very dear to me. I was with your mother when she gave birth to you. I am the priest who christened and baptized you. Dear me, I am the priest who christened and baptized your mother! And I was with her when she died, as was Lord O'Malley. You've heard of Grace O'Malley?"

"Aye."

"Do you know Grace O'Malley is the daughter of Lord O'Malley?"

"I've heard this. But I know her not."

"I'm glad to hear it, Mary. The English will no doubt find this Pirate Queen, as she calls herself, and execute her on the gibbet someday. The English would need no excuse to execute her half-sister for good measure. Come, let us drink and speak of less troublesome matters. And should anyone ask me, I've never seen you before this day."

After we found a quiet inn to our liking, Friar Thomas and I talked of many things. He told me things about my mother I did not know or had long ago forgotten. And I shared a few of my adventures in the New World, as a lowly ship's cook, with him. I told him just enough to hold his interest, but nothing of great substance. I mentioned nothing about the Twins or of my arrangement with the queen. It was clear to see the friar's sympathies would be with Catholic Spain if war broke out.

"A ship's cook you say?" he asked after I had finished my story.

"Aye."

Friar Thomas winked at me. "Ahem, I think not. But I respect your need for, um, for anonymity."

"Let us raise our glasses high," I said, "and drink to anonymity!"

The good friar drained his ale with one, long gulp. "Ahhh," he mumbled and placed his hand over mine. "Mary, you've been cautious with your words. Even so, one needn't be wise to see that your heart is burdened down with hate. Let it go. Free yourself from pain, Mary. Our Lord teaches us through the Gospels to love and to forgive one another with all our hearts. Saint Matthew gave us this simple but sage instruction: *For if you forgive men when they sin against you, your heavenly Father will also forgive you. But if you do not forgive men their sins, your Father will not forgive your sins.* Mary, I beseech you, embrace this Truth. Only then can your restless, troubled soul find the peace you crave."

The priest's power of perception surprised me. I did not think I had said or revealed that much about myself.

"Peace? Ha! I have no care for peace, Father. Vengeance is my stock and trade. I crave retribution swift and sure against any who have or would do me harm, not peace. Let the Lord forgive the wicked if it pleases Him to do so. And you Father, save as many souls as you are able, to your heart's content, but let me be the dark angel of death. Let me be the one who rips their spirits from their flesh for you. I will protect my own. This is the way of it. Such is the world we live in."

The friar shook his head in disagreement, but smiled tenderly at me too. "Mary, Mary, Mary, no good will come of it. But I judge you not. Even as a young child you were headstrong and obstinate. Have you at least considered finding a good husband and settling down? You must know of your own great beauty. You would attract many a fine suitor, men of substance who could give you a life of ease and privilege, if only you would allow it. And whether you will admit it or not, you have a kind and loving heart. I see this. I'm thinking about your earthly happiness now, not your immortal soul."

My thoughts turned briefly to that wretched day in Dublin when I fled into the streets an orphan in torn and bloodstained clothing. I decided to spare the good friar from the atrocities of that unholy night. My rite of passage into womanhood, my passage into the world of violence and bloody vengeance was my own and for no one else. Not even with Hunter had I shared these things.

I forced a weak smile to reassure the friar. "I am, I promise you, Father, most happy."

"Ah, very well, I see your mind is firm. 'Twas perhaps foolish of me to try. You'll be in my prayers and thoughts tonight and forevermore my child."

"Thank you kindly, Father. I will consider all you have said for I know that you are wise. But I make no promises. I'm curious, if you know, who were my mother's people? What clan was she from? I don't recall ever knowing."

"Ryan. You are a Ryan on your mother's side, Mary. And let me tell you, the Ryan's are a feisty brood!"

"Oh."

The friar chuckled. "Hmmm, Ryan and O'Malley blood mixed. Now there's toxic brew! There's a double dose of trouble..."

Not long after the friar and I said our farewells and parted ways, Hunter, Atwood and Efendi returned from the east with not much news. And then our men slowly trickled in. Two months after our arrival we weighed anchor and left the rocky, sacred shores of Ireland behind us. We set out for the New World once again.

And so this is how we lived our lives over the next few years. We ravished Spanish and Portuguese ships here and there, never too many at one time, and on occasion we raided a village or two just to keep the Spanish guessing. We never took too much. We never tarried long on any one island. We avoided killing and were always on the move - like the nomads of the desert. I was content to let Drake and others have all the fame and glory. We were just one of many nameless raiders preying on the Spanish in Caribbean waters. And whenever we had taken a worthy prize or two, we'd sail

back to the Old World, to England first, to auction off our plunder,
and then on to Ireland so men could see their loved ones.

    Life was good for one and all. Our profits were obscene.

Chapter Fifteen

dged in fine gold, purple clouds sailed across a sky of soft turquoises and brilliant reds on a glorious morning of breathtaking beauty as the crew of a familiar English man-o-war expertly eased their sturdy vessel into Guadeloupe's tranquil bay. Moving under half sail, the ship's helmsman pointed the battlecruiser's nose towards my three ships sitting quietly at anchor while her topmen scrambled up the ratlines and moved out along the spars to take in more canvas. My men and I had put in at Chief Paka Wokili's fair island a few days earlier to rest our weary bones, to take on fresh provisions. I had rowed out to *Phantom* only moments before from the shore to fetch a few amenities and watched as the English ship coasted into the bay.

With her gunports closed and her guns secured, the English ship glided gracefully into the center of our small fleet accompanied by a flock of squawking seagulls looking for scraps of food. Her crew let go the anchor and brought their man-o-war to rest within easy shouting distance of *Phantom*. I saw the mysterious Master Martin standing at the ship's helm. He offered me a friendly smile and waved.

Martin and I went ashore together in his launch where my old friend, the King of Guadeloupe, his long hair now white as snow, stood stoically on the beach waiting for us, curious to know more about our visitors. After I explained to Paka Wokili that Martin was a good and faithful servant of the mighty Queen of England, Spain's arch enemy, he commanded a great feast be held in Martin's honor. For the chief, any excuse to hold a banquet would do.

In the evening we ate and drank to excess around our

315

campfires set out along the shore while our Carib hosts gladly sang the songs of their people and danced with graceful movements to the sounds of drums made from hollowed-out logs and to claves and dried calabashes filled with pebbles or sand to entertain us. The merriment was grand. Even the unflappable Master Martin actually seemed to enjoy himself for once.

After we had filled our bellies and exchanged our stories, Martin leaned close to my ear. "Her majesty is calling upon all her commanders who love her," he whispered. "She is calling upon all those who love England, to rally around her banner. Our Sovereign Mistress is beset on all sides by enemies, enemies incited by papal intrigue, by foreign arrogance and greed."

"And what does this have to do with me?" I whispered back, indifferently.

"Did she not entrust you with a royal commission?"

I looked at the Englishman perplexed. "She thinks of me as one of her commanders?" I cared not one whit about papal intrigue, or about foreign arrogance or greed. Nor did I love England. But I had a fondness in my heart for the queen - and the Spanish and I were hardly friends.

"Why Mary, are you not one of the dame protectors of the realm? Yes, you are indeed, most certainly, one of the queen's trusted commanders. For prudence's sake, I think it wise her majesty not shout your status from atop the battlements surrounding London for all the world to hear - not just yet. Wouldn't you, a woman who cherishes anonymity, agree?"

"Aye, aye, I would indeed agree," I answered. "The thrust of your point is not lost on me. I prefer keeping to the shadows these days. How did you know where to find me? We haven't put in at Guadeloupe in ages."

Martin cracked one of his rare, thin smiles. But when he smiled his face never really changed. He always wore a mask. Even the lovely breasts of a striking Carib woman swaying directly in front of us to the music's sensual beat seemed to have little effect on him.

"Ah, Madam, you have spies and I have spies. I dare say a few of your spies and few of my spies are one and the same spy."

"Indeed? So, I pray you tell me what vexes my dear sister, the mighty Queen of England? I cannot imagine her majesty distraught over papal intrigue or troubled much by foreign arrogance or greed. Not that woman of iron. In any case, these matters are hardly new."

Martin raised an eyebrow. "I beg your pardon, Madam. Did you refer to the Queen of England as your *sister*?"

I smiled, pleased that I had bemused the mysterious Master Martin for once. "That is how the queen chose to describe me as I recall and who am I, a lowly shield maiden, a commoner and a thief, to disagree with Her Royal Majesty? By all means ask her if you like the next time you have her ear but, if you do, please assure Her Royal Majesty that I use the term *sister* most sparingly and only with a select few who understand discretion."

"Indeed, Madam. In any case, England and Spain for all intents and purposes are at war. England is sending ships, men and money to the United Provinces to break Spain's siege of Antwerp. Spain will respond in kind of course to keep her hold over the Netherlands."

"Ah, ha. War has finally come. So this is what brings you to the New World. You are the queen's trusted advisor and from what I know you are quite capable. Return to her majesty and advise her to make peace at once. Spain is a rich and dangerous adversary. Her majesty risks all with war against that mighty colossus. I dare say the odds in such a contest do not favor our good and pious queen."

"England is hardly feeble," Martin replied in a haughty tone. "We have ships built for rugged war, fine ships, and fighting men unequalled in all the world. I dare say our women are not to be trifled with either. Her majesty is proof enough of that - as are you, Mary."

I nodded my appreciation to Martin for his compliment. "I pray I'm worthy of such generous praise, good sir. Still, I'm a bit hazy on your purpose here?"

"Spain is building a great fleet of warships, the likes of which the world has never seen. King Phillip intends to invade England, depose our beloved Elizabeth and restore Catholicism to the islands to please that old lecher in Italy, that detestable prince of Rome. English armies and the Navy Royal have started making preparations to defend the kingdom of course. And the queen has authorized Captain Francis Drake, now Sir Francis Drake - you know of him - to assemble his own fleet, to include a squadron of private raiders for certain, irregular operations against the enemy."

"A squadron of privateers? You mean with ships like *Phantom*?"

"Quite so, my lady. *Phantom* is a fine warship with a disciplined crew and she is ably commanded by officers of uncommon skill."

"To what purpose? We're no match against a fleet of Spanish heavy galleons."

"How true, Mary, how true. But against smaller ships, at disrupting supplies and at creating confusion and panic in the enemy's own waters, you excel. You and your men have become quite adept at hit and run tactics I hear. You have a gift Mary and England is blessed with others like you."

"So you sailed over one thousand leagues to tell me to continue to do what we are already doing?"

"No, of course not. Drake has returned to the Caribbean in force, with a fleet of warships, and intends to cause some mischief. I sailed with him, though I have returned for other reasons. One of those reasons included finding you. You, your ships and men, will sail with me back to England."

"But -."

"But your *sister*," Martin interrupted, "the Queen of England, needs you now and I think it not to bold of me say that you owe her majesty your life."

"I see. The danger then is quite real."

"The danger is quite real, Mary. Permit me also to offer you this tidbit of news, news that might whet your appetite to see *Merrie Olde England* once more. The brothers you call the Twins have aligned themselves with Spain. England is not alone in using privateers. These men are traitors to the Crown and should your paths cross, well, war unburdens us from obedience to certain laws. You are free to kill the bastards if you see them and keep whatever spoils you take - without any recompense to the royal coffers."

"I see. And when do we sail for England?"

"We sail on the morrow, after an early breakfast. Oh my, I nearly forgot. The queen was quite touched by the exquisite pearls you gave her awhile back. She wishes to take this opportunity now to properly thank you."

Martin reached into his vest pocket to remove a maroon velvet pouch and dropped its contents, an intriguing brooch, into my hand.

"What is this?"

"The queen asked me to deliver this to you as a token of her affection."

The queen's gift was a beautifully wrought serpent - a sea serpent poised to strike, my serpent - cast in fine gold with a pair of blood-red ruby eyes. I owned very little jewelry and none of it had value. I marveled at the exquisite craftsmanship. I'm certain my eyes must have sparkled as I ran my fingers over the serpent's delicate scales, etched with wonderful detail.

I would like to say my men and I contributed in some meaningful or decisive way to England's lopsided victory over Spain and all her ships and fighting men at sea. But that would be untrue. In truth, my men and I saw very little action. And though I was there at the battle, which was a series of smaller, running engagements spanning several weeks, not one single clash of arms, I cannot say even now that I truly understand what happened as I only saw a fraction of the whole. Scholars and historians will no doubt have much to say about *Gloriana's Victory* over the *Armada*. This much I know at least: the English were very brave and bold. They had their backs against the wall. They were fighting for hearth and home and family, for their beloved queen and for their

Protestant faith. And they had the better ships. The Spanish, like the French I think, are more comfortable on land than sea. England is an island after all and her people have forever loved - and have always understood - the sea. But in truth the Spanish beat themselves. Ah, then again, there are those who say the Almighty had a hand in the final outcome too...

The *Grande y Felicisima Armada*, the Great and Fortunate Navy as it was called, left Spain in July of 1588 with nearly one hundred and fifty ships carrying twenty-five hundred cannon and twenty-six thousand souls, including slaves and priests, under the supreme command of Don Alonso Pérez de Guzmán y de Zúñiga-Sotomayor, the seventh Duke of Medina Sidonia. The fleet sailed for the Netherlands to rendezvous with a Spanish army there - thirty thousand strong - being assembled under the command of another one of King Phillip's favored princes, a man named Alejandro Farnesio, the Duke of Parma and the Governor General of the Spanish Netherlands. The Spanish invasion plan was simple enough on paper. Medina Sidonia's ships were to pick up Parma's army and ferry his men across the narrow English Channel to England to topple the heretic queen. After the queen's demise a brotherhood of fanatical priests, the *Tribunal del Santo Oficio de la Inquisición*, with the force of Spanish arms behind them, would be free to root out and eradicate English Protestantism wherever they found it. God's will. But before the mighty Spanish *Armada* left the warm and friendly waters of Spain and Portugal, before the *Armada* had even weighed anchor, it all went very wrong.

The English drew first blood. I was there to see it.

In the spring of 1587, Drake led a surprise attack against the Spanish when the grand *Armada* was still gathering all of its parts at Cádiz and at A Coruña. Drake's mission, handed down to him by the queen herself, was to harass and destroy whatever he could, to disrupt Spain's preparations for war. This was when I had first met the great English hero. I did not like him. He was pompous and vain. But, I must confess, my opinion of him was tainted by what I knew about the massacre of the MacDonnell clan at Rathlin Island.

And it was plain Drake did not like me. He did not trust me or my Irish, Catholic crews, men he thought of as thugs and most likely traitors. He kept us at a goodly distance.

Drake's fleet included four splendid Navy Royal galleons, one of which he made his flagship, the *Elizabeth Bonaventure*, twenty smaller ships, mostly converted freighters owned by adventuresome London merchants looking to turn a profit, and a wonderful squadron of first-rate privateers, including my *Phantom* and *Diablo*. I had to leave *Bella* behind with MacGyver in Plymouth after an errant supply barge missed the dock, slammed into *Bella's* stern and snapped her rudder off. Oh how the barge's fool of a master, stinking of liquor, cringed in terror that day when I unleashed my unbridled scorn upon his head!

We sailed south for the Bay of Cádiz first where Drake assigned my two ships the thankless task of waiting outside the harbor to guard his flank, to keep his line of retreat open if things went poorly for him inside. Ignoring the Spanish shore batteries, and their woefully ineffective fire, Drake boldly sailed his fleet into the harbor at sunset and attacked a Spanish fleet of three powerful Spanish galleons and sixty smaller carracks head-on. My men and I were forced to watch the battle as best we could from afar. We were only spectators and saw no close action, which also meant we would share no prize money.

The battle raged on all through the night and well into the afternoon of the next day. After sinking only a few minor ships and capturing four vessels of dubious value, Drake decided to break-off the engagement to look for easier prey. The Spanish had fought valiantly and had held their own throughout the first duel. They had earned our admiration.

We sailed up the coast to Lisbon next, attacking any ships we crossed along the way and shelling any shore batteries we passed. We achieved very little.

And then a formidable Spanish squadron of swift carracks in hot pursuit sailing up from Cádiz started gaining on us. Not liking the odds, Drake swung his ships due west, out into blue water, and set our course for the Azores. Drake was betting the skittish Spanish would never follow us out into the wild Atlantic - even under warm and sunny skies - and he was right. The Spanish commander had no stomach for the Atlantic's erratic mercy and refused to risk his squadron so far away from land. As I watched the Spaniard turn his ships around for home, I found myself wondering what kind of man would we face once the great invasion fleet set sail, a commander like the bulldog who tenaciously fought us off at Cádiz, or more like the tepid squadron commander who turned away from a brawl? Perhaps they were one and the same.

It was off the Island of São Miguel, the largest of the islands in the Azores archipelago, where Drake's fortunes truly soared. My lookouts were the first to spot a lone freighter plowing through the swells under full sail. I took my ships and we peeled away from the fleet to intercept her - until Drake raised the signal flags, ordering me to stand down. He wanted to grab the honors for himself. I had a mind to ignore the Englishman but, at Hunter's urging, I swallowed my pride and did as I was told. Drake and the *Elizabeth Bonaventure* overtook carrack easily. She was the *São Filipe* from Portugal and had left the New World for Lisbon laden down with unbelievable quantities of gold, silver, spices, silks and the like. Drake claimed her as his prize and wisely decided to hurry back to England with the *Filipe* in tow.

The queen was delighted by the news of Drake's successful raid on Cádiz. The *Filipe's* booty alone had made the whole expedition worthwhile. Her majesty took half the spoils for herself, a sum they say exceeded all the Crown's customary revenues for the entire year, and gave Drake ten percent of the winnings. The investors divvied-up the rest. My men and I didn't see one penny. But of far more importance to England than plundered treasure, Drake's daring raid had set Spain's invasion plan back many months, giving the English more time to prepare.

We heard stories from Madrid that King Phillip was infuriated by the setback and threw a royal fit. For years the name Drake had brought the royal court no joy. The spectacular capture of the Silver

Train at *Nombre de Dios*, the sackings of Santo Domingo, Veracruz and Cartagena, and more recent raids against the Azores and Cape Verde Islands, had all been by Drake's hand. The Iberian king so despised the cunning Englishman he dubbed him *El Dragón* and placed a royal bounty of twenty thousand gold ducats on his head, a sumptuous sum, but for years *El Dragón* had eluded all attempts by the Spanish navy to corner him.

And then after Cádiz, Spanish ambitions suffered a second, ominous blow. Spain's great Lord High Admiral, Álvaro de Bazán, first Marquis of Santa Cruz de Mudela, died unexpectedly in February 1588 on the eve of the great crusade. Santa Cruz, a principal architect of the Spanish galleon, a competent commander and gifted sailor, had been one of the precious few gems in the Royal Navy's officer cadre of pampered aristocrats, ne'er-do-wells and men of doubtful talent.

After Santa Cruz's death, King Phillip turned to Medina Sidonia, a court interloper with little military experience at sea or on land, and handed the most powerful navy ever assembled over to the duke. The king's choice was most curious. The newly minted admiral had never held command of any kind before. Medina Sidonia's first order as High Lord Admiral: delay the invasion. Spain lost more time.

When Medina Sidonia finally set out for England in April 1588 - after Cardinal Archduke Albert had blessed the mighty invasion fleet to the sounds of trumpets, fife and drum at High Mass held at the *Santa Maria Maior de Lisboa* and with all the trappings of royal pageantry - Spain suffered another bitter serving of misfortune. Only a few days into the expedition, a powerful spring gale swept over the *Armada*. Many ships were badly damaged and the Spanish were forced to return port to make repairs.

More precious time was lost - a bad omen for those who knew how to read the signs. Fortune had sent the King of Spain three.

Meanwhile the English, including my men and me, spent that spring and summer of 1588 in Devonport, waiting. I can't recall ever being more bored. Even now my head rebels at the very memory of the monotonous card games, the hours of tedious, heavy drinking and the endless weeks of stubborn drizzle. We sat in port bored witless, waiting for word from English spies planted in Spain and Portugal.

The dreaded day finally came in late July when English picket ships spotted the *Grande y Felicisima Armada* off the Cornish coast. All along southern England sentries lit the beacon fires to warn London of the coming storm.

My ships sat shackled to the River Tamar when word reached us to make ready. I scrambled to assemble my men and scoured the markets and farms around Davenport, buying up all the fresh provisions we could lay our hands on. Privateers eat better than their English navy cousins and enjoy superior health. The food is more wholesome and portions are more plentiful. My men were no exception. I never pinched on victuals. My men and I ate well.

After calmly finishing his game of bowls at Plymouth Hoe, or perhaps he was just waiting for the outgoing tide, Drake led us out under fair skies and light winds into the English Channel to take on the Spanish juggernaut with the race-built galleon *Revenge*, an impressive forty-six gunner, and eleven warships of different kinds plus his squadron of first rate privateers. Lord Howard Effingham soon joined us with thirty-four warships, including twenty-one powerful race-built galleons - the cream of the Navy Royal.

A hodgepodge of fifty English ships faced one hundred and fifty Spanish. I did not like the odds.

When I first laid eyes on the mighty Spanish fleet inexorably lumbering towards us under full sail, I felt my heart go faint. I had never seen such power. Masts and sails filled a vast expanse of sea. The enormous force bearing down on us looked invincible, looked unstoppable to me.

Medina Sidonia had his ships deployed in a huge, sweeping arc resembling a crescent moon. Or perhaps his formation was meant to be a scythe for harvesting Englishmen. The admiral had placed his powerful but slower galleons in the formation's center and his smaller escort ships, mostly zabras and patches used to protect and resupply the galleons, at the wings forming the crescent's horns. The fleet stretched across the sea for miles. Even now it is difficult for me to faithfully describe the sheer grandeur of what I saw. The Spanish must have looked down on our puny English fleet sailing out to stop them with utter contempt.

And the galleons of the *Armada* were nothing like what we had seen in the New World. These were huge battlewagons displacing nine hundred tons or more with thick, oak hulls and massive sails. They were armed with batteries of demi-culverines, guns of enormous size capable of hurtling iron shot weighing thirty pounds or better at targets over a mile away. But these brutes were also slow and clumsy compared to England's swift and nimble warships. In fair seas or foul, a Spanish war galleon will never out-sail an English race-built galleon.

Just south of Rame Head near the Eddystone Rocks, a place of no military significance, is where the battle started. We stood off these hazards a ways and opened fire on the Spanish with over a mile of water between us. We concentrated our bombardment on the huge Spanish galleons, lobbing our iron balls at them for several hours though I know not why. We accomplished very little at such long range - except to waste good shot and powder. When we did manage to hit anything besides ocean, our iron simply bounced off the impenetrable Spanish hulls. The Spanish must have howled with laughter at our foolishness. But we did learn something of interest during that first skirmish. For every shot the Spanish fired, we answered them with three or four. Spanish gunners had been excruciatingly sluggish returning fire. With a bird's eye view of the battle high up in the rigging, my topmen had been quick to spot the problem. Spanish decks were grossly overcrowded with supplies and provisions of every sort. Spanish gunners struggled hauling in and reloading their great guns surrounded by stacks of clutter, by crates and barrels and bundles of every size and kind - a fatal flaw in tactics perhaps.

Following a long day of pointless gunnery, with no ships damaged on either side, we followed the Spanish up Channel well into the night. But when my men and I lost sight of Drake and the *Revenge* in the mist and dark, I turned my three ships around and headed for Portsmouth, a port closer to us than Plymouth, to take on more ball and powder. Our magazines and shot lockers were nearly empty and I didn't trust the English to resupply us privateers.

After replenishing our stores of ammunition and buying more fresh victuals in Portsmouth, we set out on the first tide and caught up to the English fleet a few days later sitting off Calais. The Spanish *Armada* had dropped anchor in the roadstead outside of the French port to, we all assumed, wait for Parma's army. But Drake had other plans for the Spanish.

That night Drake confiscated eight ships, ships he deemed expendable including my poor *Bella*. He had in mind a sacrifice, something to warm Poseidon's cold heart. At midnight, English sailors loaded the eight ships down with pitch, brimstone and tar, set them ablaze and launched the doomed squadron downwind towards the tightly packed Spanish ships riding anchor. The English call their fire ships *Hell Burners* and to the Spanish it must have looked like hell was coming for them. Panic jumped from ship to ship as crews watched the wall of fire drifting their way in horror. Captains gave the order to cut the anchor cables and all good order within the Spanish fleet disintegrated as ships sailed out to sea to escape the rolling conflagration. When morning broke we saw a Spanish fleet in disarray, struggling to regroup. And when his ships were unable to reassemble in the fluky, ornery winds of that day, Medina Sidonia gave up on Calais and moved his fleet a little ways north along the *Côte d'Opale*, up the Opal Coast, to Gravelines.

My men and I missed all the hot action at Gravelines the following day and again I felt cheated. Drake had sent my two ships farther north to join a Dutch fleet of thirty fly boats at Dunkerque. The Dutch were blockading the French port to prevent Medina Sidonia from rendezvousing with Parma there and I was to deliver private dispatches, an absurdly menial task, to the Dutch fleet's commander, Admiral Justin of Nassau. In addition to our courier duties, we were to keep a close eye on our fidgety Dutch allies.

Gravelines was an epic struggle. The English launched an all-out assault against the *Armada*. Ships traded broadside after broadside for hours. They say that Protestant Dutch refugees, French Huguenots and local town folk turned out by the thousands along the Cliffs of Dover to see what they could see of the life and death struggle twenty miles across the Channel. They watched the battle anxiously, too far away to be able discern who was winning and who was losing but knowing all the while that an English defeat would bring their doom.

With their faster ships and better crews, the English mauled the Spanish fleet. English gunners targeted Spanish gunners, inflicting horrendous losses on their kind. Midway through the battle, Medina Sidonia's commanders were forced to replace their losses using marines after hundreds of Spanish gunners had fallen. But Spanish marines had no experience working the navy's great guns and the *Armada* suffered for it.

Two fine galleons, the *San Mateo* and the *San Felipe*, drifted away from the battle in bad condition and floated past us at Dunkerque late in the day. I took my ships and gave chase, hoping to snag ourselves a prize but with a pair of Dutch warships chasing after me. When the galleons ran aground at Walcheren, the Dutch claimed the warships for themselves and found no reason to share the spoils with us Irish.

Disgusted with the Dutch and with my own bad luck, and jaded with blockade duty, I took my ships without orders and sailed south to find the fleet. When we sailed past Gravelines we saw the Spanish still anchored in the roadstead. We gave that colossus a wide berth. We continued sailing south until we found the English fleet off Calais strung out across the Channel in a defensive line.

Bloodied at Gravelines, running short on supplies of food, water and ammunition and unable to link-up with Parma's invasion army at any point along the French coast, Admiral Medina Sidonia knew the campaign was lost and decided to return to Spain while he still had a fleet to return with. But the *Armada* was still a dangerous beast and the English weren't about to let the duke slither away scot-free. This was why the English waited for the Spanish off Calais - daring Median Sidonia to sail south through their line of battle. If the Spanish wanted to return home by the shorter, safer passage down Channel, back by the easy way they had come, they'd first need to bludgeon their way through an English wall of wood and iron.

The English knew their man. The High Lord Admiral had no stomach for another risky, bloody fight and ordered a *North About*. The duke decided to take his chances up Channel, which meant the *Armada* would need to sail north, far north, in the opposite direction of Spain, cut through the stormy North Sea and then sail around the whole of the British Isles. The choice had to have been a difficult one to make. Medina Sidonia knew, we all knew, that any voyage north around Scotland and Ireland would be a long and perilous one.

The Spanish started their journey well enough. They departed Gravelines with fair weather and in good order. The whole English fleet dropped sail to follow them. But once the last of the *Armada's* squadrons disappeared into the mist off the Firth of Forth, once the winds and currents seized the Spanish ships, making it nearly impossible to turn back, the English swung their ships around and headed due south for home. I wonder if Medina Sidonia felt the icy hand of doom resting on his shoulder when he saw the English turn and sail away. As I reflect on these events now, it was at this moment I think when God deserted the Spanish.

I did not turn my ships with the English. No. I had other plans. I asked my men to buckle on their courage and then we followed the Spanish into the swirling, ominous mist. My service to England in the war against Spain was finished. I had honored my oath to the queen. But we had nothing to show for our efforts. I had no illusions about the English navy ever paying us for our services, or compensating me for the *Bella*, and we hadn't taken even one, small prize. My officers and I all agreed we would shadow the *Armada* all the way back to Spain if needed to try and pick-off a straggler or two. The Spanish were still fair game.

After we rounded the northern tip of Scotland and headed west, skirting in-between the Orkneys and Fair Island, the winds freshened and the seas began boiling with angry whitecaps. The temperature suddenly plummeted and the skies unloosed torrents of freezing rain. For days intermittent squalls of mean temperament coming down from the cold northlands of Scandinavia ravaged and abused us. One storm after another punched and counter-punched our ships like punching bags.

Unprepared for the cruel and unforgiving North Sea, the Spanish paid a dreadful price. We watched the swells batter the *Armada's* ships to pieces. One galleon near us broke in two. We watched her bow - with no gladness in our hearts - drift one way and her stern the other until both sections slipped beneath the waves with all hands lost. Other ships struggled, trying to avoid the same fate. At first it was unclear to us why so many Spanish vessels were sailing so poorly in the squalls. The winds and swells were grueling indeed. But we had seen Spanish ships handle seas no less rough, no less erratic in the Caribbean well enough. We only learned the truth some months later. The Spanish had precious few Atlantic-class cruisers in their grand invasion fleet. Many of their ships had been hastily built and poorly constructed for what men thought would be a short voyage to France and then an easy hop and a skip across the English Channel to England. The Spanish had built themselves a fleet of flimsy channel barges for their ambitious invasion, not sturdy, seagoing battlecruisers.

Merchantmen, overflowing with soldiers, horses and supplies of every sort fared no better than the warships. Ships were taking on more water than their pumps could handle in the heavy seas. We saw more than one vessel in danger of capsizing. Sailors began pitching supplies, cannon and even animals over the side in desperation. One poor horse struggling in the waves looked up at me wild-eyed as we sailed by. We had no means to save the animal and sadly watched the horse drift off into the dark abyss neighing frantically. A few ships in difficulty, those with anchors, ran to shore for shelter. But for the ships without anchors, their crews having left them on the seabed at Calais to escape Drake's dreaded *Hell Burners*, they had to plow ahead as best they could. The risk of foundering on the shoals near land was too great.

To add to Spanish woes, food supplies were dwindling fast and had to be severely rationed. Some crews were down to boiling rope and leather to eat.

And men were cold. Too many lacked proper, warm clothing. The Spanish had left the southern latitudes of sunny Spain in July expecting to be in London in a few weeks. But autumn comes early near the northern latitudes of the Arctic Circle and even in August the air can turn bone-chilling cold out on the open water.

Disease preys on malnourished men shivering in the cold. Spaniards fell by the score to starvation and to exposure. Even with our well-provisioned ships, we lost men to illness too.

But these hardships were nothing.

Once the Spanish cleared the Outer Hebrides, once the *Armada* entered the North Atlantic, Medina Sidonia and his navigators - men with no experience in those waters - made a horrible, tragic mistake. Steering by dead reckoning and latitude is not enough to navigate the contrary winds and currents around northern Scotland and Ireland. Those waters are perilous year round as any seasoned Scot or Irish seaman knows.

Admiral Medina Sidonia had one last easy - but crucial - maneuver to make once his fleet reached the North Atlantic. He needed to turn south. After that simple maneuver his course was a straight line for home. But in the poor visibility brought on by unrelenting squalls and fog, and in his haste to get home before all his men perished from the elements and starvation, the Spaniard misjudged the timing of his great wheeling maneuver around Ireland. The unfortunate duke gave the order to turn too soon and brought his fleet frightfully close to Ireland's rugged west coast, too close to her dangerous rocks and crushing breakers. That simple error in navigation would do more harm to Iberian dreams of conquest than the whole of the English navy.

We followed the Spanish ships from a goodly distance. We did not turn as they turned, no. We kept ourselves farther out to sea in our swift and nimble ships, ships far more seaworthy than the Spanish galleons, galleasses, zabras and patches we were chasing after. I still had hopes of picking-off a prize or two. And we did find stragglers here and there, though heavy seas kept us from closing with even one. And then, on the first day of September, we saw, through thin gaps in the mist, the forbidding cliffs of Ireland looming large off our port bow, closer than what even my men and I were prepared for...

Chapter Sixteen

s my tiny fleet continued shadowing the grand *Armada* off the coast of Ireland, a second storm, an ungodly storm blowing up from the south-west and far worse than the sporadic squalls we had encountered off Scotland - a great monster unleashed by the New World - swooped down on us with a terrible, raw fury. With nearly *huracán* strength winds and wicked rollers, the frightful tempest drove the Spanish ships hard towards the breakers, cliffs and reefs of ancient, sacred Ireland, a land where Celts bury their saints and sinners side-by-side. My men and I had never witnessed such a storm before in those waters. But like a woman's heart, one can never truly know the sea.

At that very moment Medina Sidonia, no doubt to his horror, must have understood the unhappy consequences of his earlier mistake in navigation as he watched all order disintegrate within his ill-fated fleet. His captains could not keep to their stations against the towering waves spilling over the rails, knocking their ships about like fragile toys. Ships foundered in the heavy seas or were dashed against the jagged breakers where wood and bone are no match against ruthless rock. Whole squadrons vanished in the night. Thousands perished.

My own ships did not come through the storm unscathed. In the morning, in calmer seas and lighter winds, we found *Diablo* with a broken bowsprit. *Phantom's* rigging was in shambles and we had lost three souls to the sea sometime during the night. Luckless or careless I know not. I sent Atwood limping into Limerick with *Diablo* as Limerick was the closest port of any substance while I stayed out on the open water, unwilling to give up the hunt.

My perseverance was at last rewarded. As soon as *Diablo* left our company, Good Fortune found us after a long and painful absence. Hunter spotted a lone, two-masted Spanish galleass not far off in the distance and we saw our chance to snag ourselves a prize. Her lateen-rigged sails, stitched together with alternating vertical red and yellow stripes, caught the eye. She looked to be about two hundred tons or so with two banks of sixty oars. She carried no more than ten small cannon.

My men hastily repaired our rigging, spicing lines together and patching up torn sails as best they could and before long we were on the move again, sailing close hauled towards our target. Following a spirited chase we overtook the galleass with plenty of daylight left. With one shot across the bow her crew wisely heaved-to. She was no match for our deadly *Phantom*. After the galleass's crew smartly lowered their ship's distinctive red and yellow sails, her oarsman crisply pulled in their sweeps, letting the galleass coast to an easy stop. I took Hunter and a boarding party of twenty in the longboat over with me to have a look around.

The galleass's captain, a most hospitable Italian, a man of pleasant smiles and friendly tones, introduced himself in tolerable English from the aft rail as Antonio Marcus from Naples. He even extended his hand in a gracious gesture to help me aboard.

After I stepped on deck, wretched souls wrapped in dirty, threadbare rags gathered around me with curiosity. Marcus and his crew were a sorry, filthy lot. They were all skin and bones with open sores and cracked lips. Hunger and the elements had beaten each man down, including Captain Marcus - which earned him my respect. As I took in my surroundings it was plain to see the galleass posed no threat. These Spanish and Italians had no more fight left in them. As they considered me with hollow, bloodshot eyes and as I considered them, I could not find the face of my enemy among them, not one. Frail, homesick men are all I saw. I saw the faces of husbands, fathers, sons and brothers, of men who would gladly have paid me gold for a scrap of moldy bread.

Marcus apologized profusely for the sad appearance of his crew.

He explained that not long after departing Spain their supplies of food had quickly rotted and their water had turned sour. In their haste to please their king the navy's coopers, "the fools" he called them and spat, had used green, uncured wood to fashion the staves to make the navy's casks and barrels. As a consequence, captains throughout the fleet had to severely rationed food and water early on in the campaign. Hunger and illness struck the Spaniards hard soon after. Marcus had lost a third of his ship's complement since leaving Spain.

While Hunter and the boarding party disappeared below to search the ship from stem to stern, the galleass's weary crew kept their tired eyes fixed on me as I remained on deck with Marcus exchanging idle, friendly chitchat. Even though I sensed no hostility among the crew, I rested my hand on the hilt of my sword just in case and was glad for the brace of pistols Hunter had tucked inside my belt against the small of my back.

After one of my men returned from below to inform me that our Spanish trophy was of no great value, I shook my head in disgust. The galleass was carrying mostly boots, tents, cots, cooking pots and the like meant for Parma's army stranded back on the continent, things that did not interest me. Our excursion into the North Sea chasing after the *Armada* had been for naught. I had risked all of our lives for nothing. I cursed my foul luck.

Marcus shrugged his shoulders and smiled after my man finished his report. I was uncertain of whether the Italian was bemused or amused by my frustration.

But then Hunter came bounding up the companionway grinning like some silly schoolboy carrying a small chest in his arms. Marcus suddenly looked less amused when he saw what Hunter had. Hunter pulled the lid open to show me the gold *reales* inside. He had found six chests in all in the captain's great cabin hidden behind a false panel. We took the gold for ourselves of course. But I also took pity on Marcus and his men. I sent ten of my own back to *Phantom* with our treasure and had them return with clothing, blankets, food and fresh water, enough food and water for the

Spanish to get themselves back to Spain. I had no desire to see any more young men die and I had no interest in taking any prisoners.

As Marcus leaned over the rail, watching my crew and I pile back into our longboat for good, I looked up at him and waved farewell. He answered me with a playful smile.

"You Irish haggle poorly," he called down to me.

"How so?" I asked.

"We have robbed you blind, my lady," he answered good-naturedly. "You have given us our freedom. You have given us life in exchange for a few paltry boxes of pretty metal, metal of little use to us except for ballast."

I laughed and wished him good fortune as he cheerfully waved us off. The galleass was my *São Filipe*. Those six chests of gold had made the whole voyage back to the Old World worthwhile.

We meandered back and forth off the coast of western Munster for another day, trolling those murky waters for fresh victims, but found none. Whatever was left of the *Armada* had moved far south. And so we put in at Limerick to replenish our supplies and to rendezvous with *Diablo*. But Atwood had already replaced his bowsprit and had departed Limerick we learned, which meant he was on his way north for Westport to look for us.

Limerick was abuzz with talk of the Spanish *Armada* of course. From fellow mariners we learned that any Spaniards who had survived the shipwrecks and made it to shore were being rounded-up and executed on the spot by the English, along with any Irish who offered them assistance or sanctuary of any kind. The Lord Deputy of Dublin himself had issued the execution order. Except for Spanish officers and nobility, who were to be held for ransom, no prisoners were to be taken. Hundreds of unarmed Spaniards had been butchered already and more were being hunted down in the woods and hills each day. My thoughts turned to Captain Marcus and his men. I was glad I had set them free. I was glad that they would live.

Up and down the waterfront we heard talk, boastful talk, that the *Armada's* losses were staggering. Barely half the Spanish fleet would ever make it back to sunny, Catholic Spain, or so folks said. Whatever the truth, no one could deny that Phillip's expedition had been a colossal failure.

We did not tarry long in Limerick. We scrambled back aboard our ship and after we stowed away our supplies, we dropped our sails and pointed *Phantom's* sharp prow north for Westport to find our brother Atwood.

After we reached Westport, once we had properly overhauled our ships and replenished our stores of ammunition and food and the like, I intended to cross the broad Atlantic for the New World without delay. I had had a belly-full of the old one.

"Mary, Mary!" Henry shouted at me excitedly while I was squatting at the head answering nature's call. "Come quick, come quick I say!"

I pulled my trousers up and hurried back to the helm with Henry practically dragging me along. Despite his own excitement he didn't say a word. And when we reached the quarter deck, I immediately understood Henry's zeal; I understood why he had said nothing. There was no need for any words.

There on the water, coming down from the north and tacking against blustery headwinds, I saw *Medusa's Head*! She was rounding the leeward side of Clare Island for Westport. She had lost half her mizzen mast, her sails were tattered and her main spar had fallen. The massive wood laid cock-eyed across her deck, buried underneath a heap of rope, tackle and canvas. It was plain to see *Medusa* had sailed with the Spanish *Armada* through the gale. We had heard rumors from Martin about Irish privateers sailing alongside the Spanish. Bruised and battered, *Medusa's* crew no doubt was stopping in Westport to make repairs before sailing on to Youghal. This Godsend was worth more to me than our six chests of Spanish gold.

Hunter, MacGyver and Efendi, standing together at the aft rail, spun around in unison to greet me with broad smiles. Efendi had already laid out his sharp knives across the rail for a quick inspection. We had the wind, we had the currents and we had surprise on our side. *Medusa's* weary men ignored us, oblivious of who we were. They sounded no alarm; they took no precautions as we glided closer to them. They seemed content to just make port. I told Henry to quietly pass the word around: bring up the swivels and all our arms, prime and load the guns, but don't run them out - not yet.

"Good Fortune is with you, Mary," Hunter said, absently scratching the stubble on his chin. "You are blessed. When *Medusa* turns due east and her crew makes for port, Mary..."

I smiled. "Aye, when they turn due east we can come up behind them and hit their stern at close range with a raking broadside. They've got land and shallow water to their port and contrary winds to their starboard. Boxed in like that, they won't be able to do much more than sail clumsily straight ahead. We'll need to move out smartly though, not much daylight left."

Hunter nodded with satisfaction while rocking back and forth on his heels. "Quite so, my lady, quite so. Not bad for a ship's cook. We should only need one pass if we do this right. Michael, Mustafa, arm the lads, prime and load the guns as Mary says and form a boarding party - and be quiet about it now."

Ever since that terrible night of slaughter in Guadeloupe, I had imagined in my mind many times how this day might play out. I had imagined a long and agonizing end for the Twins. I wanted them to suffer. I wanted them to have ample time to reflect on their wickedness as I slowly bled their lives away - as they had done to Gilley and all the others and had nearly done to me. Now I would have my chance.

MacGyver took the helm. Efendi, Henry and Kinkae moved among the men, quietly readying the ship for action. Hunter stood at my side and barked out orders to trim the sails. But I and I alone was the captain of the *Phantom* again. This was my moment.

"Michael, a point to port," I said in a calm and confident tone.

"A point to port it is, my lady," he replied and nudged the tiller over.

"Henry," I called out. "Go to the beak-head. If anyone on *Medusa* hails us, ask them if they have a physician aboard. Tell them our captain was gravely wounded by a Spanish ball."

My Carib lieutenant, imitating the silliness he had seen Hunter and others do, bowed to me as if I were royalty. "Aye, Mum," he said and hurried to the beak-head shouting along the way: "*Enry can tu it! Enry can tu it!*"

I looked over at Efendi next. "Mustafa! When we make our turn to starboard, you know what must be done. Make every shot count."

Efendi's lips curled into a crooked smile. He offered me a reassuring nod before he made his way down to the main deck to carry out my orders.

To my surprise, *Medusa* continued sailing blissfully on towards Westport, oblivious to any approaching danger. Her crew made no attempt to maneuver away from us as we drew closer. They made no attempt to take their vessel out into the channel's deeper waters.

I reached down and discreetly took Hunter's hand. "James, what do you think?"

"I suspect," he said, squeezing my hand reassuringly, "if the Twins are even onboard they, like Dowlin - before you lopped-off his head - are poor sailors. Most likely they'll feel secure and safe in their great war galleon, especially with Westport only a few leagues away. Arrogance has killed more than one man over the ages. I smell no trick at play here - unless they intend to blow themselves to kingdom come and take us with them if we sail too close. Our tactical position could not be better."

I placed my hand on his chest. "Have a care with my heart when we board *Medusa*, James Hunter. Do not be reckless with your life."

He laughed at me. "I shall do my very best, dear lady, rest assured of that! And you, you hold back for a bit until it is clear victory is ours. Only then should you follow me over with the second wave to press home our attack."

I surprised us both when I agreed.

At one hundred yards, *Medusa's* officer of the watch - there was no sign of the Twins - took an interest in us as we closed. Henry richly played his part asking for a physician, purchasing us a little time. At seventy-five yards *Medusa's* officer of the watch waved us off and repeated that his ship had no physician or surgeon on board to help us. At fifty yards I gave the order to turn the *Phantom* into *Medusa* and Efendi had our men run out the port side guns.

My gunners jumped into action as we closed with *Medusa*. One-by-one the gun captains brushed their burning linstocks against the touchholes of their guns as *Medusa* drifted past their sights. The linstocks ignited the black powder and the powder set off the charges, propelling twelve pound iron shot violently through the air in quick succession. Heavy guns shattered the day's fragile serenity belching smoke and fire.

At such close range my gunners couldn't miss. Every man hit his target. Our iron wreaked terrible damage on *Medusa*. The first two balls smashed her rudder to pieces. Our iron shattered wood rails and cabin windows, launching shards of glass and jagged splinters through the air in all directions. And then we heard *Medusa's* Bonaventure crack. The great stick wobbled for a bit before toppling over the side with a horrible, screeching noise, taking sails and rigging with it.

Then Hunter hoisted my battle flag up the main mast. I smiled when I saw the serpent, a red sea serpent poised to strike on a field of yellow-gold, fluttering freely in the wind.

We circled around for a second pass. Only this time we came in closer. With a broken rudder and her Bonaventure dragging in the water, *Medusa's* men shortened sail and wisely brought their crippled ship to a dead stop before they ran aground. My men lined up along the rails and threw out grappling hooks to snag the handsome man-o-war. After they hauled her in, Hunter stormed aboard *Medusa* with a company of one hundred men, with our biggest, strongest fighters. I sent another fifty aloft in *Phantom's* rigging with muskets to cover them. And then I drew my sword and pistol and followed Hunter over with my fearsome Carib warriors, covered in bright war-paint from head to toe, and my muscular, battle-hardened Moors.

We easily overwhelmed *Medusa's* men defending the aftercastle and pushed them back. Most fled down the double stairs to the main deck. More than a dozen surrendered, mistaking us for English navy. Hunter and his company continued the assault while my men and I secured our prisoners and then we reformed ranks. I had six swivels brought over from the *Phantom* and my gunners hooked them over *Medusa's* fore rail. They took aim at *Medusa's* crew packed in tight below on the main deck.

"Surrender or die!" I shouted down to them.

The defenders wavered. For an instant I thought the battle was over, that we had won a cheap and easy victory. But then, emerging from the forecastle near the bow, the Twins, huge and terrifying, stepped on deck, brandishing swords and muskets. Even from a distance I could see the murder in their eyes. Scores of men came pouring out on deck behind them. The Twins rallied their crew, numbering close to four hundred, and charged at us. We fired the swivels and dozens fell. We fired-off our muskets and dozens more fell. And as we reloaded my musketeers up in *Phantom's* rigging fired-off a volley too. Still the Twins and their men kept coming. By sheer force of numbers, *Medusa's* crew pushed Hunter and his men back, back across a deck slick with blood and gore, across a killing zone fouled with piss and shit. Rivulets of blood trickled down the scuppers. The fighting turned savage, hand-to-hand. Men mad to kill locked with men mad to live tore at each other shooting, gouging, stabbing, punching, choking, biting...

MacGyver and Efendi, on Hunter's orders I knew, moved next to my side as I rushed down the stairs to the main deck. Each of us marked a target, fired, and three defenders went down.

And then I heard Hunter cry out, his voice ringing with godlike power: "Attack, lads! Attack! Beat these bastards back! *Hoorah!* Forward, I say! Forward! The ship is ours! *Faugh a Ballagh!*"

My men surged forward with Hunter, shouting the old Celtic war cry with him. "*Faugh a Ballagh! Faugh a Ballagh!*" they screamed with one, thundering voice.

I could see Hunter near the main mast wading into a cluster of *Medusa's* men, wielding his sword right and left like a man berserk, cutting a bloody path to reach the Twins. He charged ahead with no fear. He plowed into the enemy like Achilles, a New World Achilles. Men shrieked and fell back in horror as Hunter relentlessly hacked them down one after the other without pity.

But not the Twins, no. They did not fall back. Hunter's bravado meant nothing to them. The massive brothers brushed their own men aside like rag dolls in their haste to get at Hunter, killing any of my men who dared step in their way. The Twins seemed unstoppable and I gasped when they somehow managed to close in on Hunter. I threw myself into the thick of the melee with no care for my life, desperately trying to reach Hunter's side until a brute, a repulsive man, a man nearly as big as the Twins, stepped in front of me. He swung his *falchion* from left to right, barely missing my throat. Efendi, my brave and loyal Turk, brought the giant down with one powerful thrust of his knife into the man's bowels. The blade went deep. The man glared at Efendi as Efendi sliced his way from the man's naval up to his breastbone as if he was gutting a fish. The brute sank to his knees trying to scoop up his entrails as they spilled out all around him. He keeled over and died before I could slit his throat.

I ran a second sailor through the lung and MacGyver hacked-off the leg another with a battle axe. Grisly, brutal work. My man fell on his back but kept thrashing his sword around trying to cut me until I dropped to my knees and plunged my dagger into his heart. And when I stood, drenched in blood from head to toe, I saw in the fading light the vicious fighting all around me ebbing like the tide. Men were holding back and checking their blows. I couldn't imagine why. And then I saw men stepping aside to give my Hunter and the Twins - my Twins - room to fight. This was like watching a play for the second time. This was Guadeloupe again.

"You!" Remus, the taller of the two brothers cried out after recognizing Hunter. "I fuckin' killed you once, maggot."

Seized by bloodlust, Hunter took a step closer and laughed. "You miserable, foul-mouthed oaf! You disgrace! I'm the one who bested you that day. You'd be dead all these past years but for your cowardly brother who shot me down before I could finish you off! But here I stand and I come bearing gifts. Today Hades has dubbed me his trusty herald and one of his invitations bears your name. Today I will give you the rematch you long for though I promise you, you'll take no joy from it. Today your men will hear you scream when I rip out your wretched heart. Look up at the sky my friend. Take a good look at the setting sun. For this is the last you or your wretched brother will ever see of it."

Remus grunted in reply. Wielding a Caribbean cutlass, he lunged at Hunter with all his fearsome strength. But Hunter, with a quickness and raw power I'd never seen before, grabbed Remus by the wrist and cut his hand off with one, quick blow. Remus howled in agony, pressed his bloody stump into his armpit and stumbled backwards, leaving his severed hand behind still clutching at its sword.

Then the one-eyed Cyclops named Romulus, the more formidable threat by far, stepped into the circle. That man, I must grudgingly admit, had no fear and he was cleverer than his brother.

He ignored his brother's whimpering. He paused for a moment to consider Hunter and forced a friendly smile, though I will never forget the loathing I saw in his eyes. "After I disembowel you," he told Hunter, while contemptuously kicking his brother's mangled hand aside. "I am going to fuck your bitch over there. I'm going to fuck her raw. And when she starts to bore me, I'll hurt her in ways you can't possibly imagine. I'll feed tiny pieces of her to my dogs and make her watch. A finger here, a toe there, perhaps even a nose or an ear. I'll keep her alive in horrible pain for long, excruciating weeks, perhaps months, I swear it."

But Hunter didn't take the bait. He kept his cool composure. "I do the world a favor by killing you this day," he said. "Tonight your one-eyed carcass will swing from your own yardarm to rot, next to your one-handed brother. What a sight you'll both make dangling side-by-side from the yardarm. Tonight my woman and I will raise our glasses high and make a toast to your new place in hell as your mangled bodies twist and turn in the wind."

But Romulus wasn't about to take the bait either. He ignored Hunter's taunting; he ignored Hunter's blatant attempt to provoke him into rash and thoughtless action.

The two men squared-off calmly, each man carefully dancing around the other, taking time to gauge the mettle of his opponent. Hunter made the first move. He took a step forward and thrust his sword at the one-eyed Twin. He missed. He took a second step forward, lunged again and missed. He took a third step forward, feinted to the left, feinted to the right and tried running Romulus through the heart. But the Twin was not so easily fooled and he was quicker than his brother. He deftly stepped aside and parried the mortal blow.

Romulus countered, swung his body around and tried taking off Hunter's head. But Romulus's blade found only empty air to slice through when Hunter ducked. Then both men settled down and warily circled around and around each other. They slashed and hacked away, both men looking for some weakness in the other to exploit. It was a battle of two titans, of two godlike champions at the pinnacle of their astonishing powers. All of us, men on both sides, stood and watched in awe.

The duel dragged on and on. The two warriors went at each other relentlessly for what seemed like long hours. They fought each other like gladiators in the ring where no quarter was asked and none would be given and it was by no means certain at first which man in the end would prevail. They seemed an even match.

But then, after both men had exchanged many blows and counter-blows, a smile touched my lips. I saw the sweat trickling down Romulus's temple. I could see his arms begin to tire. I could see the wobble in his legs. He switched tactics too. He started fighting defensively, wielding his sword with two hands to compensate the strength draining from his limbs.

Hunter started moving with more confidence, with more power. He had conserved his strength. He had been toying with the Cyclops all along.

Romulus soon understood the terrible truth. "Lads!" he finally called out, trying to make men think he held the upper hand. "Enough of this foolishness - this strutting popinjay and I have fought ourselves to a stalemate. But we can still snuff out all the rest with our greater numbers. Kill them, kill them all I say!"

I clenched my teeth, raised my sword above my head and took several steps forward. "NOOO!" I screamed. "This abomination you call your chieftain is nothing more than a cruel and craven coward. If one man moves, just one of you - I'll show no mercy. I'll murder the whole lot of you. I swear it. And no one will question me. The English already know you've sided with the Spanish. See my men up in *Phantom's* rigging and along *Medusa's* fore rail with muskets and swivels at the ready? You're caught in a cross-fire. You'll all be slaughtered. Do not test me for I am, if you do not know it, the bitch all men dread. I am the last offspring of the last of the Kings of Umaill. *I AM BLOODY MARY!*"

Romulus searched the faces of his men. No one stirred to help him. He looked back at me and snickered. "You, the descendant of a king? Ha! How preposterous. You're the daughter of the gutter, the bastard child of a whore. I'll deal with you later, after all your men are dead, you diseased-riddled trollop! Hear that lads - I want Mary alive."

And with one last fierce surge of energy, with one last roll of the dice, the mighty, one-eyed Twin threw himself at Hunter with everything he had. He raised a knee and slammed it hard into Hunter's midriff, catching Hunter off-guard. Hunter doubled over in agony. Then Romulus raised his sword high above his head to drive the sharp-edged hilt down into Hunter's skull. For the second time that day, I put my hand to my mouth and gasped.

But what followed next stunned us all. Hunter pounced. He wrapped his arms tightly around Romulus's hips, lifted the giant up off his feet - as if he were tossing a sack of apples over his shoulder - and slammed Romulus down against the deck. Romulus's head smacked the wood hard and he let out a dreadful howl. I thought I heard his skull crack. Hunter straddled the brute, used his knees to pin the monster's arms down and rested the edge of his sword across Romulus's neck. The one-eyed Twin looked up at Hunter dazed and unsure, grimacing in pain.

And then, out of the corner of my eye, I saw Remus, his bloody stump now wrapped in linen, come at Hunter from behind with a machete in his hand, barely a step or two away. I jumped into the circle ready to plunge my sword into his belly when a chill shot down my spine after I realized that Remus was just beyond my reach. But not beyond Efendi's. Efendi's knife flew past my nose and buried itself in Remus's windpipe.

Remus didn't scream. He didn't even cry out. He dropped his machete to free his hand and calmly plucked Efendi's knife from his throat as if he was removing an irksome splinter. Still very much alive, he moved forward to stab Hunter in the back with Efendi's own blade - until I kicked him behind the knee, causing him to stumble. And before he could regain his balance, I brought my sword around my shoulder and cut off his pig head. His corpse twitched for a bit, spraying jets of blood through the air, and then toppled over.

Hunter then finished it. "Now you can join your brother," he cried out. "Time for you to die!"

I spun around just in time to catch Hunter, with one quick pull of his sword, cut Romulus's carotid artery open. Romulus gagged on his own blood for a bit until his one good eye rolled up into its socket and he was gone. Hunter had killed my man and I had killed his.

With both Twins, lying dead in a pool of blood, *Medusa's* men had no more fight left in them and threw their weapons down. At long last the ugly deed was finished. Finally the long and costly blood vendetta between the Twins and me was settled. And it was me, a meek, imprudent woman, the bastard daughter of a clan chieftain raised by a common laborer, a butcher, and the daughter of a whore, who had won.

Hunter and I embraced and kissed while my men watched and smiled. I didn't care. I was thrilled the Twins were dead. I was overjoyed that Hunter was alive and well. He didn't have a scratch on him.

And then, feeling strangely tired, I returned to the *Phantom* and let Hunter and the others secure the *Falling Star* and our prisoners without me. After every battle, always, I had lured Hunter into my bed to ravage me. But not this time. Once I was back in my cabin, I stripped off all my clothes, soaked in filth and gore, washed the blood off my face and hands in cool, clean water with soap and crawled into my bed, exhausted. With little effort I floated off into a deep and peaceful slumber.

Chapter Seventeen

nown for its wholesome food and good hospitality, we chose Shaw's splendid establishment to eat and drink and celebrate - renamed *Fúmsa an Díoltas* in my honor - the place where the Twins had first tried to kill me. And after supper, when we were all feeling mellow, we gave thought to our future and plotted new adventures. The Twins were dead and the Spanish would be licking their wounds for a very long time. *Falling Star* was mine again and we had six chests topped off with Spanish gold. Good Fortune was lavishing her bounty on me.

And I could hear the Caribbean whispering my name, whispering to me to come home. Yes, I thought of the islands as home. I could not imagine a better, richer life.

After midnight men started drifting back to the ships or headed out on the road to see their homes and families again - I had given everyone thirty days' liberty, give or take. Among my officers only Hunter stayed behind with me to finish off the wine and ale.

And then a man I recognized as one of Martin's, I did not know his name, burst in through the tavern's door. A rogue gust of wind followed after him carrying debris and dead leaves inside. He nodded when he saw me and hurried over to our table. His trousers were splattered with drops of what looked like blood and his boots were caked in mud. Sweat trickled down his brow. He paused to catch his breath.

"Lady Mary, Master Martin has sent me to find you. He's down at the old mill. Do you know it?"

"Aye, I know the place. It's been abandoned for years. Why?"

"Master Martin is there. He's been shot-up pretty good."

"What? Who shot him?"

"I know not. Three angry men tried to rob us on the highway. They looked like foreigners, shipwrecked Spaniards on the run most likely. One of them pulled out a pistol and shot Martin off his horse when Martin went to draw his sword. Martin asks for your help before the Irish or Spanish find him. He asks you to secret him out of Westport. We must hurry and get him to a friendly town under the protection of English soldiers."

"How many men does he have with him?"

"None."

"None?"

"No, Madam, none. When we came ashore he brought only me."

I looked around the tavern and counted, including Hunter and me, only thirteen of us. "How did Martin know I was here?"

"I cannot say for again I do not know, Madam. But this is where he told me I could find you."

Hunter sighed. "No peace this night for the weary. What in God's name is Martin doing in Westport?"

"I know not, sir."

Hunter looked at me. "Christ, man, what do you know?"

"Forgive me, sir. I am but a simple soldier. Master Martin does not confide in me."

Hunter nodded. "Aye... Mary, we should return to the ship to fetch more men and arms before we go traipsing through the woods at night."

The Englishman shook his head. "Please sir, no. There is no time. Master Martin has lost a lot of blood and if the Irish or the Spanish find him, well, he's an Englishman with rank..."

I took what men I had and we hurried off to the old mill. We did not wait on Martin's man, who had left the tavern before us to look for a wagon we could use to transport Martin in.

It was a dark and moonless night. We moved with haste down a winding country road with lanterns, torches and muskets in hand.

The old mill was not far off. And then, just as the dark

silhouette of the mill came into view, the woods on our flank erupted with tongues of flame and clouds of smoke. All around us the crackle of musket fire shattered the still, night air.

"AMBUSH!" Hunter screamed. "Hurry! Everyone to the mill! Run for it lads!"

"Ugh!" I cried out after I felt a sharp pain in my leg. I dropped to one knee and saw a hole in my trousers with a dark stain spreading out from the tear. A ball had grazed my thigh, gouging out a deep and bloody path.

Hunter pulled me up and put my arm around his neck. I hobbled next to him using my musket as a crutch as we made our way towards the old mill, towards a familiar place where I had often come in my youth when I needed a little solitude. Men were shouting and reloading their muskets. More shots whizzed by all around us. We were caught in the midst of a hellish cross-fire. I heard men, my men, screaming as they fell.

Hunter and I were the first to reach the mill. After we ducked inside we spun around to help the others. But there were no others. All my men were down. Lanterns and torches littered the road, marking the place where each man had fallen. And then shadows in the woods stood up, two dozen strong or more, and slowly started walking towards the old mill, pausing along the road here and there to dispatch any of my wounded.

"Mary," Hunter said, breathing hard. "There's no latch to this door and there's no time to make ourselves a barricade. Quick, up the stairs we go!"

As Hunter helped me stagger up a rickety, old staircase a voice from the woods - a voice ringing with power - called out my name. A chill shot down my spine. I froze.

"Mary, you loveless bitch! Death is coming for you! But before you die, I want you to know who it is who kills you now. First Dowlin, and then Remus and Romulus - you killed them all. They were my family. I was among the crew aboard *Medusa's Head* when you savagely cut my uncles down. After we reached Westport, you set the rest of us free - you fool. Mercy is for the weak. You should have killed us all that night and dumped our bodies in the bay. Oh yes, the man you murdered and knew as Dowlin was my father and through me, my father lives. Tonight we settle old scores in blood. Tonight we close all accounts between us. This place, this mill, is your funeral pyre. Do you like it Mary? I pray you do. I chose this spot, this hallowed ground, with great care just for you. Sit tight now. We're going to roast you and your fuckin', rabid dog alive!"

I caught a glimpse of the voice calling out to me through a gap in the old mill's framing. The tall, sinewy fellow speaking to me had an oddly familiar face.

Hunter pulled me up the stairs. When we reached the second floor we found an empty room to bolt ourselves in. We had seen no sign of Martin anywhere. The night turned deathly quiet.

And then Hunter - my magnificent, gallant Hunter, my heart's true joy - let his musket slip from his hands and he toppled over. I reached for an oil lamp and a tinderbox sitting on nearby table and frantically tried lighting the wick. It took me several tries as I fumbled in the dark. Once I had a flame, I found Hunter lying on his side with his shirt, front and back, soaked in blood. I ripped the material apart and I saw one hole in his back and one in his chest where a ball had passed straight through. I sat next to him on the floor, composed myself, and gently placed his head in my lap.

He gazed up at me with vacant, listless eyes and tried to smile. I knew the look. I had seen the faces of dying men many times before. He grabbed me by the arm and squeezed with all the strength he had left.

"Mary, how rich my life has been with you," he said in-between gulps of air. "I regret not one moment we shared together. Not one. Not even now, at this, my end. How much I loved you. You gave my life purpose and gladness. I die a happy, lucky man. I, I loved you with everything, with, with everything I had to give my, my darling, precious girl. God keep and save thee always, Mary. Whew, I'm cold. Go now, please, as I rest. Save yourself, I beg you my sweetheart."

"Shh, shh, shh, shh, my dearest," I said as I pressed my hand against his wound, trying to staunch the flow of blood. "Save your strength now my fine, fine man. We have voyages yet to make, new worlds to see, you and me together, hand-in-hand, across the deep and boundless sea."

He managed a loving smile. He kissed my hand. He closed his eyes and took his final breath. But before I could reach his lips to kiss them one last time, he died.

And then I heard angry voices just outside the door. I picked-up Hunter's musket and cocked the hammer back. But neither Dowlin's son nor his men made any attempt to break inside. They had another plan in mind. They smashed their oil lanterns against the door, against the walls and hallway floor. The old mill began to crackle and burn.

"Blood for blood!" a voice cried out. Those were the last words I heard, followed by footsteps retreating down the mill's rickety, old staircase as the fire spread.

I remained sitting on the floor, holding Hunter's lifeless body in my arms. I stroked his hair. I rocked him back and forth and wept. The fire outside the room spread rapidly. The air inside the room turned thick with choking, grey smoke. My eyes began to sting and I found it harder and harder to breathe. I started coughing. I would suffocate from the toxic fumes before my flesh would burn and took comfort in that at least.

In-between my coughing fits, I snapped my head around and eyed a back room, a room not much larger than a closet. I looked down at the floor boards in that little room where I knew there was a hatch, a trapdoor, a trapdoor that led to a hidden crawl space underneath the floor boards used to access the old mill's great wheel, to a wheel that dipped into the living waters of a stream, into waters that flowed out into the open sea, out into the rough and tumbly sea that had always nurtured me, that was life for me.

But I was unafraid and made no attempt to flee for soon I would be rejoining my beloved Hunter. Soon I would be standing at his side in a new and wondrous world. I was at peace with myself. I was content with my sad end.

351

I looked back down at Hunter, at my beautiful, shinning prince, and hugged his body tightly. I had loved this man more than life itself. My love for him was my one, pure act of grace in this cruel and unforgiving world. I could not desert him.

With all my heart I've tried to understand and love our Lord God. If He loves me, I know it not. He is either an unkind God or He is an unloving God or perhaps He is an indifferent God and if He is an indifferent God is that not the same as being an unkind or an unloving God?

I suppose many would say I am not a moral person. I have seen and spilt a lot of blood. How could any kind and loving god know me? These were my final thoughts as the heat and thick tendrils of smoke encircled me.

And then I touched my belly and smiled. I'm certain I felt the baby move.

I kissed Hunter's forehead one last time and eyed the back room again. I looked down at the floor boards in that little room where I knew there was a hatch, a trapdoor, a trapdoor that led to the open sea, out to the rough and tumbly sea that was life for me.

I have always been, and I shall always be, the butcher's daughter...

Afterword

Ships & Guns of the Elizabethan Era
- The Dawn of the Golden Age of Sail -

El Grande y Felicisima Armada
(From the Movie *Elizabeth: The Golden Age*)

When I first began down this journey with *The Butcher's Daughter*, I worried whether I would have enough to say after the first chapter or two. What little I knew about Sixteenth Century Europe (before any research) seemed, well, boring. In this, I was very much mistaken. In politics, religion, science, art, literature, finance, technology and warfare, great changes were sweeping across Europe throughout the 1500s. Genius, innovation and opportunity flourished. This was the Renaissance, the Reign of Elizabeth I and the Protestant Reformation converging all at once. Europeans were stepping out of the Middle Ages and into the modern era, into a golden age that would culminate with the Age of Enlightenment, which in turn set the stage for the American War of Independence. These were dark times too. This was an age of African slavery and Indian genocide. This was a time when tens of thousands of Catholics and Protestants were torturing and slaughtering each other in the name of God.

Christopher Columbus's discovery of the New World in 1492 changed everything of course. By the turn of the century, settlors - *conquistadors*, traders, money men, monks, opportunists, adventurers, doctors, craftsman, farmers, mercenaries, slavers, pirates and the like - were flocking to the Caribbean and beyond in vast numbers. Towns and cities were popping up like mushrooms. During the Sixteenth Century some 240,000 Spaniards alone immigrated to the Americas.

This staggering European expedition into the New World would not have been possible without a lot of ships and ships cost money, more money then what even kings and queens kept in their royal coffers. New sources of wealth were needed to fund the migration west and that need gave rise to a new middleclass of entrepreneurs adept in sophisticated international commerce and banking. These gifted moneymen cobbled together a cash-based, capitalist financial system and raised enormous amounts of investment money, money used to fund dreams, both small and grand.

Throughout history navies have played a role, sometimes a decisive role, in war and politics. In the ancient world Themistocles's war galleys saved Greece and Western democracy from King Xerxes's Persian hordes when his triremes ambushed and annihilated the Persian fleet in the Straights of Salamis after Leonidas and his three hundred fell at Thermopylae. And it was Octavian's navy at Actium that crushed the dreams of his rival Mark Antony and Egypt's Queen Cleopatra to rule the world, not Rome's legendary legions. But these were exceptions. Before the Sixteenth Century, navies were largely used to transport men and supplies from one point to another and game-changing victories at sea like Salamis and Actium were rare.

In the Sixteenth Century men learned how to mount heavy cannon (guns in naval parlance) onto a rolling deck in large numbers, revolutionizing naval warfare. The flimsy ships of the past were quickly discarded for far more potent, heavily-armed cruisers. Fleets turned into armies on the water capable of projecting a kingdom's power and prestige around the globe. And when the Spanish and Portuguese discovered gold, silver and pearls in the New World, Spanish and Portuguese shipyards began churning out larger, stronger Atlantic class treasure ships capable of hauling all that loot safely back to Europe - along with larger warships to protect them from treasure hungry marauders prowling the Caribbean Sea. Spain launched the world's first battleships. Majestic galleons and carracks displacing one thousand tons or better and carrying huge guns able to hurtle a thirty pound ball over a mile away took to the oceans.

Envious of Spain's fabulous New World wealth, and alarmed by her increasing power, England and France feverishly started building their own battleships to catch up to their great rival to the south. The three superpowers quickly found themselves locked in a deadly, high-stakes arms race. For the next four hundred years foundries forged bigger and heavier guns and shipyards built bigger and heavier ships with progressively intricate sail plans to propel them.

Spain gambled big on building bigger ships and heavier guns in her desire to command the sea lanes (the French eventually did the same). The English chose speed and maneuverability over big and heavy. In the end the English won.

Odds & Ends

The Ships

The workhorse of the day was the caravel and with a good master, these ships could sail up 10 knots, covering between 50 to 100 miles a day. The Spanish treasure fleets typically sailed no faster than about four knots.

Common ships of the day:

Man-o-war/frigate: 360 tons, 190 men
Brigantine: 150 tons, 150 men
Sloop: small, fast, 100 tons, 75 men
Pinque: two-masted, square-rigged with narrow hull and overhanging stern
Caravel: 250 tons, three-masted square-rigged or lateen-rigged (a caravela, like Columbus's *Nina* and *Pinta* were only 50 tons or so)
Dutch fly boat: fast, flat bottom, 200 tons
Galleass (or Turkish *mahon*): 250 tons, three masts and with up to 64 oars with five rowers to an

oar

Galleon: the battleship of its day, a floating castle displacing 500 to 1000 tons or more

Carrack or Nao: the largest ship of the age (up to 1000 tons or more), the bowsprit is longer, the forecastles higher, but similar in characteristics to the galleon (Columbus's *Santa Maria* was a smaller carrack (90 tons)

Pinnance: small, two-masted vessel used as couriers and transport

Patache: general name for any kind of small vessel used as couriers and for reconnaissance

Zabras: small vessel resembling a frigate

The Great Guns

The *great guns* were classified according to size and included canon royals, demi-cannons, culverin, demi-culverins, sakers, falconets, minions and others. They were cast from either iron or more expensive (more accurate) bronze. Some types were muzzle-loaded, others were breach-loaded. Someone thought to cut out gunports in the bulwarks and mount the guns on four-wheeled carriages.

Common guns of the day:

Falconet:	Weight:	200 - 400 lbs.
	Barrel:	4'
	Shot:	1 lbs.
	Max Range:	1,500'
Culverine:	Weight:	4,500 lbs.
	Barrel:	12'
	Shot:	17 lbs.
	Max Range:	7,500'

Demi-culverine:	Weight:	4,000 lbs.
	Barrel:	11'
	Shot:	30 lbs.
	Max Range:	5,100'
Cannon-petro:	Weight:	4,000 lbs.
	Barrel:	4'
	Shot:	24.5 lbs.
	Max Range:	1,600'
Saker:	Weight:	1,900 lbs.
	Barrel:	9.5'
	Shot:	5.25 lbs.
	Max Range:	7,400'
Minions:	Weight:	800-1,000 lbs.
	Barrel:	8'
	Shot:	3 lbs.
	Max Range:	6,000'

A Few Interesting Historical Tidbits

Sixteenth Century Words: I am by no means a scholar in language or words. I wouldn't know how to write as people spoke back in the 1500s. Nonetheless, I tried to avoid obvious modern words in an effort to give a touch of authenticity to the times of Queen Elizabeth. I was surprised by how many new words and phrases came out of the 1500s (or thereabouts). I used the word "traffic" for example, but "traffic" sounded too modern to my ear so I considered using a synonym. But people actually used the word "traffic" in the 1500s. The Spanish used the word *tráfico* (or *traffique* in the French and *traffico* in the Italian) to describe trade and commerce. The words "relapse" and "goodbye" are more examples. The etymology of "goodbye" is particularly interesting as people started using this word in the 1570s (how we know this is beyond me), the period in which much of our story takes place. The word "goodbuye" ("goodbye") is short for "God be with ye" though somewhere along the way "God" in the phrase was replaced with "good." There are many other examples of this throughout the book. Lout (a clown, a bumpkin), "weakling" (first coined by William Tyndale in the 1520s), "newfangled," "methodical," "livelihood," "good-naturedly," "upshot," and "shit" are all Sixteenth Century words and the list goes on.

Galleons: History is a bit murky on who originally built the first galleons. Captains Pedro Menéndez de Avilés and Álvaro de Bazán from Spain are generally credited with the revolutionary new design though there is evidence that the Venice built the first galleon, or *gallionis* to fight pirates. (The word galleon is derived from the Old French word "*galion*" or "little ship," which the Spanish used to mean an "armed merchant ship" ("*galeón*"), which the Portuguese used to mean a "war ship" ("*galeão*"). The Spanish galleons were sleek and powerful ships capable of sailing around the world and when the English saw them, they wanted them. Sir John Hawkins and three master English shipwrights, Richard Chapman, Peter Pett and Mathew Baker set about designing an improved version of the Spanish galleon and ended up with their "race-built" design (the fore and aft castles were "razed" and lengthened to improve stability, speed and maneuverability). The English builders described their ships as having "the head of a cod and the tail of a mackerel." The first of these new galleons, the 295 ton *Foresight*, was launched from the Deptford Dockyard in 1570. Following the success of the *Foresight*, the English launched many more race-built galleons in preparation for the war that was sure to come between England and Spain.

Mary Rose: As with any new and complex technology, things can go very wrong. In 1511 England launched the *Mary Rose*, a 500 ton carrack class vessel. The *Mary Rose* was King Henry VIII's pride and joy and his flagship. She was one of the first warships to use the recently invented gunport (invented in 1501). During the Battle of Solent (off the Isle of Wight) against the French on July 19, 1545, *Mary Rose* suddenly, and for no apparent reason, heeled over sharply to her starboard and capsized from water pouring in through her open gunports. Only 35 out of 400 officers and men survived. The wreck was discovered in 1971 and salvaged in 1982.

Naval Guns: The first use of shipboard artillery was at the Battle of Arnemuiden on September 23, 1338 when the English armed the *Christofer* with three small artillery pieces and one hand gun.

Gun Laying: The first recorded device to measure an elevation angle was Niccolò Tartagilia's invention of a gunners' quadrant circa 1545. This device had two arms at right angles connected by an arc marked with angular graduations. One arm was placed in the muzzle, and a plumb bob suspended against the arc showed the elevation angle. This led to many calculations relating elevation angle to range.

Gunpowder: The earliest gunpowder was a finely ground mixture of charcoal, saltpeter, and sulfur known as "serpentine powder," By the 15th century gunners were using corned powder which was pressed into pellets and screened to a uniform size.

Navigational Instruments: The mariner's astrolabe, also called sea astrolabe, was an inclinometer used to determine the latitude of a ship at sea by measuring the sun's noon altitude (declination) or the meridian altitude of a star of known declination. Not an astrolabe proper, the mariner's astrolabe was rather a graduated circle with an alidade used to measure vertical angles. They were designed to allow for their use on boats in rough water and/or in heavy winds, which astrolabes were unsuitable. In the Sixteenth Century, the instrument was also called a ring.

Mining: In 1545 the Spanish discovered silver ore in Peru and began the first mining operations in the New World.

Situado: After Francis Drake (1540 - 1596) and others inflicted great damage on Spanish interests throughout the Caribbean, Spain began pouring millions into fortifying key ports with citadels and walls. The Spanish called this system of fortification *Situado*. Between 1751 and 1810 Cartagena alone received the sum of 20,912,677 Spanish *reales*, or the equivalent of about two trillion dollars in today's terms, to beef-up her defenses.

Plantation: In the Second Desmond Rebellion in the early 1580's (both Spain and the Pope sent soldiers to support the Irish), led by Gerald FitzGerald, the Earl of Desmond, the English used 'scorched earth' tactics across Munster in retaliation for the uprising. Famine broke out and 30,000 Irish men, women and children to starved to death. After the English crushed the rebellion, Munster was colonized under the doctrine of Plantation.

The Color of Slavery: The evil of slavery was not limited to American Indians or African Blacks. King James II sold 30,000 Irish prisoners to the New World as slaves. Bye the mid-1600s, 70% of the total population of Montserrat were Irish slaves. From 1641 to 1652, over 500,000 Irish were killed by the English and another 300,000 were sold as slaves (under the guise of "indentured servants"), including children (an estimated 100,000 children between the ages of 10 and 14 were sold in the New World during the 1650s). Africans sold for around 50 sterling, Irish for only 5.

Infamous Women Pirates of the Sixteen Century: Grace O'Malley (Irish/1530 - 1603); Syyida al Hurra (Moroccan/1510 - 1542); Lady Mary Killigrew (English/1530 - 1570); and Lady Elizabeth Killigrew (English/1570's - 1582).

Motley Crew: was term used to describe the mismatched multi-colored woolen clothing worn by pirates.

Cádiz: The *São Filipe* and her cargo captured by Drake off the Azores was valued £108,000. Queen Elizabeth awarded Drake 10% of that amount. "I've singed the beard of the King of Spain" Drake boasted after his raid at Cádiz in 1587.

Game of Bowls: Legend has it that when the Spanish *Armada* was sighted off of the southern coast of England, Drake insisted on finishing a game of bowls with his officers at Plymouth Ho before setting out.

Gravelines: English ships suffered little damage at the Battle of Gravelines. Spanish casualties were much higher. Three Spanish ships were sunk, one was captured and four ran aground. Many others were severely damaged. Spanish cannon balls recovered from the site revealed the iron had been poorly cast and instead of penetrating English hulls the metal shattered on impact.

Medina Sidonia's orders to the *Armada* for the *North About:*

"THE COURSE THAT SHALL BE HELD IN THE RETURN OF THIS ARMY TO SPAIN

"*The course that is first to be held is to the north/north-east until you be found under 61 degrees and a half; and then to take great heed lest you fall upon the Island of Ireland for fear of the harm that may happen unto you upon that coast.*

"*Then, parting from those islands and doubling the Cape in 61 degrees and a half, you shall run west/south-west until you be found under 58 degrees; and from thence to the south-west to the height of 53 degrees; and then to the south/south-west, making to the Cape Finisterre, and so to procure your entrance into the Groyne A Coruña to*

Ferrol, or to any other port of the coast of Galicia."

The admiral's orders to sail "north/north-east until you be found under 61 degrees and a half" would have brought the *Armada* to the northern tip of the Shetland Islands, giving the fleet ample distance between itself and Ireland after turning west. The fleet couldn't keep to these orders though and cut through the Orkneys and Fair Island (south of the Shetland Islands) instead, bringing the fleet much closer to Ireland.

The Tilbury Speech: Queen Elizabeth's rousing speech given while inspecting the army on the eve of battle at Tilbury in Essex on August 18, 1588:

"My loving people:

We have been persuaded by some that are careful of our safety, to take heed how we commit ourselves to armed multitudes, for fear of treachery; but I assure you I do not desire to live to distrust my faithful and loving people. Let tyrants fear. I have always so behaved myself that, under God, I have placed my chiefest strength and safeguard in the loyal hearts and good-will of my subjects; and therefore I am come amongst you, as you see, at this time, not for my recreation and disport, but being resolved, in the midst and heat of the battle, to live and die amongst you all; to lay down for my God, and for my kingdom, and my people, my honour and my blood, even in the dust.

I know I have the body of a weak, feeble woman; but I have the heart and stomach of a king, and of a king of England too, and think foul scorn that Parma or Spain, or any prince of Europe, should dare to invade the borders of my realm; to which rather than any dishonour shall grow by me, I myself will take up arms, I myself will be your general, judge, and rewarder of every one of your virtues in the field.

I know already, for your forwardness you have deserved rewards and crowns; and we do assure you on a word of a prince, they shall be duly paid. In the meantime, my lieutenant general shall be in my stead, than whom never prince commanded a more noble or worthy subject; not doubting but by your obedience to my general, by your concord in the camp, and your valour in the field, we shall shortly have a famous victory over these enemies of my God, of my kingdom, and of my people."

Victory Coin: To commemorate the victory over the Spanish *Armada* a coin was struck with the words: "God blew and they were scattered."

The Final Butcher's Bill: The *Armada* lost about 24 ships against the rocky coastline of Ireland between Antrim and Kerry. As many as 5,000 Spaniards perished in the storms or were executed by the English. Medina Sidonia limped back to Spain with only half his ships in all (67) and less than 10,000 men (he lost 20,000 dead). The English lost only 100 men or so killed in battle and no ships. A staggering 7,000 English sailors however perished from diseases such as typhus and dysentery.

The "Counter Armada:" In 1589, a year after the English defeated the Spanish Armada, Queen Elizabeth sent the English Armada, also known as the Counter Armada or the Drake - Norris Expedition, to the Iberian Coast (in what was later called the Anglo-Spanish War) to finish-off the Spanish fleet. Sir Francis Drake had command of the English Armada and Sir John Norreys had command of the army. The campaign was a disaster for Drake and England. Drake lost 40 ships and thousands of men allowing Spain to reclaim her naval dominance.

Letter of Marque and Reprisal granted by King Henry VIII (1543):

> The King's most royal Majesty being credibly informed that divers and many of his most loving faithful and obedient subjects inhabiting upon the sea coasts, using trafic by sea, and divers others, be very desirous to prepare and equip sundry ships and vessels at their own costs and charges to the sea for the annoyance of his Majesty's enemies, the Frenchmen and the Scots, so as they might obtain his most gracious licence in that behalf, Hath, of his clemency, tender love, and zeal, which he beareth to his subjects, by the advice of his most honorable counsel resolved and determined as hereafter followeth:
>
> First his Majesty is pleased, and by the authority hereof giveth full power and licence to all and singular, his subjects of all sorts, degrees, and conditions, that they and every of them, may, at their liberties, without incuring any loss, danger, forfeiture, or penalty, and without putting in of any bonds or recognizance before the Counsel, or in the Court of the Admiralty, and without suing forth of any other licence, vidimus, or other writing, from any counsel, court, or place, within this realm, or any other his Majesty's realms and dominions, prepare and equip to the seas such and so many ships and vessels furnished for the war, to be used and employed against his Grace's said

enemies, the Scots and Frenchmen, as they shall be able to think convenient for their advantage and the annoyance of his Majesty's said enemies. And his Majesty is further pleased, and by this presents granteth to every of his said subjects that they, and every of them, shall enjoy to his and their own proper use, profit, and commodity, all and singular such ships, vessels, munition, merchandise, wares, victuals, and goods of what nature and quality so ever it be, which they shall take of any of his Majesty's said enemies, without making account in any court or place of this realm or any other of the King's realms or dominions for the same, and without paying any part or share to the Lord Admiral of England, the Lord Warden of the Five Ports, or any other officer or minister of the King's Majesty, any use, custom, prescription, or order to the contrary hereof used heretofore in any wise notwithstanding. And his Majesty is further pleased that all and every his said subjects which upon the publication of this proclamation will sue for a duplicate of the same under the great seal of England, shall have the same, paying only the petty fees to the officers for writing the same.

And, seeing now that it hath pleased the King's Majesty, of his most gracious goodness, to grant unto all his subjects this great liberty, his Highness desireth all mayors, sheriffs, bailiffs, aldermen, and all other his Grace's faithful officers, ministers, and subjects of this realm, and other his Highness' realms and dominions, and especially those which do inhabit in the port towns and other places near the seaside, to shew themselves worthy of such liberty, and one to bear with another, and to help another, in such sort as their doing hereupon may be substantial, and bring forth that effect that shall redound to his Majesty's honor, their own suerties, and the annoyance of the enemies.

Provided always that no man which shall go to the sea by virtue hereof presume to take anything from any his Majesty's subjects, or from any man having his Grace's safe conduct, upon the pains by his Majesty's laws provided for the same. And his Grace is further pleased that no manner of officer, or other person, shall take any mariners, munition, or tackle from any man thus equipping himself to the sea, but by his own consent, unless his Majesty, for the furniture of his own ships, do send for any of them by special commissions, and where need shall require. His Majesty will also grant commission to such as will sue for the same for their better furnitures in this behalf.

The world is fickle, friend. Some (I hope) will like this book and others won't. An artist can only offer his or her best and pray. I think Eleanor, the *grande dame* who urged me to write this book before her end, a beautiful woman and wise in many ways, would at least have enjoyed our story. I wish you a good journey...

For

Eleanor Ann (McRoberts) McMillin

Made in the USA
Middletown, DE
16 August 2015